W9-BIJ-029

PROFESSOR BAKER'S HAND GRENADE

A Novel

B. J. LUCIAN

Bookman LLC
Publishing & Marketing

Providing Quality, Professional
Author Services

www.bookmanmarketing.com

© Copyright 2005, B. J. Lucian

All Rights Reserved.

No part of this book may be reproduced, stored in a
retrieval system, or transmitted by any means,
electronic, mechanical, photocopying, recording,
or otherwise, without written permission
from the author.

ISBN: 1-59453-365-2

Cover photo of Mont-St-Michel

The characters in this story and their experiences are fictional. The cities, newspapers, government agencies, CACTUS, ordnance-ridden Lac Bleu and booby-trapped France are very real.

ACKNOWLEDGEMENTS

I am very indebted to the following authors for their many ideas and explanations relative to various aspects of French culture: Johnathon Fenby, <u>FRANCE ON THE BRINK</u>; Donovon Webster, <u>AFTERMATH: THE REMNANTS OF WAR</u>; Harriet Welty Rochefort, <u>FRENCH FRIED</u>. The Hotel de Ville in Angers and Avrille were both informative and helpful in their many E-mails and newsletters.

I am grateful to my brothers for their reading time: Brothers Daniel, James, Joseph, Matthew, Philip, Terence. Special thanks are due Loyce Winfield and Delynne Duerkes. I would also like to give a special thanks to Ms. Lindsay Bough at Bookman Publishing for the cover design.

vi

DEDICATION

To the French Département du Déminage
which oversees the removal of live unexploded
ordnance left from two World Wars.
Many *démineurs* have been killed doing this
dangerous clean-up work.
They all have our profound respect.

REAL-WORLD NEWS EXCERPTS

Menace of the Blue Lagoon.
French news. com, 2001. CENTRE from David Line. *Their (Avrille, France, citizens) fears focus on the Lac Bleu d'Avrille, the site of a former quarry and now home to many thousands of tonnes of explosives dumped there since 1924...Campaigners launched their latest protest at the Angers conference by bearding delegates from the Ministre de l'Ecologie et de Developpement Durable and plan to continue their action until "the last chapter of the blue lake is written."*

Angers: un lac explosif!
La Nouvelle Republique du Centre-Ouest, 28 May 03
Des ecologistes d'Avrille (Maine-et-Loire) organisent Dimanche la visite d'un plan d'eau communal ou reposent 10,000 tonnes de munitions.

Aftermath: The Remnants of War.
Donovan Webster, Vintage Books, 1996, page 12.
All around me, the demineurs—or 'deminers,' as France's weapons disposal experts are called—are clearing the forest of explosives, carry them to the cargo beds of four-wheel-drive Land Rover trucks we've driven into this forest.

ASSEMBLEE NATIONALE RAPPORT 3199
Par Mme Nicole Feidt, 3 July 2001

The case of 'Lac Bleu' d'Avrille, en Maine-et-Loire, which contains between 5,000 and 7,000 tons of munitions, in particular grenades dating from the first world war, is well known.

1ere SÉANCE DU MARDI 5 JUIN 2001.
Presidence de M. Patrick Ollier
Deminage du Lac Bleu a Avrille, en Maine-et-Loire
...6,000 and 7,000 tonnes d'obus, grenades et munitions diverses dont la corrosion a donne sa couleur au lac.

Pierre has been my main contact with all things French for years. He can find a cab when there are none, translate from and into several languages, advise on the current euro/dollar money market and he always knows when the next sudden *greve,* strike, will hit the Paris streets. Les *grevistes*, the strikers, have been known to hoist a few at Pierre's bar on occasion. Pierre has to be one of the most all-round informed men in Paris. He has been this way since our grade school days together in Avrille, France.

This day he feels like discussing what the International Herald Tribune has been suggesting, that France through Chirac, must compensate somehow for its gradual loss of influence in Europe and the world. France needs to demonstrate its intellectual and moral superiority, its Gaullist righteousness, its natural leadership among European nations.

"France is, after all, the leading nation of Europe, now and probably forever," he says.

"Well, that last France-Iraq dodge was a poor showing for a proud self-appointed leader, my friend," I say, sipping vodka while a tiny ice cube floats temporarily in the heat of the day.

"But you look at our leaders and compare them to the American diplomats your President sends around the world," says Pierre. "Our men know languages, customs, they know protocol, international expressions of traditional respect, diplomatic corps etiquette. And the French delegates to our embassies and to the United Nations are educated. You know, mon cher professeur, how we French note the differences and we can't help but feel justifiably superior in these areas. Have you ever sent an American to speak to us in French? Our diplomats appearing on CNN speak perfect English. *C'est vrai, non?*"

"But hasn't this made y'all rather perversely self-satisfied and seriously traditon-bound?" My bit of scarce European ice is long gone.

"And that, *mon ami*, is our strength. Our men know our language and yours and they can think and discuss in both while paying due respect to our heritage, our *patrimoine*."

"But isn't that the trouble—y'all just think alike, traditionally?" Vodka warm now.

"France trains its men to administer the nation. You have these so-called 'majors' in your universities. We have complete courses of study. You have your Harvard-Yale networks. England depends on Oxford. We have our obviously superior Grandes Ecoles."

We are interrupted by a group of men in suits and ties from the Bourse coming in for a mid-morning coffee.

PROLOGUE

So here I am, retired, attached to my beloved Mid-South University, spending a great deal of time, reading and writing and hiking. Not all at once; usually one thing at a time.

In fact it was while I was walking past the hippos in our renowned Memphis Zoo one sunny day that my musing was interrupted. I met a former student, the beautiful Laura Veronica Campbell.

Laura, or L.V., as she likes to be called, graduated a few years ago as a pych major, with minors in French and English. She had been a top student, straight 4.0, soccer player, and a student government leader. L.V. reminds people of Drew Barrymore in 'Charley's Angels.' She looks the part and could certainly act the part, especially the physical segments. Nowadays she spends much of her free time at Memphis' St. Jude's Research Hospital in the data-gathering-computer area, but manages to visit some of the children each week. She is active in the local Alliance Francaise. Laura is about five feet nine inches tall, slender, auburn-haired, attractive, with a very active high I.Q.

She saw me first and shouted out "Professor Josh" as I was engrossed in the hippos' eating process. I turned to see who it was and noticed that several others had also turned to see who called. L.V. has always been able to turn heads. We embraced. L.V. is a great embracer, and then laughed with everyone else as 5,000 pounds of hippo lurched and sagged and flopped into the pool. There the mammoth immediately became a graceful water-horse, literally *hippopotamus*.

"Like that gives new meaning to the belly flop," said L.V. And she waved a salute to the hippo, bowing: "*Je suis enchanté.*"

"And to the breast stroke," I added. "How have you been? You look so energized."

"I'm fine, Prof, thank you. Just checking on a computer glitch in the panda research lab, here. My old buddy Mitchel Joseph called me to see if I would take a look at his new computer set-up and offer a suggestion about his missing data. The lightning storm yesterday seems to have messed lab computers up big time. He wants to wrap this up today because he's leaving for Paris tomorrow; something about diving for bombs in a lake. He is an adventurer."

"Do you know where his lab is? Come on, I'll walk you over," I volunteered.

As a part time docent I often assist folks to find things around the zoo, everything from wallets to toilets, elephants, pronto pups and grade school teachers. You'd be surprised the number of little kids who report missing teachers. Teachers are pretty embarrassed when they hear the public address system: "Attention Inca Elementary teacher Susan Fessmer. Your class is here in the administration building. Your bus is about to leave."

L.V. introduced me to Mitchel Joseph. Then we all said the usual Memphis tag line:

"Keep in touch now, he'ya?" as we waved goodbye at Joseph's lab door.

I passed the hippos on my way to the parking lot. They had consigned their hourly defecation to the pool and seemed perfectly contented walking about submerged in dark brown water. Hippos are almost unbelievable. It's hard to believe, for example, that their huge lower canines fit perfectly into sheath-like pockets in the upper jaw. And they love water—any color, any contaminant.

Strapping myself in my Ford I thought about what L.V. had said. Her friend Joseph wants to "dive for bombs in a lake?" In France?

PART I

Prof Josh

My flight on Air France was uneventful except for the fact that we almost crashed coming into de Gaulle. That is, we crashed into each other. Several people were in the aisle when a large dip, courtesy of an air pocket or two, caused the plane to suddenly lose altitude and pop back up quite forcefully. A pretty French flight attendant landed in the lap of the guy in front of me. She squealed something like "Mon Dieu!" He sacrificed his body to break her fall. She was grateful. "Merci bien, monsieur."

"Bienvenue," the guy says, with a slight Provence accent. She jumped up after a few seconds and raced to the galley. As she moved up the aisle with an open garbage bag she smiled and blew a kiss in the direction of the heroic lap. We eventually landed safely and proceeded through the new style Paris customs procedures. We passengers passed through as quickly as we could walk with our carry-ons. Not a single French customs person said a word or even made a motion except to point towards the exit. The new regulations must have been easy to learn—smile at new arrivals and point, point, point.

As I am strolling towards my metro station the Montmartrobus #96 pulls up with a swerving motion common in Paris, where small cars and smoking people offer bus drivers moving obstacles. The swift braking of typical Paris traffic causes me to look up quickly. Who should be boarding #96 but the flying Laplanders, the flight attendant and her landing pad, now stretched vertically. Arm in arm, luggage and all, they were heading to Montmartre. I had assumed those two had just accidentally met on my air-pocket flight into de Gaulle. Now here they are together again on a bus that folks in Paris take when they know their way around Montmartre. They certainly seemed joyous together. Good for them, I thought, they seem like they are having fun.

My Paris apartment is in the Hotel Colbert overlooking Place des Victoires. It adjoins the Biblioteque Nationale, about which I care a great deal, and near the Bourse and Le Banque de France, about which I care not at all. Much of my work is part-time research. The other half is also research. In short, I love French archives and libraries. Isn't that normal for retired psych profs?

The Colbert staff get me right to my room for the seventh time in as many years. They call me "Monsieur le professeur" and refuse to ever call me "Josh." It takes me about two minutes to get settled and unpacked in #1, on the first floor, that is, one floor up from the ground floor. Then I am down in the bar having an aperitif, (read vodka-tonic) with Pierre Le Grand, the barman.

"A *bientôt*, Pierre," I say as he begins the noisy cappuccino machine. "*A demain.*" See you tomorrow.

Out on the Rue des Petits Champs I thought about what Pierre had bragged about. He was correct to a certain extent, of course. France does have a fine training system for its civil service people. The Ecole Nationale d'Administration, popularly known as ENA, graduates thousands of very select students (called 'Enarques') from hundreds of university-level schools. Most of France's civil servants come from ENA, and other grads lead public-sector companies, state banks, and planning groups. French Presidents, Prime Ministers, heads of government ministries and diplomats are trained for those jobs. They, like American millionaires and Senators, form an elite caste. But France, about the size of Texas, is surely not as complicated as the States.

After a brisk walk up the Avenue l'Opera, a brief check at the American Express, and some window shopping, I felt ready for a jet-lag nap. Back at the Colbert I noticed the thread in the upper door hinge was exactly as I had placed it. I managed to get an hour's rest despite constant police car sirens screaming up and down Rue de Rivoli. It seemed like a Bistro Melrose dinner night. You can't go wrong dining on Avenue Clichy. Escargots unlimited.

France is a beautiful little country bordered by eight other countries from which people can now come and go rather easily without all those gendarmes guarding every entrance and exit. Professors emeriti appreciate that freedom. France's neighbors have been its good friends, its effective enemies, and its concerned partners. Consider Switzerland, Italy, Germany and Monaco on the east, Spain and Andorra on the south, and Belgium and Luxembourg on the northeast. That represents many generations of treaties and contracts, documents and pacts, covenants and just plain deals. Many of these connections are important to the overseas departments of French Guiana, Martinique, Guadeloupe, Reunion, and island dependencies like New Caledonia and French Polynesia. And let's not forget Corsica in the Mediterrean. All of that is Republique Francaise. But the French Francs are long gone; count your euros.

My family, generations of Bakers, (*boulangers* of *boulangerie* fame), started out of La Rochelle with Champlain in 1633, with about two hundred would-be settlers. Many of them ended up in Quebec and along the shores of the St. Lawrence River. From there they became the pioneers of the unexplored interior and eventually developed into a new breed of people we now call French Canadians. The Boulangers eventually evolved into Bélangers.

Some say they deserved their name because they were from Belle Angers, that is, the beautiful town of

Angers in northwest France where the Loire River flows 625 miles from the Massif Central, past Nantes and out to the Baie de Bourgneuf and the Atlantic at St. Nazaire. Whatever the origin of the name, these were folks acquainted with rivers and oceans and so were at home on the St. Lawrence River in North America. From there my very great ancestor Abraham Martin sighted the outcropping of the Quebec heights and cried "Quel bec,' because from far below on the water the mount above did look like a huge bird beak. Anyway, we are all attached to Quebec via Paris via Angers via the Loire.

After several generations of living in Quebec, Memphis and Paris, we Bakers find our way back to Angers every year or so. My usual route is to drive from Angers to Paris in my trusty 1939 Citroen Le Traction Avant, the remarkable *Cabriola* which I keep in Pierre's garage behind the Colbert. I have always considered it pretty much his car, for after all, he does see to it that the dear little thing is kept safe and sound year round. He has my permission to use it any way he wants at any time except, of course, when I'm visiting. I know many international travelers think a *traction cabriola* is a small car with few amenities and even less humility. But my first tour of Paris many years ago cemented my relations with the *Avant*. It was my first day in Paris and I was literally caught in the swirl of nine lanes of traffic around the Arc de Triomphe. Several regular commuting Monsieurs swore vocally and in sign language as I cut them off from their usual exit. I hunched over the wheel and white-knuckled my grip, looking straight ahead. As soon as I whipped into Avenue Kleber l parked behind Palace de Chaillot for a moment of silent prayer of thanks. The most perilous part of a six-month tour of Europe had been successfully completed. I was now a certified triumphant survivor, an "Arc Driver."

A typical telecast scene of Paris, no matter what the media news focus of the day, will include a scene of little Parisian bumper cars moving menacingly at each other around the great circle. Foreigners can't believe the circle can be negotiated more than once or twice without a fender-bender or two. Parisians are equally amazed each time they exit unscathed. Approaching the Arc from the Avenue de Champs Elysée, for example, one must have a committed plan for entering and exiting The Circle. Nothing, absolutely nothing, must interfere with one's fixed track. If you need to exit Avenues Foch or Hugo (without having to drive around the circle several times) you must become aggressively war-like as you veer toward your established goal. Army tank drivers and Special Forces officers have been emotionally challenged at the Arc. *Angoissant* is our word for it: simply nerve-wracking.

Now I am more or less used to it and this day I am speeding up Avenue Marceau and taking aim for the critical half-circle that will whip me off into the Avenue de la Grande Armée. My elderly Avant is in fine condition and it is growling at the passing speeders who are shouting and gesturing and no doubt admiring my split second shot into *Avenue Armée*. Several larger cars have come close to scraping my fender paint. Suddenly a side glance brings me the vision of Laplander and the Flying Flight Attendant in an open convertible, necktie and scarf waving in the wind. In a moment they are gone, down Avenue MacMahon. Coincidence? Again? Could that really be a reocurring event happening by mere chance? What are the odds?

I exercised some mental math on the subject of chance as I circled the outside rings of Chartres, and Le Mans southwest into Angers on good roads characterized on the map as "dual carriageway with road numbers." The results of deep mathematical consideration of higher probability study resulted in a gerontological conclusion. This prof is emerging into the stage of pre-fogeyhood. Not quite an old fogey yet, but approaching serious geezer-enhanced imaginings.

I hardly saw beautiful Angers as I slowed through the city on rue Plantagenet, sped south a few miles into my childhood neighborhood, a veritable field of dreams that is Avrille. Where I live on the edge of town there is a quarry, a city dump, a municipal technical center of some kind and a marvelously famous little lake, Le Lac Bleu.

I am always happy to pull into the yard at Chateau Boudreau, our ancestral rock pile in the neat little town of Avrille, just six miles outside of Angers. My relatives, who refuse to become concerned about Boudreau, "an inherited derelict," enjoy kidding me about its looks. It appears to the cynical as justifiably abandoned. And the name does not denote a grand old castle, or manor or even a small citadel. It actually is a small, sturdy house constructed of field stone and tons of quarried slate. Local residents say it must be about 200 years old and I guess it sort of looks it. I love it.

The fields around it have been lying idle for generations despite my generous offer to the Ecole Superieure d'Agriculture. They don't seem to need additional land outside Angers for crop experimentation. Because I think France needs continued crop experimentation I have never offered to donate land for more soccer fields to any of the other ten ecoles superieur, schools or institutes in Angers which train privileged young people for commerce, production, public relations and communication. All those schools make Angers a university town and thus it has many libraries along with frequent parties, festivals, and the well-known carnival.

The Boudreau, as we call it, has six rooms: a great parlor-fireplace area, a modern, yet French, WC, a semi-modern kitchen, three bedrooms and a sun room. There are three exterior doors; the sunroom French doors, the kitchen door in the back and the very thick and heavy front door. The roof is *mansard* which means literally garret or attic with dormers, but we have always used the top floor for comfortable guest rooms.

The quite unspectacular spiral oak staircase has never been carpeted; it looks worn yet inviting. It does creak, but not in a spooky way. The grounds around the immediate exterior stone and slate walls are lined with hydrangeas. On the side lawns are flower and vegetable gardens and in the rear is our venerable *pétanque* ground. We Bakers are traditional inveterate lawn bowlers. And if we advertised in a typical British journal under *immobilier*, the Boudreau property would look like this:

Restored attractive stone villa on the edge of a hamlet, with slate roof in a superb setting of 5,000 sq.m. of woodland; the property comprises exposed beams in living room/dining room wi stone/tile fireplace, terracotta flooring, fully equipped kitchen, 3 bedrms fitted wi wardrobes (armoires); 2 bathrms, 2 WCs, oil-fired central heating; charming garden, well, terrace, veg. garden; beautiful original features. Completely habitable.

As is my custom I drove around the back and entered through the kitchen where I unloaded luggage and groceries. Then on walking through to the front, uncovering draped furniture as I went, I saw what I was supposed to notice if I entered by the front door. On the inside of the door a hand grenade was dangling from a wire at about eye level. It had been set to demolish my head.

11

I realized I was looking at a hand grenade prepared to blow when the door opened. I sat down in my favorite lounging chair and stared for a long time at the device. After a while I went to our vast collection of books on types of explosives and detonators. The French figure government professionals have destroyed about ten million unexploded grenades since 1946 when they became serious about cleaning up the countryside. Now here's a very old one someone found to display in my home. It is of German make, the type the Americans called "potato masher," because of its resemblance to a kind of kitchen ware, with its throwing handle sticking out of the canister part. It sure did remind me of my deceased brother.

My young brother had been a French *démineur*, a de-miner of unexploded ordnance left lying around the country after WW I and WW II. Jean-Luc Napoleon Baker had been one of his country's bomb-disposal experts, a member of the *Département du Déminage.* He was a specialist's specialist, willing to handle and eventually dispose of what awful materiel his *déminage* crew found. During 1991 thirty-six farmers died when they accidentally discovered unexploded shells on their properties. Jean-Luc had been nearby on one such occasion and rushed to assist the wounded. He was presented with a medal by the Département. Some time later a buried shell did its thing—this time to my heroic little brother. We never did find out the details of the accident that killed him.

A little over 100 de-miners work every day throughout France. They have a full time, never-ending job. The Department estimates that 12 million unexploded shells from World War I are buried around Verdun alone. Over 600 brave men have been killed working in demining. So now you know why my family is quite conversant with unexploded ordnance and unfortunately very familiar with the exploded kind too.

After reading up on grenades for an hour or so in Jean-Luc's munitions library, I decided to call the Angers District Déminage team. The guys at headquarters were very excited about the set-up and suggested maybe the local Police Commissioner and an Inspector specializing in firearms would also be the appropriate authorities to alert at this time. Because of Jean-Luc's reputation, two déminage guys came to Boudreau immediately, at my suggestion, to the kitchen door. They mumbled and whispered a lot and moved about the room as if the whole place were mined. Maybe they always walk like they are sidestepping invisible land mines but after some tippy-toe maneuvering they gingerly took the grenade off the door and out to their truck.

"It is a 1936 German grenade," the leader explained, "dormant, but it has been adjusted just enough to be easily awakened by a sharp pull on the wire. We will take it to our District site at Lac Bleu, but obviously this is a case for the Avrille police commissaire Lemieux, *mon ami.*"

"I am very grateful gentlemen. I am sorry I am not unpacked and ready to receive guests. May I invite you another day for a toast to Jean-Luc?"

"*Oui, monsieur,* we would be honored, some day when we are finished with our work in this area."

With that they roared off in the official unmarked truck, my grenade encased safely in a special carrier on its way to join tons of other unexploded grenades retrieved from all parts of rural France.

My next immediate task was to call Rosemarie Evangeline Baker, my brother's widow. I really had to talk to her before any more unpacking activity distracted me.

Rosemarie is an extraordinary woman. She is gorgeous, a self-reliant thirty-two-year-old widow, and one of Angers' highly regarded teachers of mathematics. My brother Jean-Luc, (whose nickname was "Boney" because his middle name, Napoleon, prompted his grade school pals to call him Boneparte) and Rosemarie were both true Angevins, Angers residents. They had graduated from the Université d'Angers and both had plans to be parents and eventually teachers in the excellent traditional Angers school system. Rosemarie is a professor in the Institut des Relations Publiques et de la Communication (IRCOM) and drives into work each Monday, Wednesday and Friday. Boney needed to work a few more years with the Ministère de Défense before he would be able to earn enough to build a townhouse north of the Maine River. Here it is largely residential around the Université d'Angers, situated north of the Maine, with its myriad college town bars, computer stores, clothing shops, restaurants, and apartments with flower gardens in every window. Both Boney and Rosemarie loved the Angers-Avrille area, and had had no plans for living anywhere else.

They had met at the Cathedrale St.-Maurice in Place Freppel when they were both studying for the *baccalauréat*. This final secondary school exam qualified them for entrance into the university. Boney and Rosemarie took "bac D", maths and natural science. They spent as much of their free time as they could together, and often studied together sitting elbow-to-elbow, so that it became common knowledge among our families and friends that the Baker and the Beaulieu families would soon be joined. After the "bac" she went on to IRCOM and Boney became a *démineur*. Telling her about the Boudreau grenade would not be pleasant.

"*'Allo Rosemarie, c'est votre beaufrere ici. Comment ca va cherie?*"

15

"Eh, voila Josh, mon vieux, I have been expecting you."

"I arrived last night. The weather has been perfect and the drive from Paris uneventful." I didn't think it was a good time to talk about the Laplanders.

"When will I see you? I can have *a boullabaisse* ready in a short time. Please come in." Rosemarie among her many talents is a fantastic cook, especially with seafood. It struck me more than ever before that Rosemarie and I have always mixed French and English in our family conversation, something neither of us ever did in our university courses. Maybe that is why it seemed pleasant to come home to Avrille and feel totally informal in a bilingual manner.

"Rosemarie dear, I will do a little shopping at my favorite *quincaillerie*. Maybe in modern Angers they are now calling it a hardware store. But at any rate I need some new door locks for this place. The ol' Boudreau needs a little attention."

"Mais pourquoi, Josh? Les Gagnes are not attentive? I will speak to them *toute suite*." She would too. "Speak" to them I mean. Rosemarie has been a wonderful overseer of the Boudreau since Boney's death and since my less than frequent visits to Angers/Avrille. And I think the Gagnes have always been fine workers, cleaning and maintaining the entire property.

"I have not seen either Robert or Elaine around here yet, but tomorrow will be soon enough. The place is clean and neat, except for one detail that is rather surprising."

I then began to quickly tell her about the dangling grenade and how fortunate it was that I entered the back door. She listened, breathing heavily into the phone in what I took for a concealed scream of anger. I promised to be there soon and asked what I should bring.

"Yourself in one piece if you please, Josh. I can't believe this. *Incroyable*. Unbelievable. Incroyable…" as her voice trailed off and I said "*A bientôt chéri*." I would see her soon.

Having visited Oulette's Lock Shop, I'm chugging along in the indefatigable Avant past the Museum d'Histoire Naturelle, aiming for Angers' Pont de la Haute-Chaine which spans the Maine river. In the Place St. Serge, just before the bridge which will put me in north Angers, there is a three car pile-up. I slow and am hailed by two gendarmes. They signal to roll down the window and ask if I am a doctor. They explain there has been a terrible accident requiring immediate assistance; while awaiting the city ambulance the bridge must be kept clear so all traffic will halt on this side of Haute-Chaine. Having no experience in emergency medical practice I pull off as much as possible and prepare to wait patiently.

In about six minutes two ambulances arrive and I stroll over to the crash site with about ten other stalled motorists. Hands in pockets, gawking, killing time, saying a silent prayer for the victims. I am noticing the remarkable efficiency of the emergency crews, thinking too about Rosemarie and boullabaisse. The same two gendarmes come running to me, motioning me to follow them. I hesitate, thinking I have misinterpreted their body language. But no, they practically drag me into the middle of the horrible scene, explaining politely but vehemently *"Cet'homme vous connais,"* or something like that, "this guy knows you."

There are at least four bodies on the ground, each one with one or two medics leaning over them. I can't see any of the victims' faces but it seems to be very serious work, commands shouted, carts banging around among crashed cars and emergency equipment. An officer approaches the two young gendarmes who brought me into the bloody circle, glances over at me a few times while talking. Then the officer signals me to approach him. As I do he nudges a medic away from where he is attending a fallen man.

"You are American?"

"Yes sir."

"You live in Angers, monsieur?"

"I have a home in Avrille; I am visiting family and friends for a few months."

"And you live in Memphis, Tennessee?"

"Yes sir," I answer, astonished.

"Well this injured man now being loaded onto the ambulance is from Memphis also. He says he knows you. If you would be so kind as to accompany me to the hospital this officer will follow in your car. I am Commissaire Roger Lemieux." As he said this he touched my elbow and gestured towards a police car. He seemed the clone/stereotype of Inspector Clouseau, only more self-assured.

A young gendarme held out his hand out and I gave him my car keys. I was ushered into the back seat and we were off, from standing still to full speed in a few seconds. This Angers driver had surely apprenticed around the Arc de Triomphe. We were a careening ship, leaning, swaying, tipping, and seemingly glancing off things as we shot across the bridge. We screeched to a single-jerk stop and the officers very slowly assembled around me and purposefully escorted me into a tiny police station.

"Coffee, monsieur le professeur?" He had ascertained my profession on the flight to this station. Now he was all calm politeness.

"No sir, merci bien. I would really like to know why I am here, *si voulez vous me dit quelque chose.*"

"*Ah, oui. Precisement.* You are here monsieur because that young man on the street said he knew you. With his last breath. You are from the same city, Memphis, Etats Unis, *n'est-ce pas*, monsieur?"

"I have no idea, sir, what you mean. I cannot think how I can help you. Perhaps if I could talk to the poor fellow we could establish some relationship and maybe I would be able to help him. I would be happy to do so right now. He seemed seriously injured.

"Yes monsieur, he was badly injured. I meant, monsieur, 'with his last breath' literally. He died on the way to the hospital so there was no reason to have you see him just then. His name was Mitchel Joseph, 2454 Aviator Avenue, Memphis, TN."

With that he handed me a wallet and the travel papers and tickets of Joseph, Mitchel. I sat down and tried to think of a logical way of explaining my scant knowledge of Mitchel Joseph, research lab director of the Memphis Zoo, whom I had seen a few times during the first few months of the Panda Pandamonium of last June. The entire city of Memphis was excited about the arrival of Le Le and Ya Ya, two young pandas from China. Joseph had been instrumental in managing the successful quarantine period. The last I saw him he was talking to L.V. Campbell. I knew nothing more about the man. I told the Commissaire and several other listening officers all I knew. They were very attentive. I handed back the papers and the wallet while I palmed the small card that read

ESAG ANGERS FRANCE
Cooperation Militaire et de Defense
Quatrieme #212

"If you will be so kind, monsieur le Professeur, to sign what you have dictated."

"Dictated? Was I dictating?" I had seen no one writing and there was no recorder in sight.

"Oui, monsieur, in order to get accurate statements we have abandoned hand written statements in favor of dictated and printed statements. All it takes is your signature, *justement la bas,*" just right there.

"Ok, let me read what I said. *S'il vous plait,* monsieur."

An officer presented me with a sheet of paper, legal size, with my few short paragraphs at the top. It was accurate, to the comma. I signed.

"Thank you monsieur. How long will you be in Angers? We may have to call upon your kind service again."

"I will be at my home in Avrille. But why would you ever need me again?"

"Because," he said, patting his holster, "your friend Joseph did not die from the car crash. He died from a bullet exactly in the brain, as you Americans say, between the eyes. Well, good night, monsieur."

"Good night, Commissaire."

Rosemarie was expecting me an hour ago. Parking in the French manner, two left wheels on the sidewalk with the Citroen's right side sort of dangling in the street, I lurch toward Rosemarie's house. She meets me at the door.

"*Vous etes en retard, mon vieux*, something happened, right?"

"Oh oui, *beaucoup de chose*. Do you have any Cointreau handy?"

"Mais oui. I can see plenty happened since we spoke earlier—you never looked so disoriented. Sit and tell."

Taking the glass in a shaky hand, I told her the whole short story. During the retelling I became aware of my emotional voice tones. I am really angry in Angers today. These events have really shaken me up. First a German hand grenade is placed in my house to kill me, then a passing acquaintance is shot in a car in front of me in Angers traffic. Qu'est-ce que c'est? What's happening?

While I try to relax in a large fauteuil armchair she lights the table candles, gets the steaming bouillabaisse from the kitchen, and pours Cabernet Sauvignon. After a prayer of thanksgiving we begin to talk about the delicious meal, how it was put together, when we last had a family gathering in Angers and in Avrille.

"How could this boy from the Memphis zoo turn up murdered on a roadway in Angers," she asks. "It seems too much of a coincidence. He must have had a reason for being here in Angers and I think that reason includes you, Josh."

"But I just met him casually a few days ago. Why had he even remembered me and quickly recognized me in a fatal emergency? And why was he killed?"

"We'll work on that," she said. "But right now let's eat."

I tried to steer the conversation to something nearer her every day interest and responsibility. She is in the middle of refereeing a national teacher's strike for the city of Angers. In her university position she is often asked to be a spokesperson for one side or the other. In this one, involving all French public school teachers, she is trying to bring about a peaceful solution by listening to all sides in the approved manner of the professional female ombudsperson.

"I get the impression that the teachers have fiercely rejected all the proposals for educational decentralization," I ask. "Is that the main issue?"

"Yes. Teachers' unions have reason to believe that if the school system is decentralized some poorer communities will end up with inferior curricula and schools, and the wealthy areas will be able to afford more and better school programs. Of course there are controversial pension requirements and pension proposals involved also. In the meantime many students have not had the proper review and preparedness for the up-coming bac exams. It is truly a typical French foul up."

She speaks about these grave issues with great calmness, thoughtfully, but with a visible, furrowed brow. She knows, of course, that 20% of French youngsters attend Catholic, i.e., private schools, where everything will stay the same no matter what the Ministry of Education eventually decides to do. And what she does in the very cantankerous public area may never really change anything except maybe some union leadership.

"Besides which," she continues smiling, "the PM Raffarin has given all his ministers a stern order: spend no more this coming year than you did last year. *Ca, c'est domage, bien sur.*"

I agree, it really is too bad for the school kids. But at least right now my strategy to talk about something other than Mitchel Joseph has helped us relax for a few dining moments away from the major event of the day. But then we suddenly stop and stare over our soup bowls and ask each other. "Now what should we do about Joseph's murder?"

Before I leave for Boudreau late that night we decide to get more information on poor Joseph. She will visit the morgue in company with a Medical Examiner friend who works there. My task will be to appear at the police station again and ask the Commissaire a few more questions. After all, I am the "friend" of the deceased.

On the way back I decide that tomorrow afternoon would be about the correct time to press the Commissaire for additional details. Surely by then the crack gendarmes of this famous capital of the Maine-et-Loire department in Western France will have cracked the 'American between the eyes' murder case. While it is probably true they don't get American murder investigations in Angers every day, they must have some expertise somewhat superior to the traffic department I met tonight. After all, Angers does have about 200,000 Angevins (residents) and is a trade and business center known for its wine and Cointreau liquer. And let's not forget its glassworks, printing plants, textiles, and on the outskirts, the very large slate quarries. Ardoisieres, slate quarries, are a big deal around the Lac Bleu d'Avrille area. Les Policiers Municipaux will undoubtedly be fully conversant with the unfortunate Mitchel Joseph's travel plans.

On the way to see the Commissaire at the City Hall complex, I pass by Place Ste-Croix and the school Les Freres des Ecoles Chretiennes, where Pierre and I spent many happy years until the age of fourteen. The Commissaire did not seem happy to see me and even looked at me as if wondering where he had seen me before. After a few moments of face-to-face *politesse*, him thinking, 'Who is this guy?' I refer to Mitchel Joseph. His face lights up and he mentions it may not be here right now. The body, he says, may be at the American Embassy. He is an artist in his craft of professional nonchalance, and gives the universal French shoulder shrug, hands out in front facing up. The shrug is saying, 'I don't know and I don't care. Can't you see I am not interested?' I grasp that and ask why the body is at the Embassy.

"Was he not an American, this Mitchel Joseph?"

"Yes sir, he was. Last night you had him delivered to the morgue. An M.E. pronounced him DAO from a gunshot to the head. You had his documents in your hand. Now you are no longer concerned about a murder in your district?"

I paused for breath and for effect.

"You see Monsieur le Professeur," he said, smoothing his little mustache and gently fingering his rather pronounced left ear lobe. "When the mayor of Angers gives me an order I carry it out. When the U.S. Embassy asks the mayor for a simple courtesy he carries it out. When your Consulate asks you to forget the bridge incident you also will oblige them, no monsieur?"

"Forget the incident?" I am stunned at his hands-off attitude regarding a murder now reduced to an 'incident.'

"Eh, alors, monsieur, our business together is now completed. I hope your stay in our city will continue to delight you. *Au revoir.*"

With that he extended his hand accompanied by the formal French bow and with an abrupt military turn he strode away. I had been dismissed by an expert dismisser.

I sat for a few minutes in the Avant and thought about what had just occurred. Obviously I would have to follow the body to the American Embassy on the broad Boulevard Foch, named after everyone's favorite WWI general. Foch, I remembered, was a household word when I was growing up. My father had been in the American Expeditionary Force, Army Medical Corps, as a translator and corpsman in No Man's Land around Verdun. He had been a life-long fan of Foch, the General chosen as Supreme Allied Commander after the German offensive in 1918, and the man revered by his allied troops. That memory distracted me.

The American Consulate at the Embassy in Angers is not a former chateau or even a very impressive building. But it has an enviable address and an American government official or two of importance. There are those who believe that every person assigned to an overseas office is a member of The Company, the Central Intelligence Agency. This is not true. Some are there to help Americans abroad and others are just good public relations people who can determine which foreigners are lying on their applications for U.S. visas. Some American career diplomats can perform several functions overseas. I'm sure I met one of those.

His name is Anthony Vincenzo Manerelli, and a more likable rigid bureaucrat clerk you will never meet. He's about five feet five inches tall, weighs a good one-hundred eighty-five pounds, a little on the puffy side, starting with his cheeks and moving down. His suit, shirt and tie seem to be wonderfully fitted over that entire roly-poly surface. In short, and he is, he smells and looks *tres chic,* fashionably Parisian. He is our United States Consul in Angers, France. It says so on his desk name plate.

After a short time in his antique-filled office, during which we exchanged remarks about our Women's USA Soccer team versus that of France in the World Cup, he came to the point.

"We have been expecting you, professor. The police commissioner told me you were recognized by the dying American. Any idea how this young man knew you?"

"Of course I do, sir. I talked to him last week at the zoo in Memphis, Tennessee. We talked about pandas. A former university student of mine was with us at the time. After a couple of minutes I left them there. That's it. That's the extent of my knowledge of the poor fellow."

"You're saying you did not have plans to meet here in Angers last night? You just happened to be driving by? Then he just happened to get hit by another car or two? Then he mentioned your name to the police? Then he took a bullet? Then you walked onto the scene?"

He paused, out of breath.

"That about sums it up," I said. "I'm impressed at this succinct summary."

He smiled and gave me the We Aim To Please Our Compatriots Abroad speech. Then he produced the wallet, pictures, money and documents found on Mitchel Joseph's person.

"What do you make of these things?"

He held them out in my direction over the top of his uncluttered desk. I pulled my chair up close and looked through all the stuff in a large brown envelope. $400.00 US, and 350 euros, a valid passport, extra recent photos, Social Security card, health insurance card, Amex and Visa cards, membership in the Memphis Zoological Society card, driver's license, and two Tennessee documents, Durable Power of Attorney and Living Will.

I placed them back on the desk. We stared at each other.

"What was our boy up to?"

"Up to?"

"Yeah, what was he doing here in Angers? If he was up to something we should know about, you should tell us right now."

I wondered if I should repeat the whole short story about my brief acquainance with Joseph. Then leave? I finally said, rather firmly, I thought. "There is nothing more for me to add. I came to the Consulate knowing there was nothing I could help you with. I thought a Consul would fill me in. For example, why was he killed?"

"Nothing else?"

"Question, you mean? Sure, I have questions. Why was he here? Why did he identify me seconds before he was shot between the eyes while lying helpless in the street? Have the local police and the American authorities followed up on any of that? Where is the body now? Have y'all contacted his relatives? Why did the police commissioner dismiss the incident just as you are doing? What are you up to? And so on. You know."

"Well," he said. "I know the answer to one of those questions. His body is on its way back to the States."

He leaned back in his chair. I could feel another dismissal coming.

"So *monsieur le professeur,* as Commissaire Lemieux calls you, you are free to go. Case closed."

He arose and extended his hand, mumbling something about enjoying my stay. At least he skipped the Gallic Shrug. Instead it was the New York Brush Off. I started for the door, slightly stunned, very angry. I'm sure my face was flushed. I looked back as I went through the door. He was on the phone, smiling.

Rosemarie had agreed to meet me in the Mercure Hotel restaurant in Place Pierre-Mendes-France, next to the fantastic Jardin des Plantes. The room is all pink and white and looks out on the Botanical Garden. Lovely place in magnificent Angers to discuss a very ugly subject. When we are seated and I have met Monsieur Richard Guyon, the assistant Medical Examiner, we order and sit waiting for the waiter to go away, which he will typically eventually do for a long period of time. Without speaking, Rosemarie passed me the copy of the M.E.'s document on Joseph, Mitchel.

DOA by a bullet fired from five feet into the mid-frontal lobe.

They were both made even more morbid by my report. In summary, the body was long gone and the local *Muncipale* and the American Consulate wanted nothing moore to do with it. My impression of the official Gallic Shrug added to the story. I told them about my brief connection with the deceased and his friendship with L.V. We agreed I would have to call L.V. today and alert her to the unfortunate events. She could call her Senator or someone else in government and maybe she could get some info concerning Joseph's planned adventure.

Mr. Guyon picked up *l'addition,* the food tab. I slipped into Old Dufferdom, becoming ever so slow at flipping out the euros. As the three of us exit the Mercure we do the French sidewalk thing—we clump together, block pedestrians, shake hands and say goodbye again a few times, while people walk around us. As we finally part for our cars I turn and bump into Laura Veronica Campbell. We startled each other. Our meeting was so totally surprising at first we just stood there and shouted each others' name.

"Prof Josh."

"L.V."

L.V., former psychology department star, looks like a million bucks, or at least like a young woman who has just come from a very expensive dress shop. A duplicate Ferragamo scarf is in a neighboring shop window for 99 euros. Her natural beauty, like a young vibrant Brooke Shields, is pleasing to the eye. People see her and break out in a smile. I comment on her fabulous appearance.

"I'm meeting Mitchel," she explains. "Right here in this Mercure lobby."

"Ooohhh," I sort of groan. She notices my voice and spirit are less than joyous.

"What's wrong, Prof?"

"L.V., honey. I have bad news. Let's go inside. I'll tell you why I am very sad right now. *On y vas.* C'mon, let's go sit."

We ordered her a *café noir* and a small bread stick, a *tartine,* to swirl about in the cup. It's something we French do when we are a little anxious; I hoped she would swirl. I pretended to sip a *Vittel menthe.*

By now she sensed a serious subject coming up and the smile of recognition had disappeared. I decided to be direct with L.V., and bank on her native good judgment and emotional stability which I had seen often during our four years at the university and the six years since.

I took the non-swirling hand in mine and as we made eye contact I told her "Mitchel Joseph is dead." Both her hands went to her face, her eyes widened, as if in disbelief, and she moved her chair a little ways away from the table. We sat that way for about a minute while I quietly filled in the details as best I could. We both teared up; she sobbed openly when I got to the part about him being already back in the States. Then she stood and asked if I would accompany her to the Concorde Hotel. We walked to my car, her arm in mine, her face covered with my large handkerchief.

In her gracious Concorde suite she stretched out on the *chaise longue* and words, calmly and precisely, poured out.

"Mitch and I were to be married in Paris next month. We have your Avrille address and we were going to surprise you at your Boudreau place one of these days. We are, excuse me, were to be married in Paris' Notre Dame, in a side chapel, not in the main arena. We knew you would be here and we so wanted to surprise you. We have even contracted for our French Memphis friend Father Charles-Henri Morreau."

Time out for sobbing. Tears of genuine sorrow, from deep down the physical and spiritual systems, those agonizing groans of grief, pain and misery, terribly appropriate under these awful circumstances.

"We had another reason for being in Angers this week, Prof. Mitch's hobby, as you probably don't know, has been for years studying and writing about the world's unexploded ordnance, you know, all those left-over land mines, and so forth. Mitch thought he could publicize the fact that there are millions of undiscovered shells remaining in France, along the

Marne and Somme rivers, for example. In fact, his ambition this next year was to apply to the French Departement du Deminage or some such outfit, for permission to work directly with *démineurs*. In the meantime he had been accepted into an exclusive international group of *Specialistes Americains*. They were to begin training next week."

"Excuse me L.V. dear, but what is this Special American group?"

"It is a scientific training program to prepare specialists in ordnance removal. It was begun by the French because they seem to have the most unexploded bombs and shells lying around their countryside. They have developed over the years the expertise required to remove unexploded shells from someone's farm, let's say. So for the last few years the French *demineurs* have been training Americans in what is called in their esoteric literature 'the French philosophy of demining.' The actual program is run through the engineering facilities of the *l'Ecole Superieure et d'Application du Genie*. The ESAG is one of the best French engineering schools. And that word *genie,* by the way, is also the same word for 'genius' in French, which applied, I think, to Mitchel."

She paused for additional Kleenex.

"Like your brother you told me about Prof, Mitch wanted first hand knowledge of the enormous problem.

He feared a cover-up or at least indifference by many governments which have not cleaned up their post-war litter. Mitch thought bureaucrats would not want their people to know how horrible the dangers are, even now in these so-called 'intermittent times of peace.' His idea was to write, maybe a book, and then European and Asian leaders would be attracted to his computer research program and training. He was going to insist on helping in the hands-on clean up, so a book was a few years in the future. I was to help in gathering computer data. In the meantime we would have a flat near Catholic U., where I have an interview next week about a possible teaching position in the *Centre International d'Etudes Francaises.* "

At this point she sort of collapsed, and after a deep sobbing outcry, lay perfectly quiet as if about to sleep. I suggested she change out of that stunning outfit and relax until I return in a few hours with dinner. She mumbled, "Okay, thanks Prof, you are a friend. Merci bien, mon ami."

I gently closed the door and began using my unused phone card. Rosemarie said she would be happy to bring one of her extraordinary *quiches,* sort of a *tarte-flan spectacle*, after I quickly brought her up to date on recent events. Before calling Pierre at the Colbert bar in Paris I scooted around the corner to select a *St-George Bordeau* from St-Emilion and a *Rivesaltes* of Roussillon. The wine store *patron* and his wife both asked about the young lady. They had seen us going into the hotel and had, in the manner of French wine retailers, pretty much covered the topic of the blond hiding her face in a kerchief and the *aînè* holding her arm. The neighborhood shop owners were usually well aware of Mercure residents, including this newly arrived 'elder.' The Mercure hotel chain in Paris seems to have its own effective gossip chain. News travels fast from one hotel to another via drivers, food and beverage managers, and, of course, between the talented and articulate Mercure hotel chefs. So before I returned to L.V.'s room I was sure many Angevins knew our whereabouts, including Lemieux, the Avrille police chief.

L.V., God bless her, always thinking, did have a great idea. She would be perfect for the highly regarded C.U. language center, which has an annual enrollment of 2,000 foreign language students. And Angers does have the reputation for the best-spoken French, taught on a fabulous campus, just one-and-a-half hours from Paris by TGV train.

Pierre's assistant said the boss was over at St-Eustache church helping a few of his steadies put up the traditional holiday lights. Those would be the regular customers who used the Colbert and St-Eustache as two focal points in their Parisian lives. And those worthies probably owed my pal Pierre, Paris' true *bon vivant,* a favor or two. He was devoted to the up-keep of this old church and attended as often as his enviable Colbert Hotel job allowed him to be away from the bar outside of happy hour. And God knows the ancient dark and dingy St-Eustache needed Pierre's generous caregiving.

Pierre loved that 1st *arrondissement* and often said if he never had to leave that district it would be okay with him. He frequently strolled the Palais Royal arcade, garden, and car-free *place*. He said it made him feel aristocratic to enter a restaurant there, as if he just happened to be passing by and stopped in for a bite on a whim, when actually he had been planning it for a week with three colleagues. Paris is almost twice as large in square miles as New York, 40.5 to 22.7 square miles, with many more churches to be looked after by devoted laymen like Pierre. Paris has 1,800 monuments, 170 museums, 145 theatres, and 380 cinemas. But you don't easily find the total number of churches in the City of Light. It is probably difficult to know nowadays because so many churches are museums, art galleries, show places, unused architectural tour stops, restaurants, etc. Maybe some one of the approximately 2,200,000 population may know how many churches there really are. Some of the 100,000 resident Americans may know. But Pierre would answer that query with a shrug. "Who cares?" He prefers St. Eustache in his own little part of the 1st *arrondissement.*

He was back in the bar next time I called. He listened to the L.V. story without saying a word except the *"oui, oh-oui, oui-oui"* he almost constantly mumbled. Then he made a suggestion which sounded like a long-thought-out plan. We would meet the next morning at Boudreau.

From a distance, Boudreau is a shining jewel in the spring morning sunlight, surrounded by a sea of wild green grass at this time of year. Others would say it is a pile of rocks with several entryways, any time of the year, sun or no sun. If it were pictured in a guidebook it would be noted as a typical Loire farmhouse. I guess the reason it is a jewel to me rather than a pile of rocks is that it is home. My childhood days centered around the school of the De La Salle Brothers who taught everything, including sports, especially soccer. Classes were challenging and entertaining at the same time. There was an historical ritual among the Brothers for rewarding academic accomplishments. Public bulletin board announcements regularly heralded the leaders in various exams. Medals and ribbons were distributed four times a year. My father had been through the same system and, in fact, had had some of the same Brothers in math and science. Parents were encouraged to drop by the school any time to talk to any teacher. My dad really liked those teaching monks. In his house the evening was family time and homework. School hours were from 7:30 to 5:00 p.m. Boudreau was locked up for the night at 9 p.m. The area was still shopping mall-free for miles up and down A11 from Boudreau to the town of Ancenis. Angers has many still-inhabited chateaux but the Bakers never were on first name terms with any of those families. So we were rather insolated as kids when my parents were alive.

The next morning Pierre drove in from Paris via Angers. I had remembered to check all the practically invisible strings at each Boudreau opening and found all intact. Rosemarie picked up L.V. from the Concorde Hotel. The four of us had a grand breakfast with our two caretakers, Robert (never "Bob") and Elaine Gagne. After we talked about the weather, the cost of an electronic alarm system, forthcoming Easter festivities, and our national women's soccer star Miss Pichon, we moved into the *salle de séjour* and sat staring for awhile at the hand grenade door, *la porte de la grenade,* as Robert named it. The inside sight of that door, with a tough wire still hanging significantly down from the top, was a stern reminder that it was time for a serious discussion.

When we were all seated comfortably in the big room, with the unpolished beams and stuffed book cabinets all around us, it was time to bring everyone up to date with the identical information. I began with the casual meeting of L.V. and Mitchel Joseph at the Memphis zoo, tried to explain the Laplanders and their various appearances, my stay at the Colbert Hotel in Paris, Joseph's murder, the hanging grenade, Rosemarie's advice, the police inspectors, the Commissaire, and the American Consulate. There were several questions and clarifications, proposed theories and suspicions. From Robert and Elaine there was mostly horrified astonishment as each separate segment of the story was introduced.

41

Robert and Elaine Gagne are my age, born and raised in Maine-et-Loire, never venturing far from the Angers/Avrille area. Their family homestead is a mile from Boudreau. We have known each other since we met on the first day of school as five-year-olds, and gradually became bilingual together. The three of us were all good in sports, especially football, that is, soccer. They both are palindrome hobbyists. They love phrases that read the same backwards as well as forward. When they were together they would say things like "Madam I'm Adam." And the other would respond with something like "Live not on evil." Robert would ask her, in front of guests, if they had any lemons. She would answer "No lemon no melon." Their dog's name, by the way, is Hannah.

When I went to the States to teach, the Gagnes took over the management of Boudreau, outside and inside. Robert is a professional landscape architect and Elaine manages her successful *boulangerie* near their home. They are best friends with Rosemarie and know Pierre from several of his former exciting visits to Angers. It was obvious they felt terrible about the Boudreau potato masher and I did my best to appear at ease with what could have been my explosive demise.

They repeated over and over, mumbling to themselves and to each other, "How could that have happened? We checked every detail of the property the morning of Josh's arrival. All doors and windows were locked."

Elaine added, going into detail, "My daughter Suzanne and I completed vacuuming and dusting just before noon. On the door we used that Old English liquid scratch cover you sent us. We smoothed over the entire door. Robert had finished watering the young trees; we locked up and went home for lunch."

After more discussion we took a bathroom break and returned to summarize and make some decisions. It was agreed that all of us could help gather information. We would work in pairs, and report back in five days. Pierre and I would be picking up the hotel and food bills and any other expenses the groups would incur. In the meantime we would not communicate except with our partners, endeavor to be as unobtrusive as possible, and keep our behaviors as normal as possible, *comme c'est la vie normale.* If there is such a thing.

Out of respect for Boudreau's 200-year-old door we called our informal investigation Operation Entrée. The teams would be Robert and Elaine; Rosemarie and L.V.; and Pierre and me.

The Gagnes would begin by doublelocking all Boudreau windows and placing inconspicuous tiny threads on all entryways, doors, windows, vents, etc. We needed to know if we had unwelcome visitors again during our absence. Then they would go about their usual landscaping, teaching, and the baking business with close attention to anything unusual up, down and around their A11 autoroute. They would visit shops and customers, stop and chat with nearby residents, check on any new arrivals or departures among acquaintances. In general the Gagnes were to be our ears for gossip. As they said, *commerages or nouvelles,* malicious or non-malicious.

Rosemarie and L.V. would do some library research, check out activities in local universities, mention the name of Mitchel Joseph, interview someone about his application to become a *démineur.* And how does one go about purchasing a 1918 German hand grenade in Maine-et-Loire, France?

Pierre and I would meet a few Air France pilots, old drinking buddies. Maybe they could get a list of flight attendants on my 1204 flight out of Boston. We wonder if French intelligence would have any additional info on the death of my brother Boney. We'll also visit Consul Anthony Manerelli and Commissaire Roger Lemieux. All three Operation Entrée duos have plenty to do.

Before we left on our missions each group of two met quietly in separate parts of the massive living room and talked about their planned moves. Then we met together again to clarify all our itineraries for the next five days. We now knew where and when everyone else would be. If we accidentally met we would not acknowledge the other group. Pierre gave us some final pointers. Beautiful Rosemarie and L.V. would certainly attract attention in academic Angers. Rosemarie would probably meet some folks she knew from the University. Pierre urged a good cover story on these extraordinary ladies.

Rosemarie thanked him for his advice and spontaneously led us in a French Hail Mary: *Je vous salut Marie...* I locked my faithful Avant in Boudreau's garage. Then we all left in three cars.

After five bustling days we met at Boudreau. We decided to have the *nouvelles de la rue* report first. Elaine and Robert Gagne would lead off with the views from the proverbial 'man in the street.'

"Rise to vote sir," began Robert, treating us to his first palindrome in five days. L.V., sharp minded as usual, laughed and said, "Way to go Robert!" The rest of us just smiled, anxious to get into the news.

"As you know I am not so the best of English speakers, but 'ere are some of the things we 'ave witness. On Sunday we attended a gathering of many of the local Angevins and Avrillais, citizens who are interested in the Lac Bleu problem. We have not kep' up with the protests and Elaine 'elped us mingle with the crowd, ask questions, listen to speeches. These are the kind of peoples who will know what is going on in and around this village of Avrille. There were about one 'undred there, mostly mature men and women, some sat in folding chairs, others 'eld up signs."

"The main discussion at the lake," continued Elaine, "was the fear that the estimated 10,000 tons of unexploded ammunition lying under water pose a huge threat to the safety of the residents. People speak casually about World War shells, and shockingly, they joke about hand grenades. One guy mentioned the large number of French who are maimed each year by land mines. There were several speakers, whose names I have written down here, who greatly excited the people. All of you have seen the autoroute construction going on. There is a theory that the road will somehow, you say 'impact'?, the continued safety of the Avrillais who live very near the lake and the new roadway. Some complications about water level and autoroute level being too similar for comfort."

Robert chimes in, "Since then we 'ave been drinking many cups of 'otel coffee at D'Anjou 'otel on Boulevard Foch. *Café au lait mauvais; nouvelles tres bien.*"

"In the shops and restaurants the locals speak of a 'powder keg,' referring to the Lac Bleu problem," Elaine added. "The other side, the government, says there is absolutely no risk of any explosion. This Lac Bleu problem is very urgent right now. It is easy for us to say that an autoroute and an underwater munitions depot do not fit together, so near each other. But we do not live near the lakeshore the way these nice people do. And of course we do not know all the details. It seems *tres complique* you know."

The rest of us joined Pierre in congratulating them on an eavesdropping job well done. Elaine, stylishly dressed in a dark blue two-piece (Printemps or Longchamp) suit, which she called her 'spy outfit,' began to serve *café au lait* and *croissants*. Robert, obviously relaxed after their report, stretched out in the French version of a 'lazy boy' chair. He really did not like any form of public or, in this case, private, reporting on a controversial topic. Joke with palindromes okay. Talk about anything remotely governmental/political and he clams up.

While sipping coffee, brought into the living room by Rosemarie and Elaine, several fresh *croissants* quickly disappeared. L.V. was anxious to begin her segment of the program.

"As y'all know I was staying at the Concorde Hotel, down the street from the D'Anjou. It is a lovely place, modern, with a brilliant young staff of chambermaids, concierges, receptionists and bar men. All are bilingual and prepared to talk about many different topics. They love government gossip and local opinion chit-chat, the more sensational and provocative the better.

We learned the name of that group of Lac Bleu activists is Collectif Angevin Pour le Trace Urbain Sud.

Their acronym is widely known: CACTUS. In simplest terms the word *cactus* means *problem* in French. In brief, it is a very prickly association. They mean to continue these kinds of Sunday teach-ins Elaine and Robert attended at the lakeside. They are said to be convinced the government will be forced by these demanding demonstrations to listen to the lakeside residents and actually take some positive anti-pollution methods.

There are movies available of divers swimming about piles and crates of the ordnance below the surface of the lake. Additional divers are scheduled to descend again to illustrate the importance of the danger. Cactus wants the lake cleaned up."

L.V. stood up to pour coffee and take a breather. Rosemarie continued.

"This Lac Bleu is a very old slate quarry, maybe 12th century, about 90 feet deep, now loaded with those well known unexploded munitions. The government has the idea to build a fine highway between Angers and Avrille. The residents of Avrille now know that the road bed is being planned to run just 600 meters or," smiling at L.V. "1,800 feet from the lake. The ordnance is only about 15 feet below the surface. So the lake water level becomes very significant."

Pierre, my best ol' buddy, cleared his throat and assumed his usual working pose as a bartender-counselor—he stood at the mahoganey table and leaned forward, elbows on the 'bar.'

"Your Excellency Judge Palindrome, Right Reverend Monsignori, ladies and gentlemen of the jury, and the talented caterer. I rise to discuss a great mystery. Our two first teams have done an excellent information-gathering job thus far and I am convinced we shall all do even more in the near future."

At this point it became clear he was finished kidding and his demeanor became quite solemn, almost like a Lieutenant talking to his Special Forces.

"It seems like it will take us some time before we can conclude anything about why young Mitchel Joseph was executed, why an attempt was made on the life of Josh Baker, and for that matter, an explanation into the death of his little brother Boney Baker. But I believe we have made some progress already. We know something about why hand grenades are so common in this area, what the public fuss is all about at Lac Bleu, and who some of the principals are.

"Josh and I had a nice talk with the American Consul, Anthony Manerelli, and with a couple of Air France jockeys. We may have a link or two to Josh's Laplanders from the pilots. By the way Josh thinks he caught a glimpse of them again today as we passed the *Palais de Justice,* which fronts on the Avenue 11 November 1918. Streets here really are history lessons.

"We picked up miscellaneous mini-facts like you did. We heard on good authority there are four million grenades in the lake. It is a matter of record that in 1965, 1997, and in 1982, there were several interruptions in the peace and quiet around Lac Bleu, centering on the left-overs of at least two world wars. Then we have the local and national politics, mixed up proposals concerning an autoroute, a city park, a tunnel, a by-pass highway, and this blessed, blustering CACTUS. Each of these subjects has a phalanx of leaders, politicians, and wannabes in each of those categories. Good and bad, crooks, self-righteous protestors and firm liberals and conservatives. Around here we call this *beaucoup de bruit*. *Bruit* says a lot about this situation: noise, racket, sound effects, and babbling din. Out job is to get to the bottom, not of the lake necessarily, but of the *bruit.*"

Pierre took a swig of cool coffee.

"So that's why Pierre and I," putting my hand on his shoulder, "will interview the Minister of the Interior and the Préfet de Maine-et-Loire. We'll interview a few *plongeurs and démineurs*. I think professional divers and deminers, specially trained by the Department of Defense in what amounts to an American Special Forces group, will have opinions which have not been aired in all the local papers.

In the next few days try to read as much local material as you can easily find around Angers-Avrille. Try *Le Courier de l'Ouest, Ouest France,* and *La Nouvelle Republique du Centre-Ouest.* Feel free to read Asterix and newspaper comics while you're at it."

The phone rang, at L.V.'s elbow. I quickly picked it up and listened as I turned very white.

"Monsieur Baker?"

"Oui, c'est moi ici."

"Oh Dr. Baker, I am Sergeant Willard Hartfield of the American Consulate Marine Detachment. You were here yesterday talking to Consul Manerelli and left your card?"

"Yes, that's correct."

"I thought you would like to know, sir, that Mr. Manerelli died this morning. By his own hand, sir."

"Say again Sergeant. Manerelli is dead?"

"Yes, sir, according to the evidence we have, he ate his 357 Sig Sauer, sir. Early this morning. I just thought you should know. You and the French gentleman, sir, were the last two to see him yesterday. Our Captain has his appointment calendar. You two were to meet him tomorrow again, sir?"

"Yes. Okay, thank you Sergeant. We shall certainly be there in the morning."

I gave the substance of the call, omitting the "ate" graphic.

"But Josh, we didn't have an appointment at the Consulate."

"I know, but we do now."

Yesterday at the American Embassy to see Manerelli we made a fruitful stop at the first floor embassy library. There we solicited the assistance of a petite brunette librarian. She was enthusiastic about flirting with Pierre and helping search files and dossiers for some background on the American Consul. We came up with several books, genealogies, and microfiche newspapers, and spread them over two large tables. Pierre also came up with the librarian's phone number which he was unwilling to spread around. He said vaguely it 'may prove valuable.'

It turns out this Manerelli, short, overweight, slick-haired, high I.Q. American Consul posted to our embassy in Angers, is a Plantagenet. History majors remember right away the family name of a great Anglo-French ruling dynasty, and its important historical derivative, *planta Genista,* a species of bush. It seems a count Geoffrey wore twigs in his hats and helmets when he went out each day. My dictionary calls them 'broom sprigs,' *genêts.* Anyway, this became a classy accessory style of male attire for a long line of English sovereigns, Henry II through Richard III.

It was then Pierre and I and the librarian (Jeanne-Clotilde Bedard, Pierre informed me) knew Manerelli was a genetically famous Plantagenet—he was locally known to never be without a *genista* twig in his hat and/or coat lapel. Very old family tradition. His *patrimoine,* honorable heritage. Not a cast metal lapel pin representing a sprig, but the actual wilting green sprig.

"This accounts for all those little shoots of shrubs he had attached to statues and display helmets in his office and waiting room," Pierre concludes.

"I think you're correct *mon ami.* He had dozens of memorabilia strung with what looked like asparagus tips."

"If you had told me what you were really looking for, I would have explained the sprigs and twigs he collected," Miss Bedard said. "He had them delivered regularly each month or so from a flower shop in Avrille's Place Lorraine. I saw them when he gave me a tour of his office at the Christmas party."

"You knew Anthony Manerelli?" I asked.

"Oh sure, many of the staff knew or, of course now, know him. We could never get the drift of all those goofy bush bits. We called them 'Tony's Broccoli.'"

"Well, aren't we the surprised ones?" I said, surprised.

"According to this geneology chart here before us, his grandmother, a McLaughlin, was descended from a member of the English royal house when the French and English were fighting over, around, and about, beautiful neighboring La Rochelle. So Manerelli was a true *Angevin,* descended from natives of the city of Angers in greater Anjou. An authentic Plantagenet, descended from Richard III.

I thought Manerelli was going to tell us a few things about grenades and Mitchel Joseph. If we had pressed him more, been more knowledgeable..."

"Maybe that's what set him off. He probably thought from our behavior we would be back to see him again. Maybe we caused him to commit suicide, Josh. Is that possible?"

"He knew we wanted to talk more about the quick exit of Mitchel Joseph's body. Joseph may have been involved somehow in Lac Bleu. Didn't Manerelli give you the impression he dismissed those two topics out-of-hand? As if he wanted no part of a Joseph discussion and definitely had nothing to say about the so-called Blue Lake Menace and a missing potato masher."

"Yes, especially when you told him Joseph was an internationally certified diver."

"You're right Pierre, maybe I did emphasize poor Joseph's role too much, but we are fishing. We don't know what his role, if any, really was. All we know is he was slain on the street. According to L.V. he was accepted in the deminer program."

"And we know Manerelli was very nervous. Maybe we'll find out more tomorrow from the marine sergeant."

Pierre made a point of telling Ms Bedard how grateful we were for her help. She assured him she would be happy to do research like this again. Something about "being less boring than the usual library afternoon."

The next morning we were in the Consulate at nine sharp.

As we entered the inviting hallway leading to Angers' American Consulate offices we passed one of those pleasant cultural exhibits that rotate from city to foreign city on a regular annual schedule. American tax payers never get tired of paying for shows of this type displaying aspects of American life as seen in photographs and artwork. The present Angers exhibit is entitled American Zoos. This particular exposition aims to show how America supports the international Species Survival Plan, by educating the public and conserving animals in danger of extinction. There are large display boards and huge photos of animal specialists working with various species in San Diego, Atlanta, Washington, and Memphis. In the Memphis section of photos is a scene of Mitchel Joseph in his lab examining a grasping paw of the inevitable panda, lying contentedly on its back, four legs straight up in the air. On Joseph's uniform pocket one can see a green sprig of something resembling a whithered leaf or clover.

I grab Pierre's arm and held him in front of the Memphis Zoo photo exhibit.

"Look closely at this picture, Pierre. Tell me what you see."

"It is a guy in a lab of some kind. He is counting panda digits, of which there are about six."

"The examiner there is the deceased Mitchel Joseph. This must have been taken in Memphis some time ago; that panda is much fatter today."

"So that is your Joseph fella, eh Josh. Seems like a handsome lad, intent on his work."

"Now look at his right breast pocket. What is that thing? Seems to be hanging out of the pocket or…"

"It's not hanging out, Josh. It is a pin or a logo, sewn on or clipped on. It seems definitely attached to the shirt."

"Yeah, I think you're right. Let's get into the meeting and come back when we have a camera to get an enlargement of that shirt pocket, "I said, punching him gently. "I think we have another Plantagenet fan."

We continued down the hall, Pierre slowly shaking his head in French astonishment.

Marine Sergeant Willard Hartfield met us at the office door. He greeted us rather formally and asked if we could wait a few minutes. The Prefet de Maine-et-Loire is on his way to talk to us.

"Do you know who he is?" asked Pierre.

"No sir," explained the Sergeant. "I just know the marine on duty took a message asking Dr. Josh Baker to meet him here. I have no idea what he wants. My problem right now is once again, twice in one week, sending an American body back to D.C. ASAP, sir."

"Well, no one envies you the body-shipping job, but I think I know why he wants to talk to the Prof here. And I do know who he is. His name is Yves-Jerome

Dufresne. He is a remarkable young politico on the rise. He is the headman in the local Maine-et-Loire area, the duly elected leader of the Angers district, which of course includes Avrille and Lac Bleu. Laval, Le Mans, Nantes and La Roche-sur-Yon are the other four major cities in the Pays de La Loire department. Rather like a county in the States. Nantes and La Roche front on the Atlantic. The world-famous port of La Rochelle is just south of La Roche. All of this makes young Dufresne a pretty important guy.

"Okay, why don't you two gentlemen go ahead inside. Manerelli's stuff has been pretty well cleared out already. I'll just go out to the front and bring the Prefet in as soon as his car arrives."

Pierre and I entered Manerelli's office. It was entirely changed. There was nothing of his there. It looked like an empty new hotel room. Not a personal item was in sight. Where Manerelli had a shop full of his own souvenirs, loaded with the family *planta Genista*, there was a different, very cleared desk, several new chairs, no pictures, and of course no helmets or statues of King Richard Plantagenet.

Pierre, as is his custom, began to stroll about the room, examining nothing in particular, observing everything for further reference. He was staring out the window with his back to the door when the Sergeant cleared his throat and announced:

"Gentlemen, may I introduce Monsieur Marc-Francois Thibault, the Minister of the Interior of France, and Monsieur Yves-Jerome Dufresne, the Prefet of Maine-et-Loire."

I'm sure both Pierre and I stood with our mouths open, our surprise registered in our momentary confusion. He gaped. I stared. Along with the anticipated county bureaucrat we now have the stunning guest appearance of two of France's outstanding leaders. The national head of the Department of the Interior/*Sécurité Civile,* which includes the environment, and the Lac Bleu CACTUS.

After a couple of long seconds we all step forward, mutter *je suis enchanté* a few times, and shake hands. Thibault gestures towards the shiny new football-shaped conference table, and, all smiles, we sit. Hartfield had left the room and closed the door soundlessly. If I could have whispered to Pierre I would have said: "What do we do now, Tonto?"

Thibault was a very well educated man. I had read in 'Figaro' that he speaks impeccable English and was used to talking to Americans of lesser achievement. For several years in his twenties he studied religion and philosophy at St. Mary's University in Minnesota and subsequently taught there. The Sergeant reappeared with several note pads, pencils, and bottles of Perrier. Thibault took a polite swig. Then he felt ready. He drew a deep breathe and began a well-prepared monologue.

"Gentlemen, let me first apologize in the name of the French nation for the outrageous treatment accorded your Mr. Mitchel Joseph. As you know (of course we didn't) he was in Angers at the request of our Ministre de l'Ecologie et de Développement Durable. He was to sign a long-term contract with that department to head up their new computer program division for the inventory to be made of France's huge supply of unexploded ordnance. But first he would have had to go through our ESAG program for American demining specialists. After that he would be working near the *sites de stockage* commencing with Lac Bleu, d'Avrille. You now know (we had an inkling) that some people did not wish him to begin training with our programmers. To prevent further publicity we made arrangements for your Consulate to return the body immediately to his parents. With, as I say, our deepest apologies."

"I would like now, Monsieurs, to introduce you, (another water swig), to three distinguished members of our *Assemblée Nationale*. They are all very much involved in reviving our government's interest in the creation of a commission of enquiry and a *stockage de munitions et d'armes chimiques* inventory office, hopefully using your Joseph's program."

With that he stepped gingerly to the door and three somberly dressed members of the French Republic's National Assembly entered the room. I assumed they had arrived after the Minister and had been waiting just outside the door for their ministerial cue. We shook hands all around with additional *enchantés*.

Marcel Boquer, the young and talented mayor of Angers, graduated from the esteemed (in Pierre's view) Ecole Nationale d'Administration as an outstanding Enarque. Miss Cécile Picard worked in the Department of Security where Joseph would have been reporting. Also in that bureau, Olivier Lambert, belonged to Groupe de Recherce.

"The reason I feel we should all meet here in the American Consulate is to give our mutual interests some coordination. Professor Baker and his friend Monsieur Le Grand, are in a position to help us salvage the important elements of the Joseph computer program. From now on we will be meeting in our Angers government offices where we will have our official inventory survey center."

At that moment the door crashed open and bullets, deadened with silencers, spit around the room. Pierre and I were the first and only ones to hit the floor alive. Three guys all in black, from hoods to shoes, shot each of the French in seconds. In the next instant they were back in the hall, trampling the zoo display as they dashed out the front door. I followed Pierre crawling

61

on the floor to the hall and caught a glimpse of them as they leaped into an open door in the back of a black unmarked van. It was all over in about fifteen silenced seconds.

In the hall two marines lay dead on top of the collapsed zoo display. Sergeant Hartfield was lying across the conference room threshold. We had to step over his body to leave the room as people from other offices came running into the main corridor. We told them to remain calm and call the proper emergency numbers. Several secretaries had to be restrained from gathering around the bodies of the three quite dead marines. A screaming cleaning lady wandered curiously into the conference room by another door. Each of the secretaries and functionaries noticed with horror the common execution style. All of deceased had been killed in the same manner: one bullet in the forehead.

It seemed like we spent the next few days with Avrille and Angers gendarmarie. They were all over us and we were all over them. We all wanted to know 'why.' Why were these French leaders murdered; why were we spared. What's going on? During days of interrogation, hourly reviews of the event were aired, recorded, cross-checked and sworn to. Dozens of additional really queer issues arose. It took an entire day for us to speculate about the Laplanders. I had to relate my suspicions of them from our first meeting on the plane to their appearance at the Consulate dressed in black, brandishing very effective hardware. I was positive they were the killers. I knew I could not prove my assertions but I made the case as best I could.

The woman's form in the tight-fitting sweat suit, her distinctive flight attendant gait and mannerisms, so well observed in the plane aisle, their entangled movements in his seat spoke of their respective body builds, height, weight, size and shape. Maybe the police did not believe the entire Laplander story but they promised to report back whatever facts they could find out about them. Pierre again suggested the police ask Air France.

The entire Avrille police force was assigned to protect Pierre, me, and Boudreau. We, and our friends the Gagnes, L.V., and Rosemarie felt very protected— and smothered. Since there are only about six gendarmes in Avrille, good ol' Roger Lemieux was constrained to begin an actual police recruiting program for suburban Angers. While that would take time, hard-pressed Commissaire Lemieux had to take on a few gendarmes from Angers and a Special Investigator from *Sûreté* Paris. The *Sûreté* conducted the daily briefings, all public media interviews, and the liaison with the relatives of the several deceased. During the week following the slaughter, Pierre and I became well acquainted with the police force, especially our regular Boudreau security guards. After the first few days though we rarely saw a genuine 'investigator' investigating. They were, we were told, incognito.

After we all read the regional and international newspapers and magazines we felt more confused than ever. As usual, the major papers each had their own slant on the killings. New York and Los Angeles reported it similarly but the Maine-et-Loire press was more sensational than *Le Monde* and *Le Figaro.* The political parties each had a slightly different view with the *Union pour l'Europe* and the *Parti des socialistes europeens* being generous with their coverage. All ran pictures of the Consulate's entrance hall and there were many familiar scenes in the magazines of Lac Bleu, the underwater pictures taken by divers, and the roadway controversy. If the idea of the killers was to internationalize Lac Bleu's *CACTUS* it was 'mission accomplished.' Their attempt to prevent any further investigation into the La Bleu controversy would prove useless.

We agreed that the Gagnes would be our eyes and ears at the now-famous lake. They would visit the site work each day, and get as close to the lakeshore as the military would allow. They were willing to drop the name of Boney Baker, deceased *demineur,* whenever feasible. They were personally interested, as nearby residents, to get some feeling for the 'powder keg' theory versus the *'il n'y a pas danger'* theory.

They took little informal polls and were quite ingenious. They managed to learn a great deal about how Lac Bleu people felt. Residents said they would be safe because the government and the new ecology appointees would see to that: 46%. Thirty percent said the construction of the roadway should be halted immediately—too near the daily water level of Lac Bleu. Twenty-one percent were convinced a longer but safer by-pass road would do the trick. Most had no opinion about whether a new airport would justify a new autoroute or a new park 'for the people.' Two percent thought the government already had an inventory of what is buried in Lac Bleu. Five percent were convinced the Assemblée Nationale needed a new commission *pour faire quelque chose,* just to have something to do.

Two weeks after the bloody fiasco we began to put a picture together. Within the picture frame were two opposing sides: CACTUS and the ASSEMBLEE NATIONALE. Commissaire Lemieux assigned the Boudreau group to continue working the CACTUS angle, trying to get a clue as to the genuine feelings of the leadership. He and his faceless boys would follow up on a few distinguished members of the Assembly. He was not at all convinced my Laplanders were involved. But whatever the killers' motives, they had managed to quiet further discussions of the demining problems of *la belle France.* Maybe Lemieux's investigations had something to do with the complete absence of demining in the French media.

Pierre and I split up. I walked the streets of Paris. He did the same in Angers. L.V. and Rosemarie worked Avrille. Armed with artists' sketches of the Lap and with Air France glossies of the Lander we circulated dozens of pictures of the Laplanders. Air France personnel and many of their passengers recognized the Lander but no one ever gave us a response to the Lap's police sketch.

"Have you seen this woman?" often got a French nod with gestures. Actual meaning from men: "No, but I would like to."

"Have you seen this man?" resulted in the shoulder shrug and the pursed lip response. Actual meaning: "Of course I don't know. Stupid question."

The Lander's name in Air France Flight Attendant School files is Céline Lorraine Beauchaine. Born in Aix-en-Provencee and presently said to be residing in Paris Montmartre, thirty-one years of age, she was considered by her superiors to be outstanding in every aspect of the training. Her work evaluations are outstanding. She is popular with flight staff with whom she has worked and is a marvel in emergencies with sick or drunken passengers. She has always been popular with male passengers and was known to have accepted an occasional drink at a post-flight *rendez-vous*. She has not returned to work since the Consulate shooting. Her roommate, away on a flight to the United Arab Republic, reported her missing after several days. Beauchaine was long gone with all her belongings and a few of her roommate's things as well. Commissaire

Lemieux alerted the Aix and Paris offices, faxed her picture with a request to hold for questioning. He was not confident of ever finding her again. He seemed to think that if a flight attendant cleared out her apartment and left abruptly it was with a new acquaintance found among the male passengers and little police attention was paid to these 'excursions,' as he called them.

The morning, after we received this Beauchaine report, L.V. too was gone.

**Frequent the company of
the elders; whoever is wise,
stay close to him.
SIRACH 6:34**

PART II

L.V.

At 4 A.M. I was out of Boudreau and on time for the early morning public bus from Avrille to Angers, right into *Place Marengo and the Societe Nationale des Chemins de Fer Francais,* train station. From there it was easy to catch a few minutes of shut-eye on the way in to Paris' *Gare de l'Est,* then on to the Montmartrobus to *rue des Abbesses.* Once on that lovely, short little street I offered a prayer of thanks for France's most convenient and best run public transportation system.

I feel very much at home here, having spent my senior year and two summers gawking and strolling up and down Montmartre streets. My apartment had been on rue Lepic and Madame Defarge was there again this morning as usual, preparing the day's distribution of the world's warmest *brioches.* She has devoted her life to creating and marketing these remarkable little breakfast buns throughout this Montmartre neighborhood. About this time each morning three-wheel delivery bicycles are loading up at her place and scooting out into the village streets. I feel like a new woman as soon as smell a fresh *brioche* and escape being run down by sleepy delivery boy. And so it happens; I a rejuvenated. Madame Defarge rules on Montmart The Village, as it is called by its devoted resider

69

Suggested logo/slogan for Madame Defarge's bicycles would be like: "Outside The Bun."

Happily she remembers me and we hug, laughing and shouting. Now I know I am ready for a day of detective work. Beauchaine, you witch, get ready. L.V. is on the hill, in The Village.

After two buns and coffees and loud conversation in Madame's style of street-smart French I tell her why I'm here. She has great sympathy for demining stories and quickly has an idea where to look for Laplander Flight Attendant Beauchaine.

"If she lives in the Village she will most likely be around *Basilique Sacre Coeur* sometime this coming weekend."

"But," I answer Madame, "I am not sure she like attends Mass or ever goes to church."

"I do not speak of Mass. Fine, if she goes you may spot her. But I speak of the many celebrations this week. Chirac himself will be here, with several Ministers and members of the clergy. It is a political rally with rides *pour les enfants,* food stalls, speeches, free drinks, clown acts, dozens of those Marcel Marceau imitators, and in the evening dancing in the Place de Tertre."

"So you think Chirac will draw out the blond bimbo we are looking for."

"This is possible, *ma chérie. Mais ce soir, vous-restez avec moi.*"

I am pleased to stay overnight with Madame Defarge because right now I am too tired to look for a Village rental. She gives me a key to her apartment and I am soon drowsy in her little guest room. I go over in my head the note I left yesterday for Prof and Rosemarie.

Chateau Boudreau

Dear Prof and Rose, I am leaving to look for the Beauchaine Witch because I can circulate easily in Montmartre. If she is there I will find her like in a few days. I am glad to be able to help y'all in this mess. I am most grateful for your hospitality and generosity. Will call in a day or two when I get settled. Don't worry about me. Don't look for me. Good luck in the work! Y'all are great. L.V.

After one more *brioche* I am out of the Defarge apartment at 6:00 AM. My idea is to circulate, stroll, window-shop, linger over coffee, and people watch. The nice colored photo of The Witch Beauchaine furnished by Air France is always at the ready. On this day I am on rue Lepic, around number 54 where Vince

Van Gogh lived with his brother Theo in the late 1880s. I am about to enjoy a simple lunch of a multiple egg omelette with coffee and Perrier when I am suddenly lifted off my seat by strong hands under each armpit. My chair crashes to the sidewalk and the table's contents are all over. I try to turn to see who is holding me up by the armpits but another hand strikes me sharply in the face. In a matter of seconds I am thrown in the backseat of a curbside German limo and we speed off. In about two additional seconds I recognize the blond-headed woman in the front seat. It is, for sure, Beauchaine herself. She turns in her seat and shouts at me.

"Well, you have been looking for me. Now you found me. Be careful what you search for, little Miss Campbell."

"Yeah, you're right. I like did find you. But you can call me L.V."

"Sure thing, L.V. You're locked in back there for this short trip. Be good and we won't have to gag you just yet."

They both seem to concentrate on safe and moderate speed through Montmartre byways, up Caulaincourt, right on Mont Cenci and into the back of little St. Pierre church, practically in the shadow of Sacre Coeur, under a large shade tree, out of sight from the sidewalk. Beauchaine opens the door and roughly pulls me out the door. The Laplander has parked next to a French Alpine Renault A110, and we're all three into that without hesitation. They just abandon the limo, not even bothering to close the doors. This time I am thrown in, gagged with everyone's favorite gray duct tape, and told to lie down. Beauchaine drives as one who is comfortable racing fearlessly through Monmartre streets. After several near pedestrian hits and two actual car-fender scrapings she seems delighted, all smiles, laughing and gesturing to everyone in the street. I sort of enjoy the experience too because this is my favorite part of the Village. I pop my head up once and the Laplander gentleman cracks me "up 'side da haid" to use a traditional Tennessee expression.

We are now stopping in a small cobble-stone square judging by the surround sound. I'm dragged out of the car, up two flights of stairs. Someone opens a door and charming Miss Beauchaine says "I am now going to kick you in the ass." I immediately go flying through the door, propelled by a hard right-foot goalkick placed in the geometric center of my cherished *derrière.* There is no goalie to catch me and my landing among the contents of a coffee table full of knick-knacks hastened my deep resentment of this witch, whoever she is. Since I can't talk I mumble uncomplimentary French expressions. Another slap "up 'side da haid." I flop on the floor and remain there.

The next morning I am awakened by a small *baguette* landing forcefully on my forehead. There is a carafe of red wine near the door. The mouth tape is roughly removed. I eat and drink their classic *petite déjeuner.* When I ask for the *toilette,* my hosts are cordial. After that short break I'm back in the guest room.

Around 9:00 that morning I find out where we are in the village: La Place M. Ayme. A tour bus parks under my window and the guide begins to talk about a wonderful Frenchman named Marcel Ayme. I remember doing a term paper on him at St. Mary's. He lived near here until his death in 1967. As I recall Ayme wrote many stories and one of them has to do with a man who has the ability to pass through walls. He was enjoying his special skill until one night he became stuck and died, suspended half in and half out of the wall. In this exotic little square there is a life size sculpture created by Ayme's friends with this very vivid statue of a guy with like one leg and arm and his head and shoulders sticking out of a permanent wall. The rest of his body is incased in stone and concrete. It is a very impressive scene and the tourist audience is all 'uhs and ahs' and talking about the great photographs they are getting.

In the next hour several more buses stop by. Then the Laplanders come in, sit me a chair and demand to know why I was looking for them.

"I really don't know why I am looking for you. There was a killing at the American Consulate in Angers. Right? Well I heard about it, I managed to get a copy of your photo and your sketch, and came up here to look. There is probably a reward. I could use a few euros."

"Why did you come straight here?"

"The Air France pic of you in your uniform had 'Montmartre' stamped on the back. I like the Village anyway. It is really the *vieille ville* of France, the *commune libre* of which freedom loving French are very proud. But you dudes know all that, right?

At this point the quiet Mr. Lap pulled me up by the shirtfront and ripped it off, along with my jeans. Beauchaine tossed them over in a corner. They shoved me back down, now clad only in my Victoria's Secret outfit. And Topsiders. While Lap paced up and down before me Lander Beauchaine left the room and returned quickly with two glasses of what smelled like *Cointreau.* As they sipped they paced and spoke softly.

"You know I think we are about to create the most attractive street manikin in the Village."

"You know, my dear, I have gathered all the necessary equipment here. But we will have to feed her because they say this job requires lots of concentrated energy."

75

"Good," Beauchaine says, "you feed her, I'll get her dressed. We want her on the spot by noon."

"I'm off after a few *jambons,* assuming ham sandwiches are acceptable for you two beauties on a Sunday afternoon."

The Lap left to shop. I have yet to hear his name spoken. Beauchaine now gives me directions.

"Stand up on this fruit crate. Stand straight. I am going to attach this mechanism to the inside of your thigh. It is your urinal for the next several hours. When you feel the need to tinkle just let it flow naturally. It will go down this little tube into this strapped-on container. You can adjust the top part to suit your own comfort and efficiency. Now go ahead and adjust it. Okay, that's good. A little drip here and there will not matter. But you need to look relaxed and smiling at all times. And be convinced, Miss Adventurous College Graduate, you are going to look good out there.

"Now this thing straps around your other calf. It is a small water bottle which will cool off your bare legs when you move your left elbow gently, unobtrusively, against this neat little spray lever. Now try that. Fine, that'll work."

"Okay, now for the gown."

Out of the closet comes a gorgeous long-sleeved, floor length white gown of some kind of plastic material, flared at the bottom, with a turtle neck and hood attached. I can see at a glance it will be a sweatbox in the day's 90 degree heat. She flips the whole outfit over my head in one expert move and stands back to look. Then she fixes the neck-head material to look naturally draped, and fluffs out the bottom hem just over my topsiders. As she walks around the crate, admiring her manikin, Lap comes back with the food. They allow me to sit clumsily while we brunch on ham sandwiches and *vin ordinaire*. Lap expresses his satisfaction with my outfit and now he takes over the show.

"Today you are appearing as Miss Démineur. You will be holding in your right hand a World War I hand grenade. The sign at your feet tells these Parisians and visitors a few words about the Lac Bleu debacle. A small table next to you will have stacks of free copies of various Maine-et-Loire newspapers telling the story at length. We will get you propped up on your crate in the space to the left of the Sacre Coeur front steps. Thousands of people will see you today; you will be in innumerable family pictures. All you have to do is smile. If money is placed near the sign at your feet gently wiggle the grenade, not threateningly, but barely, as if it is being moved in a gentle breeze. Can you do that? Well, let's try. Give us a demonstration how you can stand absolutely still and silent, staring out over the hill into Paris below. No change of expression, not an audible murmur. You are a mime. Mimicry means without words. Okay, gently wiggle the grenade."

With that my *couturière* presents me with a bottle of skin moisturizer. I spead some like on my face and arms.

I am then told I will be watched at all times by one of them, in various disguises and from various places, in the afternoon throng of Montmartre visitors. Beauchaine hints that if I behave myself and do exactly as told they may explain later what we are supposed to be doing here. With that we complete the short walk to Sacre Coeur and I stand on the designated spot just outside the front door. As he gives me a hand stepping up on the crate Lap whispers as he hands the grenade up to me.

"I think this has been disarmed but try not to drop it."

So here I am on this nice sunny afternoon doing my impression of a captured, paralyzed, unconscious, elegant human statue, the Queen of all *Démineurs*. Occasionally I have to gently wiggle the potato masher and squeeze my elbow against my rib to spray my bare legs beneath this sauna dress. The environment is noisy and terribly hot with great swaths of dry heat bouncing off the marble wall behind me and reflecting up from the white stone walkway beneath my platform.

From up here the view of Paris is marvelous, of course, but the folks in the shade further down the hill, singing and picnicking, are having more fun than I. Some couples do the so-called "French thing," get all entangled on a blanket in the midst of strollers, regardless of kids romping, dogs racing, people shouting. Every once in a while I think I see Beauchaine or Lap at different levels of the long Basilica steps or mingling with loungers on the grassy hillside. They seem to be moving and blending in with the tourists while never taking their eyes from me. Are they expecting me to attract someone they want to meet?

The *Maine-et-Loire* newspapers are going pretty well. The pictures on the front page of the underwater scene at *Lac Bleu* must be more generally appealing than I first thought. I hear the words *obu* and *menace* as people walk slowly past me and on into the Basilica. Some people are actually talking about the menace of unexploded shells.

Groups of teenagers have been standing around commenting on the hand grenade. An elderly man leaning on his walker has been explaining to a few family photographers the nature, origin and development of the modern grenade. A young lady hands him a cold Evian and while they are right in front of me I feel something touch my left topsider under the hem of the dress. Then the walker and his young lady glide quickly to the other side of the square. They now turn and stare at me. Operating out of the far right periphery now I see Beauchaine appear behind the walker. Remaining expressionless, I move my left topsider a fraction of an inch. There is something heavy there, between my feet. I assume Beauchaine has seen the walker's move because she is strolling over to stand in front of me with a camera.

My undercover spray bottle is about empty. I am very warm. Elapsed time in this stance? Maybe three hours. I may cramp up any minute. As I am wondering what would happen if I fainted on the job. Lap approached from my extreme right side and startled me by extending two hands, one for me and one for the grenade which disappears into his pants pocket.

"All right dear, that's about all the time you can stand today, don't you think? Step right over here, cheri, we brought the car close by for you."

He sounds like a loving father or dedicated drama coach. Beauchaine appears out of the crowd that usually disperses when a mime ends a shift. My leg muscles are cramped, my throat parched. As I leave the box I notice the thing at my feet is gone. Beauchaine has a very fast hand.

On the way back to the apartment they discuss how hot it is on Montmartre today. You would think they were out for a Sunday's fun time in the village with their eccentric daughter the human statue. They seem pleased with events and promise a complete French dinner if I promise to behave in silence. I promise.

Beauchaine allows me to "shower," (sponge bathe), and then presents me with a new pair of her jeans and a T-shirt clearly proclaiming *Regarde le petit toutou!* which I understood to mean something about looking at a little dog. They skipped bathing and the three of us stroll around the Village, through the attractive little *Place Dalida,* dedicated to the famous French singer who lived nearby. We finally end up famished at Bistro Melrose on Clichy. Here we ate well, starting with scallops with rice and several Stella Artois beers. I had a kind of flank steak which came in under the name of *onglet de veau,* while they had the chummy *fondue bourguignonne,* splashing boiling oil all over the table. They chatted in French about the weather, food, politics, and poodles. Actually, I think they forgot I am bilingual and understood all they said.

"Do you realize," Smith asked Beauchaine, his face full of fondue, "that there are about 5,000 restaurants in Paris?"

"I did not know there are that many. Five thousand?"

"Yes, and the first one seems to have popped up in 1765 through the intelligence and initiative of a Monsieur Boulanger?"

"Oh, not that thick food story again. Do you believe that?"

"I read it in <u>Paris Confidential </u>by Warren and Jean Trabant. Yes, I believe. Boulanger called his soups *restaurants,* that is, "restorers." You look up the word 'restorers' in your Larousse and you will find the word 'restaurant.' His heavy soups were meant to be medicinal remedies, capable of restoring good health. When rich people were sick they ordered a Boulanger soup at his sidewalk food stall. Voila, the term 'restaurant' came to be used on the streets of Paris."

I tried hard to look uninterested, gazing about like the idiotic daughter of two well-heeled residents. After some classy sounding dessert tarts, six kinds of cheese, and much Beaujolais, (they really like the *Fleurie),* she decided we should take a taxi back to the apartment. I was given a mattress in the corner and lying awake for some time I began to understand what we were supposed to be doing.

"I think the kid did very well this afternoon, don't you? After all, it was not an easy task standing there in the hot sun in that airless outfit?"

"Yes," Beauchaine said, "she came through for us alright. But make sure you know she is just a young American adventurer, probably in love with her professor of yore, and who was prepared to marry Joseph the Plantagenet."

"Honey, I understand what you mean, but, hell, babe, she is easy to look at."

"Ok. Let's review what we have to do next. First of all, what do we do with the half a million euros?"

"Well, I presume we turn them in to *Le Directeur* as usual and wait for him to dispense it as our expenses warrant. *'Con de Manon!'*"

At this point I learned that ol' Lap was a reader of the French classics. In this choice phrase relative to Manon Lescaut by Abbe Prevost he is definitely not honoring his boss, whoever he is.

"Ok. You're well read. Now can we decide what to do with little Miss Mime here. I don't want her hurt."

"We will have to bring her back to her simple-minded friends at the professor's chateau. We will have to tell them the whole story and try to make them understand this is more than a simple hand-grenade alert."

"You propose to tell them," Beauchaine almost shouted, "who we are and what we were trying to do?"

"Correct. They, and Miss Mime, should know we had them under total surveillance since the prof left the States. He should know we made sure he observed our performance on the plane, our driving madly around the Arc with him, and all the other times he may have seen us. The house has been bugged and security-wired since before he arrived in Paris and we should emphasize the involvement of our *Sûreté de l'Etat* to impress upon the group the seriousness of the Lac Bleu game."

"I don't know," Beauchaine sort of whispered. "I don't know how they will be able to accept us now after all these exciting, for them, little events. They will be very angry and so will Miss Mime here when she finds out we let her find us."

I couldn't help but gasp, in my sleep as it were, away over in my air-less corner. Thanks guys, I really thought I had found y'all. I was so disappointed I had one of those sleep-jerks, rolled over and pulled the sheet over my head. They went right on talking.

"Let's hear you explain Manerelli's death, genius." Beauchaine was speaking to Lap in an aggressive tone, as if challenging him to a debate here and now.

"Yeah, I know, that will be difficult. So will the murders of the Ministers and Sergeant at the Consulate. I am willing to bet the prof's friends think we were involved in that. They will have to trust us when we say some things can get out of control in the Sûreté as in any national police force. We will frankly, nay humbly, admit we may have a mole in l'Etat. The Americans are certainly aware of that possibility. They live with that kind of crap much more often than we do. And remember the hardest part will be explaining to the prof who's who in this horrible struggle over sunken ordnance."

"That's a lot of explaining and convincing, my partner," Beauchaine said yawning. "Let's rest up for a few hours and take off for the chateau around seven."

At seven sharp the next morning we are tooling out of the village, down through Paris and flying out at great speed along the 300 km to Angers. And what a car! These two do not want to be seen in vehicles of the State and so their car of choice is one of the most rare in the automotive industry—a 1938 Amilcar B-38 Roadster. It is a blur of forest green, outside finish and inside leather. Beauchaine says something about being incognito as far as *Sûreté de l'Etat* is concerned but we seem to attract no little attention along our dash from Paris to Angers. We must look like a typical congenial rich, French family, mom, dad, and quiet daughter. Beauchaine says the body and chassis are of aluminum-alloy construction and talks about a four speed gearbox. The Lap shouts out that it drives superbly. The canvas convertible top folds totally out of sight. So here I am, having plotted on my own to find these two characters, returning to Boudreau in their friendly custody, sitting

like their pal in this outrageous classic car. And now I
have to face Prof Josh and his worried (?) friends.

Prof Josh

I never thought anyone could be more worried
about the adventuress known at Memphis' St. Jude
Children's Research Hospital as Laura Veronica
Campbell than I. But I'm wrong. Commissaire Roger
Lemieux seems to be very much more worried than I
am. He has his small force looking for an American
5'9" blond in Angers and his fellow Commissaire in
Paris covering Montmartre. I think Lemieux has a
more personal motive than his Paris counterpart for
whom such a search is rather commonplace. In the few
days she has been gone on her search for Beauchaine,
Lemieux has exhibited more than professional curiosity
into her brief life history. I have told him everything I
know that may help him in the search for either the
Laplanders or L.V. But he wants to know mostly about
what kind of a person L.V. is. I rather think her natural
charm has made our Avrille police commissioner pretty
curious.

When the three of them pull up at Boudreau in this
vintage forest green roadster we are all pretty
dumbfounded. We are mostly put off by the obvious
congeniality that exists among them. In the short time
it takes to introduce our Boudreau group to the touristy-
looking arrivals one can see they are friends of L.V.'s,
as if she is bringing two ol' buddies over for lunch. It

takes several minutes of embarrassed introductions and foot-staring before Rosemarie, God bless her, announces we should all come inside for an *apéritif.* I lead the way into La Salle de Grenade while Robert and Elaine rattle wine glasses and come up with a few microwaved *tartes.* Chairs are shuffled about a circle and we sit for a few seconds just sipping and ogling L.V. and Beauchaine. With the smell of coffee filling the air I begin to make sense of this strange gathering.

"It seems I have seen you folks on various informal occasions in the past few weeks," I began, addressing the Laplanders. Then smiling slightly, "Would you be so kind as to tell me who you are and what you are doing?"

"My name," the Lap began, "is as I said outside, Matthew Smith. I am a native of St. *Paul-de-Vence.* My partner here is Celine Lorraine Beauchaine of Annecy. We are agents of *La Sûreté de l'Etat.* Our assignment has been to keep a strict surveillance on you since your brother Jean-Luc, the *démineur,* was killed. It has been hoped by our government that your presence back in France would help clarify many of the problems surrounding Lac Bleu issues."

I looked from him to the appealing Celine Beauchaine.

"Well," I said, "it certainly is nice to know whose side you are on."

"Which side is that, by the way?" This from a very sulky Pierre, dressed as usual in stone-washed dark blue denim, shirt, jacket and pants. He loved telling foreigners about the true origin of denim from Nimes, France. Shipped crates to the U.S. were stamped *De Nimes,* from Nimes. Americans began to call the crates 'denim' and the name stuck to the material itself.

"We all have a great deal to explain to each other," said Beauchaine, "so let us begin with my falling into Matt's lap on the bumpy ride over here. Obviously we were keeping close track of you but my fall on Matt was unrehearsed and totally, clumsily, accidental. We thought my airlines experience of ten years ago would be enough to get me through the overnight ride. Then we realized you are very observant, *Monsieur le professeur emeritus.* We knew you made us on a few occasions so we just played it for laughs and kept you well in sight, informally, as it were. We had to prevent any further harm coming to a member of the Baker family. That was our original goal. And still is."

"Why does Prof like need so much protection?" L.V. was sitting on the edge of her seat.

"The simple answer," replied Beauchaine, "is that our enemies think Prof knows as much as Boney did. They killed his brother because of what they thought he knew. Most likely that's why your friend Mitchel Joseph was killed at the Angers bridge. We still need to explore what Prof knows. They really are convinced he must know. At least two men have already been killed because of that information, whatever it is."

"But," I asked, "what do I know that would be worth killing me for, something I had in common with two men I had very little contact with over the past few years."

"That's why we are here to help," said Matthew. "Personally, I think it has to do with the Plantagenet or Genista Brotherhood. We'll see."

Celine Beauchaine then went on to review for us the Sûreté activities of the past few days. She described the events that led Matt and her to wiretap Boudreau throughout, how everything we uttered from the moment I arrived was all clearly recorded in the Avrille office of Commissioner Lemieux. We were and are under sophisticated French electronic surveillance. They joked about my 'invisible' threads at all windows and doors, and the stress they were under while removing the explosive charge from the old but live German hand grenade they really did find fixed inside the front door. They were positive I would as usual enter through the kitchen of Boudreau and notice the grenade later. Its effect would be to put me on the extreme alert, which it did, without exposing Matt and Celine too soon from their surveillance of all of us Boudreau friends. L.V. precipitated that by finding them, with Madame Defarge's willing participation.

After another half-hour of these and related events being thoroughly rehashed by all parties the Gagnes excused themselves to begin preparing dinner. L.V. wanted to help but Rosemarie gently signaled her to remain seated. And just at that point our local Commissioner Lemieux appeared at the front door. Operation Entrée was indeed operational.

Two kinds of wine, a Roussillon Rivesaltes and a St-Emilion Parsac, helped pass the small talk around while Robert and Elaine quite quickly whipped up lots of veggies in their *soupe au pistou. Baguettes,* and several kinds of local cheese, kept the conversation to a minimum until the endive salad appeared with plenty of Roquefort cheese and walnuts mixed with Rosemarie's original vinaigrette. Coffee was served in the Salle de Grenade.

The discussion continued with Matthew Smith.

"I believe I was about to mention the Plantagenets," he said, sipping French roast. "We had L.V. work last Sunday as a mime at Sacre Coeur. She did well, by the way if you ever need a living statue. We correctly assumed that we were being closely watched by the Genista Brotherhood which is intensely interested in getting all of Avrille's sunken ordnance dilemma cleared up. Their leaders know who we are, (indicating Celine Beauchaine), so they left us, at L.V.'s hot feet, a half-million euros. This is their way of influencing us to work for the cleanup on the side of the Avrille residents. If we were an American political party they would be active at Democratic or Republican fund-raising banquets."

"Why not just give the money to the national government or to the Prefecture de Maine-et-Loire for a Clean-Up Fund Drive?" asks the ever-practical Robert. After all, you know, like a sort of Gift Fig?"

"A what?" Celine blurts.

"A 'gift fig,' a palindrome meant to clarify the absolute 'no strings attached' nature of the money given by people who, in this case, want to see local ecology improved." Robert was always very patient with his pleasantries and mind-stretchers.

"A Gift Fig is a Fig Gift. I never did quite understand Palindromes," smiled Celine Beauchaine. I was beginning to see her as a person, now completely separated from the "Laplanders."

"I don't think any of us understands how anyone can be opposed to the Lac Bleu clean-up," L.V. volunteers. "Is it a large, deep hole filled close to the top with unexploded munitions from World Wars I and II? These had to be collected by brave *démineurs* over the years to protect innocent French farmers from blowing themselves up accidentally. Isn't it true that even today, every once in a while, more grenades and bombs are unearthed and disposed of by these army specialists. Do you mean to tell me that over the past eighty years or so all the French governments have avoided facing the decision to get rid of this horrible pollution? Incredible." And she added, *"formidable."*

"Monsieur le professeur, may I say something, please?"

"Of course, Commissaire, by all means. You are now a member of Operation Entrée. We would like to hear anything on this complicated subject from your viewpoint."

"Thank you sir. I feel we all have a great deal to learn about this very old local French subject, which unfortunately exists in many countries around the world. When wars are over the armies leave dangerous *matériel* lying about. Consider, for example, land mines in Cambodia, Kuwait, Vietnam. And the facts include this: just under one hundred French are killed or maimed each year by unexploded ordnance. We certainly do have a great problem. But now it is even more exacerbated, this is a word, non?, exacerbated, by politicians accepting political monies from road-builders who wish to make a highway close to this famous Lac Bleu. Our local problem is: the Avrille residents are opposed to the government's proposed roadway near the edge of the lake. This historic group of Genistas want to help the residents in their fight against Elysée."

"You have let the local people rally on Sundays, demonstrate, have their pictures taken holding signs, shout into bull horns, bring in outside speakers, and in general have a fun weekend criticizing the government," said Pierre. "Doesn't your department represent the very government these Avrille citizens are scolding? Has no one above you in the police told you to curtail the rallies?"

Pierre had shifted in his chair to face Commissaire Lemieux. The policeman nodded politely as he was being personally addressed, slowly stood and turned to face the group. Lemieux is tall for his French generation, five feet nine inches, straightbacked, handsome, short-cropped hair, with television announcer teeth. With thumbs in his Sam Brown belt he said:

"And I hope no one ever does give me such an order. I quite fully agree with the demonstrators and carefully watch that no violence erupts. You see, Pierre, I too feel that if the water level is lowered, as it may be with the new road nearby, maybe only 5 or 6 hundred meters away, munitions may be exposed to air and sunlight, and danger to the townspeople of Avrille will be increased."

In the brief moment of silence that followed that convincing declaration Elaine and Robert made as if to fuss with the coffee pot. Just as they leaned forward to move, a shot crashed through a French door and Lemieux collapsed onto L.V. and they both tumbled to the floor. In that second Pierre yelled "floor" and everyone did just that, floored it.

After a moment or two I whispered, "Stay down. I'll have a look around. L.V. remove Roger's tunic and see how badly he is hurt."

I crawled to the kitchen door and glanced out over the back field. No movement. After checking the other three directions I suggested they could sit up and stay away from windows and doors. As they all assumed sitting positions with backs to the stone walls in an irregular circle in front of the fireplace I noticed a most peculiar thing. All of them were properly clutching a handgun!

L.V. spoke first. "His shoulder is really torn apart. The bullet seems to have gone through. His shoulder belt is torn so maybe it took some of the impact. Anyway, he's coming around." Elaine had crawled forward with water and a towel and Pierre was examining the wound. "What do we do now Prof?"

"Make him comfortable right there where he is. Pierre, Robert and I will have a look outside. Come on guys, we'll use the kitchen door."

Robert, of course, knows every inch of the property, so he took the lead as we half-crouched our way over the 100 yards to the tree line. In this way we worked our way around Boudreau and back into the kitchen. We had seen or heard nothing. Lemieux was on the phone, leaning against L.V. and being tended to by Elaine. Smith had rearranged the furniture into something resembling a fort. Beauchaine was cleaning her government issued handgun with parts all over the coffee table.

"Do you realize," she said, "that this group is extremely well armed? Besides our Sûreté official sidearms, these guys are loaded. Robert and Elaine both have little Beretta 9 mm pieces. Lemieux has his regular .357 Sig Sauer service weapon, and Pierre and you always have your Heckler and Koch 9 mm automatic in your pants, which explains why you both walk funny."

"And let's not forget this little 9 mm Glock," said Rosemarie, whipping up her skirt to display a neat thigh to which was securely attached a loaded leather holster. "I really never thought about having to use it in an emergency like this. Boney gave me this leg arsenal and for some reason I decided to wear it today." She gave the well-known Gallic Shrug and the pursed lip exclaiming "phew."

Lemieux finished his calls, muttered something to Beauchaine and Smith, and addressed us all from his half-sitting position.

"I will check in to my office right away and get some attention from our assigned M.D. Then I will disappear. I have been reassigned to an Avrille motor vehicle unit from which I will be discreetly in charge of this investigation—the shooting, but more importantly the CACTUS controversy. The Maine-et-Loire Prefecture and the Angers Municipale really believe this *Lac Bleu d'Avrille* quandary has to be resolved. So this is my tentative, ah, how you say, 'game plan?'"

"By all means proceed Commissaire, ah, Lemieux, ah, Roger," I said smiling."

"Merci Josh. Beauchaine and Smith have to return to their Sûreté boss, now that their cover is uncovered, no?"

"We'll face the music back in Paris, but we will make every effort to keep surveillance on this scene," Smith said.

"Good," Lemieux continued, assuming the air of a strict French *gendarme* in the midst of a great traffic jam.

"Now Elaine and Robert should go back to their house, become occupied with other non-Boudreau things and stay away from this place, which will look abandoned, as if we all gave up and left. L.V. should become a sincere graduate student, work with the local Avrille historians and librarians as if following up some kind of history project. Maybe you can reside with Angers professor Rosemarie who should return fulltime to academic duties."

Both ladies smiled at each other and nodded agreement.

"None of you must let on to anyone that you are the least bit interested in *la pollution du lac*. I will give you a number to call at a set time every few days. Otherwise forget all you have seen and heard about *menace durable*. Understood?"

"What about Josh and Pierre," asked L.V.

"I will meet with them separately. We should say our goodbyes now and for your own safety do not acknowledge each other in public from now on. *Au revoir*."

After hugs and best wishes all round Robert and Elaine loaded perishable Boudreau food for the short ride to their place. As they slowly pulled out Robert waved and shouted his daily palindrome "So many dynamos."

"I think he means all of us, we are all dynamos," said L.V. "That Robert is one sharp guy." Then Rose Maire and L.V. borrowed several books from Boudreau's library before peeling rubber out of the yard. Smith and Beauchaine said a few words to

Lemieux and quietly drove off in their company's weird little '38 Roadster.

Lemieux then told us he was being picked up by a couple of his trusted men in a few minutes. He wanted to clear some ideas with us. He thought L.V. could do useful research by keeping a close daily journal on the contents of each newspaper and radio and tv station relative to anything about demining. Maybe she could get some interviews with inquiring reporters in line with her graduate journalism course. Robert and Elaine could once again join the Avrille residents at their regular town meetings. No doubt Rosemarie would be able to ascertain the mood of university students relative to Lac Bleu. He wanted Pierre and me to openly visit the offices of the *Ministre De L'Interieur Securité Civile*, the *Département De La Securité Public Explosives,* and the *Secretariat General Pour L'Administration.* We definitely needed information on why a highway so near a munitions-laden lake was a government imperative.

The three of us were about to lock up Boudreau when the phone rang. The message in rural French was brief.

"Robert et Elaine sont mort. Bonne chance."

Robert and Elaine are dead. Good luck.

I screamed out the message, slumped over the dining room table and wept. I banged the table top for several minutes, angry, flushed, weak with helplessness, while Lemieux and Pierre stood stunned. I sat up, maddened and sick. I hollered to God. Pierre called the Gagne house. No response. Then he ran to his car, drove over to their house, saw them lying by the side of the road. Some passing neighbors were on the scene respectfully spreading their coats over the bodies. Pierre returned in a few minutes and I could tell from his ashen complexion the caller had told the truth.

Lemieux's driver came as we exchanged contact dates, times and telephone numbers. Pierre and I loaded a few suitcases into my open Avant and headed for a quick silent drive to Paris and the Colbert Hotel. After a few minutes we were approaching the A 85 cut off east to Tours when a large black van came along side and at 75 miles an hour attempted to push us off the road. I resisted as best I could but the little lightweight Avant was no match for a few tons of German manufactured delivery van. We went flying off into a deep ditch and came to rest in a field of high grass several yards below A 11. As we sat dazed, thankful for our seatbelts, we noticed the van had pulled up a few meters from where we departed the highway. Three guys dressed in those killer outfits—black ski masks, black gloves, black running suits and black boots and, sure enough, black handguns equipped with silencers—were approaching from the roadway above us.

Pierre and I leaped out of the Avant and rolled into the tall grass, handguns at the ready. He immediately gave orders. We split up, he moved to his right and took up a position a few yards from the rear of the now smoking car. I crawled off to my left so that we could get them in a cross fire. They opened fire and I heard Pierre shout some obscenities in French meant to give them the impression they had hit him. They were now about twenty yards from where I was hugging the ground in the ditch. They fired again, a volley from all three of them into the car. At that we both popped up and fired. Two of them dropped and tumbled down into the ditch. The third guy emptied his clip at the car and into the grass all around us before he struggled back up toward their van. At that point we both shot him in the legs. He rolled back down into our ditch and ended up staring into my H & K 9 mm. which I placed heavily against his forehead. He seemed to stare at me for a moment then closed his eyes and passed out.

Pierre appeared from around the back of the car holding two new guns in one hand and his own in the other. He tossed their guns in the Avant.

"Those two are dead, mon ami. So is your beautiful little red car. We'll take this guy in the van and get out of here right now. Let's go."

Cars were beginning to slow down, coming and going on the Paris and Tours routes. Rubber-necking is a universal hobby. We carried the wounded gunman to his van, Pierre got a tourniquet on each leg, and without answering any questions from onlookers, I pulled off the shoulder and onto the highway to Paris at a very cautious speed. We moved into the north-flowing traffic to Paris without calling any attention to our common looking van. We settled into a nervous adrenaline-filled drive but I knew Pierre's mind was conjuring up our next series of emergency moves.

So here we are realizing all bets are off, this is a new ballgame. Some group or other really doesn't want us to help CACTUS and they are willing to kill anyone who does. I was convinced these three van drivers succeeded earlier this afternoon in causing Robert and Elaine to have a fatal crash and wondered if LV and Rosemarie and the Surete pair are still alive. What will Lemieux think of our plans now? We must all be wondering who is directing this operation.

As we approached Paris Pierre called a gendarme friend on the handy van phone and learned these new German imports are classified as *camions,* that is, trucks. This model is just out and the owner is one Jules Labonte. Our wounded passenger's wallet had a nice picture of himself with a woman and two children, the Jules Labonte family of Avignon, where Jules is a bartender at the Café Parisienne. As I inched the van down the rue de Richelieu toward the Colbert's back parking lot Pierre was giving Jules the new ground rules.

"Now Jules, we are going to take care of you and nurse you back to health. Your leg wounds will get all the best care my friends can give you here in the hotel. If you try to escape we will have to kill you just as we did your two stupid buddies back there. If you recover politely and cooperate with us you will be freed in a few weeks when you are okay again. In the meantime you will tell us all about why you tried to kill us and what other *merde* you have been involved in. So you prepare to talk to us at great length, leaving nothing out and you will be back with your family soon. *Comprenez-vous?"*

Jules nodded, evidently in pain. But he was not losing much blood.

"I should tell you Pierre ol' boy, I do not have any nursing skills. I teach Psychology, remember?"

"Don't worry Josh. Jules will be a good patient under the care of a few registered nurses I know well. They are body-builders and professional wrestlers on their days off. At work they help people. On their weekends they hurt people. It will be up to Jules here to cooperate. *N'est-ce pas, Jules?"*

Jules nodded. We carried him in through the service entrance and got him settled in a vacant room. One of Pierre's "nurse-friends" arrived and we all agreed on how this arrangement was going to work. It seems the nurses owed Pierre plenty of favors and could be trusted. We had ham sandwiches and beer sent up for the nurse and his patient while we shopped for the requisite pharmaceutical materials Jules would be needing. Lionel, the 300 pound nurse-maid, who said he knew what to do with two simple leg wounds, one in the calf, the other in the thigh. Pierre and I walked over to the always glorious-looking Gallery Vivienne mall for a light supper, some Provence Cassis, and phone calls to the surviving Operation Entrée group. All were getting settled in their new roles and horrified at the news of the Gagnes. I gave only a sketchy account of our gun battle.

L.V. and Rose Marie would have twenty-four hour protection. The Sûreté pair was extremely angry and vowed revenge. But on whom? After reviewing new game plans with Lemieux, Pierre and I retired to our Colbert rooms. I sat on my bed and palindromes kept coming into my tired brain and exhausted body. For some reason I thought about 'Olson is in Oslo.' And then I cried for a long time for my very great loss, my good, loving, devoted, loyal, childhood friends, Elaine and Robert Gagne. I hadn't done this in recent memory —I cried myself to sleep.

In a few days we had reestablished convenient communications with the Operation Entrée team. Beauchaine and Smith sent us technical phone experts with a carload of equipment for future use. I studied the manuals. Pierre went back to his confessional, the

Colbert Hotel bar and lounge. L.V. and Rose Marie had a rural/academic routine which seemed promising. Lemieux kept in close touch and reported the Lac Bleu Avrille scene was quiet. Jules Labonte made good progress under the care of rotating weight lifters and body builders who moved a treadmill and stationery bike into his room.

At first he didn't know anything about anything. Gradually, as he realized we were law abiding citizens with normal lives and jobs who fed and cared for him in a human manner he remembered a few details. He came to know that he was not going to go free until he helped us. The nurses aided in this learning process.

One night, when I was feeling like Inspector Jule Maigret, we awakened him at 2:00 AM and asked him a simple question.

"Why did you three guys want to kill us out on A 11?"

"We were each paid $10,000 to cause a wreck. Since you two did not suffer much at all when we drove you off the road our instructions were to kill you then and there. Our weapons had been supplied by whoever gave me the German van. I was to be back in Avignon in a couple of days. God knows what my family must be thinking right now."

Pierre always did his questioning nose to nose, in a half whisper, always succinctly.

"Who in the hell recruited you in Avignon?"

"I work for a trucking company, LeFleur Hauling, a legitimate outfit I worked for last year in a typical Avignon-Paris-Avignon run. I delivered computers up here and furniture to Avignon. This time the company promised me two helpers and a van. Orders for running your little Avant off the road came at the last moment. So did the guns and my two helpers who I had never seen before. They must have really hated you two."

"You stupid bastard. You shot at us."

"Yes, I shot into the ground near you, remember? I tried to flee, remember?"

"Oh, we remember, *mon ami?* Are you saying, Jules, you meant us to live or you just presumed the other two clods would wipe us out?"

"Honestly I thought you two were dead. I didn't want any part of that. I was about to leave the other guys there. After you shot me and grabbed the van I knew my two trucking buddies were dead. Are you guys marksmen or something?"

After similar sessions we were convinced Jules was an innocent, sharp-minded, hard-working family man, a gullible victim who would probably drive any truck without asking many questions. After all, as Pierre's customers keep telling him, unemployment is 9% these days, probably higher among truckers who seem to participate on occasion in a *movement de greve.* In plain English Jules has been a *gréviste,* one of those most irritating, spontaneous strikers, for which France is so well known. He smilingly admitted he had been on strike last year when he parked his truck in the narrow street at the entrance to the Place de l'Horloge, Avignon's beautiful square in the shadow of the Papal Palace.

"That was a dirty trick, right Jules?"

"It did disturb the tourist trade."

"Disturb, hell Jules," emphasized Pierre, "you French truckers are bums and thugs. You're lucky we don't work you over right now for the inconvenience you have caused innumerable tourists over the years. But instead we are going to ask you to make up for those striking sins by helping us. You have info. We need info. You are going to get us info! *Comprenez-vous, Jules?"*

Jules, smiling again. "You guys know I got into this accidentally. You know I did not intend to hurt you. I am appreciative of the care you have given me, even against my will. Yes, I will try to help you."

"Good. For starters once again, who hired you? What were the nationalities of your two deceased buddies, who by the way have not appeared on the evening news yet, have they?"

"I believe the two guys with me in the van were Algerians. Looks, manners, eating habits, accents. Algerian."

"Okay, let's say they are Algerian. Who hired you?" asked Pierre.

"La Fleur Hauling. All I had to do was drive a day or two in the Avrille-Angers area then return to Avignon quite a bit richer."

I moved close to his face and asked quietly, "You were under the direction of two guys you do not know to earn some money for your family. Do you think that makes you a respectable guy? You were involved in an attempt to kill us. Are we supposed to be cordial to you? You will do anything for money, maybe try again to kill us? Can we trust you at all?"

We took a break. Pierre went out for wine, bread and cheese. It gave us all a chance to think about a possible Algerian connection to us and to Lac Bleu and to Genistas. CACTUS wants to clean up the munitions pollution. Road construction companies don't care about that; they are concerned with things like government highway concrete contracts. And we are almost killed by Algerians?   And their driver from Avignon has never heard of Lac Bleu. *Quelle mystère!*

**Avoid not those who weep,
mourn with those who mourn.
SIRACH 7:34**

PART III

Pierre

It's true, I did go out for food. Several things prevented me from returning to the Colbert, to Josh and Jules. I walked hastily across the street and into Place des Victoires where my good friend Henri L'Heureux always had a supply of good wine, cheese and bread any time of the day or night. His place is simply called *LIVRES,* a truly exciting name to attract the curious. I have always supposed he sold books to his many patrons who regularly enjoyed afternoon refreshments with Henri, a shrewd fat man of jovial temperament. There were bookshelves, some books and posters lying about, but mostly he sold conversation. As I entered the shop he seemed unhappy to see me and his greeting was downright cold. He grabbed my lapels, spun me around and pushed me out the door.

"What you doing here, Pierre? You should be in hiding or with a police guard."

"I beg your pardon. I came here for wine. What's your problem?"

"There are two hefty Algerian-types in the back room. They let it be known they want you and two guys named Jules and Josh. Sounds like a comedy team but it is not funny. Whatever you've done get away from *LIVRES.* Now please. Run. Fast. Vite! Vite!"

"Okay, I'm going. But why am I running again?"

"These guys are *escrocs,* crooks, killers, with ill-fitting suits and bulging shoulder holsters and mean manners. *Affranchi! Arcan!* Vite! Vite!"

Henri L'Heureux was not Happy Henry as he gave me a shove toward the center of the Place, using his splendid slang vocabulary for 'thugs' and 'hoodlums'. Just then two men came charging out the door, guns drawn. They literally ran over Henri as I took off running across the *rue du Louvre,* into the *Hotel des Postes,* out a side door, into the front of St. Eustache church, out the sacristy door onto *Rambuteau* where taxis cruise to pick up Stock Exchange personnel. As I leaped into the first cab in line, I saw the bad guys getting into a black Mercedes, signaling their driver to do a U turn, and pointing toward me. It would take him a few seconds to perform that automotive feat while avoiding the taxi line in front of the *Banque de France.* I yelled "Place des Vosges" in the driver's ear and let a twenty euro bill flutter onto the seat beside him. "Vite, monsieur, vite." I knew if I made it safely into the narrow streets of the historic Marais district even Interpol could not find me. It was but a hectic four-minute Right Bank ride. As I alighted I told the driver 'merci bien,' and 'get lost.' He roared out of the Marais. I stood for a moment, gazing at the most marvelous of all Paris' grand squares, Place de Vosges, built by Henry IV in the 1600s and, today, the center of *laissez faire* living in the tolerant 4th *arrondissement*. The first thing I had to do was call Jeanne-Clotilde Bedard at the Angers public library. After a quick look around the vast, enchanting, four-sided garden, I went directly to the first telephone booth available. Right now I needed to know if Ms Bedard would let me contact her parents. Jeanne had told me they own a spectacular Vosges apartment.

"Hi Jeanne, this is Pierre. *Comment ca va?*"

"Allo, Pierre. I am fine. How nice of you to call. Where are you?"

"Jeanne, I am in Place des Vosges. I thought I would greet your parents if that would be okay?"

After some awkward pauses Jeanne-Clotilde practically commanded me to call her parents. She will be coming to Paris this next weekend, she said, so maybe we can get together. In the meantime she promised to tell her parents about me right away. She added they would like to meet a friend of hers from Angers, especially a renown *hotelier,* native of Paris, about whom she has spoken from time to time. I was to call them around three in the afternoon. In the meantime I really had to find something to eat while avoiding two or three guys tailing me.

111

It seemed safe to stay within the Vosges and stroll with shoppers, tourists, and workers on their breaks. I pulled my coat collar up and window-shopped in the ground floor arcade stores, with hands in my pockets, as if I had not a care in the world. Lovers, or at least persons who knew each other very well, sprawled about under the perfectly shaped linden trees on immaculately manicured lawns. Others sat with their feet in the fountains. On the north and south sides of the square are the original royal pavilions. Everything in the Vosges is laid out perfectly symmetrical: the walkways, buildings, and the arcade which surrounds the entire square. This would be a great place for a field trip with a high school geometry class. The only nonsymmetrical parts of the Vosges are the people.

After a few cups of French roast and a medium baguette with marmalade, I felt better and began to scan the strollers. I thought about what Jules said about Algerians. Why them? What could modern day Algeria have in common with Lac Bleu in Avrille? And just then I saw him.

He was one of those burly guys I had been running from. He saw me at the same instant at the Place Vosges's east entrance. He came bounding across the street full tilt, not a graceful runner, but definitely a linebacker type with his eyes unfortunately focused solely on me. He ran right into the heavy, fast, rue de Turenne traffic which traverses the whole of the Marais district from the Seine straight north. He never had a chance. A newspaper delivery truck smashed right into him. The man bounced from the front bumper up and onto the roof of the van and back onto the Turenne pavement. Cars braked and slid and fender-bumped for several blocks. While a crowd gathered and drivers dismounted to ascertain damages and accost each other, I was next to the body when the *Service d'assistance medicale urgence* vehicles managed to get through nine minutes later. When a gendarme asked me if I was with him and if I knew him I replied *"Oh oui,"* and was allowed to accompany him to the hospital. He was unable to speak and many bones were seen to be broken when the attendants cut off his clothes and administered an IV and oxygen. I sat leaning against the inside of the ambulance and the attendants hardly noticed me.

When we arrived at the hospital I recited all the personal information quietly garnered from the man's wallet. His name on his cards: Mamoud Salamat, 33 years old, citizen of Ech Cheliff, Algeria, in France on a student visa. No family listed; no other personal info. How related to me? We are business associates. Insurance? Colbert Hotel, courtesy Pierre Le Grand, Director, Concierges Training. I used my real I.D., and as "Monsieur le professeur," was allowed to remain by Mamoud's side. It seemed the man was not long for this world. One of the desk clerks tried unsuccessfully to contact the Paris Algerian Embassy.

During Mamoud's X-ray session I talked to Commissaire Lemieux in Avrille very briefly. He is not one for phone conversations, sensed I was onto something important, and merely said, "I will be there soon." I promised to stay close to my new business partner.

Mamoud was half awake when he was returned to his room. I asked him in French if he would like to talk. He blinked, smirked, and replied: "I am supposed to be chasing you, trying to kill you. You want to talk. You could kill me right now. I know you have a gun."

"Yes, I have a gun. But I am more interested in a live Mamoud. Why do you chase me?"

"You are neither clever nor stupid. You don't hide from us very well, and you don't seem to understand you are marked for death. But you remain where you can easily be found. Why are you not running right now?"

"Why am I marked for death, Mamoud?"

"You, like your brother, stir up those *genistas.*"

"How is that a concern of an Algerian?"

"The *genistas* call attention to the damnable Lac Bleu unexploded munitions. We want the *genista* group to drop opposition to the pollution problem, quiet down and forget about their 'problem.' Algeria will then negotiate a 'rescue'of the Avrille munitions legally, take them off French soil, and solve the French *deminage* difficulty."

"Algeria wants to clean up Lac Bleu, buy the munitions for its own use?"

"In a nut shell, yes."

"Mamoud, are you an Algerian government representative sent here to arrange a legitimate sale of World War I and II arms?"

"You could say that."

"No. I really could not sanely say that."

Hospital lunch was served. Mamound was given some meds in a little cup, and after an impolite tirade about French food, he slept. I dozed in a chair until awakened by Lemieux and L.V.

"Hey, Roger and L.V. Good to see you." We hugged and shook hands. We're taking no chances.

"L.V. thought you might need an American 'pat on the back.'"

"I could use some. So could he, my friendly assassin Mamoud Salamat, here to negotiate for the Algerian government for the Lac's munitions. He thinks I am Prof Josh."

"He's part of the group that like fired on our Operation Entrée meeting at Boudreau?" asked L.V., beautiful eyes wide and searching.

"What do you think, Roger?" I asked.

"When he awakens I would like to have a talk with Mamoud. I don't understand why this little lake is so important to his bosses in Algiers. I will share some ideas with you later. In the meantime let us, how you say, 'grab a bite?' I can call in a few *gendarmerie* boys to keep an eye on this 'diplomat.'"

It was obvious ol' Rog was picking up some American English from L.V. He talked to someone on his phone and in few minutes two splendidly dressed and outfitted young national policemen appeared. Roger outlined their duties. No one enters except a hospital doctor or nurse. One man remains in the room, One stays outside the room door. No exceptions.

I had heard of a *sandwich grec* place in the Vosges arcade and after a short walk we found three vacant old metal chairs in a tiny restaurant which serves these large Hungry Homme lunches: hamburgers. L.V. ordered one of her favorites, Poire Belle Helene, a large pear covered with vanilla ice cream and chocolate sauce. Neither of us had even heard of it before. L.V. had had a roommate named Helen and said she always ate this dessert in her honor. Roger and I had the H.H. special. We were back in the hospital within the hour.

The two policemen were right where we left them, polite but unsmiling. L.V. suggested "they look like they need a pee break." Lemieux agreed and told them to take a cigarette stroll outside and be back in fifteen minutes. The Commissaire was anxious to continue conversing with Mamoud Salamat. But Mamoud was having no more conversation. He was very dead.

L.V. grabbed the phone and began demanding the attending staff come immediately. Lemieux and I raced out to find the *gendarmes* casually leaning against the wall under the entrance archway. Only one nurse had come in the room for a minute or two, they said. She had adjusted the patient's pillows, taken his temperature, and left. By the time we arrived back in the room L.V. was being assured by three staff that no one had entered the room while the police were there. The patient's chart remained unchanged. Lemieux told the two young *flics* to take statements from the staff while he made a few phone calls. The medical examiner arrived in a huff, followed by several others, and poor unfortunate Mamoud Salamat, still under French arrest, was wheeled out to be thoroughly examined for the formal 'cause of death' paperwork. No one called the Algerian embassy.

My cell phone rang. Jeanne-Clotilde Bedard wanted me to come to her parents' Vosges home for dinner at 7:00. I said I would have to call her back. Lemieux was furious at himself for what happened and apologetic to me for having brought L.V. into an obviously dangerous situation. I agreed L.V. should not be so involved in this but I also felt it was necessary to point out to him that Prof Josh had the most complete confidence in L.V.'s many talents. I assured Lemieux L.V. could handle this.

Several newly arrived *gendarmes* were now patrolling the Hotel Dieu corridors, looking for someone answering the description given by our two room guards, who by now were totally ashamed and worried about their future in police work. The usual police bulletins and descriptions were being efficiently circulated in Paris. Lemieux and I both knew no killer 'temperature-taking *infirmière*' would ever be found.

Prof Josh

Pierre had been gone for several hours before Jules and I began to have a semi-cordial conversation. In a way I felt sorry for Jules. He was caught up in these events strictly against his wishes. And he really wanted to get back to Avignon.

"So Jules, did you understand what the two Algerians were saying?"

"They spoke French."

"Don't you understand French?" I asked.

"Yes, but this was Algerian French. Heavily accented with mixed slang of their country. I did not get it all."

"Well tell me what you did get. Just relax there, stretch out, close your eyes, and just say whatever you remember them saying. Right now don't concentrate on the context. Just say whatever you can recall. Maybe we can put it to good use later."

"Okay, but it will be bits of conversation, you know, words I was not supposed to be listening to, so I could never ask them to repeat what I missed. Here are some miscellaneous ideas they mentioned, some serious, some just joking.

"They talked about French women a lot. French women taste and smell differently...They hate the food...They want to empty some lake...The lake is filled with stuff they need...If the lake is drained the garbage can be 'rescued...' If they cannot drain the lake they will blow it up...or something like that."

'Okay, good, "I said. "Relax and imagine yourself at the wheel while they talked back and forth."

"They know many immigrants, Algerians, Moslems, who are unemployed here in France...with no rights...some of their friends want to work on some

big road project...road near a lake...the same lake that
will be blown up or drained...I'm sorry, Professor, in
heavy traffic I was not paying attention all the time."

"That's good Jules. Relax now."

That's more than we knew before. These guys were
here to eliminate Pierre and me because in their minds
we stand in the way of their completing this mission, if
we can call it that. We are somehow seen as protecting
the lake's old munitions from any outside disturbance
so we must be killed. Like my brother Boney? Like
Mitchel Joseph? Like the Gagnes? But why do
Algerians feel the lake should be emptied? What has
this little lake in an Angers suburb have to do with
France's former colony? And what about the French
military, very ably protecting the lake from any
agitation? Certainly the Algerians know the French
government has been collecting and depositing
munitions in this lake since World War I. What's the
big rush to murder people over its existence now?

I found myself sharing more and more of this
strange Lac Bleu pollution story with Jules. As we
continued to review and speculate on the situation the
phone rang. It was Pierre, excited at being alive at
Hotel Dieu just outside Notre Dame. He wants us to sit
tight until he calls back.

"Speaking of Algerians, Jules," I said, "that was
Pierre. He's watching over a very damaged one right

now. My friend Lemieux is coming in from Avrille. We'll hear more later. He's ordered our lunch from a local *boulangerie* and they will deliver a meal to us soon. For some reason he's not using Henri's book store food today."

Ol' Avrille Roger took over several details. He sent a car to the Colbert to pick me up and drop off two uniformed police to keep Jules company. He suggested Pierre accept the invitation of the Bedards at the Vosges apartments. Roger then invited L.V. and me for a short walk from the hospital to the nearby Palais de Justice. There we sat down for a serious chat on a shady bench in the shadow of the Sainte-Chapelle. The *Conciergerie* in the Palais complex always reminded me of its 4,000 prisoners held during the Revolution, including Marie Antoinette in 1793. That's why, of all the Paris places I have visited over the years, I never strayed far from the exquisite Chapelle. Now in the Palais de Justice with a Commissaire the conversations were not about beauty, art or history. Roger had some suggestions for us and wanted a somber place to present them.

"After talking to several of my comrades here in Paris and in Angers and Avrille, I have come to the conclusion that you two are in danger of your lives because of your brother Boney's *deminage* work and because," nodding to L.V., "your connection with this *genista* Mitchel boy. They both wanted to see the Lac Bleu quarry made safe. This stand posed them against

French government inaction on the one hand, and definite terrorist action on the other. And all this over the disposition of the sunken ordnance. Or *quelque chose.* Or something. I'm not sure."

He paused for a moment to let this conclusion sink in. I guess by now it seemed so obvious to us we had nothing to add, at least not at this moment in these solemn surroundings. We didn't have long to wait before his next idea was broached.

"We can let this Jules Labonte go back to his family in Avignon. Jules is very grateful for your kindness while he has been your captive, and all our information indicates he is basically a good man. I have a contact in Avignon who will keep close to him. Jules knows if he ever has a run in with the French police again I will open this little van trip and he will go to prison for a long stretch. My contact thinks he can turn Jules and make him into a useful informant."

"So we forget about Jules?" I asked.

"For the time being, yes," Roger answered.

"And my gorgeous Avant is forever lost to me, full of bullet holes and in a police junk yard, as evidence?"

"I will see what I can do to return it to you, Josh, my friend, but the restoration will be your responsibility."

"I'd like it back, Roger, if you can spring it. This car is a relic. I would like to repair it. It will be my hobby when I am an old geezer."

"Geezer?" asked Roger.

"Gerontological slang for an old man," said L.V. "It will be many years before he enters that stage of life but I feel he will eventually get that car repaired. And the odds are he will become, also eventually, an old geezer."

"Good. Then we have concluded the first part of this meeting: We may turn a foe into an informer; you two are definitely bound up in the CACTUS struggle; and you may get your precious Avant back. Now for the interesting request."

L.V. looked at me. I shrugged and looked at Roger.

"My department knows both of you are U.S.-certified divers. We would like you both to undergo additional government training with the blessing of the Minister of the Interior. He has given us two places on the *Plongeurs de la Sécurité Civile* divers' training program. You would live and work with our *démineurs* so you will be protected at all times.

"Why us?"

"Our Ministry feels that our enemies have taken a few severe losses and Elysée will soon begin diplomatic overtures to Algeria with no mention of recent events. The elusive Algerian Ambassador to France has agreed to talks."

"Why us?" both L V. and I asked again simultaneously.

"There are many reasons and we can discuss them at length over dinner. Then I must return to Avrille, where I still have a Motor Vehicles office to run. Some thoughts for your consideration are these. Your movements," motioning to both of us, "have been made known to our Ministries. Your friends Beauchaine and Smith have been hard at work at the Sûreté's intrigue desk. A committee in the *Assemblée Nationale* wants to hear from you. The *Sécretariat General Pour l'Administration,* and the American Specialists learning the French philosophy of demining want to help you because of your brave stance in recent events and because of the losses of your well-known brother and your fiancé. And I must mention there is some official government distrust as to what you two really know about Lac Bleu contents. The Sûreté proposes that you have much more information about reasons for these deaths."

"Thank you sir, I am flattered," said L.V. "But what will I do besides float among sunken bombs?"

"Thank you sir, I am not flattered," I said. You make it sound like we are involved in some hidden plot."

"Sorry if it sounds that way, professor. You will be gathering information using our new underwater handheld computer technology which you will study, practice and learn well. We want to know how many of what bombs are down there. You will be an inventory team on a census crusade. We need to determine what will happen if the lake level is permanently lowered, and what to do if the munitions are exposed to air. Of course, you will not be in charge. You are to be members of a very specialized team, a commission of inquiry, as it were—if your diving skills are up to qualifying standards."

This last was said with a sly Lemieux smile while he gazed up at the pinnacle of the Sainte-Chapel.

"I think L.V. and I should think about this for a few days, Roger. I realize now you and others have been thinking about us and Lac Bleu more than we knew. You yourself are always planning ahead and I'm sure we both appreciate your thoughtfulness. Suppose L.V. gets back to her work at Anger's libraries with Rosemarie and I stay with Pierre at the Colbert for a few days. I will write up a report on what Jules had to say and on what Pierre has learned. Can we meet, say, next weekend at the Colbert?"

"Oui. C'est ca. Je suis bien d'accord."

He was in full agreement, three times. We shook hands. L.V. and I hugged. I grabbed a cab on the rue de Lutece for a quick ride to the Colbert. I left them standing on the corner at the Pont au Change. Lemieux was on his phone alerting his driver. L.V. and I exchanged waves. I think her other hand was resting lightly on his arm.

Pierre

After Josh, Lemieux and L.V. left it was time for me to keep my dinner engagement with the Bedards. Jeanne-Clotilde had been insistent on my arriving at exactly 1900 hours because her parents were unaccustomed to receiving gentlemen friends of hers and they wanted to make this a truly celebratory occasion. Everything was to be timed perfectly, including my arrival time, the preprandial hour, the food service, and all the traditional French amenities accompanying an important occasion. She made a big thing out of the fact that her parents, with the help of only one maid, were doing the cooking themselves.

In my room at the hotel St-Paul-le Marais on rue Sevigne I took stock of my clothes. No doubt I was ill prepared to attend an unintended formal dinner party. I called my old son-of-a-*maquis* friend, Ted Milford, both of our parents having been extremely close when they were *maquisards* during their underground resistance days against the Nazis. The children of maquisards naturally formed groups of like-thinking French children much like some southern Americans gather for reenactments of Civil War events. So Ted, short for Theodore Perham Oblique-Milford, was gracious enough to lend me what we hoped was the appropriate outfit for the Bedard evening ahead.

I arrived early back at the Vosges to have time to walk through the arcades again. I wanted to get a good idea of where everything was in relation to the Bedard apartment #14. Jeanne had said it was on the 'first floor', that is, one floor above the arcades on the ground level. From the middle of the Vosges gardens I could pick out the two gracious windows of their apartment overlooking one of the fountains. The stairwell seemed ancient but immaculately cleaned, decorated, and carpeted. Pictures of famous Frenchmen were lighted. Victor Hugo was prominent and his contemporary, Sevier, was also honored at the first stairway landing. I rang the Bedard door at one minute after 7:00 PM.

Monsieur Bedard opened the door instantly, as if he had been waiting right behind it. Jeanne-Clotilde Bedard appeared at her father's side. She was dressed as if for a gala ball and I was glad to have Milford's Choice Apparel. He had guessed correctly—they were presenting a very formal appearance.

Jeanne introduced me as 'Monsieur Pierre Le Grand de l'Hotel Colbert.' The beautiful manner of her presentation made it seem I own a chain of international hotels. For the moment I felt rather important. As I stepped into the magnificent foyer, Madame Bedard materialized. As I took her hand, kissed it gently, and said *enchanté* a few times, it became apparent this was not just 'having someone over for dinner.' This was an important event for them and I would have to adjust accordingly.

Monsieur made it clear from the start that he was going to do the talking and that his wife, daughter, and guest would listen. He made this clear by never pausing in his monologues. He began his discourse on the health benefits of wine. I could nod in agreement on that point. Bedard was born and raised in Perpignan, the capital of the district of Roussillon, and was an expert in the science of winemaking. He spoke of the superiority of his district's table wines, mentioning Corbieres du Roussillon and the Roussillon Dels Aspres, neither of which I had ever liked. I had an idea that his region produced about three-fourths of France's naturally sweet wines. Fortunately at one point in his lecture-wine tasting presentation I could muster up some enthusiasm for the Cotes-du-Haute-Roussillon while longing for a vodka-tonic.

The maid interrupted him at the comparison between Roussillon wines and the 'California product.' She was never introduced, of course, but they referred to her as Rita. She was beautiful. Monsieur explained he has been training her for a career in food catering since her parents were killed in a traffict accident. His wife and daughter looked down as he suggested Rita was a Bedard charity case.

There was more wine at the table. Two different glasses for two special wines. No water in sight. I was prepared for the classic French menu which gradually appeared. We began with *soupe,* proceeded to *coquilles St. Jacques,* and into the most wonderful *blanquettes de veau.* Then somewhere between the frog legs in butter and multiple cheeses, Monsieur began a one-man discussion on the Lac Bleu *bruit.* He is convinced, he said, that groups like CACTUS create a lot of clanging noise to attract attention to something that deserves no attention whatsoever. I glanced at Jeanne who was, like her mother, silently passive. After about an hour of this, *gateau St. Honoré* appeared. It happens to be one of the Hotel Colbert's signature desserts because we honor the patron saint of pastry cooks. So I was finishing the 'honoré' with spirit when Rita arrived with the coffee. I think I managed to refuse politely Monsieur's insistence on calvados and/or cassis with the French roast. "I just am not your average French brandy drinker" I said. "Probably the American influence," I suggested. Mother and daughter smiled demurely.

Those two ladies disappeared, (to help Rita with the dishes?), and a now even more intense Bedard led me into a large but cozy paneled library. Local furniture seemed to be on display as in a showroom; stark, unused, not very comfortable, designed to keep the sitter awake and attentive. Monsieur began, or rather continued his monologue, this time on a more personal note. He spoke impeccable French, very rapid-fire, with the occasional saliva spray in my direction.

"Now Monsieur Le Grand, I must tell you I know a great deal about you and your friends with whom you have spent the last few weeks. You all would like to see the Lac Bleu discord cleared up. I understand your interest in this since your friend's brother was accidentally killed in his demining work. But it is my duty to strongly suggest to you, sir, to leave this CACTUS issue die a natural death by withdrawing from the scene."

He paused for a breath and I interjected "I'm sure I can't withdraw. I am committed to further France's clean-up work, sir, and my friends are also dedicated to the CACTUS cause in which we believe."

"That would be a mistake, Monsieur Le Grand. Jeanne-Clotilde has told her mother and me that you are an intelligent and reasonable man who had the misfortune of being in the wrong place at the wrong time. I am sorry about your recent experiences in which, I believe, you came close to death."

"I and my friends came close to death because people who are interested in the contents of Lac Bleu are international terrorists. We have no idea why they are so violent and I deeply resent any attempt to pass off our experiences as just 'being in the wrong place.'"

"You must understand that you are prolonging antagonisms long laid to rest."

"Excuse me, Monsieur Bedard. You and your family have been very hospitable this evening. I am here because I happened to meet your daughter in the library. May I ask, sir, what is your interest in my personal life and its connection to Lac Bleu?"

"My interest, Monsieur le hotelier, is MY interest. Perhaps a small clarification will help."

He then went on for a long time 'clarifying.' He was indeed very angry with me and with CACTUS thinking. The more he talked the louder he became, and soon he was screaming invectives. He knew all about our group. He mentioned Josh, L.V., and Lemieux, who, he said, would be out of a job very soon if he continued his present conduct. He quoted at length from the National Assembly's 2001 resolution 3037 about a commission of inquiry at Lac Bleu. During the tirade he moved about the room, animated, with arms waving, dodging the numerous chairs and coffee tables.

"There will be no more underwater investigation of that damned lake. Taking an inventory of the contents, reviewing the depth of the water and the height of the roadway, the public demonstrations, estimates of the risks to the populace, all these are terminated. The issue will not be acted upon in the Assembly. Monsieur, your curious work here is finished. Go back to Paris and take your meddling friends with you."

"Monsieur Bedard, are you threatening us?"

Suddenly, without making a sound, the ladies were in the room. They each took an arm and gently led him to a sofa.

"Papa sometimes becomes excited about his many projects," Jeanne said.

Her mother held a glass of water and was giving the old man several pills to swallow, which he did without another word. Rita came in and with Madame led Bedard from the room. They left, closing the library door. Jeanne and I stood a few yards apart silently staring at each other.

Finally, I said, "Your father is a very angry man, Jeanne. I am terribly sorry for causing such an uproar. Believe me, I don't think I said anything that should have caused such an outburst. Undoubtedly there is much I do not know about your father and the Lac Bleu controversy."

She agreed there was no way me or my friends would ever understand the intricate military-industrial-political-historical complexities that excite her father and his group of 'don't rock the boat' former politicos. They want the last 60 or more years of governmental demining policies to remain unchanged.

Rita knocked on the library door and when Jeanne responded *"entré"* Rita informed us that the elder Bedards had retired for the night and send their profound regrets and best wishes. It was time for me to leave. Rita gave me a gorgeous smile as she withdrew with a *"bonne nuit monsieur Le Grand."* Jeanne saw me to the door with a polite, gracious, almost affectionate *au revoir*.

Back in the Vosges garden I walked around the arcade again, reviewing the strange events of the evening. After a while I found a taxi for the short ride to the St-Paul-le-Marais. I knew I wouldn't sleep much. Actually, I was awake most of the night wondering how in the world Bedard knew us all so well.

Prof Josh

Pierre had a private meeting room set up for us at the Colbert for Operation Entrée. L.V. and Lemieux were there on time. The Beauchaine-Smith team arrived a little late, full of their usual enthusiasm for intrigue and skullduggery. They explained it was one of those *En Ville Sans Mon Voiture* days, "in town without my car." French cities have been trying to cut down on needless driving and heavy air pollution by designating certain days when cars will not be allowed in specific city sectors.

The Colbert management served breakfast of several kinds of coffees, teas, cheeses, jellies, and warm *crossaints*. We talked and snacked around a large table while we each reviewed his or her experience of the week. Pierre had the floor for the longest time and challenged all of us to say how and why Bedard knew about us.

Several possibilities surfaced. Our two professional *Sécurité* agents reluctantly admitted that we were all under some suspicion by Angers authorities because of our obvious behaviors involving car wrecks, shootings, kidnappings, and strange disappearances from time to time. And then there was Mademoiselle Bedard, old Bedard's research librarian daughter. Maybe she gave her father the impression we were about to disrupt his cement contracts with A 11 highway construction colleagues. *Sécurité,* it seems, is well aware of Bedard's many interests.

Both Beau and Smith were explicit in their warnings about our safety. Lemieux expressed some solace by saying that, for the time being, we would probably be left alone since the Algerian thrust had been a complete failure with their Lac Bleu men dead or scattered. Pierre had to inject a few sour notes from Monsieur Bedard, the most important being the eminent dismissal of Lemieux as Commissaire. Both agents reassured Roger that he was safe in his present position in Avrille. The meaningful glances between Matthew Smith and Roger Lemieux gave me a 'heads up.' I sensed they were about to spring something. L.V. had not noticed the look with which those two guys signaled each other.

"L.V. can I ask you something?"

"Sure, Matt. What's up?"

"I'd like to know the extent of your diving experience."

"My diving experience? You and Beau and your security outfit already know that. Roger does too."

"Humor me. What diving have you done?"

"You mean my open water and cave training time in Belize? What has that to do with anything?"

"Well L.V., *Sécurité,* through the good graces of Avrille's police commissioner, has obtained a place on the forthcoming Lac Bleu dive team. A National Assembly committee has ordered the inventory that was defeated in 2001. Project Inventory is now on."

She looked at Roger, "Y'all really want me to dive Lac Bleu?"

"We actually wanted both you and Josh. But he has begged off and is into another aspect of this Operation Entrée. We really want you L.V., if you are willing to qualify, and willing to work as a subordinate team member with *Plongeurs de Sécurité Civile*. You will be under the supervision of ESAG ANGERS. This is what Mitchel Joseph had planned to do. The Ministry trusts our recommendation and has given you his place on the team. What do you say?"

L.V. was astonished. She looked out the window for about 15-20 seconds, then slowly reached over to the arm of the chair where Roger Lemieux was trying very hard to maintain an impassive expression. He moved his hand to cover hers. We all just sat there staring at Roger and L.V. Finally she leaped up, did a few typical American cheerleader moves, and screamed "'Go Bleu, Go Bleu!' And in honor of Robert Gagne: I am 'Too Hot To Hoot.'" The serious spell was broken. We all stood, laughed, and congratulated L.V. on this honor, while she hugged Smith and Beauchaine. Operation Entrée had just taken a new lease on life.

Beauchaine

L.V. stayed in Paris with me and Matthew for the next week. We ladies had some shopping to do: dive clothes, gear, and things. The Agency gave us clearance to completely outfit one diver whose equipment and written report would become the property of the Ministry. I was able to learn a great deal about this beautiful American girl whom I knew only briefly in The Village where we were just getting acquainted. Now I was fascinated that she has accomplished so much in a short time. During her university summers she had found time to take psych courses, do internships, and become proficient diving the Caribbean coastline. The terrain there is rough and full of caves especially in the rain forest of Belize's interior. Her papers, which, as she had guessed, the Agency has obtained, testify to her experience as a trained diver. She has been tested in some of the best caverns and certified as a technical diver with Nitrox. In a few more summers she would have certification as a Master Diver and as a Rescue Diver. Her future ambition is to teach young people diving, especially Wreck Diving.

L.V. had a very good idea of what she wanted and went about several Paris specialty shops snatching articles from the shelves with little assistance from the shop personnel. We soon had several large bags and boxes containing her choices: 1st Diving Systems Full Face Mask because she prefers the comfort of not having to bite the mouthpiece; a Viking Comfort Drysuit; 120 feet of cable with waterproof connectors; Neptune II NIRA with colored micro videocamera; Duratex gloves; Drysuit underwear jumpsuit; Drysuit hood; fins; and a Light Cannon 100. All surface equipment and other secret gadgets were to be supplied by the Ministry.

After a brief stop at her favorite Village watering hole, *Au Lapin Agile,* we hit the road for Rosemarie's apartment in Angers. And on the way a few side trips seemed in order.

As every French school child knows this area of Western France, especially our section, Maine-et-Loire, is chateau country. L.V. and I both love history and architecture so we decided to spend the afternoon touring a few of our favorites. We only had time for Saumur and Montreuil-Bellay this day but we vowed to return for more in-depth visits. Saumur, a town of 32,000, is known not only for the splendid Chateau Saumur towering above the Loire, but also for its outstanding cavalry school. Montreuil, just 11 miles south of Saumur, is a most pleasing little town. Here the chateau is a tough-looking fortress with at least a dozen turrets and ramparts which were needed in 1025. Montreuil makes a statement: the best defense is this defense.

After we unloaded all the gear at Rosemarie's and said our goodbyes, L.V. just had to get off one more palindrome: "A Slut Nixes Sex In Tulsa." She expects everyone to think the way she does—fast.

L.V.

After Celine left me at Rosemarie's place I volunteered to cook dinner with whatever, sight unseen, we had in the house. It was a personal challenge and an act of kindness on my part—I really wanted to do something nice for Rosemarie. Also because I began to like realize I would not be seeing the Operation Entrée team for a few weeks. Fortunately Rosemarie's house at the Catholic U. campus has a large fridge, loaded with food. In that sense she is a very modern woman, one who doesn't have time to shop every day during the regular semester. Neither does she have the inclination to count calories when a special dinner is being prepared. So I went all out to be very French.

My *Hors d'Oeuvre* was a simple *Crottin chaud en salade,* goat's cheese melted on toast with salad. Then I served a small *sole*, fried and served with melted butter. She insisted at that point on pouring us some Burgundy, *Nuits-St-George.* I know nothing about wine and would have preferred a Miller Lite but held my wine glass up and watched for the "legs" as I tilted it this way and that. Rosemarie knows I have no idea what that ritual means, but we both enjoy laughing at little wine ceremonials anyway. She praised the minced beef but we had the most fun with the *crepes flambées.* My clumsiness almost cost her a very cute set of kitchen curtains.

That whole dinner prep and presentation took almost three hours. Later, while sipping some Christian Brothers brandy from my Stateside luggage horde, I began to realize how much I love being in France.

My *plongeur* training course is to be total immersion, no pun intended. I will be living with other divers in a barracks at the Lac Bleu military compound for the entire four weeks. There are two other women in this session with ten male trainees. The notes Roger had given me were intriguing. The whole demining debacle France has been in for so many years is reviewed in detail. I have to study. I fell asleep reading.

The Demining Department began in 1946 under the Interior Ministry. Deminers work all year long, recovering unexploded shells all over France. They make 11,000 house calls a year. People call them to come look at a strange shell-like object in their farmyard. In 1991 thirty-six farmers died accidently running across live explosives. In an average year five deminers are killed, 11 hurt. Overall, since its formation, the department has lost 630 men. During that time over two million acres of French land have been cleared of unexploded munitions. It is estimated that 900 tons of explosives are found each year, unpublicized. The stuff is all taken away, eventually detonated, again unpublicized. I am beginning to feel the passionate intensity Prof Josh feels about *déminage.* His young brother Boney and my love Mitchel are numbered among the very brave men peculiar to this aspect of life in France. Now I am getting into it— hook, line and sinker.

A white Land Rover picked me up the next morning. The driver was in the uniform of the French Foreign Legion. He was polite but taciturn in the best military manner. I enjoyed the view of the 'outside' as we went directly to the Lac Bleu army base where I would be 'inside' for one month. Now I realize how unusual it must be for Avrille's citizens to gather and demonstrate against the presence of 10,000 tons of grenades and bombs in their lake. Their government has left the subject alone for many years. Now here comes this beautiful little town going 'agin the gov'ment.'

I met my fellow *plongeurs de la Sécurité civile* during our first lunch together inside the base. We were a serious, nervous group during those first few hours. The other two lady divers were from Southern France, one from Sisteron and the other from St-Remy-de-Provence: Camille Delattre and Claudine Touret. Both have had some experience with sea mines along southern coasts of France. They couldn't have been friendlier. We were a close threesome from day one: Me with my USA school-French, them with tricky Southern French accents. We were in for a lot of kidding by our male counterparts. Camille and Claudine were the first ones I heard describe France as "one gigantic booby trap," referring to the proliferation of deadly explosives. The guys, of course, gave hefty Camille the same title.

Our first official lecture was given by a man from the DST, *Direction de la Surveillance du Territoire.* As I heard him speak I tried to fit him into like a comparable Stateside government position. Then, over breaktime watercooler-type gossip with a few of the guys, it came to me. DST is pretty much the States' FBI. He waxed eloquent about what he called *le residuum,* the refuse and trash left over from World Wars I and II. He wrote the number 15 on the overhead and yelled, for emphasis, that "15% of WWI shells were unexploded duds, still lying all over France." Then he wrote a large 5 and said that WWII had improved explosives so that about 95% of them actually blew *themselves* up. That means, he said, that most of the shells we find that did not detonate in the intended manner are from 80 years ago. He ended by what seemed like a military poem: "What we deminers see is our unwanted inheritance of war." He was like an American football coach encouraging us to win one for the Gipper. And somewhat like General Patton inspiring his tank corps. I must say, I was like touched.

Camille and Claudine were both very sharp ladies, maybe too scholarly for diving work. They loved philosophical discussions about what Camus or de Gaulle really thought about anything. Both were single at this point in their lives, and it became apparent during those first training, conditioning and lecturing days, some of the male deminers would like to change that. Camille was physically attractive, with a noticeable top, small waist and long perfect legs extending her height to five feet ten inches. She was athletic and coordinated and was easily able to run and jump better than a few of the male divers. Claudine was chunky and shapeless, pretty much the same silhouette from shoulders to ankles with few curves in between. She was tough and strong and way ahead of me and Camille in typical gym activities. Guys would gape at her bench presses. They would ogle Camille, no matter what she did. I notice a few of them staring at me from time to time but I pretend to know no French and just shrug, "...*je ne comprend pas.*"

An important gentleman from *l'Ecole Superieure de Guerre* gave a talk on shell identification. His name, here in my notes, is Bruno LaRose. He's like some kind of an expert on the unexploded ordnance strewn about France with special knowledge of the contents of Lac Bleu. With overheads and deactivated samples, he described 75mm shells of WW1. He compared British 155mm shells and American 75 of WWII. He warned us we would find many German grenades in piles and crates in the lake.

That afternoon he spoke about German shells, especially the Minenwerfer, the large German shell still occasionally found buried in the French countryside. But when he came to his favorite topic, the German Train Gun, he became visibly upset. He showed us overhead pictures of the Train Gun and said things like "imagine, my friends, a gun that could throw a 420mm shell nine miles." It was a distance break-through in its day and quite scary for the French population. He ended with, "But you all know nations' ability to hurt each other has progressed beyond rail road tracks."

The next few days we swam and became acquainted with our equipment in the dark polluted lake. We were trained to familiarize ourselves with the lake's contents from photographs and from scuba observations. We practiced the real thing each afternoon, at first in half-hour dives with attention to decompression techniques specific to the regulations of the *Sécurité Civile*. There was slight chance of explosion, of course, but our trainers were making sure nothing bad happened when they sent us into a little lake loaded with an estimated 10,000 tons of munitions. It is a fact that the lake is filled with unexploded ordnance and that the *Département du Déminage* has secluded piles of materiel like this Avrille collection in other parts of France. This particular collection is the only one in a polluted quarry-lake 84 meters deep, near a populated area next to a highway. The *Département* intends to continue the collection of unexploded munitions wherever they are found. The trouble with this Avrille lake is that so many people know about it. And hate it.

We were in the middle of our second week of diving practice when orders came down that we were to begin the official inventory. We were prepared. We were equipped and trained in the use of the latest micro-tele-video-cameras, various communication units, and many of the French secret accessories and techniques.

It was astonishingly high tech. Thanks to our instructors our recent education had filled us with confidence and capability. Our Divemaster, LeRoy Journet, regularly praised us three women. I had to learn to speak and receive in full duplex mode automatically—in French. This took several hours of extra practice on my part. Listening and responding to the rapid staccato French jargon transmissions was the hardest aspect of the course for me. Anyway, we respected Journet for his frankness during our practice performances, his marvelous diving technique during demonstrations. I will never comprehend how anyone can grasp his mumbled speech; it's as if he prefers to speak without ever opening his mouth. The guys called him the 'ventriloquist' when he was out of receiving range.

Now the group was able to move capably among munitions stacked in rotting crates and over piles of grenades that were stuck in mud but still looked menacing because of their numbers, in the thousands. Getting used to the artificial light or the polluted darkness took a while. All of us loved the *comraderie*, the dangerous work, and, (I in spite of myself), the French philosophy of *déminage*. I began to understand why in 2002 twelve American specialists came here to learn this business. And I never forget that this is what Mitchel Joseph had wanted to do—dive Lac Bleu with the official deminers. I think he'd be proud of me.

Soon we were diving for two hours every other day
under strict observation. During the third week we saw
the ventriloquist in action. He and Camille were
hovering over a pile of British 155 mm shells, sending
back pictures and rattling off inventory numbers and
confidential identifications when someone suddenly
screamed *au secours, secours, mayday*, and some other
words that implied serious trouble. Two other
instructors immediately appeared and surrounded
Camille. They all made for the surface as fast as they
could. I was about fifteen yards away and was
astounded at how efficiently they all did that. Shouts
were coming from the tech guys on the surface. It was
deafening. I had no idea why Camille was surfacing
and began to follow her up. Through the darkened
polluted water I could sense others also surfacing
quickly too. Maybe it was a drill. Maybe a Loch Ness-
type monster had appeared. Like I was scared.

Prof Josh

Mme Catherine Didier said this was the first time
she was meeting with an American Professor Emeritus.
I said it was the first time I was being admitted into an
Assemblée Nationale sub-sub committee. Didier did
not smile. Ever. She asked Pierre and me if we wanted
a beverage. We both declined and noted she seemed
eager to continue this discussion in English. Her
English was Oxford English. The committee room
chairs were the uncomfortable Louis XIV restored and
reinforced type which make for short meetings in

France. Maybe that was why she let two sharp-looking over-dressed young men stand a few feet behind her chair.

When we were settled and her expensive skirt was meticulously adjusted over her lovely legs Didier got to the point.

"Here is a copy of my original resolution 3037. As I said in my report number 3099, too many French are still dismayed by the large number of unexploded bombs lying around our country, threatening our citizens. We are encouraged that international publicity has come to expose our problem, and we trust that friends like you, Monsieur, and you Professor, will encourage our lawmakers to take action toward a cleaner and safer countryside. To get that action underway does seem to require a Commission of Enquiry. When we set up the official Commission I would like you two gentlemen to act as advisers to my staff. The pay would not be much but the good you will do will be rewarding, I believe. Please say you will help."

Pierre and I looked at each other for a moment and then nodded 'yes'. We would be honored, of course, but would have to know much more about what would be required of our time and energy. We explained our academic and employment obligations. Didier seemed pleased, stood, shook our hands, and introduced us to her aids, the standees, identical twin young men in their

late twenties, her nephews Jean and Paul. She thanked
us with a promise to meet with us *a la prochaine fois.*
"Next time," Pierre mumbled, as she left the room in a
determined aerobic-power walk. Around here Didier
seemed in good shape, good condition and definitely in
charge.

Jean and Paul were hilariously informal. As soon as
their aunt left they loosened their ties, moved the chairs
in a circle around a table and uncorked some very fine
Turning Leaf wine. As we sipped and listened to them
imitate their aunt's English it became clear they were
not as devoted to the work of the Assembly as she is.
They told us they are in the Paris Assembly doing
penance for having done less than 4.0 in their years at
the Christian Brothers' Manhattan College in New
York. Jean and Paul cannot wait for the next August
vacation to return to their college haunts and,
incidentally, find jobs in some east coast travel agency.
They eventually, not too soon, want to operate their
own J.P. Didier Tours in France, Belgium and Italy. In
the meantime they are stuck with Aunt Catherine until
such time as she reports to her brother, a manufacturer
of auto parts in Rennes, that his errant sons can be
trusted with their freedom. And with family money.
That may take another year. Right now they are living
it up as best they can while on this *Départment du
Déminage* assignment. They claim they have learned a
great deal and have helped Auntie present report after
report.

"But we have worked for our occasional *liberté*, my friends. We have had to visit, with an entourage, a Northern France camouflaged demolition center near the exquisite little village of Le Crotoy. This is where the Somme enters the English Channel. You guys should put this spot on your itinerary. Would you believe 300 tons of unexploded ordnance is destroyed annually on the tidal flats? Think about it. You could learn a lot."

"Thanks, Jean," I said, "but Pierre and I have other jobs as well as a basic interest in demining work. You know about my brother Jean-Luc, "Boney," and about my American friend Joseph. So you know I am interested in whatever the *Département* does to clean up France. What happens at Le Crotoy?"

"Well, you really have to admire these tireless *démineurs*. There are only about 120 or so spread over 18 French districts. You would think they could use additional trained manpower. After all they lose about two dozen each year, either killed or wounded. Around Le Crotoy they work the tides. When it is low tide heavy machinery digs great pits far out from shore. Using heavy machinery, tons of ordnance is lowered into the hole and wired to explode. When the tide returns the entire pile is deep under water. And suddenly B L A M! The entire load is blown with great towers of water signaling to the coast that another successful load is finally gone."

B. J. LUCIAN

"And the collecting and planning-coordination for the next great BLAM?" asks Paul.

"On-going as we speak," says Jean.

"So you boys, as loyal sons of France, understand the CACTUS problem. You just don't want to get too involved. Is that about it?" asked Pierre.

"That's probably true," replied Paul, "but before we do anything else this Assembly session, Auntie says we need to make sure you see some *déminage* action for which we have government clearance. We are just wondering how daring you gentlemen want to be. We have been told about the goons from Avignon. If that experience didn't turn you off, you can learn more about the entire demining system as she is practiced in La Belle France by allowing us to show you the inside of a so-called Site-Techno-Collecto-Center. But before that, Auntie wants you to see, first hand, the village de Chatelet-sur-Retourne in the Ardennes. Over 500 inhabitants had to be displaced from Chatelet during a demining cleanup fiasco and it is Auntie's favorite example of what can go wrong. She emphasizes it in her Assembly Report of 2001."

"A report by the way which made little impression on the members and is all but forgotten by the Administration. By all except our devoted Aunt Catherine," added Jean. "I wish they would listen to her. She is, like our mother and dad, brilliant. But, alas, she is a brilliant *femme.* "

"Thank you gentlemen. This California Turning Leaf is excellent. Pierre and I have to leave now but we will definitely take you up on the site visitation proposal."

We exchanged phone numbers and email addresses. The twins asked a kind of official usher to see us through the complicated Assembly labyrinth and out onto the walk along the Seine. We will be seeing more of these Bronx-trained young Frenchmen.

Smith

We French sometimes think the Sûreté is more than equal to the power of the three letters F and B and I. The Brits come close on occasion with their CID. But never mind initials. We say *La Sûreté de L'Etat* for State Security, and we add *Nationale* to that when we are seriously speaking of The French Criminal Investigation Department. And that's how it was when my charming partner Celine Lorraine Beauchaine and I were again thrust into the quaint *Operation Entrée* and the gosh-darned Lac Bleu fiasco.

As I understand it a hasty call came in from Commissaire Lemieux asking us to come out to the Avrille lake immediately. We make record time from Paris to Avrille again in our flamboyant, unmarked,

Sûreté vehicle to meet with Diver-in-Training L.V. Campbell. She introduces Claudine Touret. Camille Delattre, the rescued diver, is still in the emergency section of this elaborate French military hospital. No one seems to know why she had to be rescued. No clue as to what went wrong. As usual we split up, Beauchaine taking Claudine off to one corner of the waiting room while L.V. and I talked near the vending machine.

"What's going on L.V.?"

"I don't know, Matt. One minute we are diving around, doing our jobs under the critical eye of the Master Diver LeRoy Journet when all hell broke loose with shouts and deafining signals and up comes a very limp Camille in the arms of two male divers. She is rushed into the base hospital and I've just been standing here awaiting word and like hoping you guys would arrive."

"Did anyone get to talk to her?"

"Well, I sort of broke in between the two guys holding her. They screamed at me to back off. Instead I leaned over Camille for a split second and put my mouth near hers to begin mouth-to-mouth resuscitation."

"They had not begun mouth-to-mouth immediately?"

"They began the automatic machine the second they got her in the ambulance. That means she was deprived of any proper administration for about twenty yards, maybe a minute or two. Those carriers moved fast."

"Did you go in the hospital with her?"

"No. The carriers were really angry at me for pushing them and touching Camille's lips. I mean, they cussed me out in several languages, I'm sure. But I'm glad I did it."

"Of course. You saw an emergency and reacted correctly. The divers saw the same emergency and thought only of the breathing machine, not our typical USA mouth-to-mouth."

"But if I had not touched Camille I would not have this."

"What is that?"

"I have no idea, but it sure looks like a diamond. Here, take a look."

"You're right," I said, putting one hand on L.V.'s shoulder while holding a small shiny object in the other. "Where did you get this?"

153

"From Camille. She had it in between her lips and when I briefly brushed them with mine she sort of pushed this out into my lips. It took about two seconds and she was being carried while I was trying to maintain my balance between those two carriers. I don't think they noticed. It was only after they slammed the door on me here in the waiting area I had a chance to examine it. Seems like a diamond. Could it have been a tooth filling? Why did she have it in the very edge of her lips, almost visible, but not quite? It seemed as if she was getting ready to just spit it out. Was it in her mouth during the dive?"

"Well first, let's talk it over with Beauchaine. I think she knows a little about diamonds. If this is genuine, then she may be able to say what our next step should be. Right now we need to focus on poor Camille."

Lemieux came in and nodded to the group in the waiting room. He was in casual dress, that is he was not in uniform, but not exactly informal. His tan slacks were impeccably pressed, expensive, and of Parisian cut. His shirt, almost a U.S.-style golf shirt, was brown and white cashmere. His tan neck scarf was probably Italian. He really looked sharp.

"Hello everyone. I will ask for an update on Camille's condition," he said as he brushed by L.V. on his way into the forbidden doctors' area.

After a few minutes he returned smiling. "She is sleeping now. She will recover but we can't see her until tomorrow sometime. These military doctors are a little more possessive of their patients than your typical M.D. They feel Journet the Dive Master should be her only contact tonight. We might as well retire now. I will call L.V. as soon as I get the okay from Journet in the morning. Then we can decide what the group would like to do. In the meantime, you L.V., and your buddy Claudine Touret are still under strict training regulations. You dive again tomorrow at 0800. *Bonne nuit a tous et bonne chance.*"

And with that "Good night to all of you and good luck" from the sturdy Commissaire, we left the base hospital. L.V. and Claudine were not happy campers as they boarded their jeep for their quarters. Beauchaine and I decided to stay at one of our favorite places in nearby Saumur, the Hotel Anne d'Anjou. It has a truly grand staircase beautifully situated in this elegant mansion on the Loire River. We discussed the 'diamond' for hours.

"How did this, whatever it is, get into Camille's mouth?" began Beauchaine.

"Let's suppose she had it on her person, didn't want to lose it when she realized she was on her way to an ambulance, and slipped it into her mouth."

"Okay, but she would have had to remove her diving mask, all the headgear, and her big gloves before she could handle this tiny object," Beauchaine continued. "Maybe she could remove nothing—she was gasping for air, let's say. The rescuers would have done that. The Journet men undoubtedly ripped off her breathing equipment, loosened the suit's collar, tossed off the gloves, etc., in the first few seconds of the rescue. Nobody looked in her mouth in the first few seconds. They were intent on getting her into the base ambulance. This little bit of glass could have been in her hand inside the glove which they hurriedly discarded. Suppose she was not unconscious and had enough sense to quickly and naturally wipe her mouth and deposit this tiny piece of glass. When L.V. appeared it was only natural to get rid of it the way she did. Camille did not want Journet's boys to get this little glass thing, whatever it is. What do you think?"

As usual I was amazed at Beauchaine's imagination. She did make sense. It could have happened that way.

"Okay, Celine, suppose that scenario is logical and possible. What's the best way to determine what this is?"

"Right, it would help to identify what it is. It will be a big help when Camille can talk to us tomorrow. In the meantime, Smithy, can we not shower up and eat? As is customary, I'm starved."

And so, like typical busy French workers, we went to the nearest *La Quick,* the major French fast-food restaurant chain. And, also like busy workers, we took our time and sat and talked over a few beers for an hour or so. The *quick* in the company name means your food arrives rather quickly but you are free to stay as long as you wish, discussing, arguing, sipping wine or beer. No one seems to rush out of a *La Quick.*

Back in my room at the d'Anjou hotel I was able to find the following ABC News report on the computer.

Belgian Diamond Theft estimated at $100 Million

Authorities put a price tag of $100 million Thursday on the jewels, gold and securities stolen this month in what is widely considered to be the theft of the century in Antwerp, the world's diamond-cutting capital.

Police are still looking for the goods taken from 123 of the 160 high-security vaults at Antwerp's Diamond Center and the burglars who actually broke into the building Feb. 16, 2003.

The next morning I called Prof Josh, the only guy I know who has been to Antwerp many times, either as a tourist or lecturer at the prestigious University. From him I learned that the 500,000 inhabitants call Antwerp the *Metropolis,* with no apologies to Brussels. After Rotterdam it is the largest harbor of Europe with enough 16th and 17th century architectural masterpieces, monuments, and paintings to keep anyone wide-eyed for weeks. The Prof mentioned "It really is the diamond center of the world, you know, Matthew, and Belgian researchers have discovered a method to identify a diamond's origin." He went on to explain that each stone has a chemical makeup unique to an individual mine, a kind of 'print' that permits experts to determine a specific mine-site of origin. Also, as the world's leading diamond trading center, Belgium could produce statistics concerning the country of origin of the diamonds entering and leaving the country. So it could be possible for Sûreté to begin the research necessary to determine where this diamond, if it is a diamond, came from.

With Prof's encouragement I decided to transport this bead or glass that sparkles like a diamond to a local Paris *diamantaire,* a dealer or cutter that maybe Lemieux could recommend. The Operation Entrée group have agreed to keep a very low profile; no one outside the group, except maybe Camille, knows about the thing she passed on to L.V. If and when we find out the value of this tiny shiny object we may be able to make some connection to the controversy at hand, the munitions-laden Lac Bleu.

Beauchaine said she would be happy to join me in a visit to a Monsieur Dominic Barardelli, a diamond cutter who is known to the Commissaire as an honest broker with a history of proven secrecy. We now had a discussion we would remember for years to come: what is the best way for us to carry this bead-like gem-looking sparkler. Should we just be off-handed and casual and carry it in my wallet or her handbag? Or do we need a Sûreté attaché case with a wrist cuff and a complicated combination lock? After some coffee we decided, out of respect for Camille and L.V., that I would carry it in my mouth.

Lemieux made an appointment for us in Avrille's short Avenue J. Vaugoyeau to meet Monsieur Barardelli who teaches part time at the neighboring Ecole Jean Piaget. This is an interesting section of Avrille near the pretty *Parc des Poumons Verts* and the historically important *Avenue de Onze Novembre 1918.* We found a good spot to park our venerable vehicle on "Vaugo" in the bumper-to-bumper manner when both doors were suddenly opened and both of us were pulled out of the car and pushed up against the sides of a Mercedes van. I looked around. Where was everybody? It was 1300 hours on a dark, drizzly day. I could see no witnesses except a third guy, holding a gun on us.

In seconds we both had hands all over us searching our clothing and bodies in a most professional and thorough fashion. For once Beauchaine was not talking while the guy searching her was mumbling obscene French slang. After a few minutes the three guys agreed they had not found what they were looking for by the frisking exploration technique and pushed Beauchaine into the back seat where they insisted she disrobe entirely. At this point she silently kicked her forager in the *précieuses.* He collapsed, moaning. The gunman entered the back seat and proceeded to extract every piece of clothing from Beauchaine. Every article was examined, deftly scrutinized, somewhat torn and shredded, and then thrown in a pile at her feet. The gunman was frustrated and smacked her hard across the face. The injured fellow began to straighten up a little and his buddies chided him for letting his guard down. Beauchaine was allowed to dress and then tied, hands and feet, with all-purpose duct tape. Now I was shoved in the backseat and gave up every stitch I was wearing. Again, frustration and a smack in the face. Then, amidst much bad language they pushed us both out onto the curbing and raced off. I was groggily standing with my pile of clothes at my feet while Beauchaine was struggling to rip off her duct tape while lying rather helpless behind a low hedge. At that moment a school van came down "Vaugo" and we both just laughed and waved. The driver slowed but did not stop. We were humiliated, bruised, angry and disheveled. The kids waved back.

After I was again in pants and shirt I sat down to tie my shoes. Then it dawned on me. I did not have the mysterious gem in my mouth. I looked sheepishly at

Beauchaine. She knew immediately. "My God, you swallowed it."

We were able to retrieve it later that night after a large pizza and several beers.

Monsieur Barardelli agreed to meet with us the next day. But now we had doubts about him being so very honest as Lemieux had advertised. Who else knew we were going to meet him at Jean Piaget school? And what would happen to our Sûreté jobs if our boss found out we were treated like amateur trainees? And why was this tiny rock I was carrying really important? Beauchaine and I decided Prof Josh should come with us to meet Barardelli. Maybe Prof's academic prestige would help us right now more than our agency colleagues. We all wondered aloud: "Who else knows about this?"

Prof Josh

We arrived at Barardelli's office in the science building of the school at the appointed 1000 hours. His secretary met us and assigned us seats in a waiting room. She seemed familiar to me, reminded me of someone, but I could not right then decide who it could be. She was professional in that cold detached manner that French academic officials often communicate to strangers. In the States we would say she is inexorably in control.

After a few moments Barardelli appeared and ushered us into his inner office. Smith and Beauchaine showed him their Sûreté badges. He nodded and made sure we had no desire for coffee, tea, or Perrier. He said, "Miss Bedard will be happy to get whatever you would like." That's when it hit me. She resembles the Miss Bedard who told Pierre and me about the Plantagenets in the library that day.

After a few minutes of the usual polite small talk the old prof got right to the point. "You wish to consult me concerning a stone of unknown origin, according to my good friend Commissaire Lemieux. I will be happy to help you and him in anyway I can. I owe Lemieux a great deal for his past kindnesses. My work in this area is like that of a priest or lawyer, total secrecy guaranteed. Now how can I help you?"

With that Smith withdrew a jeweler's gem case, opened it, and presented it across the desk to Barardelli. He took the case in his expert hands and deftly turned his chair to a side table. He placed Camille's find under a freestanding microscope, a hand held microscope, and a very bright light. His face was expressionless. He handled tweezers, velvet cloth, a couple of large reference books, and special thick glasses as if they were sacred instruments in a religious ceremony. He said nothing for twenty minutes. Then he spoke, almost in the tone of Maxwell Smart, "Very interesting." Turning back to his desk he replaced the object, closed the little case and slid it across again to Smith.

"Very interesting, Mr. Smith. You have here a rather common diamond, about 1.66 carats, worth in your neighborhood jewelry store about $3,700-$4,000. Do you three know anything about diamonds? No? Well, in the Clarity, Color and Cut tests your diamond does quite well. Of course, this was a hurried analysis, a sort of 'while you wait' job, but generally this is what we know about this diamond. Clarity is a diamond's position on a scale of flawless to imperfect. Yours has no imperfections internal to the diamond. Very few diamonds are flawless, of course, so a skilled grader under 10X magnification, in his diamond center lab in Antwerp may see a blemish here, but I doubt it. Size, color and relief characteristics will eventually determine the clarity grade."

He looked at us, awaiting a question or comment. There were none. He continued.

"As to color, in the normal range, grading color involves deciding how closely a diamond's body color approaches colorlessness. The colorless grade is the most valuable. As far as cut is concerned we don't know the full value of this piece until we see the finish, that is, the polish and details of facet shape and placement. A good cutter could do wonders with what you have here Mr. Smith. Any questions?"

"Yes sir," I said, "we truly appreciate your attention to our diamond here. As you probably know we are not about to buy or sell diamonds. We would really like to know the origin of this diamond."

"I knew Lemieiux would not send two Sûreté people here just for an appraisal. I understand your work goes beyond Cut, Color and Clarity. So here is what I can tell you about origin.

"In the first place this diamond probably came to Avrille via the diamond centers in Antwerp and/or Israel. It may have originally come from Angola. As you know Angolan governments have been at war for many years, with the Portuguese and with its own local factions. Angola possesses large diamond reserves. Two of Angola's factions have been the Liberation of Angola (MPLA) and the National Union for the Total Independence of Angola (UNITA). There are times of uneasy peace, and periods of civil and economic chaos. But the winning faction will be the group which controls the diamond mines.

Angola's diamonds are considered to be of the highest quality. Most are smuggled to Antwerp which handles 80% of the world's rough diamonds."

"Why 'smuggled'?" asked Beauchaine.

"Because legal *diamantaires*, such as the Belgian Diamond Banks and Diamond Bourses, will not be associated with illicit or conflict diamonds. Much of the MPLA and the UNITA diamonds are traded and sold in violation of the Angola government's restrictions as well as those of the United Nations, governments and industry resolutions. But wars need funding. So diamonds are mined and sold for arms. Ilegally."

He paused and smiled wryly. "This information is available to anyone with a computer. The connection between diamond mining and war is well defined, my friends."

After a few more polite comments about his office décor and original paintings by local artists he supports, we withdrew with many *au revoirs* and *je vous en pries,* and *remerciesments.* We three were grateful for his factual comments and succinct report concerning the international market in diamonds. It is now more important than ever to hear Camille's explanation of this valuable diamond she somehow came up with in Lac Bleu. We decided to send Beauchaine directly to the military base for an update on Camille's recovery and obtain from the doctors a suggested time when Sûreté could debrief her. As Beauchaine pulled out in the Sûreté car, Smith and I decided we needed a cup of coffee to help us analyze what we just heard from Barardelli. I was anxious to try out my Bedard-resemblance story on him. We found a comfortable faux Italian garden café down Avenue Durand, just across from Jean Piaget. Lemieux promised to gather the Operation Entrée group at Boudreau in two days.

**Insult no man when he is old,
for some of us, too, will grow old.
SIRACH 8:6**

PART IV

Prof Josh

Rosemarie Baker and Pierre LeGrand were on hand the next day to help me get Boudreau back to looking its intriguing best. We aired it out by opening all the French doors and windows, then swept, polished, vacuumed and washed everything in sight. Rosemarie and L.V. Campbell, our two academics, volunteered to put on a fine noonday meal for the enlarged group of Operation Entrée. Commissaire Lemieux has decided to consider using our group for continued investigation rather than open it to a public official police investigation. He, quite correctly, would like to keep us out of the media's attention for several good reasons. One of his firmly held beliefs is that the whole Lac Bleu investigation and all that it implies for France is best kept out of the limelight until we can determine who has gems hidden among the ordnance.

So on the following Monday, Boudreau was ready to receive our group and all rooms were made ready to have guests stay as long as necessary. L.V. and Rosemarie arrived early with numerous bags and boxes of fresh food. Pierre had met them in Angers and assisted in the transportation and unloading of groceries in Boudreau. Lemieux arrived in his unmarked Jeep and posted two gendarmes at the entrance to the property. Matthew Smith and C. L Beauchaine came bouncing into the house carrying several bottles of Burgundy *Beaujolais,* including some *Brouilly* and *Morgon.* The group was enlarged, literally, with the presence of diver Claudine Touret who was escorted by twins Jean and Paul Didier. Those two presented Boudreau with about a year's supply of Chartreuse, that delectable green liqueur of herbs and spices produced by monks in the French Alps.

Lemieux called the group together in the great room while most were still involved with coffee and *brioches.* It was clear our Commissaire meant business.

"Please sit everyone. We have a lot to talk over and the sooner we begin the sooner we will know that what we have to do is *très difficile.*"

He permitted himself a slight, barely detectable smile, but I noticed L.V. caught it, being attuned now to the man's unexpressed humor. She smiled broadly back at him and said, "In honor of Robert Gagne, 'Do Geese See God?'" It took a few minutes to explain to our new arrivals the late Robert Gagne and his palindromes and how L.V. is continuing the Boudreau ritual. It seemed like the palindrome was the opening prayer to a formal service as Lemieux cleared his throat and began.

"I should say at the beginning that I am here in an entirely unofficial capacity as a friend of Prof Josh. I have no authority to do whatever we may agree to do.

Officially, I am Avrille's answer to a used-car salesman, being limited to our Traffic Control Department. I am the commander of six men, two of whom are presently stationed at the entrance road to Boudreau, controlling traffic. They believe I am attending a birthday of some importance. They were demoted when I was assigned to my present duties because they were loyal to me during my disagreement with a Monsieur Bedard whom I have never met. I trust those two men. I assume I can trust all of you to keep completely confidential the nature of our business here."

He paused for emphasis. Each of us froze, some with coffee cups in mid sip.

"Prof Josh and his best buddy Pierre have assured me you can be trusted to keep our secrets. All our lives will perhaps depend upon that. You should know that this is therefore an unofficial investigation for which we have no actual permission. We are not ready for the *Sureté* to come crashing in because we are not sure who all our enemies are. But we are indeed very grateful to the departmental boss of Beauchaine and Smith for allowing them to continue to share their expertise with us. Thank you, guys!"

He nodded that almost imperceptible smile in the direction of Smith and Beauchaine, both of whom just waved a *brioche* in silent acknowledgement.

"Briefly, here is my plan, subject to your agreement. Make any comments and ask any questions. This is what I have in mind."

He outlined at some length a plan whereby we would put divers, Claudine Touret and L.V., into the munitions-laden Lac Bleu to search for diamonds. With these illicit diamonds some illegal arms trading could be supported. If diamonds are indeed in Lac Bleu the government would probably listen to the need for cleaning out the lake. If the lake can be cleared and thoroughly cleaned, water sports could return to Avrille, *déminage* could proceed to other sites, and a vicious controversy could be terminated. As it is now various factions are willing to kill and destroy whoever or whatever stands in their way of buying and/or selling arms to the highest bidders, with diamonds as the currency. We assume some of these bidders are in Angola and other parts of Africa. We know Algeria is interested. There may be other little wars here and there around the world we don't even know about right now where there is illicit diamond trading for arms. It just happens that here on our doorstep such awful business has become involved in France's legitimate activity of de-mining. Powerful factions have kept Lac Bleu in its miserable state for very many years. "We want to get government working for Avrille's citizens."

A long discussion followed the Lemieux remarks. Many questions were clarified while Rosemarie and L.V. worked behind the closed kitchen door. It was well after noon before many aspects of the work were clarified. The twins were to reassure their aunt she must continue to harass members of the *Assemblée* to act on her resolution. Jean and Paul would act as her phone committee to begin seriously attracting votes. Pierre promised to re-visit the Bedards and continue his acquaintance with the family because we really think much of the anti-genista feeling stems from that quarter. L.V. and Claudine would continue diver training and if the program did not start soon other measures would have to be taken to look for a diamond cache in the lake.

It was 1300 hours before diminishing questions from the floor allowed Lemieux a chance to call a WC break. A "simple lunch" was announced by Rosemarie and the twins uncorked the Burgundy. We sat around the huge table and talked about food. A few of us had read Under The Tuscan Sun by Frances Mayes and that was the topic of interest. Everyone agreed Rosemarie should begin her Under The Avrille Sun. Much has been written about the French love of food, of their devotion to long dinner conversations *a la famille.* Operation Entrée epitomizes two things: French love of sitting down to a meal and French dislike of private handguns.

We began with *soupe a l'oignon gratinée,* baked French-Canadian soup. The main presentation was *escalopes a la crème,* on thin slices of veal. My very own recipe for *tourtieres*, a meat pie with the best local ground round, was expertly interpreted by L.V. So it was what the twins called a hearty dinner, a veritable feast, a veri-table feast. Of course we had the house salad, apple tartes from the boulangerie, and (again) the inevi-table Camembert, Breton biscuits, and apple cider, wine, and coffee later.

Pierre

During the first two days I wandered back again into the Place des Vosges I thoroughly enjoyed acting like the tourist from Provence. I visited art galleries, antique shops, cafés of all kinds, and sauntered around the entire square. It is not difficult to imagine this oldest of Paris squares, with its immaculate symmetry, as a neighborhood of typical bustling Parisians. On Sundays many hundreds of Parisians and foreign tourists still cause it to be shoulder-to-shoulder meandering, and jostling is very much the common practice. Bumping and shoving in enclosed spaces is common in Paris accompanied by an occasional polite *"Je suis désolé."* "Sorry."

But I'm not here as a tourist. I am waiting to catch a glimpse of Rita, the Bedard maid. In order to look for her and try not to be too distracted by the moving scene around me I take up a station at the southern gateway to the square, called by historians the King's Pavilion. I would love to spend some time in Vosges #6, the former home of my hero Victor Hugo, now a museum. But right now I am attending to #14 where the Bedards live, actually in the Hotel de la Riviere. Apartments are said to cost a fortune in this most desirable of all real estate locations. How much must living permanently in one of the most expensive hotels in Europe amount to per annum? Monsieur Bedard must be very wealthy indeed.

On the third day of my people-watching in the Vosges square I spotted Rita. I had been changing my garb each day and today's outfit was banker's day: dark coat, French cuffs, pinstripe trousers and black leather attaché case. Except for the absent bowler I looked like the guy in Magritte paintings, made famous later in a Pierce Brosnan movie called the "Thomas Crown Affair."

I was able to follow her out the north gate, down the rue des Francs-Bourgeois and into the historical library of Paris, Hotel de Lemoignon. I became very interested in the newspaper section just inside the door as I watched her from behind the latest copy of La Monde. Rita moved right through the reading room to a section in the far corner where 17th century books are displayed. After a while my trick knee told me it was time to sit. I found a chair at a large table where my back could be against the French World War II Victories section of the ground floor library and I could observe well in all directions. After an hour of browsing various De Gaulle biographies I decided to wander down into the earlier French victories, maybe in the 17th century or so. I was being very careful not to

frighten Rita or give her the impression she was under
hostile surveillance. But how to make this seem like an
accidental meeting? "Sure I drop in here often to catch
up on my reading?" No. I decided to approach her,
cough, announce my name and hers and hope she
recalled my unhappy visit of last month. But as I
approached the French Crusades shelves she came
around the corner of that section and scared me.

"What took you so long, Monsieur Le Grand?"
Perfect unaccented English.

"How do you do Miss Rita. I am sorry I do not
know your full name."

"I am Rita Mary Tomasino. Please call me Rita. I
am a Miss but Rita will be fine."

"You knew I was following you?"

"I saw you two days ago at the King's gateway.
You do change your wardrobe often Monsieur Le
Grand."

"Pierre, please Rita. And yes I do, especially when
I have to talk to an important person in Vosges who
does not know me and to whom I have never been
introduced. I really have to talk to you on behalf of my
good friends who are so opposed to whatever Monsieur
Bedard professes. We are not sure how you will accept
criticism of his political stance as loudly advertised that

night. I am here to ask your help. May we please go where a prolonged conversation will not be a disturbance to researchers? S'il *vous plait?"*

Rita then gave me her beatific smile and again asked "What took you so long?"

We walked up Rue Payenne and ordered croissants and coffee in the first café we came to. When we were comfortably seated and had ordered, we sat directly across from each other at the typical tiny French café table and just stared at each other for several seconds. And sure enough we both began to speak at the same instant. Both of us laughed and indicated the other should begin. More unwavering peering. Finally she started:

"I was in my final year in Language Studies at the Sorbonne two years ago when I ran out of money. I answered an ad the Bedards had placed, I was interviewed twice, once by Monsieur alone and once by all three together. I was hired, they pay well, my duties are quite easy and living there is obviously a good way to see Paris. Period."

After a few more minutes of sipping and munching and staring at each other I decided to respond in the same manner.

"Ok Rita. I was in my bar in the Hotel Concord, Paris, when my best friend Josh Baker offered me a job and after one interview I decided to help him investigate the death of his brother and several other friends of ours. Monsieur Bedard gave that amateur investigation additional impetus. Now meeting with you adds even more incentive. You are correct. This is a very good way to see Paris—and enjoy my investigation."

"It is obvious Pierre, we have a great deal to talk about. I know about Jean-Luc's death and that of your friend Mitchel Joseph. I have followed CACTUS and Lac Bleu in the newspapers of the Northwest. My family, back in Breaux Bridge, Louisiana, are devoted *genistas.* So you see I was really expecting to see you again. We have many things in common, *n'est-ce pas?"*

"Yes, indeed we do Rita, and I am overjoyed at that. So you are from Louisiana. Cajun country?"

"Yes, born and raised in sugar cane country, on a large farm, French in the home out of respect for my grandparents. I was a tomboy, riding horses and helping in the cane fields. I began seriously studying French history at De La Salle High School in New Orleans. The Brothers there helped arrange my entrance into the Sorbonne. Since being with the Bedards I have learned a great deal about demining."

It was time for me to tell her about Operation Entrée. I gave her the names of our group and emphasized how closely we had been working together while dodging bullets and bombs. I told her clearly how much we needed her help.

"How can I help?"

"We need to know who we are up against. Who or what is it that wishes to see us dead. The answers may be with Bedard. In his head or in his office. In his excitable state that night he said many things only an insider would have known. We hope you can find out more about his hatred for *genistas* and his faith in a government administration which refuses to help the residents of Avrille. Rita, really, we are asking you to spy on Bedard for Operation Entrée. You don't have to commit this minute. Think about it. It could be dangerous."

"I will think about it Pierre. Now I must go and begin supper. Remain until I am gone up the street. I will join you next Tuesday if you dress like a Matisse painting. South gate. 1400 hours. *A la prochaine fois,* 'til next time."

Tuesday I arrived early to people-watch. The Vosges changes its appearance every day depending on the crowds, the seasons, the weather. But it especially changes on weekends and holidays. On this drizzly fall weekday there were few tourists shuffling about and the arcade lunch crowd was thinning. It was easy to spot Rita coming out of an antique shop. She had a canvas shopping bag in one hand while she held her pretty scarf at the neck with the other. She spotted me from the shop door, walked right by me without stopping or looking. I proceeded to follow her until she sat down at an outdoor café on rue St. Antoine.

"This is one of my favorite neighborhood places away from the Vosges. Is it okay?"

"Rita, wherever you sit I am honored to occupy the same table. How are you?"

"I am fine thank you, Pierre. We can sit here and talk. We don't have to order anything."

"Good," I said. Then we began again to stare at each other. Smiling. After while she said, "I think I know how I can help you. All Monsieur's papers are kept in large locked metal filing cabinets in his office. If I knew what to look for I could find it if it's there."

"What would he do if he ever found you looking in his files?"

"I suppose he would have me arrested as a thief and I would go to trial and jail. I think he has powerful friends in Justice. If I were lucky he would just fire me."

"And there is the possibility with his temper he could attack and injure you physically, right?" I said.

"Perhaps, but I know my way around the place and I'm willing to take a chance on avoiding him. What do I do?"

"Well we don't know exactly what he knows and how he knows it. So first, we need to learn what he may have in the files that relates to *Déminage* projects, government contracts for the Lac Bleu roadway, correspondence with Assembly members relative to the proposed resolution 3037, and so on. You would have to arrange a time when you could read through what's there, maybe make a note or two. When we get an idea of what he has on record I can decide what our game plan will be. What do you think?"

"Yes, I can try to do that when they are away or asleep. But wouldn't it be easier if you were there to identify the contents directly instead of me just repeating what I find? You would know immediately just what is valuable to your cause."

"Correct. But how do we work that?"

"Simple. While they are away in Barcelona next week you can let yourself in the house and read files to your heart's content. I will have to be with them. But I made a duplicate set of my keys. Don't you types have little cameras that take pictures of people's private papers? Most television shows make such spying look like child's play. *Allons-y.* Let's go."

"You mentioned the files are locked, Rita."

"Yes, but I figured these common metal file cabinets have Mickey Mouse locks, no? Geez, I can't do everything for you."

We both laughed and agreed to meet next Tuesday, the day before the Barcelona trip. In the meantime, next Sunday, her night off, we would have dinner together. We knew it would be best for me to stay away from #14, and she was positive the Bedards knew nothing about her so-called social life. We decided to meet at the Ambroisie, #9 Place des Vosges, which is one of only five Paris restaurants with three-star Michelin rating. It is discreet, in the truly French manner, romantic, and requires reservations weeks in advance. My cousin Tommy, who owes me several favors, is the *maitre d'hotel*. Rita laughed delightedly; we stared across the table awhile. Smiling, she preceded me back up St. Antoine to the Vosges.

With some advice from Smith and Beauchaine I decided to dress as a waiter for my #14 entrance. They suggested that waiters from the cafes and restaurants around the Vosges arcade are not that uncommon among the homes/apartments on the upper floors. I had my white shirt, black trousers, black shoes and socks, and a large wrap-around apron. Some utensils on a tray helped the outfit look legitimate.

The stress began when I arrived at the Bedard door, #14—A-3. I had to set the tray down outside the door while I fumbled with the key provided by Rita. That certainly would have looked strange to a passing resident but fortunately no one seemed to be in the halls at 0002 since most people in Hotel de la Riviere are in bed at 2 A.M.

I managed to close the Bedard door soundlessly and with a small flashlight found my way around the furniture. Rita had clearly sketched the house layout and in a few seconds I was at Monsieur Bedard's office door. This involved two more keys and a quick move to the left wall to shut off the security system. So far, so good.

I waited in the dark for a few minutes and listened intently to the clicking of a large electric clock. As I became accustomed to the dull glow from the Tournelles street lights I thanked past Paris mayors for their security measures. Paris is the City of Light in more ways than one. Darkened offices are partially lit at night and we burglars appreciate it.

I put the door keys in my back pocket and concentrated on using a bundle of "openers" I had borrowed from my official Hotel Colbert security-locksmith. After several tries the top drawer opened and I was able to begin the actual search. After glancing through folders of government tax forms, car and furniture purchase receipts, travel brochures, and medical bills, I began to mumble to myself "nice try Petey, forget it." In the third drawer of the second file cabinet a dossier caught my full attention. It was labeled:

CACTUS: Collectif angevin pour le trace urbain sud.

In this fat folder Bedard had collected over several years the complete history of the Lac Bleu controversy and all its' attending links. Each file was bound separately and labeled in caps. In each file was a 3½ floppy disk from McKinnon Software Mobile Fax and Data Connection, Inc. That seemed unusual—there were no computers or copy machines in the office. But the dossier hard-copy titles I photographed were impressive:

DEPARTEMENT DU DEMINAGE
TECHNICAL CENTER: MARLY-LE-ROI
DGSE: DIRECTION GENERALE DE LA
    SECURITE EXTREME
MENACE DURABLE—AUCUN DANGER
SITES DE STOCKAGE DE MUNITIONS
HISTOIRE D'ANGOLA
SECRETARIAT   GENERAL   POUR
    ADMINISTRATION

Monsieur Bedard was indeed a complete researcher. No doubt he had a few secretaries or research assistants. His wife and daughter?

Among the papers the name LeRoy Journet appeared several times. No time to read details now. Some pages were devoted to *La Lettre du Génie no. 36: Le Groupe de Défense; Sécurité civile, exercice subcom; La formation scientifique et technique de l'ESAG.*

My keys, flashlight, and camera were neatly packed in my pockets. The files were closed and everything was in its place at the desk. I reset the alarm. As I made my way toward the door, feeling a good job had been completed, I heard some conversation outside in the hall. It was then I realized I had left the tray with its clean cup and saucer on the floor next to the door. Stupido Petey.

Two men were talking. They could not figure out why such a thing would be outside the Bedard place. After all, they are in Barcelona and they are very neat folks. It is highly unlikely, they said, that Monsieur would have placed a tray in the hall. Besides, said one voice "this was not here when I made my rounds two hours ago." They would make a note of it and mention to Monsieur next week. "In the meantime we will return the tray to the proper café with a severe warning to the offending café owner."

"Except, Monsieur," said one voice, "there is no café name on this tray."

"That is very strange," answered his buddy. "We should notify the hotel management. But maybe not now. Tomorrow would be soon enough, no?"

"Oui, Jacques, *demain matin. Mon Dieu que je suis fatigue.*"

"Bonne nuit, mon ami."

One of them rattled the cup and saucer as they moved away from the door with the tray. All was silent. I waited for fifteen minutes before opening the door ever so gently. No one in sight.

But as I came around the corner on the street level two night watchmen were waiting for me. And I was still wrapped 'round in my apron. As Josh has often said, the best defense is a good offense.

"Mon dieu Monsieurs, you took my tray? I have been looking for my tray!"

"You left this tray at #14. Why is that Monsieur?"

"Mes amis," I said, trying to look indignant and helpless at the same time. "I have a weak bladder. I was just looking for a WC. When I came back, voila, no tray. I am responsible for this expensive serving set. I am most grateful for your attention to detail. Merci, Merci. There is only one WC in this entire building?"

This was all sputtered in rapid-fire Provencal. The two guards looked me over carefully. I told them my name; it came out something like *Amatore Supplimentaire, de Rotterdam,* with a pronounced lisp. I slowly lifted the tray from the guards' table, muttering thanks. I bowed to them and backed out into the street where I turned around and slowly walked away, with a slight limp.

I vowed never to do breaking and entering again. It can be nerve wracking.

Prof Josh

Jean and Paul Didier met me at *Le Grizzli* in Les Halles, Paris, on rue St. Martin where a specialty is the cured ham from the Southwest. They were both eager to fill me in on their recent Assemblée research so after much hand-shaking, shoulder-patting and "greetings from Aunt Catherine," we settled down into what they called The Dual Didier Seminar. They did not seem to notice two well-dressed gentlemen at the next table who seemed very interested in our conversation. The Didier boys were very intelligent but not very street smart.

"First the good news," said Paul, who was immediately interrupted by Jean.

"Your group, 'Operation Entrée' you call it, no?, will be pleased to know there is an organization of scientists in southern Alsace devoted to training science students in the complexities of de-mining. They call themselves ARTID, Association for Research of Technical Innovations in Demining. It is a non-profit organization devoted to guiding young scientists in ways of inventing innovative de-mining tools for use in the field."

"That certainly sounds promising," I said, "but what is the government doing?"

"Aha, I knew you would be astounded to hear this, *mon vieux,* er, excuse, respectfully, sir. The French government has given the Angers ESAG the task of formation, training and development of *démineurs.* The program is called *Département du Déminage Humanitaire.* So we do have a center for mine-training action."

Then they both spoke at once.

"Have you heard about the forthcoming strike?"

"It could be as early at this afternoon."

"That's like asking have I heard about the forthcoming soccer season," I said. "These aspects of French culture regularly occur from time to time, no?"

"Not this variety. We are referring to the French diplomats and other government representatives in our embassies and consulates—on strike!"

"I'm a little rusty on my government studies. Can government strike?" I asked.

"Anyone can strike, Professeur," said Jean.

"Anytime. Anywhere," added Paul.

Then we began a serious discussion on French freedoms. These two young men, products of the best education abroad and in their own country, held forth on the caricatures of France.

"We have a five week vacation, 35 hour week, public-sector strikes. We are over centralized, over taxed, tradition-bound, and pretty well self-satisfied with our important historical leadership role in Europe. But that is changing I suppose as we enter the early two-thousand years."

'Hey, guys, wait a minute. What about our great train and post-office systems? Best in the world. Certainly these two public services put the U.S. to shame, no?" I was trying to penetrate their natural cynicism.

"Okay," said Paul, "we exaggerate. We really do appreciate our country and its place in the world. But you must admit France does have its obvious faults on the world-wide screen."

187

Eventually I worked the conversation around to some of the compelling dossiers I found in Bedard's house. Without telling them my source I asked them what they thought about a tunnel instead of a roadway through Avrille. They didn't seem to care about that until they realized I was referring to CACTUS and a diamond or two. An intense discussion ensued concerning the controversial motor route which they knew would pass very near to Lac Bleu much to the disgust of the Avrille citizenry.

Jean's phone rang. He listened for a couple of minutes, turned very red and then quite white. He said, "*Je comprends,*" and flipped the phone back into his coat pocket. He pushed his Amstel aside, stared out into space and then at Paul.

"Aunt Catherine has been kidnapped. No ransom. Just make sure her Assemblée resolution of Lac Bleu enquiry dies. Or she will. *C'est tout. Fini. Au revoir.*"

He was out of breath and said those words in short bursts of obvious anger and anxiety. He was scared and almost speechless. Paul seemed petrified.

I tossed some euros on the table and said, "Come on guys. We'll go to my Colbert suite and make some calls. *Allons-y.* Let's go. Now." I snapped my fingers near their faces. I walked between them, arm in arm, urging them forward.

In my apartment we sipped coffee in silence. Then that twin thing happened. They simultaneously said: "I know who did this." Without looking at the other they said it again.

I left them sipping black coffee and called Lemieux from my desk phone. I tried being as succinct as the kidnapper had apparently been with Jean. Maybe we French are so used to convoluted speech, terse statements seem breathtaking. Lemieux said he would be here in a couple of hours.

Lemieux reassured me. "How you say, sit tight? *J'arrive.*"

When I hung up and returned to the sitting room the Didiers were gone.

L.V.

I was talking to Rosemarie outside her classroom at Angers' C.U. when Jean Didier came rushing up to say I had to go with him immediately. Paul, he said, was gunning their Renault Laguna right out in front and we had to go right now. He gave the *Je suis désolé* nod, I'm sorry, to Prof Rosemarie, who smiled and said something like "I'll see you later." I only knew these twins casually but since Prof Josh liked them they couldn't be all bad. The 1995 Laguna, a true French car, starts at top speed and is prepared for neck-wrenching stops all along the way. We raced back to Paris and up to Montmartre.

Even crowded together as we were in the front seat it was difficult to understand them over the roadway din and their stepping on each other's shouted lines. Their aunt had been kidnapped they said and they seemed to know who did the deed. The deed had something to do with diamonds so I was, in their minds, involved. Another reason they wanted me along on this little skirmish or whatever they called it was because I knew the kidnapper, one LeRoy Journet, my diving boss.

"We're going right to their house and confront them. We know they know that we know who did the kidnapping of our Aunt Catherine. They will be expecting us to arrive and to be ready to deal for her return." Both of them contributed some other overlapping statements lost in the rushing wind.

We roared into the otherwise respectable Avenue du Chevalier near the spot where some of my best mime work took place. A few quick illegal turns and we were at the door of St. Pierre de Montmartre, next to the Sacre Coeur.

"Why here?" I screamed just as Paul turned off the ignition. Several pedestrians turned to wonder why someone shouted that in English for the entire street to hear. Oh, a rude American girl with two great-looking French boys.

"These Journets have a thing for St. Pierre churches. You'll see. *Allons-y, "* said Paul. Or Jean.

We leave the car at the ancient church whose origins go back to the sixth century. Up and around a few side streets, we knock on a door. An elderly lady appears. She is evidently in the midst of some serious cleaning work. The boys ask for Monsieur LeRoy Journet or his son Isidore. Monsieur is at the Avrille Quarry, the traditional name for the munitions-laden little Lac Bleu. As for Isidore, she was more wary.

"What do you want him for?" she asked.

"We have a medal of honor to give him from our University days. He has been named an outstanding graduate and we will invite him to the presentation feast. He will be happy to see us Madame. This is his Queen for the occasion, Mademoiselle La Branche."

She looked the boys over carefully and then smiled in my direction. "Young Isidore is on retreat at Mont-St-Michel." She explained he is a fine young man contemplating the priesthood under the guidance of his uncle the Abbot. We all thanked her and Jean begged her not to tell M. Journet about the surprise to be bestowed on his wonderful son.

Back in the car, Jean at the wheel, they reviewed their relationships with the Journets. In their French university days he came to know the Journets quite well. It seems Isidore was a physical bully in the soccer matches, not a big brain in class, but popular because of his father's political influence. These Didiers acted as class clowns on occasion, appearing and disappearing as the other twin, changing reversible jackets on the spur of the moment to take each others' tests or scoldings or girl friends. Most of their classmates were never really sure to whom they were speaking when they met them separately or together. Jean and Paul over the years, since they were teenagers, had worked out many marvelous routines. They used the same speech patterns on purpose to confuse. Some days they appeared in identical dress and represented themselves as the other twin. Other times they came to school in totally different outfits. Then when some poor kid like Isidore had pretty well identified one or the other, Paul and Jean quickly switched clothes in the school bathroom. Isidore, and thus, his father, were embarrassed more than once by these antics when Isidore, The School Bully, was made to look stupid before his peers.

These two dudes got a big kick out of telling their university jokes and stories and the hours flew by, literally, as we sped north-east on N 12 to Fougeres. A short jog brought us to Pontorson where we had a most delicious meal. Jean ordered *a la Breton* for me: salmon (butter, wine and shallots), crepes Suzettes, Camembert, and non-alcoholic cider. This was my first time in Northwest France, on the historic coast of Normandy, and the Bay of St. Michel.

"We have to keep our wits about us," they said. "We have no idea what to expect here so be prepared to improvise." We left the Renault in Pontorson and took the tourist bus out to the most enchanting sight in France, Mont-St-Michel.

The Mont's silhouette appeared through a fine mist as we approached the border between Brittany and Normandy. The gigantic rocks rising out of the water with the statue of Saint Michael 560 feet above do give you pause. The causeway has eliminated tide-anxiety which used to bother St-Michel visitors; we were driven right to the main entrance without worrying about the swift tides taking our car. This former very influential Benedictine monastery of the 12th and 13th centuries is now a national monument. We joined a busload of enthusiastic tourists for the basic daily tour. The twins believe in the adage Three Is a Crowd. They thought that male twins and a blond companion would attract more attention than any ordinary blond with her guy. For that reason they bought me a huge *chapeau* and sun glasses while one of them turned his jacket inside out and separated from the walking tour group by several yards. They called this "separating by ones and twos." Most likely we were the only people on the tour who were looking for a kidnapper.

We trudged up the Mont's Grande Rue hardly listening to the professional guide up ahead. Souvenir shops and petit cafés line the narrow streets. There are a few private homes, too. After all, about a hundred people actually live permanently on this islet of magnificent Gothic-Romanesque architecture.

Paul, I think, was with me, Jean was bringing up the rear with a group of pre-geezers from Duluth, Minnesota. Our goal was to follow the tour guide and pay attention to open doors, dead-ends, various towers, chapels, cloisters and rooms where we might secretly spend the night. At the end of the tour in the ancient Almonry-gift shop we would ditch the guide, mingle with a new group and miss the bus.

At four o'clock it was becoming difficult to mingle as the last of the tour groups were beginning to board their buses. Shops began to close and last minute sales were rushed and concluded. "All aboard," a loudspeaker announced in several languages. "Everyone should be outside the main entrance by four-thirty. Please board your buses and cars now." It was time for us to find a place to hide until further exploration could begin in the quiet of the night. Jean said our motto was "Find Journet, Remember Auntie Catherine."

Jean and Paul agreed that a good place for a hidden night's lodging and searching would be one of the 11th century crypts built to support the transepts of the main church above. The doors were not securely locked, the air inside was not too bad, and there was room for us to rest among discarded chairs and old pews. How these guys discovered this during the guided tour I will never know. They selected the Crypt of Thirty Candles. We were on the middle level, right behind the former Knights' room. We settled down to await the guards on their rounds, which were described in the voluminous literature supplied by the gift shop.

After about an hour of sitting around in the dark guards came by opening and closing doors, gates, windows, and anything that could be unlocked or locked. We heard them coming up Grande Rue because they shout to each other *"Trés bien!"* as they secure each area along their designated route. Tres bien, literally, "very good," that is, "All A-OK here." Jean explained that while these guards have electronic devices hanging on their belts and sticking out of their pockets, the historical monuments ministry preserves the 17th century manner of guard-shouting. Paul thinks the shouting gives the guards themselves confidence and self-assurance as they walk slowly around hundreds of curves and corners, cloisters and halls, towers and ramparts in a dark, spooky many-leveled complex.

We hid behind stacks of chairs and benches when they rattled the door of our crypt. *"Très bien."*

We had the impression their guarding is rather perfunctory but Jean said they do carry guns and are trained marksmen. After all, he said, the Mont is a huge national monument-treasure chest. Anything of value stolen from the Abbey, for example, would be worth a fortune almost anywhere among Europe's underground art collectors. Two guards met for a cigarette break outside our door. After a few minutes they separated, one moved across to the Knights' room and down that way. According to our bookstore map the other guy was going around to the opposite crypt. We needed to get to the off-limits area where the few remaining Benedictine monks lived so we would be able to question Isidore Journet, unloved fan of the Didier brothers. We removed our shoes and left them just inside the crypt door.

Paul opened the door silently. He went out into the pitch-black hallway and stood still. We all listened for any more shouts. He whispered *"Allons-y"* and we moved quietly down the hall. After a few turns we came upon a signboard on an iron stand in the middle of the hall: *Interdit*. So far the Mont map was helpful, it brought us right to the off limits rooms. We went around the sign and Jean approached the very first door. We froze motionless as Paul passed him a set of what looked like fancy corkscrews. Jean knelt and began noiselessly fiddling with the lock. Suddenly with a great shout of "Gotcha, you bastards" the door flew open, lights went on in the hall and in the room, pistol safeties were audibly released by two guards. There, in the doorway a young monk stood with hands on hips, smiling broadly, and repeating "Gotcha, you bastards."

Jean dropped the keys and stood. Paul said feebly, "Hi there 'Dore."

"Get in here you two dumb asses. You two," addressing the guards, "can take off, and thanks for a job well done. *Très bien.*"

The guards had a good laugh, slammed the room door, turned off the hall lights and walked rapidly away back down towards the shops. No one had noticed me standing in a dark corner behind some pillars. Wait 'til I tell Beauchaine and Smith how my Sacre Coeur mime experience proved so very helpful. But then I thought, "Like now what the heck do I do?"

After staying behind the column for several minutes I eased up to the door and listened. It sounded like an annual frat party, the Didiers making jokes and laughing, Isidore commenting seriously on how dumb they were to come in here at night. Isidore was taking the offense and the twins were supposed to be on the defense, for after all, they had broken several Mont-St-Michel rules. But they were playing it for laughs and kidding Isidore about being a monk-in-training.

"You guys are in serious trouble," Isidore shouted. "In the morning the local police will take you two into custody. You can't get off the Mont 'til then so just shut up and let me alone. I have locked you in. Now

I'm going into my bedroom. Good night to you double
dumb asses."

After that outburst I heard the twins speak
simultaneously.

"Okay, we'll be quiet but first you have to tell us
where our Aunt Catherine is. And then enlighten us on
why you and your dad hide diamonds in Avrille's Lac
Bleu. And, if you don't tell us all about both of those
things we will scream and holler and accuse you to the
police. Kidnapping charges. Locking us in this
dungeon."

Someone was coming and I scooted behind the
pillar. It was a monk and he saw me. The floor was
cold and a little slippery for my shoeless feet but I took
off as fast as I could round the next corner and up some
steps. He was right after me, yelling into a cell phone
about an "intruder on the stairs to the upper church
level." I outran him on the Great Inner Staircase and
following our tour guide's clever observations of that
afternoon I hunkered down at the top and when the
monk dashed by me I doubled back down the stairs to
the middle level and back towards the Candles crypt. I
was about to push open the crypt door when a deep-
throated scream came from the middle-level Inner
Staircase I had just left. It was a horrible shout of
awesome anguish and it faded away as if someone was
gradually turning the volume down. Then everything
returned to Mont silence.

I ducked quickly into the crypt again, found my shoes in the dark, relieved my self in the facility provided, that is, in a hole or drain in the floor, a type of lavatory not unknown in modern France. That fantastic scream in the silent darkness and the unscheduled full-out run to get back here to my hiding place had really unnerved me. I kept thinking, "Like what could that strange sound have been?" I took out a somewhat smashed health bar from my jeans pocket and stretched out over three little rattan chairs. As I relaxed and chewed, it suddenly hit me. In the history of this place, our guide had said, there was a time when La Mont was a prison. Yeah, during the French Revolution. And there was a prisoner named Gautier who leaped off the little terrace now named after him at the top of the Inner Staircase. He leaped to his sure death from high up at the Church Level. In fact *Gautier's Leap* is marked on the tourist map. Could it be? Had the monk chasing me miscalculated the turn on the dark stairs and fallen to his death? Was that his falling scream I heard? That was my last sleepy thought of the day until I awoke the next morning to the sounds of tourists chattering on past towards the Knights' Room.

I arose and stretched, arranged my wrinkled blouse and combed my hair. As the tour group sounds faded the door sprang open and Jean dashed in.

"Good work last night my dear L.V. You hid masterfully. Now you have to get off this Mont and fetch your Prof and Lemieux."

"What's the rush? What happened with Isidore?"

"Dore is totally distraught this morning, he is agitated and almost frenzied. It seems his uncle, the Abbot of this little monastery, is not around. When he missed the early morning rituals a monk came to our door, also quite disturbed, and had a long whispered conversation with Dore. I get the idea they have no idea where the Abbot could be. It seems absences on the part of an Abbot are unheard of."

Then it was my turn to explain the unofficial Olympic Track and Field tryout the Abbot and I had last night. I explained the race route, using the gift shop map. I left out the scream or cry since I was not sure there was any connection between the Abbot, the strange noise and his sudden disappearance.

He hugged my disheveled body, congratulated me again for my "adroitness," *dexterité, en francais*.

"Here are tickets for another Mont tour in case you are questioned. This is a bus ticket back to Paris. Take my phone card and use it if the bus makes a wee-wee stop. Report all this to Lemieux. We will be keeping Dore in our sights from now on. Paul has a plan to extract any info Dore may have about diamonds and

Aunt Catherine. If Dore contacts his father, your diving instructor, *pere* will surely come racing up here. You should not be around. Try to get into the diving group's regular schedule as if nothing has happened. You are getting good at this sort of thing. *Au revoir.*"

After a quick hand shake and cheek touch he was furtively opening the crypt door. Just before he shut me in again he reached into his coat pocket and tossed me a small *baguette.* "Isidore is probably too excited to eat his monk's breakfast."

I figured the first public bus trip back across the causeway would not be for an hour or so. I tried to relax. The morning breakfast was delicious but reminded me it would soon be time to have a real meal. That's what I was thinking about when the door slowly opened and a very bright light lit up the pee-smelling crypt. Two guards, the same two I saw last night, did remarkable double-takes. First they blinked at me for a second. The next second they exclaimed something like *maudit!* They were as startled as I was. But only for two seconds. Both came at me, one wielded the huge flashlight, the other a gendarme's club. I was like now what do I do? Fortunately my Nikes were laced tightly this morning and had good leverage on the crypt floor. I had one second to assume my fighting stance learned in martial arts class at St. Mary's. This seemed like a good time to maybe perform a little.

The flashlight dude came first. I feinted left and kicked his right hand hard. The light went flying and lay there lighting up our feet. I turned 180 degrees and again kicked the bewildered guy holding his wrist and cussing. My crotch kick must have been very painful. He stumbled forward right in the path of his partner who had put away his club and pointed his standard military sidearm at my chest. I stopped, stood up straight, smiled, raised my hands above my head. He came forward, told me not to move or he would kill me. He nudged his partner moaning on the floor. For the second he was distracted I lunged at the gun, twisted his arm in a most unnatural direction, cracked him in the face with the gun, and kicked him behind his knee. He crumbled on top of the first guy. I pocketed the gun. They were groggy enough to allow me to take their handcuffs and put them on their wrists behind their backs. They should be in a French prime time TV series: Two Fat Flics.

I shut the crypt door and locked it from the inside. I then told them to sit up against the wall or I would kill them right now and no one would ever find them. My French was not perfectly grammatical but they seemed to get my drift. They were about thirty-five or forty years old, inept, scared and very hateful. I managed to empty all their pockets of wallets, radios, ammo, and other personal items like cigarettes, matches, etc. I stuffed all, except their keys, into the hole in the floor. They moaned and swore. Some of their expletives are not in my dictionary.

I motioned them to keep quiet while I sat on an old pew and tried to think about my next move. I figured these guys would kick on the door as soon as I left and someone would investigate. In fact, they may be missed right now. It was too early to board a Paris-bound bus so I decided to talk to them.

At first they were like too angry to respond with anything but verbal abuse. I called them each by name, told them I was not dangerous and just wanted to leave the Mont as soon as possible. I mentioned I was a friend of the Abbot. At this they both looked up and then at each other. Apparently they knew about the Abbot's absence. Maybe they knew what had happened to him. After a few minutes of staring at each other and at me, one of them mumbled, "Gautier's Leap."

I pretended I didn't understand. The crushed crotch one said in French, "You killed the Abbot. You will be tried for murder." I decided it was about time for my exit. But first I wanted to give these two a handicap. After gagging them with their socks I dragged them over to the corner of the crypt. Then I carried and pushed and lifted all the church pews, individual kneelers, dozens of broken chairs, a very old organ and a high bishop's chair into that corner. They were surrounded on all sides and from above by furniture which, when stacked, made a fine barricade in the traditional *Les Misérables* fashion. When I finished I could hardly see them beneath what seemed like a neat storage method. I removed the battery from their large flashlight, tossed it onto the pile, and locked the door from the outside. I quietly entered the Knights' Room hallway just as a group of tourists were completing the first tour of the morning. I joined them as they proceeded to bus number 43 for Paris. While I bent over to tie my shoe, the guard's keys slipped from my hand into the Bay of St-Michel. *Tant pis!* Like *too* bad. Bummer for the bad guys.

Prof Josh

L.V. called from Pontoron on her way back to Paris with a Mont tour group. It took Lemieux about five minutes to arrange a fast police car out of Avrille. We surely broke a speed record getting to the Mont causeway. On the way we had discussed at some length what our moves would be once we were into the Abbey. But those plans changed when we were met at the tour gate by regular Normandy gendarmes who objected to a police chief from Avrille investigating the disappearance of the Mont-St-Michel Abbot.

"We are not investigating anyone's disappearance," Lemieux explained. "We are here to meet our friends, Messieurs Didier, who are visiting Frater Isidore, nephew of the Abbot."

"We would prefer you tell us the truth from the beginning," replied the security guard. "You see these gendarmes here. They are holding the three gentlemen you mentioned. They are accused of being implicated in the disappearance."

"I and Professor Baker request a short conversation with the Didiers. Then we will all leave," said Lemieux.

"You are wrong on all counts, monsieur. Only police of this Prefecture will talk to them. And this Professor, a civilian, will not be allowed anywhere near the three suspects. If you wish, sir," he said turning to me, "you may take the regular morning tour and then depart. You sir," bowing politely to Lemieux, "may accompany me with the understanding you have absolutely no jurisdiction."

"Good. Let us proceed," said Lemieux grimly. "Prof I will see you later right here at this gate. Say in about an hour?"

I nodded as he, with two local gendarmes and two security guards, moved off. I stood there pensively until a new tour began. I managed to nonchalantly join various guided groups as I wandered up the Grande rue, the so-called pilgrim's route, up to *Eglise St-Pierre* and up to the abbey gates.

With my newly purchased Mont-St-Michel *carte*, the kind France is well known for among map-makers and tourists alike, I set out to find Gautier's leap.

Actually I wanted to find Gautier's Landing, not his jumping off spot. That seems to be well annotated. But if, as L.V. reported, the Abbot screamed as he repeated Gautier's dive, I wanted to find the landing zone. If she were correct in her assumptions a body should be directly beneath Gautier's little terrace. And while the leaping point is on the charts, the landing is not mentioned. Maybe too gruesome. Or maybe too inaccessible?

One of the tour groups on the West Terrace was totally into photography. I mingled with them as they moved slowly with a guide repeating his memorized details as boringly as possible. I looked straight down from the Leaping Terrace and figured out how I could get to Gautier's Landing Site, unmarked on my *carte*. It would be in a small, sloping thick grove of beech trees at about the Mont's middle level, that is, beneath the abbey church and above the level of the Crypt of the Thirty Candles. When the boring tour spiel moved on towards the Cloister I retreated down the Inner Staircase, jumped a few *interdit* signs and slipped under a large apple tree. The ground is hilly, to say the least. From the apple tree I walked hunched over past an *Interdit Absolument* sign and into a hillside grove of beech trees. At this point no one on the terraces and paths above could see me standing under these trees. I crawled farther among some bushes growing on a steep slant and looked in all directions. There were no sounds and no sights: just bushes and trees. This spot could not be seen from the abbey resident buildings and certainly not from the walkways below. I sat down to catch my breath and look around. I loosened my collar and flipped my beret onto a bush. Then I pulled my hand back sharply. On the bush was a small wooden cross hanging from a leather cord. On the ground, lying against the base of a beech tree was a shiny bald head. Another tree prevented the body from sliding further down the slope. It was securely wedged in this tiny grove, eyes staring down the hill. The right hand was clutching a small flashlight. The garb was that of a Benedictine monk of Mont-St-Michel.

After a few minutes of prayer for the deceased I untangled the cord from the bush and held the cross. I turned it over and gasped. There imbedded in the wood was a twig, the *genista* plant of the Plantagenets. This good monk had been making his silent statement like Manerelli and the others in Avrille; he was for cleaning up the leftovers from two wars.

I gently wiped my fingerprints from the cross and rehung the cord on a branch. My beret replaced, I now had to figure a way out of this little hillside cove without being seen. It may have been too difficult to explain how I was able to walk down here without seeing those 'no trespassing' signs. I decided to sort of slide down this steep little grove and try to immerge near the Abbey's gardens. At this point the Abbey walls rose up on one side of me for a few hundred feet. The area was in dark green shade. After a few clumsy yards I sort of staggered into some trimmed hedges and was met immediately by several camera-laden tourists. We smiled at each other and discussed Mont plant life until a guide yelled that we should "keep up with the group please." I brushed myself off and noticed there was a great grass stain on my right knee. It showed up clearly on my khaki slacks. I tried to mingle closely with the camera buffs. We caught up with the guide who was conversing with two Prefecture gendarmes.

"Where have you been?, asked one of the young officers in Normandy French. I pretended not to understand and nodded, smiled and said "Yes, lovely day."

"We were attracted by the exquisite flowers, sir" said an Englishman, indicating the group. We all smiled.

"You were off limits and away from your guide. He is very upset."

"We apologize," said the tourist.

"You fell," said the second gendarme, who was pointing to my knee.

I mumbled "clumsy" and attempted to demonstrate how I tripped. With that the gendarmes waved us on and the guide continued his monologue where he had apparently left off. When he paused for questions I asked him about St-Aubert.

"Did he really begin Mont-St-Michel?"

He turned to the group, repeated the question, and became entirely engrossed in his clear, lengthy response. I managed to slip away.

Lemieux and a few gendarmes were waiting for me at the main gate. After a few final pleasantries we said our goodbyes and thanks. In the car, this time at a more sane speed, Lemieux explained the scene with Isidore, his dad, and the Didier twins.

"This may come as a surprise to you Josh: the Abbot of this place is a *genista*. He and his monks, including Isidore, are all anxious to see the *démineurs* in complete charge of cleaning up Lac Bleu as a token gesture of how interested the national administration is to clear up France's unexploded munitions country-wide. That pits Isidore the young monk, against his father, Journet the dive-master. After much arguing neither could convince the other so Journet the elder departed in a huff. He will not return to visit his son here at Mont-St-Michel ever again, he said. And, incidentally, he was not the least bit interested in the whereabouts of the missing Abbot. As for Madame Catherine Didier, he professed complete ignorance. The Sûreté, our friends Beauchaine and Smith, are scheduled to interrogate him further."

It was then my turn to surprise Lemieux. I told him the complete story of my hour of exploring the ruins of the Mont. He chuckled and commented on how typical "An Hour With Prof" can lead to an unusual adventure. That, he suggested, could be the title of a French television serial. We agreed that the local gendarmes will soon discover the body beneath the Gautier terrace. It would certainly not be prudent for us to tell them where to look. Whether they care about his being *genista* is not important right now. But if it becomes public the influence of historic Mont-St-Michel may help the demining cause.

"But I have another question for you Josh. Do you know that the Museum of Natural History in Angers is sponsoring an ALGERIA EXPOSITION? It will run from October through February. During that time many entities, companies, schools and corporations will engage the private and public sectors in the million-year-old history of Algeria from prehistoric Maghreb to the present. There will be hundreds of Algerians visiting the Angers area. Among them will be diamond dealers. I was wondering if your friend Jules Labonte would like an all-expense paid trip back to Paris. He would mingle with various Algerian delegations and along with L.V. keep an eye on our suspected diamond cache in Lac Bleu. We could arrange for his cover very simply. He could again drive another load of computers for the LaFleur Hauling Company, computers to be used for the historic exposition. He would be able to be around the Angers exposition and

Lac Bleu in an official technical capacity. What do you think?"

"Wonderful, my friend," I replied. "And who will pay for all this?"

"Under the heading of Assistance to the Department of Demining it will go through just fine."

"Excellent, Commissaire. Now what about Madame Didier?"

"Her two charming nephews have been of little help, thus far. Isidore was a dead end. Sometimes I think Jean and Paul are also dead ends. Anyway, I believe it is time for us to visit the *Ministre de L'Interieur Sécurité Civile.* They have not said a word to the media thus far. Assuming none of your recent antics reach the press maybe we can surprise Elysée with news of our own."

"There is something very serious about the Madame Didier disappearance, Roger. Suppose members of the Assembly begin to decide voting issues by calculating what their chances are of being abducted until that issue is resolved? Not ransom for money. Just ransom for votes. The Assembly member to be returned unharmed when the final tally is gaveled *'finis.'* In this case the *finis* would guarantee the depths of Lac Bleu would remain a marvelous hiding place. For old bombs. For diamonds? For terrorists' funds? *Ca va?"*

211

"Yes, that sort of adds up alright," said Roger.

"So what's our next step."

"Operation Entrée meets at Boudreau in three days," he said without hesitation. As L.V. would say: Step on no pets."

"I think it's wonderful that L.V. is teaching you all these useful palindromes, Roger."

"I do too, my friend. She is a natural teacher. I feel I am learning American English."

Three days later Boudreau was ready for the Operation Entrée meeting. Rosemarie Baker, my stalwart sister-in-law, and her gloriously nubile daughter Delynne, did a masterful job of preparing Boudreau. There was the very agreeable odor of raspberry in the grand salon. Near the Porte de Grenade was a table spread with light snacks, including walnut bread and lavender honey. On the bar they had set up the coffee, with special glasses for the kir and a pastis, presumably for post-discussion consumption. Over the east wall, to the right of the fireplace they had cleaned and remounted the joy of my rather eclectic art collection: a numbered copy of Claude Monet's Ships Riding on the Seine at Rouen, 1872/73. It shown brilliantly in the light fixture arranged by Robert Gagne just the week before his unfortunate demise at the hands of the anti-*genista* monsters. It is a little more than 14 x 18 inches. The original resides in the National Gallery of Art in D.C., in the Ailsa Mellon Bruce Collection since about 1970. I find it hard to believe that at one time I actually thought of seriously bidding. When it was sold I left the auction room in tears.

By 11:30 the group began to arrive for discussion and lunch. Pierre had slept in Boudreau's great guest room. Commissaire Roger Lemieux arrived in his nondescript car with Miss Plenitude herself, Laura Veronica Campbell. Roger has been referring to her as Miss *élan,* as in 'impassioned enthusiasm.' He told me privately "I had to look it up."

Celine Beauchaine and Matthew Smith drove Rita Mary Tomasino in from Paris in their ancient French masterpiece. Pierre introduced her to the group as the "important woman who enabled me to enter the Bedard fortress." The group settled down in chairs and sofas in our usual semi-circle facing the fireplace. A dummy grenade was presented by Beauchaine as a Salle de Grenade trophy. Lemieux praised Rita for helping us gain Bedard info. It was obvious that Pierre really appreciated her advice and assistance. It was also clear he was not anxious to commit a B & E again.

"The files, Rita, that Pierre came out with are very helpful to us. We have been able to tie ol' man Bedard into several suspicious Algerian diamond merchants. I can now understand how much he must hate our questions concerning exploded munitions if they indeed threaten his government-protected hiding place in Avrille. You have to admit if you need to hide something for a year or two official Departement du Deminage lairs are, how you say, efficacious?" We all nodded yes. Lemieux paused.

"I don't think I understand why Monsieur Bedard doesn't just place his diamonds in a bank vault," Rita said.

"Well, in the first place Rita they are probably not all his. A consortium of some kind owns them. Another group placed them in the Lac and is responsible for watching over them. That's why they panicked and killed poor little Camille Delattre."

"Killed?" we all called out.

"Yes, my friends. In the hospital room. A bullet between the eyes." And nodding to me and L.V., "like young Mitchel Joseph and the Ministers at the Consulate."

"Why so drastic?" asked Rita.

Beauchaine stood for a moment to get another cup of espresso coffee with warm milk. She said, "They thought both Joseph and Delattre interfered directly with their plan to sell the illegal diamonds to a terrorist group who will buy arms and pay handsomely those

214

who have facilitated the exchanges along the way…like Bedard seems to be doing as far as the *Sûreté* can observe."

"And this whole 'hide the diamonds in the bombs' game is taking advantage of a legitimate French government effort to clean up WW I and II debris," added Smith. "Beauchaine and I have been over those Bedard papers with several of our top people and it is clear that illegal diamonds for terrorist arms is an on-going industry around the world. Our little Lac Bleu in Avrille is a small scheme in the overall movement. But even though small, terrorist heads will roll if and when we crack the plot and make arrests under French authority."

"So why don't we do some cracking?" asked miss élan, the literal miss enthusiasm.

"The usual reason," Beauchaine said, giving us a Gallic shrug. "Our superiors are waiting until we can arrest as many as possible. They are not interested in merely cleaning up our Lac. They are interested in closing down dozens of other misuses of legitimate demining sites throughout France. Interpol will probably have the final say on when we actually 'crack.'

"So what do we do in the meantime?" Lemieux was up and facing the group. "We have plenty to do, with the proper authority. Authority because it was here in this room that a murder attempt failed and the *Maitre de Boudreau* has a right to be angry. He and Pierre survived a later attempt by Algerian assassins. Early on, the Gagnes were killed to discourage us from looking into demining any further. You are all still deputized by me, Avrille Commissaire, to assist me in this work. In that capacity we continue our work. Each of you has a talent to assist my meager police force. Right now I would like Prof Josh to tell you about his adventure at Mont-St-Michel."

I went over the Mont story of the deceased Abbot, emphasizing the wooden cross and the sprig of plant life imbedded in it. L.V. almost fell off her chair when she explained her race from the Abbot and his probable scream as he apparently fell from Gautier's terrace. Lemieux added his story about visiting the Journets and Didier twins in the young friar's room. After that we all sat there for a few minutes looking at the fireplace in silence.

After a thoughtful pause I looked at L.V. You could almost see a palindrome coming. She stood, stretched her model limbs, smiled slightly and said: "Don't nod." Be alert everyone. "Don't nod."

Everyone laughed, rose, and informally began to gather around the table Delynne had been quietly loading with steaming dishes. Rosemarie and daughter had *omelette a la Normande* (which includes diced apples in Calvados) and *Navarin d'Agneau,* a delightful

French lamb stew. We were all about to sit when Rita said something that made us stand still for one moment more.

"Now maybe I am beginning to understand why the three Bedards have been training with various sidearms. When they give me a day off they drive out to a professional shooting range with a former army arms expert. He told me once they are all very good marksmen. Oh well, can we eat?"

Lemieux

The meal conversation centered around the Bedards and their unique family hobby, as Rita called it. It is unusual in Paris to find an elderly mom and pop shooting team and a 30 year-old-daughter who shoots, according to the unnamed expert mentor, at an Olympic Gold Medal level. I asked Rita if she would please follow-up on that topic and find out where they go to shoot and with whom. Between courses I used Boudreau's office phone. I called my Commissaire friend in Avignon and made arrangements for Jules Labonte to once again be assigned to drive some Algerians to Paris. They should be here next week. A call to Journet resulted in a progress report on L.V.'s diving skills and her ability to work as a team member in the on-going Lac Bleu program. The head office of the *Sûreté de l'Etat* directed my inquiry to the French Criminal Investigation Department. I was assured of the continued services of the Beauchaine-Smith team. I summarized the results of my phone conversations. No police commissioner anywhere could have a more congenial and effective group of deputies.

When I arrived back in my office I was met by a pile of faxes from the Brittany-Normandy police. They decided to release to the media the accidental death of the Abbot of Mont-St-Michel. There was, of course, no mention of his peculiar *genista* cross so the report to the public was strictly non-political with all arrangements facilitated by the Benedictine Order. I hastened to alert L.V. that there was apparently no knowledge of his late night race with her. However, there would be some consequences at the Mont. Several army-trained guards would be added to the Mont corps, and the daily tours will now conclude at 1500 hours. A phone call to the Mont revealed that the young monk Isidore Didier will be on a closed private retreat for several weeks.

In the days immediately following the Operation Entrée gathering Prof Josh and Pierre began to concentrate on key National Assembly deputies. They presented a concerted effort to lobby for Catherine Didier's formal proposition for the creation of a *commission d'enquete,* the long-delayed inquiry into the inventory of buried munitions. For the most part assembly deputies listened and promised to 'look into it soon.' They indicated that it would be easier to bring the resolution back to the floor for discussion when Madame Didier herself reappeared.

A few of the 321 members of the second assembly of the French Parliament, the Senate, seemed somewhat more interested in Didier's whereabouts. Pierre has known Claude Delorne and Jacob Warneau, successful Senators, who, from time to time, have made use of the services offered by Pierre's hotel bar. These gentlemen indicated that the Minister of the Interior and the head of the Sécurité Civile might be of unofficial assistance. In the Assembly corridors and lavatories, lunchrooms and parking lots, Prof was able to participate in casual chat with these two VIPs and other, lesser powers. In French that kind of talk is *bavardage* or *papotage*: gossip, rumour. It is the natural hobby of most legislators. The gossip men engage in while urinating, washing hands, lighting cigarettes, etc., when accumulated and synthesized can be useful. After a few days of this sort of research Josh and Pierre were convinced the Didier twins knew where their Aunt was being held. Probably in their own home in rue Charlot.

Charlot is in the northern part of Le Marais, the 3rd arrondissement. Josh and Pierre are acquainted with this recently gentrified little corner of Paris where 17th and 18th century buildings are home to wholesalers and manufacturers, as well as to Asian, Jewish and gay enclaves. At first they scouted the narrow streets carefully around #12 Charlot. Some are too narrow for anything but biking and walking. Among the bakeries and art galleries they found the best way to approach the Didier residence. It is a charming recently renovated four-room residence with parquet floors, exposed stone, a complete kitchen, and an ancient unreconstructed lift. It was this peculiarity that prompted them to become 'Acme Elevator specialists from London.'

"Where did you get all this authentic-looking equipment?" asked Josh, when Pierre pulled up in a tiny rented van.

"From a costume shop just down the street. I hope the Acme jackets fit us."

"Why don't we just knock on the front door in the normal manner?

"Because," Pierre explained, "the boys are not there. Haven't been there for several days. The antique shop owner at #10 will let us into the elevator machinery room. Andiamo."

They were admitted with ease and began puttering with tools near the lift machinery. When the shopkeeper left they rode up to the Didier floor and Pierre's 'magic keys' quickly had them inside. Within two minutes of prowling about the rooms they came to a small bedroom and Madame Catherine Didier. She was handcuffed to a bedpost and seemed drugged or at least very listless. She seemed to recognize Prof and putting her finger to her lips pointed to a large recorder on the nightstand. Pierre turned it off. Catherine let out a great sigh, a nervous laugh, and a whispered "*Vous etes bienvenue!"* They had suspected they were welcome but were dismayed to learn from her right away that the twins would be returning soon. Josh had plans for a quick getaway.

"Pierre let's get her stuff together and get her out of here. We don't have time to clean her up here. Just put this blanket around her and tell any neighbors you meet you are taking her to the hospital."

"Hold it Josh. What are you going to do?"

"I will await our friendly twins. I think I can talk to them, stall them. They are obviously working for those opposed to their Aunt's Assembly work to investigate the demining sites. That puts them, if we are correct, against us and with the Bedards. I'll try to keep them talking while you get Beauchaine and Smith over here. Go!"

Pierre gathered Catherine into his arms, walked quickly into the lift and the last Josh saw of him from the window he was tooling rapidly down Charlot in the direction of the Seine. Josh locked himself in the apartment, cased the kitchen, found some stale croissants, and settled into a plush chair facing the door. He thought to discard his Acme jacket and tools under the bed. His H & K 9mm was tucked in his belt at the back. He tried to assume a casual air, picked up a television magazine and crossed his leg. When Jean and Paul arrive, he thought, I will appear to be waiting to visit with them, having been let in by the helpful neighbor.

> **My son, hold fast to your duty,**
> **busy yourself with it, grow old**
> **while doing your task.**
> **SIRACH 11:20**

PART V

Prof Josh

"*Merde que j'ai horreur de la semaine de velo,*" yelled Jean and he and Paul came charging into the room, each carrying a bicycle.

"You hate riding a bike anytime, not just during the perfectly logical Bike Week."

"Why does the Marais need a bike week? Our driver gets a week off for no good reason while people go peddling their brains out bumping into each other in these narrow streets, and…"

"Well, hello Monsieur le Professeur," said Paul, very surprised.

"Professor Josh!" yelled Jean. "What are you doing here?"

They plopped their bikes down against the far wall and stood aghast. I waited, smiled, ready for any further reaction. They continued to stand, glaring.

Finally, Paul: "What's going on?" His eyes flicked towards the closed bedroom door where his aunt had been.

"I was in the neighborhood and decided to drop in. The neighbor let me in."

Playing it cool. They are hoping I have not seen their aunt?

"Well, we are glad you dropped by. But," looking at Jean, "the antique dealer has no right to open our door. He's your friend Jean. Is he going to allow anyone to walk in here. Please speak to him for God's sake." Turning to me, "Coffee prof? Chardonnay?"

"Chardonnay would be fine, thanks Paul."

Paul pours three little glasses in silence. They are really confused. I am playing it cool, toss the magazine aside, study the wine 'legs' in the glass. These guys are definitely not used to embarrassed silence.

"Well, that Mont-St-Michel is really something, isn't it?" This from Paul. Silence. At this point L.V. would have thought 'Paul is appalled.'

"Yes," I replied. "What ever happened to Isidore and the Abbot?"

"When we left Dore had to go into some kind of a retreat. The Abbot has been found, I heard. Seems he may have fallen from Gautier's diving platform. Really too bad," said Jean.

"What have you heard Prof?" asked Paul.

"About the same. Excellent Chardonnay."

Another pause of perplexity. Their brows were actually furrowed.

"I suppose we should be getting something to eat. It's not often we have a Professor Emeritus visit for dinner, eh Paul?"

"Right, my brother. Let me check on the cat for a moment and then we can go to our local sidewalk café, Prof, if that is okay with you."

Paul walked down the hall where we had found Catherine. I heard a door open and close.

Jean was very nervous, paced about a little, talked about these new traffic rules concerning *En ville sans voiture.* He really dislikes being in town without his car. Paul returned and headed for the door. *"Allons en route."* They exchanged a split second glance. In the time it took me to get out of the soft chair and walk towards the door I noticed they were both armed. In Memphis jargon they were both carrying. I could feel my Heckler & Koch nine-mm automatic pressing against my sweaty back.

Jean led us to La Salle Bakery, a small café around the corner from their house. They are well known by the staff and were shown to what seemed to be the

Didier table. We all ordered onion soup but different desserts. I had *crépes flambées*. We all said "I'm really not hungry." Obviously we were all quite tense. As we rose to leave they made the first move toward honesty. Paul had gone to the WC and when he returned he was behind my chair. With practiced adroitness his hand was down my back and on my gun. When he came around to his seat he held it under a folded *Figaro*.

"Well professeur, let's be honest. We know you know about Catherine and now we know you know we know she is gone from our house. Now we need to know where you have taken her. We need to know what you have told the police. We assume your *mec,* your buddy Pierre, is in on this. Speak up Monsieur, vite, vite."

"Okay, you guys, you really thought you were hot shot, smart, double bastards. Well, now we know you have goofed big time. Catherine is safe, the Assembly will reconsider her Resolution, and you clowns have broken a dozen laws in the last few days which the Sûreté knows all about."

I stared hard across the small café table and put on my bluffing visage.

"The prof can be angry and vulgar, Paul. What do we do with him? The ol' bullseye in the forehead? What do you think? We should move fast."

"Jean, as usual you are too spontaneous. Relax. Order some coffee. We'll walk him back to our house, just for today. His friends will miss him and contact us. We will not have seen him since the Mont. The police will search our place and find nothing. Of course we'll have to send him where we sent his little brother, the meddling American Joseph, and a few others. But our deal with Algiers will continue. How about that Professor Emeritus? Too complicated for you?

Coffee came and remained untouched. After fifteen minutes more they motioned me to stand and walk back toward Charlot. Jean walked beside me, gripping my jacket sleeve tightly. Paul walked behind with my gun clutched in the newspaper. They talked in their usual congenial manner. I had to do something before arriving back in their house.

As we neared the Didier house a group of about fifty teen-aged girls in the uniform of a private English school came bursting out of rue des Coutures. They had evidently just come from the Picasso Museum and they were all talking at once about the great artist. Their noisy group was going to intersect my pathetic death-march guards. Jean attempted to pull me to the side to let them pass but I refused to be dragged. We met the young ladies head on and they flowed on both sides of my execution squad, all laughing and shouting. In their midst my right fist came in contact with Jean's face and he slumped down among the girls who yelled

227

and laughed as they stumbled over him. My left hand grabbed my paper-wrapped gun, knocked Paul's glasses off into the crowd, poked him hard in his right eye and ran. I was able to make it through the giggling human traffic up the narrow Coutures and into the Picasso Museum. The museum docent warned me they would be closing soon as he accepted my elder citizen fee.

I found a pay phone and called the Colbert. Pierre was there making Catherine comfortable. The hotel doctor had pronounced her vital signs good but she was undernourished by about three *brioches*. Pierre's hotel staff would take care of her in complete anonymity. He agreed to have a police car at the Museum door in about fifteen minutes. It was not difficult for Pierre to round up a couple gendarme friends. They were probably right there at his bar but he didn't say that exactly.

Twelve minutes later the familiar French police siren was heard and then a screeching car skidded up to the Museum entrance. Two gendarmes leaped out and were immediately under heavy fire from across the street where the twins had taken over a *boulangerie*. The gendarmes reacted well. The Didiers are not Bedard-style marksmen. Neither policeman was hit after a rapid exchange of ten shots or more. One of the twins was hit and fell into the bakery window. We think the other left by a side door and out onto rue de Turenne. The policewoman in the car called in the situation while two of us grabbed the one wounded twin from the badly shot-up bakery. *Service d'Aide*

Medicale Urgence, SAMU, and the fire service medical team, *Sapeurs Pompiers,* all arrived quickly. Jean had a bullet in his right shoulder. I recognized Jean because he had a bruised face and bloody nose. Which reminded me Paul couldn't be doing too well either with a sore eye and without his glasses.

When I turned around to thank the gendarmes Beauchaine and Smith were at my side. Beau was stowing her gun, smiling.

"Finally after hours of innocuous computer garbage comes a call from a voice we can relate to. How are you prof? Having a typical Emeritus day?"

"Hi there Beau. Always good to see a friendly face after a gun battle."

"What's been happening, Prof? Bring us up to date," said Matt.

"Be happy to do that. Come to my place at the Colbert. There is someone there you should meet."

The last I saw of Jean that day he was giving me the finger from the back of the dreaded *fourgon,* the police van. The local gendarmerie were spreading their men on foot and in cars throughout the Marais's Museum neighborhood. Matt called Lemieux from his car and we arrived at Colbert for the cocktail-two-for-one-hour.

I was interested in interviewing Catherine. First I asked about her health. Her daily medications and several changes of clothes had been retrieved from her place and she was in rather good spirits considering what her ingrate nephews had done to her. She was as gracious as usual and with an aperitif in hand we talked about the twins.

"Will you be pressing charges against Jean and Paul," I asked.

"No, I don't think so. I have called my Assembly committee secretary and he has explained to the police that my absence of a few days was caused by a severe case of *la grippe*, gastric flu. I am recovering at the home of some friends, I told them, and the location must be kept from the media. I will return to my office in a few days and mention nothing about my wonderful nephews. Really, I would very much like to administer *un coup de pied au cul,* to each. You understand?"

"Yes Madame, they certainly deserve at least 'a kick in the pants' as Americans say. And I hope you recover quickly from your influenza. But right now Jean is in jail and Paul is being hunted. The charges are numerous but the major one at the moment is the attempted murder of several gendarmes. Kidnapping/abduction, etc., will come later."

"What do you think of those two Professor? Are they among the disturbed types one reads about? How would you assess them? I know you dislike typing people but just in general and for me here, informally, what can we say about their mental/psychological state?"

"Just for my mental records, Catherine, is it true they are both baptized with the same second name, as in Jean-Theophraste and Paul-Theophraste?"

"Yes, professor, that is correct. Their mother wanted them to be distinctive, to stand out from the crowd."

"Well from what I understand about their early childhood they were orphans at the age of eleven. Their parents, compulsive gamblers, were killed in an auto accident and you took over their education. They were reluctant high school military academy brats in New York. At Yale they did enough studying to graduate. Since being back in Paris they are very involved in gambling and maybe took one trip too many to the Deauville tables."

"That is true. Deauville is a beautiful place to become a pauper, similar to your Tunica, Tennessee, according to L.V. And by the way, professor, I also subsidized their graduate schoolwork. They now have a postgraduate diploma, the DEA, *Diplome d'Etudes Approfondies*. They are very intelligent young men. They told me they studied the mathematics of chance."

For an hour or so we talked about the twins, her visits to them in the States, their pranks, foibles, and failed romances. Catherine said that for some years now they haven't held paying jobs and live moderately "by their wits." As we talked a picture formed of the twins' pathological gambling. This disorder is often self-destructive, usually begins in adolescence, may include a childhood loss of a significant adult. The senior Didiers were known to be risk-takers and cocaine addicts. The twins are extreme sports enthusiasts with a tendency to major depression, typical of this impulse control disorder. Catherine suggested that the twins, at least Paul if he is still on the loose, have numerous contacts and options at a time like this. Paul, she suggested, is most likely already in hiding far from the Marais. And Jean has a battery of lawyers among his gambling pals.

"Perhaps it's time for a siesta, Madame. We will talk again tomorrow. I am very glad you are alright and I appreciate your candor about the family. You understand that any description of behavior and diagnosis of this kind is pure speculation. Maybe one day the boys will want to voluntarily enter treatment."

L.V.

Monsieur Le Roy Journet has kept us divers-in-training very busy. He says his job is to make us into high tech professionals but I have a strong feeling that several in this so-called training program are

232

professional dudes who are there to report every move Claudine Touret and I make. The daily program itself is fun, altering lectures, training films, and actual underwater work. Claudine happens to be as bright as Camille was built. We study the books on techniques and equipment manuals together. She knows diving well. Journet and his male diver-buddies have not yet noticed that I know French and sometimes they talk complacently within ear shot. Claudine and I are beginning to realize that if we get too close to a certain part of the lake the other divers crowd us off in another direction.

In the program library we have been studying newspaper coverage of the 2002 Lac Bleu phenomenon. Le Courrier de l'Ouest ran a series on the underwater photography of Yves Gladu. Two of the photos on 25 July are called *vrais* documents, real, true documents, showing piles of explosives in a crate. Both Gladu and Erwan Amice, of the French navy, speak of the lake as genuinely risky business. These two experts would say Claudine and I are diving, once a day for about an hour, in an authentic *menace,* a menace in any language, in this case even spelled the same in French and English.

The Program Lectures are always interesting. This week a representative of the Organization for the Prohibition of Chemical Weapons (OPCW) told us the Vimy, France, story. He quoted from an Assembly report to reinforce the shock of the evacuation of 12,000 inhabitants of the town of Vimy and its neighboring villages in the Pas-de-Calais. It seems the OPCW received information about the leakage of chemical agents from some stored weapons left over from World War I. The chemicals are mustard gas and phosgene. The OPCW rep praised the French authorities for their rapid response to this emergency. The toxic waste was destroyed in line with the relevant national regulations. The citizens of Vimy and vicinity, as well as French legislators, will not forget the incident. Like neither will the brave *démineurs*.

Anyway, it was after this Vimy lecture that our crash course crashed.

Claudine

Or as you Americans say, we took a dive. We gave up. We had to. It was awful.

The day after the Vimy lecture who shows up at the diving office but one Isidore Journet. I knew Dore during our early school years. He was, I remember, remarkably unathletic. The kids made sure he knew we knew he was gay. He hated sports but he was tough. So when he surprised his father in the office some of that long-suppressed toughness came out.

I had been tying my shoelaces on the bench in the hall near our diving quarters when he suddenly dashed through the door looking furious.

"Is my dad in?" he shouted, without even looking in my direction.

"I don't know, Dore, how are you and what's with the monk's outfit?"

"I can see you haven't become any more intelligent since we were ten years old, Claudine."

"No, I'm still slow. Congrats on the *soigné* brown oufit. And, oh yeah, nice to see you too Dore."

"Hello and goodbye. I'm going in to see my dad."

With that he charged into the room, leaving the door ajar. I sat on the bench and watched and waited, wondering how the Journets, father and son, interacted. It became clear in about one minute that this was going to be a fight to the finish. Dore accused his father of undermining the good *genista* anti-pollution work of his now deceased Abbot. The father told Dore to get back into the Mont and mind his own business. Dore accused his father of harboring illegal Algerian diamond dealers while waiting to profit greatly from the sale of the Lac Bleu diamond cache. At that point a full-fledged *bagarre* broke out, a literal *bataille* between *boxeurs*. Chairs and books crashed to the floor, framed photos of the Program's graduates fell from two walls. These guys sounded serious. I edged toward the door and peeked in. Journet senior was staggering back under a rain of quick accurate body blows to the face and chest of his much faster-moving son. Each time he hit his father and dodged a return blow Dore would shout words like "bombs, grenades, Vimy, shells, mines." Before I could intervene, Journet senior threw a heavy desk replica of Rodin's The Kiss. It caught Dore on the left temple and he dropped. I crashed into the office, leaped over strewn furniture and knelt beside Dore. He looked gray and bloody. The dad sat right on the floor where he had stood behind his desk, dizzy but still alive. Dore moved to squeeze my hand and pulled me towards him. I looked into his face, wiped away blood and spittle. He mumbled and when I leaned my ear to his mouth he whispered "The diamonds are…" He was dead.

L.V. came jogging by, saw the door open, looked in and grabbed the phone from the floor. She called emergency, Lemieux, and Prof Josh in that order. Attendants arrived with stretchers. Journet senior was taken off to the Avrille hospital. Dore went to the local medical examiner. Finally the military authorities arrived from somewhere off the grounds.

Prof Josh

The young Benedictine novice Isidore Didier was buried two days later in a private ceremony at Mont-St-Michel. The next day the National Assembly voted to reopen debate on Catherine Didier's proposition to create a demining commission of inquiry. Consistent with that resolution the Sûreté was asked to conduct an inventory of storage centers. That is how I was appointed by Catherine to assist agents Beauchaine and Smith in their visits to various *sites de stockage de munitions.*

The papers that week featured several stories and interviews of the triumphant anti-pollution assembly member. She is always elegant when posing for the camera or speaking informally with reporters. Madame Catherine Didier is well known in Paris social circles for her *coiffure,* which can refer to one's hairstyle or headgear. Both terms apply to Catherine. She says that's because she has taken her patron saint, Saint Catherine of Alexandria, Egypt, very solemnly. The saint was beheaded for her faith under Maxentius around the year 310. A custom then arose among young ladies of Normandy to honor the Saint by wearing an elaborate hat or *coiffe* on 25 November, her feast day. This, the papers reported, is why Madame Catherine Didier wears a fabulous hat and/or remarkable hairstyle each day in the National Assembly.

The Director of the *Direction Générale de la Sécurité Extreme* assigned us to the famous Maginot Line *site de stockage,* exact location of left-over stock piles a State secret, of course. Named after the planner of the fort, War Minister Andre Maginot, it eventually became a symbol of lousy planning. But it was an extraordinary engineering achievement with French soldiers living forty feet below ground in an amazing series of interconnected forts built along the Franco-German border. From 1927 to 1936 engineers and hundreds of soldiers worked on these magnificent fortifications only to leave the Belgian border open. The world soon learned what a rather useless fortress *La Ligne Maginot* was when the German army swept through Belgium and came around the back of The Line.

So that's how beautiful Beauchaine and efficient Smith and I came to Northeast France in their glamorous company car. We enjoyed a day in Reims' cathedral and Epernay's chalky caves tasting champagne. We had long talks with locals about their demining issues. They were eager to talk about friends and neighbors who were *démineurs,* especially during delicious restaurant dinners. Over a beef stew braised in beer we reviewed various signs we had seen in our *site de stockage* search: *terrain interdit, cordon rouge, keep out; touché pas: ca tue.* We listened to locals talk about how hard they work to keep the place totally disguised. Military camouflage and secrecy are not natural states. Some very direct signs for foreigners are necessary: THIS AREA BOOBY-TRAPPED. These graphics become the subjects for many American cameras. In Nancy, over pea soup, *Potage St-Germain,* we learned that Verdun has an estimated twelve million unexploded shells in its sacred ground. We were met by a driver in a Land Rover. Jacques Favrau reminded us that the work of the *démineurs* is not to be publicized. I put my small notebook back in my pocket.

Favrau is a long-term vet of the Demining Department. He has served in the technical center at Marly-le-Roi, the closed forest east of Paris where he was engaged in weapons testing. He smokes the most rude cigarettes incessantly. His breath, he tells us, does justice to Krieckenlambic, that strong bitter Belgian beer, cherry flavored. Nowadays he conducts VIPs around, not near, demining projects, even whipping his Land Rover from one end of the Maginot Line to the other, a distance of 200 miles. For our education he used back roads, explaining, as we passed vast open fields, that his main responsibility is chairing a committee of young military engineers. They are supposed to arrive at new methods for disposing of sea-mines along the French coast. As we drove towards Metz he philosophized aloud, as if he were by himself.

"C'est un vrais scandale...qu'on laisse des armes... dormir...".

As he drove with his left hand he fingered his 357 Sig Sauer service weapon.

'Yes, it is a real scandal," he said, answering himself. "Leaving all those munitions lying around, hoping they will disappear by themselves. But they won't disappear, you know," turning to Smith. "No they won't..."

239

Just as he finished 'won't' the Land Rover hit a mine. We all went flying. Beauchaine and Favrau were in the front and they hit the windshield, or vice versa. Smith and I went out both back doors and landed on opposite sides of the demolished Rover. My first thought was 'I may be permanently deaf.' The unexpected roar was ringing like mad in my head. I had landed hard on my left shoulder. My arm hung, useless. I staggered to Smith who seemed okay except for his right knee which he bashed on the car door on his mine-assisted way out of the back of the car. We sat looking at each other for about five seconds. Then we both yelled "Beauchaine." We clumsily staggered to the totally destroyed front of the Rover and found her lying unconscious in a ditch. Smith crawled next to her and held her in his arms. Favrau was in a hedge, mumbling some of the most ingenious French invectives ever fabricated. He had several cuts on head and shoulders, but he could stand, albeit wobbly.

He leaned against the twisted rear of the Rover and shouted several versions and meanings of *foutre* and *merde*. He soon became hoarse and slowed to a whisper, sunk slowly to the ground and passed out.

We lay there right where we were for some time, shocked and numbed. Smith yelled out "I think she is coming round." Favrau and I crawled near to them. Smith was patting her face with water from his ever-present Evian bottle.

"My radio is broken, my friends," said Favrau. "I am sorry it is of no help to us out here. We are far from any village."

"I can walk," I said, "if you point me in the right direction."

"Walking seems to be our only choice. You see this road, how you say cut short or short cut, is far from a main road or farm."

Poor Favrau, the dynamic military leader, really seemed dejected. I was hoping he would soon snap out of it and come up with a productive idea or two. I was about to say something like, "Well, you can't win them all," or, "Demining is a work in progress," when I saw a cloud of dust from the Metz direction. A vehicle of some kind was approaching rapidly. I shouted, "Hey guys, our rescue squad is arriving." As we watched, the dust cloud became two large American vans, the kind U.S. Colleges use to haul sports teams. Favrau said "How did they see us so quickly? Remember not to mention *déminage*. You people can be from a real estate company. *Comprenez?*"

"Sure, no problem," said Smith. "We'll just tell the truth: we need a hospital. Then we just need to get to where we will rent a car and continue our observations. I'll pay them for their help. Not to worry, sir."

Beauchaine sat up and Favrau and I stood, rather dizzily. Nothing more was said in the few minutes it took the vans to approach. Then our surprise and shock was intensified. Each van was occupied by four people in black tight-fitting 'hi-jack' outfits, including those blasted ski-masks. They leaped out with guns drawn.

Our group froze, motionless and silent. We probably looked beat up and grimly astonished. We couldn't believe our eyes. The rescuers in black also maintained silence. With the back doors open they pointed with their guns and waved us toward the vans. They gestured Smith, carrying Beauchaine, into the lead van. Favrau and I followed the pointers into the other. Without a word they slammed the doors, revved up and roared off in the general direction of Metz. As they swerved off the main motorway into a service area one of them drew the back curtains closed. While the driver kept a Sig Sauer on us the other climbed into the back area with a large roll of duct tape. Favrau attempted to protest but was immediately knocked unconscious. We were both taped with our hands behind our backs. I could have adjusted to that but worse was yet to come. Propping Favrau up against me he taped us over our mouths, eyes, and ears. Our ankles were taped tightly toether. The sound of duct tape being peeled from the roll will always be a frightening recollection. The driver took all our guns and tossed them into an ample glove compartment.

The two vans pulled out onto the main road again with Favrau and I banging into one another trying to keep our balance on the armless seats like two sacks of soccer balls. Our driver was evidently well acquainted with this route. He swerved and curved at good speed, passengers bouncing about in total darkness and deafness. After about an hour we slowed and in a few more minutes we stopped.

The doors were opened and several hands unloaded us onto what seemed like wheel chairs. We could hear nothing. I could feel the seat and the movement. I was hoping Beauchaine was ok. Maybe this was a hospital. But maybe not. We were too trussed up for any medical attention. So where were we? We seemed to be on a smooth ramp or parking lot and apparently accelerating down a slope. After a few more minutes of rolling we were stopped and our feet were freed. A very strong arm and shoulder lifted me up and set me standing. Whoever it is, I thought, this guy is a body-builder with excessive upper-body musculature. He lifted me and set me down with ease. But without sight, hearing, or hand touch, my nose was working overtime. The sweat smell of this guy was being challenged by his French cologne, a concoction strong enough to anesthetize a rhino. Was this to be a robbery, kidnapping, murder, extortion or could it have anything to do with demining?

I felt and smelled several others bodies around me. We began to walk down stairs. Many stairs. Four flights. Were we forty feet underground? Why? And where can you find a building near Metz that has underground facilities? We were jerked to a stop and bumped into each other. I think Beauchaine was in front of me now. She does have a distinctive aroma that shouts 'joy.'

Sliding my feet, as if to keep my balance, I thought we were on gritty or sandy cement flooring. Again we were pushed, shoved and hoisted into vehicles. I don't know who else was where but Beauchaine was plainly beside me. Again one could feel movement, wind, this time in an open vehicle with no doors or windows. It was dusty and someone beside me had a long bout of sneezing.

After about ten minutes on these little race cars, or golf carts, or whatever they were, we stopped near what had to be dining facilities—overwhelmingly strong cabbage smells. Once again we were assisted to stand upright and close together. This time my feet detected what felt like narrow gauge rail tracks. To make sure I stumbled and began to guess where we were.

We were led into a room with stagnant-air circulation problems. Our hands, ears and mouths were ripped free of tape. There were a few pain-filled sounds. Then I rubbed my wrists and mashed ears. All okay, but my shoulder seemed out of its proper rotator cuff. And I'm not even a golfer.

Next we were made to sit side by side at a kind of bench-picnic table arrangement. Metal plates of food were at each place and a spoon was placed in our right hands. Of all things! The plates were filled with macaroni and cheese, great mounds of it. After two spillings we learned that water glasses had been generously provided. All this time there had been no conversation. But, judging from the sounds, we ate plenty. Usually I hate macaroni and cheese.

Were we still in France? Most definitely. We were being held in France's treasured military masterpiece: the Maginot Line.

After finishing our lunch we were again led out into the carvernous-sounding tunnel and again I stumbled against someone and learned one more thing about our captors. This one was definitely of the female persuasion. I was immediately pushed against a wall by the muscleman while duct tape was wrapped around our wrists. I could hear the tape being applied to my comrades.

We were addressed in French.

"We have brought you here to ask you a simple question. We will keep you here until you tell us where the diamonds are. You will now be put in individual rooms and left there. After tonight we will kill one of you if we don't learn the answer. After ratification of your answer you will be released. But tomorrow one of you dies if you ignore our simple question: Where are the diamonds?"

"Let's just kill one now. The others will talk."

"Well, okay. Anyone wish to answer now?

Silence from us.

"Okay, into the four rooms. We will ask again in a few hours."

"In the meantime," I said, "this woman needs medical attention."

"When she tells us where the diamonds are she will be attended to. Good night."

The four rooms he referred to were former officers' quarters, near the mess hall. They were small but probably adequate for smallish French Lieutenant-type officers of the nineteen thirties and forties. We were locked in from the outside. There was no light, toilet, table, or cot. Just a bare room. I began to realize that the Maginot Line, THE French fortress, is so huge that parts of it can be taken over by criminals like these guys and the authorities or caretakers may not even know anyone is occupying this section. There is little chance that anyone outside this group of kidnappers, diamond thieves, murderers and terrorists, ever comes near this section. It is undoubtedly INTERDIT-posted.

For the first few minutes inside the room I thought of my companions. Favrau and Beauchaine had really been injured and were probably very uncomfortable right now. Smith was most likely feeling his way around the room, touching the walls, searching for furniture. Favrau I pictured preparing to break out by charging at the door head first.

This extraordinary fortress has been famous for what it did not accomplish but to this day it is popular among French, German, and British tourists. The nearby town of Thionville advertises its l'Horizon Hotel where visitors can purchase a package deal of two days touring the fortress and environs plus one hotel overnight. It will never be as popular at Mont-St-Michel but it does have its historic attraction for World War II enthusiasts. There is on display everything the French needed to survive underground while being totally prepared for an attack from Germany. There are tunnels with practical cars on small gauge train tracks that can transport you to the army's kitchens, infirmaries, communication center, power station, maintenance shops, and the ever-popular gun turrets which clever machinery could raise up from ground level prepared to shoot the enemy. Unique vanishing pill boxes, movable bunkers. It really was ingenious. Of course only a small portion of the many miles of secret passages are open to the public today. Favrau, Beauchaine, Smith and I were occupants of the CLOSED TO THE PUBLIC section.

B. J. LUCIAN

After about an hour of total darkness my officers quarters lit up and two visitors appeared at the door. The first one in was the large muscleman who had been lifting and shoving me about. His size and aroma were unmistakable. When he stepped from the doorway into the room Jeanne-Clotilde Bedard was right behind him, still in black, mask removed. Muscles was mean looking; Mademoiselle Bedard was smiling.

We spoke in English. Muscles was silent. He didn't seem to be interested in the conversation, probably not being able to understand much of what was being said. He was there strictly because of his bodily strength. Bedard, on the other hand, had plenty to say. She greeted me as one would an old friend, except for the cheek-cheek ritual.

"Well, hello," I said. "How unsurprised I am to see you. Again."

"What do you mean 'again?'"

"You know what 'again' means Miss Bedard, secretary to the late Dr. Barardelli, diamond expert."

"Oh, so you did recognize me. Even in that very short time in his office? I must remember to change hair dressers."

Then she continued. "I know you made me today in your clumsy attempts to gather as much information as you can. You have good stumbling skills, don't you? I assume you know exactly where you are."

"Well, not exactly, but we must be someplace along the two-hundred miles of the Maginot, no?"

"Correct. And you also know exactly what we need."

"No actually, Mademoiselle, I don't."

"I think you do. We haven't a great deal of time to discuss the details."

"Why not? Your boss said we have until morning. Pull up a chair. We'll chat. And by the way, do we need Muscles here? What's he, the interpreter from your intelligence branch?"

"As I understand it, you are a Frenchman teaching in the States. You and Pierre are old friends. You are both *genistas* and opposed to existing munition dumps and want them cleaned up. My group does not care whether they are cleaned or not. But right now these *sites de stockage* make wonderful places to hide things. You accidentally discovered our *cache diamants,* at Avrille. We want all the Lac Bleu diamonds back. Simple enough for you?"

"My dear young lady, you are totally misinformed. We do not have your cache of diamonds. We know now that you know that we found one. Uno. Un. The brave diver who brought that one diamond to the surface died mysteriously in the military hospital. So we were unable to ask her where exactly in Lac Bleu she found it. Since then, with all the Journet troubles, we have not had a chance to find them. We just have the one and the Sûreté suggested they keep it for us."

"You are lying."

"No. We don't have it. But we are going to find the cache, somehow. And then you will be indicted for a series of crimes that will include your illustrious sharp-shooting parents Bertrand and Nicole. You are such a model Vosges family. Isn't your father in with the boys at the Elysée palace? You can check with the Chirac government. It is time they reward the Département du Déminage, perhaps with some diamonds.

"Between you and the Sûreté team we will get our information," she replied, after a slight hesitation. And by the way, that stupid Favrau is already dead. It was his unlucky day to be assigned you three to view the demining sites. His body is so far underground in this Maginot tomb he will simply be on the roster as AWOL forever. I will go now to interview the Beauchaine woman. Seph, my guard-companion today, is rather anxious to interrogate her."

"Come back anytime. Don't be a stranger."

"If I come back to this room it will be to kill you after the Sûreté agents have talked."

"I bet the alumni association of Wellesley is proud of you."

She left, still smiling. Seph was right behind her, still flexing. After feeling my way along the four walls for some time I sat down in a corner and tried to think. I was asleep when the door crashed open and Seph and Bedard were there again.

"Hello there you two. A truly sharp-looking couple. You were just passing by and decided to drop in. Again?"

"We came back because your Sûreté pals are useless. Seph was a little too harsh and they seem to be dead. So it's just you *professeur*."

"I don't believe you. Your boss said we had until morning and it can't be more then about midnight, *n'est-ce pas?* He will not be pleased with you Bedard. You are messing up badly on such a simple mission— get some info."

Bedard motioned to Seph and his giant fist flashed before my eyes and crashed into my forehead. The back of my head hit a wall. I folded limply into the corner and lay stunned.

The door slammed, lights went out, and I lay with a #1 headache, one hand on each head bump. As I began to regain some consciousness my olfactory sense went on full alert. A noticeable scent of Channel #5 was very near in the darkness.

Jules

The "V" in *Train à Grande Vitesse* (TGV) stands for speed, something or someone in a *Grand* rush. On the train from my hometown of Avignon north to Paris one can notice the speed; this train rocks at 100 miles per hour. Considering the usual airport delays this is certainly the easiest, fastest, and most pleasant way to get from Avignon to Paris. You get the idea there is a great deal of open farmland in my country. It is lovely to see, even at this remarkable speed.

Chief Lemieux said "get here as soon as possible." I was to rent a large van in Paris and meet him at his headquarters in Avrille. "Why?" I had asked. Answer: "Because the Prof is convinced you know how to handle Algerians."

So here I am humming *"Sous le pont d'Avignon, on y danse, on y dansé...,"* relaxed in the TGV. I know Americans sing *"sur,"* "on" the bridge, but the proper word is *"sous,"* "under" the bridge. There was a little tavern on an islet in the river where the LaBontes danced literally under the bridge.

Anyway, when I last saw these guys, the Prof, Pierre and Lemieux, they made me promise I would be attentive in LeFleur Hauling and report any activities that seemed out of the ordinary. This time, after three hours, I'm on the carriageway in a new German van, (capacity eight adults). I was happy to see delightful L.V. and Lemieux in Avrille but was astounded to hear the nature of this mission.

Lemieux

I have a theory and it involves Jules making contacts with his LeFleur co-drivers. There must be a connection between the Algerians who tried unsuccessfully to kill Prof Josh and Pierre on the highway and the Avignon Algerians in LeFleur Hauling Ltd. If anyone can come up with some credible ideas it will be Jules. That boy is not as simple as Prof made him out to be. The Avignon commissaire has made that very plain to me. Jules is an accomplished private detective. And besides, key members of the Operation Entrée team seem to be incapacitated. We need Jules now.

In the meantime I was able to obtain a *mandat d'arrêt*, a search warrant to search for and 'discover' and retain any illegal documents in the Bedard household. Many 'old friends' of the curious monsieur

Bedard were amenable to talking about his work of preserving Lac Bleu exactly as it is, diamonds included. His esteemed dinner guest, monsieur LeGrand, will be able to attest to his threats and his enthusiasm to shut down the *genista* movement. We were thinking Pierre's tiny tape recorder would refresh everyone's memory. But as it turned out, the Vosges *mandat* resulted in more excitement than we expected.

Following Pierre's very exact directions, we offered the two night watchmen a few euros for a complete late-night dinner at La Coupole in Montparnasse. They promised to stay there for a few hours while we took care of business in the building. With many reassurances concerning their important Vosges job, they departed and the building was quiet.

Our plan was to knock politely on the Bedard door, present our warrant, and proceed to 'search' for the documents Pierre had originally 'found.' But much to my amazement and that of my three gendarmes, Bedard's door was open and he was welcoming us with a wide gesture. *"Bienvenue"* he almost shouted. My men holstered their sidearms and we all smiled an insincere "Bon jour." Bertrand Bedard was, to say the least, prepared for us. He had planned *une surprise* complete with negotiations.

"You are wanted on the telephone, Commissaire."

"Allo," I said, "to whom am I speaking."

"I am Jeanne-Clotilde Bedard, monsieur. I know who you are Commissaire. You are the man we wish to negotiate with, here and now, quickly and quietly."

"Negotiate?"

"My father will explain the details. Please be assured, monsieur, that your friends are prisoners here with me, and all three are near death."

"Which friends, *s'il vous plait?*"

"Your very good friend, the Professor and his two sûreté, *les fouteur and fouteuse de merde.*"

"Such foul language mam'selle from such a refined young lady."

"Deal with my father. *Au revoir.*"

"Well Commissaire, you are now 'up-to-date,' as the Americans are fond of saying."

"Up-to-date on what? She said I would deal with you. Please explain."

"Please sit, monsieur. *Vous aussi,*" he said to the gendarmes. Just sit anywhere. We will not be long.

"You and your professeur and his *hotelier* have brought us to this point. I tried to tell him to drop this silly Lac Bleu exercise, as he undoubtedly reported to you. But you persisted. Now you will have to pay for your stubbornness. And you too gentlemen," he said, nodding to the officers.

"You see the diamonds you have stolen from the old quarry belong to me and my associates. We want them back. *Immédiatement. C'est tous.*"

"Well, monsieur, I cannot do that. I do not have them. I do not know who does. As far as I know they are still wherever they were when I came into this case. *Et voila, c'est tous, vraiment.*"

"*Bon.* If you do not tell me right now I will call my daughter and she will have your three friends killed. *Tant pis, n'est-ce pas?*"

"I honestly did not know anything about any missing diamonds. The one brought up by Camille is in a sûreté vault. I know of no others. Josh, Smith and Beauchaine somehow fell into terrorists' hands and are probably being asked the same question. I assume with the same results—zero. But where are they?"

"You are a fine officer, monsieur, but underpaid. Now we can make you wealthy. You have heard of the Antwerp diamond robbery of last February. At least one-hundred and thirty safes were systematically emptied. The diamond center of Antwerp and its 30,000 workers are still in shock. The media calls it the Crime of the Century. Some of those millions could come to you and your department. So you see, you have stumbled into a *pétrin* much greater than you anticipated. Your American friends would say you are up a creek without a paddle. Your situation is immensely more significant than any remote little lake filled with munitions. It is what is buried among the bombs that now interests you and me.

Okay, monsieur Lemieux. We know you are not here to discuss enforcing laws concerning veils in French schools. We are discussing your life. Where are the diamonds?"

Everyone in the room was extremely tense, including madame Bedard who was listening behind a huge tapestry. As I stalled and pretended to organize my response, one of my officers, young Nicet Suchon, God love him, shifted his big *arriere-train* in his tiny Louis XIV chair. A shot from behind the tapestry caught the good man right between the eyes. I supposed madame Bedard thought shifting his enormous rear meant he was drawing his sidearm.

I screamed "Hold your fire. Everyone stay calm. And you madame come out and make no more mistakes. You, madame, have just murdered an innocent man, an officer of the law, who has a pregnant wife and two children. Put down your gun. You are under arrest."

The curtains and tapestries fluttered and Madame Bedard appeared, a sight to behold. She looked like an insane Bonnie, with Clyde standing by her side. She was holding a hefty gun in each hand, hair disheveled, skirt and blouse filthy. She seemed drugged and unsteady on her feet. But her eyes blazed right into me, right where she wanted to place the next shots. Her arms were extended straight ahead, both guns unwavering. She snarled and drooled while taking a shooter's determined stance. Old man Bedard and my men froze in position, all holding sidearms, staring at this repulsive and dangerous crazy person. Ol' Bedard was himself a little startled. Gone was any semblence of *haute société de Place de Vosges*.

"Nicole, *ma cheri. Calmez-vous.*" Turning to us. "*Ne vous enervez pas!*"

Once again, for a moment, there was a total calm, a breathing out by the gendarmes and ol'Bedard. Then madame screamed "Zut alors" and shot both gendarmes, Fulgence and Antonin, whose last actions in life were to shoot, albeit in the air, as they fell. Ol' Bedard and I both stared for another second, each unwilling to execute the other. Following a split second after madame's last two shots another came from behind the tapestry and madame fell dead at the feet of the gendarmes. Rita came silently into the room behind ol' Bedard, put her gun to the back of his head and muttered some very meaningful words into his ear. He dropped the gun and seemed to deflate onto the *chaise longue.*

"I'm sorry I came late. They had sent me out for *baguettes.* This is terrible. Your men are dead."

Rita handed me her gun, knelt near the officers and cried and cried. I cuffed Bedard and phoned my office. Bedard seemed to be as deranged as his wife had been. He kept mumbling, "In the polls 65% of the French would remove the veils. 65%. 65%." I was sick to my stomach. Cordite in a closed room really stinks. I kept thinking "Where in the world are Prof Josh, Smith and Beauchaine?"

Prof Josh

It really was Chanel #5. In the absolute darkness I had been testing my surroundings by slowly waving my hand in front of my face. Nothing. So I reached out very timidly in every direction and touched wool. Then a running shoe. It had to be the rude kidnapper, pride of the Vosges Bedards. What in the world is she doing here, sleeping curled up beside me on the floor of this Maginot officer's room.

Then my wandering hand touched the cold steel of a small weapon, maybe a 9mm Beretta. As I lifted it from the floor a little fist smacked me right beneath the chin. I was so surprised I dropped the gun, grabbed my pocket handkerchief to stem the flow of blood from badly bitten lips.

"Yikes, babe, not so rough! And what are you doing here anyway?. Shouldn't you be out killing people? Or are you on a terror break?"

"I have to follow orders and wait 'til the morning deadline. I decided to wait in here, away from the goons I have to work with. We have time. Let's talk professor. Certainly you have some knowledge about those Lac Bleu gems."

"Can we turn the lights on?"

"If it will make you more talkative, by all means."

Her fragrance faded as she moved away. When the lights came on she was holding the gun in one hand and arranging her hair with the other—from the opposite side of the room.

"Okay, let's talk prof. The gems, remember?"

"Well, I have some time yet. How about a little background? Why are you, a trained academic research librarian, spending your time with thugs involved in a diamond heist?"

"You wish to waste time with my life story? This will not prevent you from being slain when the boys come back to question you one last time. If you give them an answer they will check it out with colleagues under my father's direction in Paris, Angers and Avrille. While he confirms your info you will continue to be held here. After that you go free—or die, of course."

"Okay, I understand the orders and constraints. Now, about you. Why are *you* here?"

"I have been raised in the Vosges as you know. My father has been, all my life, an underworld character I guess you'd say. He is very wealthy and very untouchable by French law. He deals in smuggled diamonds, among other things, but it is these damn diamonds your friends have found that make him nervous and unpredictable. My mother and I have helped him. If he is ever caught we will also be arrested because we are totally involved in most of his dealings."

"Who killed the government people that day at the U.S. Consulate?"

"That was me and the unreliable, self-conflicted Didier twins. We assumed French government agents would desist from asking further questions and forget about investigating the finances of my father and his associates. You noticed the case was pretty well covered up and the press did not pursue it hardly at all. Your government did my government a favor, diplomacy being what it has been between them, and quietly refused to expose the situation to its ultimate conclusion. They did the same for the Mitchel Joseph, Manerelli and Delattre elimations. You should understand that sort of thing. The U.S. has taught the world all there is to know about cover-ups. In fact, that term *cover-up* is now used by the international media and governments everywhere. And well understood by all. In French we have a meaning for *etouffe:* to smother or cover-up. Anything else?"

Jules

According to the Angers *Lettre d'information* of 06 Oct 03 this is Algeria Year in France. The Angers municipal library is providing to the public numerous exhibitions of the history and contemporary culture of Algeria.

As I'm cruising toward Angers I try to recall from *bac* classroom drills those modern States which have French as their language: Mauritania, Madagascar, Cambodia, Laos, Morocco, Tunisia, Vietnam, and, of course, Algeria, French Africa, Switzerland, Belgium, Guinea, and island paradises in the Carribean and the South Pacific. Quite a record! I also remember our professors emphasizing that French governments were not always very anxious to let the colonies separate. In fact, France tried to prevent decolonization during those years filled with cries of independence. Algeria was a gigantic trouble spot for France for years.

And now, here I am, going to a French Algerian celebration to make contact with Interpol agents who are on *qui vive*/surveillance for some diamond smugglers who specialize in demining facilities. As if the Département du Déminage doesn't have enough trouble of its own, unearthing very old but very live ammo.

The municipal libraries were hosting this international exhibition which included seminars on the cultures and histories of the two nations. I parked the van and proceeded to the lobby of the main library. When I gave my name to the staff librarian at the welcome table she handed me a packet of materials and a name tag. Lemieux had even thought to pay my participation fee. I went into the lecture hall and found a seat in the last row. I was reading through the day's events when two men came in and sat next to me, I mean one guy on each side. Clean-shaven, dark suits, Italian shoes, obviously carrying. Both said "good morning" and began to read their programs. "Total beans," said the guy on my right. "Doleur" I replied.

"Let's stroll into Seminar Room #4, down the hall. Easy does it."

They rose and went out different doors. After a half-minute I strolled, sort of meandering I guess, reading some of the bulletin boards and attractive librarian-type graphics along the halls. The two Interpols were seated at a large table in # 4 and signaled me to join them. I locked the door and pulled out a chair.

"Over here," said the most talkative. "Big room, large table, lots of Evian bottles, and three committee members *tete-a-tete* over program logistics."

"Very nice," I said imaginatively.

"You are Labonte. We are Jones and Carr, Interpol."

We shook hands.

"We need to move fast now Labonte. We have received a message from our man in Verdun. Your friend the Professor and two Sûreté agents are being held in the closed part of the Maginot Line by associates of a Mademoiselle Bedard, diamond smugglers under the direction of her father."

"This is all news to me fellas. I was under the impression that 1) I am returning a favor I owe Commissaire Lemieux of Avrille, and 2) I am to use my supposed expertise with Algerian racketeers of some kind to assist Interpol wherever I can."

"*Ah bon*," said Jones. "We welcome your assistance and have a high regard for Lemieux. We'll brief you on the way in your van. *Alons-y.*"

As we passed the welcome table the staff gave us a quizzical look.

"Family emergency," said Jones. The librarians gave us those consternation smiles that said: *un silence gene,* shocked, gaping jaw.

Prof Josh

I think Bedard actually dozed again. This taking prisoners to the Maginot Line can be exhausting I suppose. It must have been around four in the morning when the door again burst open. Bedard leaped to her feet, switched on the light again and, imitating American gangster movies, said to Seph The Smelly; "He ain't talkin' Tony, maybe we should rough 'im up a little." I immediately thought of my bloody lip and left rotator cuff and felt like applying for an exemption from this round of questioning. But Bedard intervened.

"Sit back in your corner prof. You know our family are expert shooters. I feel like giving you a demonstration."

"No, that's okay. I heard you are all quite good. I'll pass on the demo."

"Shut up prof. I need the practice. Put this cigarette in your ear and face me. Now."

She tossed me a cigarillo. I stuck it in my ear. She turned her back, bent over forward, aimed and fired through her legs. The little cigar disintegrated. I pulled the stub out.

"Nice shot."

"Thank you. Feel like talking?"

"I don't know what to tell you."

"Diamonds from Lac Bleu."

"Have no idea."

"Okay, Seph, you try."

Seph picked me up, twirled me about above his head a few times and threw me into a corner. I landed on my left shoulder and bit my lip.

"I still don't know," I mumbled.

The door opened once more and the boss-team leader stepped in with two other guys about the size of Seph.

"It's time professor. I'm about to go over to the lady. If she is stubborn you will hear a gun shot. Ready for that, are you?"

For the first time I was able to notice that the three huge goons had no side arms. Just the leader and Bedard had guns. If we were ever to survive this situation I would have to get one of the guns because I certainly could not physically challenge the three monsters. Stall, Josh, I'm thinking. Stall.

"What makes you think the lady knows anything? I'm on a National Assembly sub-committee to look at munitions sites. That was in all the papers. That's why I was on this ill-fated excursion. But you know Mademoiselle," forcing a smile at Bedard, "I'm a visiting Memphis psych prof. What would I know about international black-market jewelry or whatever it is you are looking for...

No one really heard that last word. The door came crashing in, off the hinges, knocking Bedard's boss down and out, flat on the floor on his face, under the door. Three guys in coats and ties charged in, jumping on the door and leaping at Bedard's three apes. She was so surprised, I was able to grab her gun hand with both of mine. We proceeded to wrestle. For the gun. Each time I spun around trying to get the gun away from her I observed a new aspect of Kung Fu, Kickboxing and Savate, called *boxe Francais,* the French art of foot and fist fighting. It was three against three, with Bedard and me being relegated to a mere pre-preliminary match. The six guys were out to do severe bodily damage.

As I held on securely to Bedard's right arm I saw good 'ol Jules of Avignon fame and two other men in stylish black suits and street shoes viciously attack big Seph and his two pals. Seph yelled French slogans as his fellows recovered from their initial surprise. From reading, not from practice, I knew that the martial art of Savate emphasizes precision kicks to vital bodily points with Western boxing techniques neatly integrated. Savate is a popular ring sport in modern Euro Europe.

The Boxe Francais association would have been proud of the quick reaction and recovery time of its three accredited advocates. But the three suits and their Taekwondo and Kung Fu hand and foot moves were swifter and more damaging. In a few minutes of lunges, feints, moans and grunts, the kicks, punches, throws, joint locks and pressurepoint strikes of the new-comers dominated. The room became quiet except for heavy breathing. The three goons were handcuffed and sort of tossed in a pile against one wall. Bedard finally stopped talking when she knocked herself out; her jaw somehow struck the gun we were both holding. A limp Bedard had her wrists tied behind her back. The boss of the losing side was dead under the door.

Jules helped me up and introduced me to the two Interpol agents, Jones and Carr. Jules and I immediately dubbed them Steven Seagal and Chuck Norris. It turns out all three of them have been studying and practicing various martial arts for many years as self-defense sports. In the future they wish to participate as arts instructors, school owners, and video stars. They all looked at me and at the prone Bedard.

"I have been *reading* about the martial arts, also for many years. Let me go down and get my two *Sûreté* friends."

Bedard let us remove her key chain. We found Smith in good shape, Beauchaine dazed with badly bruised arms and legs. She perked up a little when Jones offered to help her walk. Carr made several phone calls once we reached the surface. It was good to see the sun and breathe fresh air. We all sat under some trees awaiting our transportation back to Paris.

The transport turned out to be the French AS532 Cougar helicopter. The Couger in the 2006 restructured army is designed to provide high performance mission readiness. It can carry twenty-five commandos. Our rather beat-up group piled in as if we had been under enemy fire for weeks. There was continual banter and emotional relief.

"*Zut alors,*" I said, and repeated it a few times. "Well, I'll be darned. We made it out of a very serious situation."

"*Zut alors*?" asked Beauchaine?

"Yeah," I said. I don't mean it literally. I just like the sound of that expression. "*Zut*." "*Zut alors!*"

It gave me great pleasure two days later, after a restful night at the Colbert, to visit the Bedards, father and daughter. It was wonderful to see them as honest to goodness *prisonniers,* separated from each other, in the interrogation rooms with Interpol personnel. Mother Bedard, the Witch of the Vosges, was quietly buried by distant relatives in their Nimes plot. Rita, the unsung heroine of the Bedard household, was debriefed at Paris headquarters and allowed a week in the Vosges before moving to an apartment near the Place des Victoires. Bedard's Seph and the other Maginot thugs were flown back to Algiers in handcuffs. Favrau's body had not been found. The agency boss had generously given Smith and Beauchaine a week's vacation. Pierre and I raised a few vodka and tonic salutes to Operation Entrée. I talked to Rosemarie and L.V. at length, both busy with their academic work at the U. in Angers. Rosemarie commutes often to her Avrille *boulangerie* while L.V. continues her daily dives in the Lac. Journet has been replaced by a commander of the French Foreign Legion. Lemieux, back in tranquille Avrille after attending the funerals of his men, was overjoyed to hear the rescue story with Jules as the star. I mean he loved to hear the whole story, over and over, including all details, especially my feet dragging techniques. Then he became the story-teller. L.V., of course, heard everything from Lemieux, especially the part where he decided to import private detective Jules from Avignon. We agreed on a Boudreau planning session-dinner for next week. In the meantime I wanted to help the Paris police in the hunt for Paul Didier. But most of all I really felt compelled to continue my deep interest in studying legislative and alternative means to clean up the thousands of unexploded bombs.

L.V.

Roger and I have been successful in coordinating our free days, either in Angers or Avrille. This day we were jogging in *Le parc naturel regional Loire,* on excellent running paths. Both of us enjoy the other's company while staying in shape with some form of physical activity. While authentic joggers, exercising during their power work-out, don't converse with another runner, Roger and I do chat while moving and while resting. The French have adapted the word "jogging" into their sports vocabulary, as in *aller faire un jogging, faire son jogging matinal,* to go for one's morning run.

"I had a long phone talk with Prof Josh this morning," Roger started, as we rounded a gentle curve and a slight incline. "He seems to have recovered from last week's *incroyable* Maginot experience."

"Yes, he and Pierre are in Aix-en-Provence this week. Josh needed to get away from being a full-time crime-fighter and Pierre persuaded him to go to their place in the South. They are co-owners of what sounds like a marvelous retreat. Maybe we'll get a chance to visit them there some day."

"Provence is lovely. I can see myself retiring there one day—in the distant future of course." Roger smiled, and as he said this he glanced sideways at me.

'You've been running this park trail for years? "I said.

"At least once or twice each weekend, L.V. I love this Loire area. We have beaches, water sports, biking and hiking trails. And, of course, chateaux galore. Is that right, "galore?"

"Yeah, perfect Roger. Galore suggests *en abondance,* abundance or abundant, Galore means there are plenty of chateaux.

"Thanks. You have been very patient explaining English words to me. You Americans seem to make up new words every day, on purpose, I think to confuse foreigners who are trying to learn the language. Changes, all the time. Synonyms. And your slang is impossible."

"Yeah, that's true," I said, "but don't forget I have a dictionary of French slang and colloquial expressions, most of which I could not repeat to my mother."

"Oh, *oui, c'est vrai,* but you make them up each day. Lately I heard some Americans in my station appealing a speeding ticket and they said the arresting officer was a Monday morning quarterback. *Quoi?* We did not know how to answer this accusation. They paid the fine and left. None of us knew what this means."

"Okay, Roger, I can explain that phrase, but it may take a while. You will like it because it is a sports expression with a rather precise meaning. But first, let's not forget in France you guys have the *Academie Francaise,* which gives y'all an ultimate authority on every single word in the dictionary. Something about *les Quarante.* Like there are actually forty people who check each word?"

As we passed under a number of overhanging branches, who appeared from behind a huge tree but Paul Didier, renowned fugitive. He had leaped into our path, arms outstretched.

"Slow down you two. Time for a break."

"Paul," I shouted, "What the hell are you doing here? You really are nuts."

"Thank you, my dear. You look ravishing in that outfit. You too, sir. Can we sit here for a moment?"

"The Didier twins, Rude and Crude, "I added.

He seemed perfectly relaxed, clean-shaven, expensive jogging suit, new Nikes, de Federico sun shades.

"What are you trying to do?" Roger said in a low voice, the stern police commissioner now. "We could overcome you right now and take you into custody."

"I know you could beat me up any time you want. But I have a gun and I notice neither of you is packing, as Miss L.V. would say. Secondly, I must tell you, if I am not back with my friends in one hour they will make my Aunt disappear again. Voila, this time a national scandal. Headline in La Monde: 'Madame Didier names the Avrille Commissaire as her lover-kidnapper.'

Roger sat on the bench with arms crossed, legs stretched out in front of him, I sat on the grass beside the bench. Paul stood and sat and stood, as nervous and determined as ever.

"L.V.'s right, you know," Roger said, staring straight ahead. "You have no chance of evading the police, the Sûreté, the Interpol, local bounty hunters. You will be killed."

"Yeah, well that is always a possibility for everyone, no? Right now the topic is diamonds. You guys probably don't even know what you did when you stole our loot from the Lac. I am in deep yogurt because the Algerian mafia think Jean and I have them. I thought old man Journet had them. Dore died thinking the twins screwed his family once again. But the joke is we really don't have them and we think y'all's cute little diver here took them from among the munitions. I can see she doesn't have them with her right now. So doll, wherever you have hidden them, you and your boy friend here need to get them up fast or dear Auntie will vanish and you two will be ruined. What say you? Let's deal."

"*Petit fripe qui parle*," plain spoken Roger sputtered brusquely, referring to Paul's ability to talk through the lower end of his alimentary canal.

Paul took that as a "No deal." He disappeared into the forest. Actually, he seemed to be a ungainly runner.

"Let's get back to our radios in the car, L.V. I'll call my office and Interpol. See if you can raise the Sûreté friends. Our English lessons will continue, no? I need to know what means "Think outside the bun.""

We raced the two miles back to the cars. He won. When I told him "Nice run dude, you won," he answered with his first palindrome: "I did, did I?"

Prof

Pierre and I have always wanted to have a place in Southeast France. When we were little kids together

B. J. LUCIAN

we talked about owning property in Provence. Several
years ago this old *mas* became available. I had just
begun to teach in Memphis and he became a partner in
the Colbert. But over the phone we decided to buy the
place upon the recommendation of Rosemarie.

Farmhouses in this area are called "mas" and
pronounced "Ma." Pierre got such a big kick out of the
word that he has always referred to our grand and
ancient farm as Ma. A few times a year we visit Ma.
We clean up the place, rake, garden, paint, repair, shop
and cook for ourselves. Ma has a roof of Canal clay
tile, with pale yellow, orange and beige outside walls.
It is gorgeous in the morning sun. Our model Mas is *Le
Mas des Santolines,* a four star *Gites de France.* We
know we will never reach the heights of stars Marie-
Claude and Jean-Pierre have achieved near Uzes. But
we have no qualms about copying some of their classy
style.

Most of our summer work clothes and tools remain
at Ma so we have little baggage on the TGV from Paris
to Avignon. There we rent the ever-reliable 2 CV for
travel throughout the South. It does narrow streets with
ease. We often drive to Nimes first and ceremoniously
view the grand Pont du Gard which the Romans built to
bring water to Nimes. I am in awe of that 500 year old
phenomena, no matter how often and from what angle I
see it. Then we visit markets and buy, buy, buy,
visiting St-Remy-de-Provence on the way because we
like to argue about Nostradamus who was born there.

We were still talking about one of his prophecies when we pulled up to the farm gate. Pierre jokingly reminded me to check the doors for hand grenades. Excellent idea, I thought, but how would we do that since all three of the doors and six windows are locked.

Pierre is thinking aloud. "Should we look around the place before we bring out the groceries? Should we have hired a local groundskeeper? Are we not about a kilometer from the nearest farmhouse?"

"Ok, Mr. Caution-conscious. Let's approach stealthily. Crouch down and crawl in the Lavender field. Take Ma by surprise."

Pierre gave me his left eyebrow arch. "Smart ass," always accompanies the arch. "You know we have to be careful. After all, you have the diamonds from Lac Bleu."

"Yeah, I have them in my nose. It costs me a million every time I sneeze. Now be careful. Remember, since we were here last, ol' buddy, a few more snakes and lizards may have moved in."

We slowly approached the house. There was some normal disturbance in the dovecote as we came near Ma's door. I touched the knob. It was ajar. We each produced our recent loaners from Lemieux, shiny new Sig Sauers. I motioned Pierre to circle the house. I went the other way and we met at the back door. A blue 2 CV stood next to the open kitchen door. No noise except the pigeons. Then a voice behind us.

"Drop the guns, boys. God, I've always wanted to say that. Now step inside."

We both turned, saw Paul, and backed into the house. He kicked our guns aside while following us. Pierre nonchalantly pulled out a kitchen chair and sat at the table. Defiant and angry.

"What's our next move, Tonto?" Pierre can talk between clenched teeth.

"Don't be funny Pierre," screamed Paul. He was very anxious, jittery, in a strung-out mood.

Pointing with his gun, he told me to sit. It was then I noticed the kitchen and the dining room had been tossed. Furniture, books, dishes, lamps, phone, all heaped in one corner. Cabinets emptied, pots and pans and kitchen ware flung around the room. Now I was angry.

"For God's sake Paul, you think we hide stolen jewelry here? *Vous etes fou!* You really are acting like an idiot. The Lac diamonds have never been here. We have no idea where they could be."

"I know you told stupid Bedard that same story. But you were rescued just before you were about to reveal the whereabouts of your loot."

"How do you know what I told Bedard?" I said.

"I know everything that happened in the Maginot. I was able to talk to my friend Seph. At first he didn't recognize me in the stolen Guard's uniform I wore. But then he told me about the fight and rescue. He's in Algeria now, poor guy."

"You are a ludicrous S.O.B., Paul. Desperate too. That's your downfall. You can't think clearly being so desperate. Calm down, stow your gun, sit and listen for a change."

Pierre, who had been staring at the floor all this time, leaped at Paul, knocked the gun out of his hand, and flung the kitchen stool at his head. Paul ducked and dashed out the kitchen door to pick up our guns. Pierre grabbed Paul's Browning 9 mm from the floor. We were out the front door and into Ma's forest before Paul began firing into the trees. The chase was on. Two vacationing classmates with one gun against one social deviant with two guns.

We dodged through the overgrown forest as fast as we could, pointing instead of talking to each other. Nevertheless, I'm sure anyone in the area could have heard our noisy crashing through the dry leaves. We might as well have been shouting "here we are, shoot in this direction."

After a few minutes of intense running I signaled us to a stop behind two giant Luberon oaks. Paul was walking a little to our left, stopping every few steps to listen. Then he began again, stomping with his *avoirdupois* through the natural forest debris. We whispered.

"Maybe," Pierre said, "if we ran all out for a while he would give up the chase. If he continues we can set up an ambush."

"I don't expect him to run too much further. He is not athletic. I think he is already pretty pooped."

"Okay, let's go about twenty yards further in. By the way," Pierre said, in a barely audible murmur, "I think I saw a little green dragon back there. Are there alligators in this forest?"

A bullet thumped into a tree a few yards away. We both agreed Paul had no clear shot in this situation. We trotted to our right and found a slight rise covered with a species of prickly plants we had never seen before.

"Stay here Josh. Get down. I'll move just over there. If he makes it this far I must tell you, my friend, I will really have to shoot to kill. This guy will not take any prisoners at this point."

A loud smack, into a tree far to our left. I lay quiet. Pierre disappeard into a clump of young oaks where several huge fallen trees formed a natural fortress. It was a silent forest for ten minutes. Then right in front of me I heard him coming, slowly, step by step. There was no way he could see us or hear us, but the crunching leaves told me he was walking straight toward me. The lizard family nest, on which I was lying face down, were squirming to get free.

"I know you guys are around here," Paul shouted. "I heard you farting." He giggled like a little kid. "No one will find your bodies in this place. Thanks for the guns. I may be desperate, but you blokes are hopeless. Just one notch above ol' Dore himself. *Ecoute mes petits mecs!* Talk to me about the diamonds."

He sounded like an incoherent druggie now, really reckless and extremely dangerous. He shouted additional insulting non-sequiturs about God, the universe, and diamonds. As he screamed invectives he was taking baby steps towards my bushy hide-out. He was out of breath. He advanced four more steps, wheezing. No doubt, this was more exercise than he'd had in a long time. Listening to him gasp I thought maybe he'll just drop right here, exhausted as he must be. One step closer. I could see him now, holding a gun in each hand, but his arms were not stretched out in front of him. In fact, his arms were at his sides, feebly raised between gasps.

I timed my throw so that the foot-long lizard struck his chest when his arms were down. He let out a scream, dropped the weapons and fell backwards. Pierre and I were on him in seconds, flipped him over and tied his wrists with Pierre's silk necktie. We waited for him to catch his breath. But that never happened. We turned him over and saw his unfocused eyes. Pierre felt for a pulse. Nothing. Paul had died. From fright?

Pierre

It took a few minutes for both of us to realize what had happened and to calm down. We sat on the ground, leaned against trees, and prayed for the deceased Paul Didier. *"Je vous salue Marie, pleine de grace, le Seigneur est avec vous…maintenant et de l'heure de notre mort."* "Now and at the hour of our death." After three Hail Marys we made the sign of the cross over the boy.

We decided the authorities would want to see the body in this exact spot so we gave up our first idea which was to carry Paul back to the house. Instead Prof would remain right where he was and I would drive back to Aix-en-Provence to the local commissariat. I found my way back to the CV and chugged as fast I could into town. I dusted myself off, arranged my jacket and wiped my face. This was going to sound so weird I wanted to at least look rather normal.

"Bonjour monsieur," I said to the first uniform I met outside the police station. "Comment ca va?"

He smiled and asked if he could help me. I felt like saying, "You won't believe this, but..." However, his accent, local or foreign, caused me to be serious.

"I would like to speak with the officer in charge, please."

"I am he monsieur. Would you like to step into my office, she is right here."

I followed him, struggling to understand his French.

"I am Commissaire Bruno Guedon. *Votre nom, monsieur?*"

'My name is Pierre Le Grand, sir."

The chief sat behind a desk and seemed to undergo a personality change. He began to speak loudly, rapidly, and incoherently. I think I understood a word or two only. Suddenly he stopped and said "You do not comprehend to what I am speaking to you?"

"No sir, I'm sorry. I am from Paris. I have a summer home in Aix-en-Provence."

"Ah oui, c'est ca. Bon, on parle Anglais n'est-ce pas?"

"Oui, merci, monsieur le commissaire."

"Bon," he replied again. You see I am born and grow here all the life. I am Occitan. We of us from Occitanie, Southern France, try to clung to our *Langue D'oc.* We are proud of our heritage and make the fun with visitors from other parts of the France who do not regard us. Please excuse to us when we speak our mother language. We are stubborn very little minority. *Maintenant,* what is your visit?"

I then began to explain what had happened starting with our arrival at Ma. I spoke slowly and watched his eyes. He seemed to understand. Explaining all about the Didiers would be difficult, let alone our connection with the Département du Déminage.

I paused to wait for questions. He hit a button on his desk, two elderly gendarmes appeared, and all three of them dashed out into a large police wagon. They gestured for me to sit next to the driver. The commissaire drove as if we were the only ones in this part of the country. I drive fast in Paris, but I cringed now. It was the first time I experienced the phrase from the musical 'Oklahoma,' where the song says chickens and ducks and geese better scurry. In Occitanie men and women and children scurried when they saw the

Aix police van. Some people just barely made it to safety.

Prof Josh stood when he heard four guys tramping through Ma's old forest. After the introductions and Prof's predictable look of curiosity, the commissaire repeated his devotion to *Langue D'oc*. This time he added, no doubt for the prof's sake, that he was an Occitaniste, an expert defender of the language.

Prof then went through the details of the final few minutes we had with Paul. He described the exhausted appearance of Paul, trying to hold two Sig Sauers up in front of him; my fortress in the trees; Paul's bullets in nearby trees, his laying on the lizard in the bushes, and his decision to throw it at Paul.

"Describe the animal, please sir."

"I think it was about a foot long chief, bright green with blue spots on the sides. It is an ugly species."

At this point the chief looked at his two gendarmes, smiled, and asked how the throw was made.

"What do you mean, 'how'?"

"Well, you throw like this," he imitated a clumsy toss of a hand grenade. "Or do you lance it as an American baseball pitcher?"

Prof picked up a short, stout, tree limb and, balanced on his right leg, lifted his left leg high, reared back, wound up, and flung the piece overhand twenty-five feet. A fast-ball right down the middle. I yelled "Strike!" The three police broke into applause and joyous laughter. Prof and I just looked at each other.

"Bravo, monsieur le professeur. We are the, how you say, fans, of the baseball. We have a Occitan team, taught by an American teacher, a De La Salle Brother, in the summers he trains us."

After some more baseball talk one of the gendarmes took some pictures of the scene and some of me and Prof and several of Prof posing with the chief. They loaded the body into the police van and passed on our offer of coffee or Pastis 51 in Ma. As they prepared to leave the Chief said he had three things to tell us besides "enjoy your stay here."

"First I must tell you that the lizard you lanced so well as overhand American pitcher was of the genus *Lacerta,* perhaps the four-limbed *Ocellata.* Also, it is good to know that Aix is pronounce *aches.* As in American, how you say 'aches and pains.' No? And, yes, we will see you tomorrow in our office for the writing of this incident on our *nouveau* Windows 95, with the HP LaserJet 4000 printer. *Au revoir.*"

Prof went into Ma, put his feet up on a broken chair and poured a small glass of 51.

"There goes the most unusual man we may ever meet."

Prof

The next few vacation days in beautiful Aix were filled with police interrogations which we admitted were justified, detailed, time-consuming. We learned from the police and the newspapers that we were on the Paris front pages for a few days. Mme Didier was interviewed at great length at the Assemblée. She included some complimentary remarks about us "in their undisclosed summer retreat." Paul was buried in the Didier family plot in Paris. Jean was not allowed to attend but he watched the ceremonies on prison television. Lemieux spoke with <u>Le Courrier de l'ouest,</u> in which he emphasized that paper's early interest in the CACTUS controversy of last summer. He was quoted as saying several times, "Avrille...le bruit que pourrait faire le lac Bleu." These widely publicized personalities resurrected interest in the Département du Déminage in the print and broadcast media. My brother Boney and Mitchel Joseph would have loved this publicity trend.

Pierre and I used the newly reconnected phone and our hand-held cells. Pierre called Rita every day, describing the area with gusto. He described the *Parc National Regional du Luberon* and urged Rita to contact *Tourisme de Vaucluse* and "come on down," a phrase he likes from an America television shopping show. He told her they could explore the region by bike or horse, on foot or on the seats of the 2 CV. I couldn't believe his enthusiasm for the place as he waxed eloquent about villages, ruins, castles, forts, and the Ma. After a few days I began to realize he wanted Rita down here period.

Lemieux and L.V. wanted us to think about what we could be doing right now to further our continuing investigation of the lost diamonds and the CACTUS controversy, Avrille Versus the National Government, munitions versus cleanup. I was glad L.V. was continuing her daily dives in the training program. One day I described to her the Lavender, *Lavande,* fields here, mercifully beyond the actual French Riviera. Of course, L.V. already knew true lavender, *Lavandua Angustifolla,* has the essential oil used by perfume makers. It is difficult to surprise that young woman. Maybe Lemieux can. She was stumped, however, on the origin of the town name, "Aix." Sources say it was named after the founder, 122 B.C., Roman general Caius Sextius who named it Aquae Sextiae, after himself.

Pierre and I walked in the *vieille ville* each day, talking about the surrounding tree-lined avenues and 14th century Aix. We admired the unique walnut doors of the Cathedrale de St-Sauveur, where we lighted a candle in honor of the Mother of Jesus and said a prayer for the repose of the soul of Paul Didier. In a café we heard Occitan at the next table and were drawn into an interesting discussion with a student group called Garderem l'Occitan. They were preparing to demonstrat the next day in Aix. They are indignant because only four new teachers of Occitan have been hired for a total area of 32 departments with 12 million inhabitants of whom 1.5 million speak Occitan. We promised them we would support them next time we were in Aix. We usually ended up our walks in bookshops and antiques stores, agreeing to disagree on our next *déminage* move. One day we actually walked and talked and ate so much we thoughtlessly sat on the edge of the 1734 hot-water fountain, which splashed 93 F water on us and our new books. *Blasé* investigators, to be sure. It was time for us to return to the scene of the crime.

Rosemarie promised to have a Boudreau feast prepared a week from now. She and L.V. would do what they really love doing—shopping in the local markets, always humming on Thursdays. We would furnish Pastis 51, pride of the South. August 15th we loaded the 2 CV for the 45 kilometer drive to Avignon and then the TGV to Paris.

We both dozed for the first part of the train trip. Later I served coffee from Ma's thermos and enjoyed reviewing the week's excitement, the fear and the fun of it. Pierre began to contemplate his return to the job he loves, his new title as General Manager of the Hotel Colbert. He is always glad to hear about any *déminage* developments because they get him out of the confines of the straight-laced hotel business. After a few days he can't wait to return to the management of one of Paris' grand hotels. This most recent trip to the South was precipitated by Diane Keaton, Keanu Reeves and Jack Nicholson of Hollywood, USA. Their movie executives had contracted for the use of the Colbert for a romantic Paris rendez-vous between the principal actors of the popular movie "Something's Gotta Give." Pierre thinks the three actors are very nice people and did their best to avoid being overbearing or snobbish. But the movie company's activities disturbed the normal operation of the hotel for days with miles of cable, camera equipment, lights, crews and camp followers all over the place. The hectic result was Pierre needed time away from that lobby. Hence, our quick trip to exciting Aix-en-Provence.

Sometimes, during his regular Paris work day, Pierre just walks out the hotel door and strolls slowly, with his hands in his pockets, down rue Vivienne to Le Vaudeville where he orders his all time favorite *soupe à d'oignon,* superior onion soup. After an hour he walks back to the Colbert for many additional hours. He admits to saying "no" along that route, to the occasional vagrant or prostitute. One day he returned to the hotel and said "no" to the first two employees who approached him. He later apologized. Aix is good for him, no doubt.

As the TGV neared Paris we resolved to pay more attention to the Avrille citizens and their munitions problems.

Lemieux

I had several reasons for gathering Operation Entrée at the new and improved Avrille Gendarmerie. We all wanted to hear about the Aix adventure, I wanted to show off the recently installed law enforcement technology, and I needed to up-date the group on the forthcoming CACTUS Revival. Our station is not usually equipped for feeding more than a couple of hungry gendarmes. So we scheduled the meeting for a Saturday when we could make use of the best caterer around, Rosemarie Baker, *chef extraordinaire,* and C.U. professor. Since the completion of our Gendarmarie's two-story wing this occasion would be a combined dedication of, and public introduction to, our auditorium.

"I honestly thought this construction would never be completed," Prof Josh said upon congratulating me. "It's my ingrained belief that any government work will drag out over time and finally be forgotten. Here you are with a fine new auditorium and computer center. Congrats Roger."

"And completed on time, my friend," Pierre said. "A miracle."

"Your two technicians at the closed circuit tv surveillance desk are hot dudes too. That's an improvement," said L.V.

After a few seconds of eye contact between us, L.V. and I both blushed and laughed.

"I am getting used to this lady's sense of humor," I admitted.

"I am still adjusting to it," Josh added. That made me feel better.

While I explained the latest technical amenities the station has, Smith and Beauchaine arrived, mouthing the "ohs" and "ahs" tourists often do. In the equipment room I explained the *Euro-laser,* which enables us to control vehicular speeding. Our task here is to complement the National Police and be a primarily preventative station rather than aggressively investigative. We have two cars, now, out cruising the main roads, preventing speeding accidents. Another car is devoted to school area safety. These are all newly funded responsibilities for this town. We will be challenged by the up-coming CACTUS Revival. Our job: traffic and order.

I told them, "I am planning a few more days of *En Ville Sans Ma Voiture.* "

"You will be much more effective, Rog," said Smith. "This elevates your station status from a small suburb to a high tech resource. Great job."

"You certainly must have made an impression on Paris headquarters," added Beauchaine, hugging me. I explained that the two new "hot" technical young men have just returned from a course at the national tech center in Crotoy. I could tell Operation Entrée members were impressed. I know I am.

"OK, enough of this. You people all know you are welcome here anytime. Now we will begin our little meeting, *n'est-ce pas?*"

"*Oui mon capitaine,*" said L.V. "Like right this way, dudes," or something like that.

We filed into the wood-paneled Cezanne Meeting Room, where the two techies, Tim and Ter, served coffee. The table is football-shaped. (Prof: "I like the sport symbolism."). The lighting is recessed and controlled from a device at the head of the table, where I sat and played with the switch, showing off just a bit. I explained that we French have insisted on calling our computer *ordinateur,* and computer science is *informatique.* P*rogrammeur and programmeuse* reflect distinctive masculine and feminine computer programmers. Prof always loves to hear about *Acadamie* dictionary decisions.

Just as we were settling down from the informal tour to a serious session, our other guests arrived. Mme Catherine Didier was announced by Tim. She floated into the room like any French woman in power politics would—with graceful ease and confident air. She is always a magnificent example of *trés chic.*

"Bonjour," she said and bowed and extended her hand to all. Apologizing for being late, she took the chair offered by Prof Josh, who slid over next to Smith. I explained that we were just getting started on the topic of CACTUS Revival. She smiled and said she had some good news. It seems her Assembly resolution has a chance of passing this term. Its passage would call attention to our country's *déminage* dilemma. For this purpose a few powerful committee members will be announcing their support. These worthies are, "for example," she said, the Ministre De L'Interieur Sécurité Civile, the chairman of the Groupe De Recherche Et D'Intervention Au Déminage, and the Ministre De Département De La Sécurité Public Explosives.

For the next hour we discussed the Revival day, dedicated to the *demineurs* who have given their lives to protect the people of France. Emphasis will be on Avrille. Public announcements will remind the 14,000 citizens of the date and time. The crowd will gather at the old quarry, site of the now famed Lac Bleu. The event has been referred to by the press as CACTUS II. That label in itself should bring the nation's media. There will be speeches of course. Several politicians have sent feelers, suggesting they "would be pleased to address the good people of Avrille and environs." Food will be provided by local venders who will be free to advertise with printed handouts, placards and signs. The local De La Salle band will play. The Diving School will present a techniques and equipment exhibition. Games and prizes for the children will ease some of the seriousness from what could become a gruesome trip down murky memory lane for senior members of the community. We all made sure we knew our parts in the day's activities. At 1800 hours we broke for preprandials and a Rosemarie buffet.

Prof Josh

The big Revival Sunday dawned clear and warm. People began arriving at 1000 hours with lawn chairs, beverage coolers, and baby carriages. At 1030 the band began a short concert and then played La Marseillaise. As in the States, the French take their national anthem seriously and most people enunciate loudly. After speeches by the Mayor and the Prefet de Maine-et-Loire, M. Lambert Picard, the crowd came to life. The grandstand was set up on the lake's edge so that "Bluesy," an inflated floating dummy of some kind with its fingers giving us the two-fingered victory sign, came into view behind the speaker. If a mascot ever diverted audience attention this thing became a champion distraction. It floated by on a gentle lake breeze. The papers carried pictures of Bluesy on their front pages next day, arms straight up, two fingers spread in the V sign. Kids loved it.

Dozens of signs were hung from posts, trees, arms, and necks. GO COLLECTIF! AUCUN RISQUE? PLUS JAMAIS CA! UN LAC EXPLOSIF? LAC BLEU ET A 11. LE LAC BLEU, MENACE DURABLE. Etc. If the speeches were to be boring at least there was plenty to look at while dozing in the hot sun. Politicians, who were not asked to speak, were seated on both sides of the rostrum. The Secretary General for Administration was there beside Ministers of Ecology, Interior, and Security Development. Under Secretaries of various ministries sat behind them with members of Mme Didier's Commission. After one more martial band number, the main speaker arose.

Mme Catherine Didier, Chairwoman of the National Assembly's Commission of Enquiry approached the rostrum amidst polite applause. This is how the press reported her speech.

Mesdames et Messieurs

Je suis tres content de vous voir ici aujourd 'hui.

Two years ago there appeared in our national news media an expression we had not heard before: Menace of the Blue Lagoon. The papers reported that citizens of Avrille publicly raised the question of the time-bomb ticking in their backyard. Your fears focused on this lovely little Lac Bleu. It is a former quarry and now the site of many throusands of tons of explosives dumped there since 1924. You strongly suggested that danger to you would be increased if a proposed Angers autoroute were constructed to pass just 600 meters from the lake-lagoon shore.

You all know about the city of Vimy in the Pas-de-Calais and how 12,000 people had to be evacuated because of the risk of explosion there. Recently, in the Ardennes, 560 inhabitants had to be evacuated from a village near Chatelet-sur-Retourne. We do not want these events to be repeated here in Avrille. We will continue to follow the Principle of Precaution.

Our President Jacques Chirac has told us to take the initiative. He wants us "to use our responsibilities with discretion, using them with authority, generosity and initiative while always listening to what your fellow-countrymen have to say." You have been doing that in your discussions here. Now you are understandably anxious for results. I will do my best to help your situation. Pray for me and my fellow Assembly members.

Finally, my friends, I would like to say a few words about our marvelous men and women of the Département du Déminage. You know that France has remains and reminders of numerous battles on dozens of battlefields from two world wars. Much of the total munitions used by German, British and American forces landed in France, unexploded. These left-over reminders remain unexploded ordnance to this day. Imagine please that there are 900 tons of bombs found on French soil each year. Our government chooses not to publicize the dangerous disposition work of our brave demineurs. One in five of these military heroes is accidently killed each year while working to clean up this sad national situation. Over 600 demineurs have been killed since the Department began in 1946. Many farmers and other civilians have been killed by bombs sunk into their very own land. You want to prevent any more accidents? Continue to push for government policy change. Get your lake cleaned up. I and the Assembly and Senate will help. God bless France. Be well in Avrille. A la prochaine. 'Til next time.

The people struggled up from their picnic blankets and lawn chairs, cheering and clapping for one and one-half minutes. That is a very long time in French political history. Mme Didier was superb in accepting the recognition her words deserved. She bowed graciously and exited the platform, the picture of smart elegance. She was escorted on the arms of Smith and Beauchaine. Her chauffeur and bodyguards awaited her at the car. She had them drive slowly while she waved with the window down.

Operation Entrée was now spread throughout the crowd. I called Smith on the phone Lemieux had given each of us.

"I feel like a spy in 'The French Connection.' Karl Malden, wasn't it?"

"This is not a movie Prof. Could you wander around to the east end of the lake? I'll move slowly around this side and meet you. Say ten minutes?"

"Check," I said. Lemieux had told us "Over and out" is *passé*.

My phone rang. "Prof, this is agent 67. I am going into my space suit now so I will be out of reach for a while. *A la prochaine* as Madame would say."

"Okay L.V. Dive well and take care."

Walking around the grounds was a pleasant task. Families were having fun, awaiting the next talk at 1400 by the CACTUS leaders. Most dads and moms were feeding kids and sharing baguettes and *confiture,* various jams and jellies, cheeses and *jambon de pays,* that special country-cured ham. Ballons were popping, wine bottles were opened. Small groups of men were actually in serious conversation about the lake's contents. Some kids had gathered to watch the diving class receive last minute instructions before descending for one of their last dives of the training course. L.V. had done well as a diver, but we had learned nothing since Camille's demise. The diamonds were still missing and Operation Entrée still accused of having them.

I caught a child's soccer ball with my head. On purpose. The kids thought I would like to repeat the trick. The ball again came directly at my head. I have always hated heading the regulation ball in an actual game. We called it Adviling, as in Advil. Anyway, this little game ended when a dad rescued me by calling his kids. We smiled and waved to each other. It was just then I noticed three men in unusual clothes huddled together near the trees, away from the hundreds of happy neighbors. Avrille men were in summer shorts and golf shirts. Hats, some stylish, some big floppy models, were everywhere. The three I saw wore long pants and layers of shirts and sweaters, as if they just arrived from Duluth.

"Smith," I radioed unobstrusively, and probably clumsily, "have you seen the three guys in the clump of trees?"

"No, I'll kind of waltz over your way. Stay where you are."

After a couple of minutes, while I stood and surveyed the picque-nicques, Smith casually came close.

"Okay, I see them. They are so very obvious, standing and gawking at the crowd. Come on, we'll go over and talk to them. Maybe they just arrived in town and are trying to understand what this gathering is all about? Ready?"

"Ready."

As we sauntered and talked quietly the three strangers began to withdraw further into the trees. We had definitely spooked them. Now we were looking directly at them and continued to walk in their direction. As if on a given signal, they all broke into a run through the trees. We chased them. They easily beat us to the road and roared off in a mid-size van. French license plates.

"Now what the heck was that all about Prof?"

"Zut alors! I have no idea, Matt."

He was on the phone to Lemieux. The CACTUS speeches were about to begin.

Avrille was being honored today by having two extraordinary gentlemen present at this Lac Bleu public hearing. Monsieur Jean-Yves Raveneau, successful mechanical engineer and inventor, and Monsieur Erwan Amice, well-known professional diver of the Institute Universitaire Européen de la Mer. L.V. has met them both during the summer's controversy and speaks very highly of their stance to assist the local citizens.

Smith

Beauchaine and I have been spending a lot of time with Jean Didier and his lawyer. Jean is considered a very special prisoner these days because his Aunt is a very important lady in the French social and political systems. We are assigned to investigate all aspects of the case because bullets flew (at us) and because Jean is suspected of being an auntnapper. And dear nephew Jean is playing his wounded shoulder for all it is worth on stage, screen, tele and radio.

"Here we go again," complained Beauchaine. "This spoiled brat will do anything to obtain special privileges while in jail. To be freed or put on some kind of probation he would gladly sell out or squeal or bribe or lie. Why are we continuing to talk to him anyway?"

"L.V."

"Like, wha'd ya mean, L. V?"

"Because, dear partner o'mine," imitating Beauchaine's bad imitation of L.V.'s slang, "Jean is threatening to expose L.V."

"Expose to what? Or for what?"

"His lawyer, one of the few in Paris not on strike this week, has suggested that Jean knows enough about some nefarious deeds of the beautiful Laura Veronica-mime-diver-author-linguist-martial arts practitioner, to get her into serious trouble with French law. The lawyer I've been dealing with, René Breaux, is convinced he can succeed."

"Nefarious?"

"Yeah, infame, en francais, my dear, that is, 'despicable.'"

"Whoa, Tonto, what's the charge?"

"Well, it seems Jean's lawyers have hired a private detective or two. At Jean's urging they toured Mont-St-Michel and informally talked to several guards, two of whom recognized L.V.'s college yearbook photo. They have specific charges of physical harm inflicted by her. L.V., according to the guards, beat them up terribly, bound and gagged them and locked them in a storeroom. They lay imprisoned for two days. They were injured emotionally and, they agree, physically.

Plus the private security company fired them both. How's that sound?"

"She beat up two guards?"

"The prof says she was some kind of martial arts winner in varsity competitions during college and for a year after as a professional instructor."

"And the guards were professionals, armed, full-grown men?" Beauchaine is loving this story.

"Apparently. You must have known, Beau, that our little mime is a rather extraordinary female."

"Yes, I have gathered that over the past months, kind sir. But this is a serious charge. If the lawyers can convince a judge that two French gendarme-type guards at the country's most pretigious money-making monastery were overcome by an American Aikido black belter he will throw the book at her. National pride, don't you know."

"I agree. But at the same time she would receive movie offers too don't forget. This incident, true or false, could be a lucrative career move for her."

"Okay Matt. But today let's prepare something for Jean's lawyers. We meet them tomorrow."

And we met and met, and met again. Once Jean was able to attend, hobbling in as if he forgot he was just wounded in the shoulder. He actually did have a sprained ankle, he explained, from slipping in the shower. A gang shower.

Lemieux gave us the name of a good criminal lawyer for L.V., a guy who has beaten Rene Breaux in a few cases. The man's name is Jules Labonte. We don't know if he is the same person Lemieux brought up from Avignon, the guy who crashed into the Maginot line just at the right moment to save us three weeks ago. Lemieux had said he was a 'private investigator,' whatever that means in Southern France. Right now L.V. needs a good courtroom lawyer, not a martial arts expert.

Beauchaine

In the meantime we tried to build a defense for our client who has not yet been informed of all the exciting details about to enter her academic world. We will have to question L.V. on how she became involved with the Didier twins on their infamous trip to the Mont. Why did she accompany them? What was she to do there? And what happened to cause the alleged fight with the guards?

Isidore, the young monk who was the object of the Didiers' attention, is now dead. His murdering father is in prison, in a cell far removed from Jean's. Paul, a key

305

player in the drama, is also gone in his very own peculiar manner. The news services reported some drastic Mont personnel changes after the mysterious death of the Abbot. L.V., in her naiveté, still thinks she was forced into the Mont trip by the Didiers to assist somehow in Catherine Didier's rescue. The Didiers wanted her with them as a witness to their sincere love for their missing aunt. Some of the missing diamond complications concerning the twins have so far escaped her. And after all, she says, they treated her well during the Mont episode. She feels very bad about Dore's untimely death at the hands of his father and Rodin. This distraction prevents her from appreciating what harm Jean could do her in a court of law.

After a week of time-consuming meetings with Attorney Breaux, Smith and I could again return to our primary function as caretakers of Operation Entrée. Our boy Jules, lawyer *extraordinaire,* arrived at the Paris Colbert. Prof and Pierre joined him in preparing for his jousting with Jean's now swelled force of five non-striking *avocats.*

Labonte and L.V. wanted to settle out of court. Breaux and Jean wanted a huge Paris trial.

Both sets of lawyers, with Smith and me sitting in occasionally, met often on friendly terms for hours. After all, Breaux and Labonte liked and respected each other. They were both aware of the unusual publicity possible if and when a young American girl was sued by a young Frenchman from an influential family. Reputations could be made and ruined. There was wariness in their interchanges but always formal lawyer-style politeness evident at all times.

So during the informal discussions and at-the-table bargaining sessions it became clear that Breaux was commited to do anything to a) get Jean out of the slippery gang showers, and b) get back at Prof Josh for killing Paul. Jean's team went to Aix, interviewed the chief of police and came back to Paris convinced they could easily prove chicanery on the part of Prof and Pierre and incompetence on the entire Aix gendarmerie. They felt there was a good chance Prof Josh could be charged with murder. Pierre would be implicated. An incompetent Occitan conspiracy would be easy to prove in a Paris court; impossible to ever prove among Aix's Occitans. The Paris lawyers and detectives discovered genuine loyalty and affection for Prof and Pierre among Aix citizens...

Smith and I found the two unfortunate former Mont-St-Michel guards in Pontorson. They identified L.V. immediately from a book of female faces. One poor fellow said he was ready to testify against "the fighting phantom," or impolite words to that effect. His partner said he had been seriously injured and is on imported Viagra. In telling us about these two guards L.V. had neglected to mention stuffing all their personal possessions down the storeroom hole. That was perhaps the most hurtful indignity and inconvenience she inflicted. But so far the guards' misfortunes have not been emphasized by Jean's staff. We encouraged the guards to remain silent if further lawyers appear. We suggested a fine Christmas gift from a prominent Paris hotel would be theirs if they remained anonymous for a few weeks more. Their wives seemed to think this would be fair since the two husbands have been lying around the house. They said things like *"se trainer par terre,"* dragging oneself about. We had coffee with them and left with a feeling of having established good *rapport.*

We left our business cards and drove back to Paris. Smith volunteered to communicate our hotel promise to Pierre of the Colbert. We knew it wasn't funny but we both noticed how the one guard did still have to walk very slowly. L.V. must have been in good 'arts' form the day of the Storeroom Sedition. It has been referred to that way in Smith's copious notes.

Prof Josh took it upon himself to explain to L.V. one day at Labonte's staff meeting how the French courts work. He outlined the development of the judicial system and brought us all up-to-date on the modern system, since the French Revolution of 1789, by the Code Napoleon. He told her lower courts have wide jurisdiction. "Yes," Prof said, "there are intermediate courts of appeal, but we won't be needing them." We all hoped and prayed he was right.

One day L.V. finally got to confront her accuser. Jean told his staff and ours that L.V. was responsible for the death of the Abbot. She should be properly tried for murder.

"This woman," he said, "did not come into Dore's room when Paul and me were forced in by some guards. She hid or something because we did not see her until the next morning. During that night the Abbot walked the long halls, saying his rosary as usual. The Mont lights were out, of course, and this woman came upon the Abbot and pushed him over the edge. It's that simple."

"Why would she do that?" asked Jules.

"Because she thought the Abbot was in on the kidnapping of my Aunt."

"Who told me about Dore being in on the kidnapping?" asked L.V.

"Paul probably."

"You are sick, Jean. You need psychiatric help," said L.V.

"Well," said Breaux, "the autopsy showed the Abbot died of a long fall."

"Which proves nothing concerning L.V. Rene, you can surely see that," began Jules. Anyway, let us suggest here some of the reasons why we cannot take what Jean says as anything but irrational. You are asking us to withdraw all the charges against Jean. This is categorically denied by us. You want the Professor to pay for the ruined bakery. Denied. Instead we will prosecute for illegal firearms, attempted murder of the Professor, Agents Smith and Beauchaine, and various pedestrians, as he shot wildly from across the street. We will show the Didiers were involved in gem thefts, (L.V. looked surprised), kidnapping, blackmail, attempted murder, and a few other crimes we have not listed yet here in the Dossier."

"Jules, the guards were and are injured by your client."

"We know that full well, Alfie," another Jean attorney. "The guards approached her with guns and night sticks. She defended herself as best she could, a girl against two armed men."

"You will not win," Breaux stated. Remember, Jules, Jean has been shot by one of these agents while trying to protect his brother who could not see well without his glasses and was in the line of fire. Your fire. These are the same agents who ruined the bakery. And further, Jules, my friend, do you know who the Didiers are? In far off Avignon, in *France Sud*, do you pay attention to the Assembly?"

"We are grateful for your bringing up the Didiers, Alfie. I have here a legal document signed by Catherine Didier which states that her nephews kidnapped her, held her captive in their house until rescued by the Professor and Pierre LeGrand. Let me read a sentence."

"I wish to prosecute my nephew Jean Didier for kidnapping me."

"Plain and simple language, no Jean? And we have a second kidnapping charge filed by our client certifying that she was taken to the Mont by the Didiers against her will. Now if that doesn't signal a totally flawed case you have, here is another. Monsieur Le Roy Journet also wishes to prosecute your client for constantly harassing his son Isidore Journet over many years. Your boy here, Alfie, has been carrying on an extended fraternity prank gone wrong by tactics designed to annoy, intimidate, bully, and threaten. young Journet. It was mental, psychological, cruelty, heaped on a school chum of impeccable academic and behavioral success. We have witnesses lined up and anxious to tell the terrible truth about *pauvre petit Jean*. Now, Alf ol' man, honestly…"

Attorney Alfie was speechless. His other lawyers were red-faced and surprised. Jean was his usual arrogant self, gaping, open-mouthed.

"We should call a recess, Jules. I will be in touch with you. Good day, ladies and gentlemen."

Prof Josh

We never saw Breaux and his team again. He sent us a formal letter in which he stated that he withdrew from the case when he realized how much disinformation he had received from Jean Didier. His partners convinced Jean to drop all his charges, hope for early release based on good behavior, and just shut up.

The guards' families were visited by some Colbert staff and assured of a fine Christmas week in Paris. At a Boudreau dinner Operation Entrée enjoyed L.V.'s blow by blow account of her Storeroom Sedition. She ended with a description of her hand built barricade made of church furniture, and a palindrome: We Panic In A Pew. I finally got around to recounting the discovery of the Abbot's body, with the sprig of *genet* embossed into the wood of his cross. We decided to have a Mass said for his eternal salvation.

This has been an historically hot summer. People died in the abnormal, intensive high temperature. Air conditioning is generally lacking. Headlines read: FRANCE TRANSPIRE! Jules returned to Avignon, to his several careers. L.V. was preparing for her last test dive and graduation from the diving program. That's when the three guys from the Avrille demonstration day reappeared, this time dressed as ordinary Angers business men. I mean business men with extraordinary bulges under their French blazers. They looked ill-fit and ill-fitting. And they were almost as conspicuous as they were the first time we spotted them. Lemieux says they are Harkis, Algerians who fought and worked with the French during the Algerian war. The Harkis were subsequently given French citizenship. When the French left Algeria in 1961 tens of thousands of Harkis were massacred by the recently independent anti-French Algerians. Ever since, the Harkis have been trying to get recognition from France. This year, for example, the Angers Museum of Natural History is presenting a program entitled: Algeria: Two Million Years of History. Given our experience with the murders of Robert and Elaine Gagne I would say the Harkis can use all the positive public relations they can find.

The Avrille-Lac Bleu Government Diving School's graduation was staged to impress the local citizens. The main message: "The national government's Département du Déminage is doing all it can to train divers to work in and around munitions sites." Their motto for this distribution of official certificates was PLONGEE POUR VIE. Posters were up all over town. Representatives were present from diving schools in France and abroad. Diving associations were here to present prizes sponsored by the private sector. The diving organization L.V. was most interested in seeing was the National Association of Underwater

Instructors, U.S.A. She had done her high school scuba training in Conshohocken, PA., and has a NAUI certificate framed in her C.U. room in Angers. She says the NAUI recognition "reeks of prestige."

The French Foreign Legion Commander, Laurent Flaurent Boulanger, was splendid in his dress uniform. Rita, who was present with Pierre, wanted to know why he did not appear in his diving gear. "Would that not have been more appropriate?" Pierre suggested then each of the two lady divers would have had to be in bikinis. "Also more appropriate." Rita said, "Tant pis!" The program was being filmed for French television.

After the national anthem, a few speeches about the motto, (the motto committee was asked to stand for applause), each individual diver was called to the podium for a few words of praise from the Commander. L.V. was one of the first to be called to the podium via the strict system of 'alphabetical order.' "Mademoiselle Laura Veronica Campbell."

L.V. walked up the steps to the podium with a wonderful half smile on her gorgeous face. She was wearing an original light blue Rosemarie creation. Together they had worked for days on her total look for this occasion. Rosemarie has become the big sister in this act. She stood off to the side, too excited to sit calmly with our group.

The Commander motioned for L.V. to stand beside him. She looked out over the audience, blushing. First the Commander read her complete name, nationality, rank in the class, (second), and future plans. At that point he looked up and said:

"Unfortunately Mademoiselle Campbell will be returning to the States. Fortunately she will be a diving instructor there. As of this moment she has active status in the NAUI."

He paused for a smattering of polite applause. Then he proceeded to tell us she had kept the best personal Diver's Training Log in the class, for which she will receive with her certificate the Significant Achievement Pin recognized and respected by divers throughout the world. After all the trainees had been presented at the podium to receive their two minutes of fame standing with the Commander the special awards began. Several of the male divers were rewarded by various French manufacturers of diving equipment. When L.V. was recalled to the podium the applause was enthusiastic, two notches above 'smattering' this time. Now she was gleeful and totally enjoying the kudos, smiling in all directions, as the Commander announced her distinction.

"And now for the last special award it is my pleasre to present Major John Burns of l'Ecole Superieur et d'Application de Genie. Major Burns."

"Ladies and gentlemen, as you know ESAG has been offering specialized courses to American military personnel in what is called the "French philosophy of demining." This group has decided to present Miss Campbell with a gift from her American colleagues. These two gifts embrace the best diving equipment available for her future teaching. The first box here, (just set them down there guys, thank you), is the Oceanreef Neptune II Nira Diving Full Face Mask, retailing in the U.S., by the way, for $680.00. The second box, (thanks Ralph), is the Oceanreef Diver Communications Unit, designed for use with the Neptune II mask, valued at $780.00. Congratulations Miss Campbell. Please accept these gifts from your diving colleagues in France's remarkable ESAG, with our best wishes."

This time, standing ovation. Then she was ushered to the microphone by the Commander.

"Commander Boulanger, Major Burns, ladies and gentlemen. I am very grateful for all I have learned these past hectic weeks. The program has been interrupted by tragedy and death but my fellow students assisted greatly in my adjustment to the sorrow and to the culture. I am grateful to them all. These gifts from the ESAG divers is especially meaningful to me because the man I was to marry died before he could begin his study at that distinguished school. The Commander referred to my future. I have accepted a job at a diving school in Lake City, Florida, starting next year. I will be leading dives and dive trips to some of the world's best dive sites. Y'all come. Thank you."

**The sign of a good heart is a
cheerful countenance; withdrawn
and perplexed is the laborious schemer.
SIRACH 13:25**

PART VI

Prof Josh

Just as that 'y'all come' was heard over the sound system, the 'thank you' was muffled by a slow building crescendo of deep bass sound, like the start of a giant throat-clearing.

It seemed to come from inside the earth. In a split second the underwater grumbling became clear to all for miles around. Lac Bleu blew up.

The jolting concussion was like a collision between people and hot water. We were flung to the ground, which shook and rattled. In the next instant we were soaked and struck by flying debris landing on the crowd from above. It rained bits of iron and steel, pieces of wood, chunks of rock and clumps of mud. The smell of sulphate was heavy in the air. The sound was horrendous. The strong wind from the blast felt tropical. Lac Bleu had erupted.

The geyser-like stream of water and metal kept coming, the ground's convulsions went on for several seconds. I was deafened by the several explosions, but when I looked up, flat on my stomach, I could see people with their mouths open, hysterically screaming. The sound from beneath us blocked out all human speech. We weren't deaf. We were engulfed in a hot wave of unfamiliar sound like a ghastly voice-over, drowning out all our cries. The upheaval could still be felt rumbling beneath us as we lay. A few more seconds and the barrage began to soften, like a volcano gradually quieting down. Another few seconds and a thousand Avrillais began to yell. Now we could hear each other clearly. The Lac was smoldering, bubbling, but quiet, as if it were pouting. After all it had really lost its temper.

As people began to sit up and look around they shouted names of people they had just been sitting near. That's when panic set in. Mothers repeating children's names, kids crying, some elderly folks wandering among the fallen, out of their minds. The first few minutes after stillness returned to the ground we were able to see what Baghdad looked like in its worst days. In front of what had been the stage there were only piles of broken boards. All about me on the ground were chunks of sharp debris, pieces of various kinds of killer explosives, now finally detonated. Bodies were slowly rising, dazed and dizzy. Others leaped up, energetic, helping their neighbors. Many were dead, pinned to the earth by large pieces of metal. Shrapnel, landing on us from above and some flung horizontally close to the ground, had cut many down. Bits of clothing from bodies blown apart were everywhere. The hot water had caused a smelly mist over the field. As I arose from my mud puddle I put my hand on someone's ring. I felt so weak and sick I picked it up and deliberately dropped it. It was warm to the touch.

This is a tragedy of enormous proportions I remember thinking. The death toll will probably be in the hundreds I thought. I took a few steps and tripped and fell back onto the soggy ground. Lac Bleu had finally spoken for itself, as if saying, "I was angry. I blew up. Now I'm cooling off."

Avrille's Lac Bleu had, as of today, followed the other cataclysmic *déminage* sites that were gradually and inexorably becoming more and more common in the French way of life. What the nation had hoped would never occur has now become a part of French culture—another ghastly explosion. I rolled over in the mud for another few seconds, thinking of how many good and brave men had put their lives on the line for this monumental collection of unexploded ordnance. How discouraged and frustrated they must feel.

Out of the haze a beautiful face appeared close to mine. L.V. was smiling.

"Howdy, dude Prof. Like authentic excitement, *n'est-ce pas?*"

As she smiled she curled her lips and there in her teeth she was holding what looked like a sparkling diamond. She laughed and put the splendid little sparkler in my hand.

"That's in payment for being an Emeritus. Like, when you look around these grounds, Prof, you will find plenty of these little gems. They must have been in a container of some kind and like they were literally blown out of the water. The survivors are scooping them up instead of tending to the wounded. How's that for good news and bad news?"

"Our Operation Entrée people are alright," she continued. "Pierre has a broken ankle from a flying grenade casing or something. Rosemarie and Rita are with him over near the trees. Roger is organizing a triage center. Commander Boulanger and Major Burns were both killed. All my wonderful new equipment is totally destroyed. I was lucky. I fell down the stairs and then the whole wooden stage flipped over on me. It acted like a shelter for the first few seconds. I had to practically burrow out from under. Like what luck."

"I am so glad to see you L.V. Your dress is ruined, but you're okay. Thank God. Let's go. We have work to do, friend. We'll help Lemieux organize the wounded."

She helped me up and together we waddled over to Lemieux's triage station. Several of his men were already bringing wounded to one place and moving the dead bodies to a different section of the field. Two gendarmes were administering tourniquets, arresting bleeding as much as possible in these panic conditions. Two surviving ladies were talking to the wounded, calming them, cleaning them up. A couple priests appeared and pitched right in. Phones were working.

Ambulances and medical teams began to arrive from Avrille town and Angers. By nightfall, the five *Départements* which border Maine-et-Loire were joining them: Vendee, Sarthe, Mayenne, Loire-Atlantique, and Indre-et-Loire. During the night dozens of police cars, ambulances and fire trucks came and went, back and forth from nearby and far-off hospitals. Traffic police set up roadways and roadblocks. Lemieux directed the whole operation with a few of his own subordinates. This emergency went on all night. There was no moon and the 'gem pickers,' as they were soon tagged, were on hands and knees with flash lights. I never knew every citizen had a *lampe de poche* for just such an emergency!

Day II of *Avrille Cataclysmique,* as the media quickly dubbed the event, brought television reporters, photographers by the dozens, journalists looking for the 'scoop' interview. They used words like tragedy, calamity, and disaster to focus in on "the early statistics of the *A.C.* " Of course there was no accurate count yet but viewers and listeners saw and heard plenty: "207 died from the force of the explosion; 57 were blown to bits; 45 are in hospital, seriously hurt; 38 are reported missing by their families and friends. The death toll will rise to over 300." These kinds of broadcasts changed every half-hour.

The Harkis did yeoman work, assisting greatly in moving bodies and caring for the wounded. One of the three was the apparent leader. He checked in every hour or so with Lemieux, suggesting 'me and my men' will be ready to help any way we can. He spoke a very educated French. Lemieux did use them. Around noon he had them set up refreshment tables, distribute food, carry dazed elders, help parents find their kids. Marami Hakim and 'his men' never rested throughout Day II. Smith and Beauchaine noticed that. The *Sûreté*, meanwhile, coordinated various arriving police investigators who wanted to get right to the reason for the explosion. Smith prophecied that would become clear right after the JFK assassination conspiracy is laid to rest.

"In other words, never."

Day III of the Avrille Cataclysm dawned bright and clear. Lac Bleu seemed dormant. The international press coverage suffocated Avrille. Diane Sawyer, Tom Brokaw, and Paula Zahn, each with his or her own tv crew, walked around the grounds with colleagues from Paris, London, Rome, Bonn, Madrid, and Brussels. Each news group staked out a portion of the field as soon as the bodies were mostly collected. Make-up artists and hair stylists for each crew were much in evidence. That's when Lemieux announced 'enough is enough.' He arranged for reporters and all the media equipment to be moved, 'no exceptions,' to De La Salle school gymnasium. Only police investigators were allowed onto the cordoned-off grounds. L.V. was asked to help them understand the most recent diving developments. She described the Program for the various press media in the school and then toured the grounds with the French police. Friends of Major Burns from ESAG were doing what they could to help explain how this could have happened. I met the family of the Commander. Others also expressed condolences. His brother wanted to stand right where his big brother Laurent had been standing when all hell broke loose. On that spot several Boulangers wept and prayed and wept again. Then they were all escorted to the gym for interviews.

By this time the French papers were calling this *le detonation classique.* The International Herald Tribune began with LAKE DEVASTATION. Stories and editorials poured out venom on the government ministers who, just last summer, had said things like: *Aucun danger, tant qu'il y a de l'eau.* There's no danger as long as there is water. Satire and cynicism mingled with sharp criticism. *MENACE DURABLE? Oui, menace durable,* said one headline in a West France newspaper. One such paper ran this in huge font: *Ou se trouve les gaffeurs?* Where are the blundering idiots?

Important visitors included Chirac and several of his key ministers. Catherine and a number of her committee members took a quick tour of the devastation. French television had pictures of her standing where the stage used to be. Journals with active archives like TIME, Newsweek, and Figaro delved into last summer's headlines. Many used quotes from pro-CACTUS articles.

PREDICTION A L'AIR LIBRE, LES EXPLOSIFS SERAIT PLUS DANGEREUX C'EST EVIDENT QU'IL FAUT DEMINER.

POUR LE NETTOYAGE COMPLET DES TONNES DE MUNITIONS SOUS L'EAU TONNES D'EXPLOSIFS STOCKES DANS LE LAC BLEU D'AVRILLE

One prominent French comic reasoned this way: "It is a real scandal to leave these arms lying around dormant. Well now, Monsieur, they are not dormant." Shrug shoulders, "phew."

Late on Day III the *Assemblée Nationale* passed Resolution 3037 by a large majority. It stated that a commission of enquiry should be formed forthwith in order to inventory the sites where munitions are stored, including chemical weapons, and ascertain the dangers presented by those sites. Catherine Didier was pictured in Le Monde with both arms raised in victory. Actually it was a perfect imitation of an American referee's football goal signal. Auntie Catherine looked splendid.

Angers, Avrille and surrounding towns proved valiant in distress. The vaunted medical services of the French were put to the emergency test and found supremely capable. But medical services were not the only aspect of this horrible event that required outside assistance. Dozens of police from nearby departments were needed by Lemieux to curtail looting. This is always the seamy side of disasters of any kind; the Lac field was the target of poachers and thieves who seemed to appear out of nowhere and then multiply. Of course there was plenty to draw them: clothes, wallets, purses, stray coins and paper money were strewn everywhere. Shiny bits of broken glass received primary attention. Some 'glass' was actually jewelry, such as ear rings torn from the deceased by the blast. But some of the 'glass' was of gem quality. Stretcher bearers stopped for a minute to pick up a bauble or two as they went about their merciful duties. Some looters, posing as bereaved relatives bent to the ground in grief, were seen to have two very active hands and stuffed pockets. Lemieux was enraged. He posted police with orders to arrest filchers. A few were immediately incarcerated and stripped of all clothing. Looters soon disappeared. The International Red Cross supervised personal belongings on Day III. One Retrieval Station accumulated twenty-three wallets, most of them empty.

By Day IV the ground had been thoroughly searched and picked clean by organized lines of gendarmes and Avrille church groups. Broken metal and bomb parts were carted off in police vehicles for further analysis. Searchers were asked to turn in diamonds at the Police Station set up on site. It was quite impossible to estimate the amount of the Diamond Disgorge, as one writer called it. It seems to be the general belief that the tragedy came with some blessings for those families fortunate enough to profit from the 'disgorge.'.

At one of Lemieux's morning meetings with various law enforcement entities involved in some way with the Avrille catastrophe the question of lost diamonds was raised. "What will the owners of that cache do," a police captain asked, "now that their illegal plans have been literally blown out of the water?"

"Who are we dealing with here?" another queried.

"Were these diamonds the property of terrorists, arms merchants, or big-time smugglers of illegal gems, to be placed on the international market?"

A gem discussion between the Sûreté agents and three Interpol men was a learning seminar for the local authorities. Further talk revolved around basic questions, such as how soon would it be possible to search the lake for unexploded ordnance? Chemical content of the sprayed water? Won't the water table have to be inspected, water analyzed? Can the deminers clear the lake once and for all? Is there a chance of another blow?

Lemieux always called a halt to a meeting after one and one-half hours. Careful recordings of these meetings were duplicated and circulated among the key agencies. Pierre commented that in the States the book and movie rights would already be up for bid, and journalists would be dreaming of big bucks for manuscripts. He was probably correct. However, all such speculation became strictly hypothetical when, on Day V, the Elysée Palace announced that all political, administrative and juridical aspects of the Avrille 'incident' were to be directly handled solely by the Département du Déminage under the immediate authority of President Chirac's special delegate. During his speech on the tele his condolences went out to the good citizens of Avrille, and he thanked everyone for their brave assistance in the clean-up procedures, mentioning Captain Roger Lemieux with commendation. Within one week the plastic tape used for cordoning-off the field was replaced by an eight-foot high electric fence; three dozen Army engineer privates worked around the clock. The shiny new wired fence encompassed the lake/quarry, the picnic field, and the entire base, now designated TERRAIN INTERDIT! All further diving programs were terminated, public tour offices were disbanded, strict military protocol would be enforced. This new *Base Militaire* would be called *LAURENT BOULANGER*. Chirac made it clear that these changes were all part of the planned military 'restructuring and professionalizing.' The plan is to change the external capability needed for crisis prevention. The planned force level will support 50,000 troops in a NATO-led operation. Avrille is designated *quartier general*. Joint exercises will be conducted under the leadership of the Joint Chiefs of

Staff, that is, CEMA, *Chef d'Etat Major des Armées*. The operational language? English.

Avrille, with its new army base headquarters has entered the big-time military world. Camp Boulanger will change not only the military map, but the lives and culture of every Angevin and Avrillais.

Lemieux

I was asked by General Louis Haute-Maison of the Joint Chiefs, to retain the three Harki Algerians under a special emergency edict of military law. But that was not necessary because they came first to me to ask if we could set up a weekly series of meetings. I would represent French law enforcement and they would represent the Algerian equivalent of the American CIA, by which orgainization they had been trained. It was to be an informal body with the objective of clearing the air, as it were, and keeping all our communications open for the good of all sides concerned with Lac Bleu. *Sûreté* agents Smith and Beauchaine had their Operation Entrée appointments extended to join the three Harkis, whose 'names' were Marami, Alque, and Benudo. Only God knows what their parents had once actually named them.

"First sir, I must thank you for agreeing to see us. We feel, as our governments truly do, that terror is best fought with cooperative neighbors," began Marami.

"I feel the same way, *monsieur*. Much can be accomplished by continuing to converse. Please proceed."

"Well, sir, firstly I must tell you why we are here in Avrille. We traced a known terrorist here, to this town and then to this demining location," continued Marami.

"And have you found him?" asked Lemieux.

"We had him in our sights. He was here poised to do some harm. I mean he was not here vacationing as so many German and British are. We had him under our surveillance for several days. He has, however, disappeared. Perhaps he was killed in the blast. Perhaps he made us and relocated. Perhaps he has gone to ground in the area, awaiting another chance. Maybe the new military base has thrown off his calculations, what with its new security. At any rate, we have lost him. The trail, so hot last week, has dead-ended."

Marami was deeply saddened to have had to report the loss of a terrorist's trail. There is always that nagging question as to just exactly when to pounce upon a subject being kept under close watch. Too soon and the watchers learn little. Too late and the foul deed may be done. Of course we don't now know whether the guy they lost was supposed to blow up the lake. If that was his job he certainly succeeded. If the lake blew on its own, so to speak, we have two questions: Why did it blow? And, where's the terrorist?

"Anyway," continued Marami, "we were to pounce when and if he came into contact with any diamonds. Our superiors had no clue about the eminent danger of a huge munitions explosion. They had a rumor that a diamond cache was in the Avrille lake-quarry. If diamonds were actually involved we were authorized to arrest him for immediate transport to Algiers. The charge would be 'illegal diamond smuggling.' We would not wait for French extradition proceeding and permission to bring him with us. He would be forcefully removed immediately or killed. It was a straightforward grab and run mission. We are not sure what to do now and seek to talk to you and your superiors."

"You are understandably hesitant to report his disappearance to Algiers. Who was this guy you're looking for?" asked Smith.

"He is called Ahmed, with many AKAs. He is number one on our Algiers list of the usual suspects."

"We will assist wherever we can," I said. "Please leave us these pictures and other materials you have here. We will study them and get back to you. We think you will like Avrille if you stay. If you have to leave I would appreciate your informing my office."

I was impressed by these three guys. I have not met many CIA-trained government agents. Marami spoke excellent English and French and probably a North African language or two.

"There is one more thing we will leave with you Commissaire. One of our agents came across this book or journal, you call it?"

Marami handed me a spiral-bound note book. I thanked him and we shook hands. Alque and Benudo were leaving the room. Marami stopped in the doorway and turned to wave.

"It is the journal of Jean-Luc Napoleon Baker, sir. My government thought it belonged here. Goodbye."

Then he stopped short again.

"I almost forgot. This was the book mark. It keeps falling out."

He put something light and small in my hand. It was a broom twig. *Genista*.

Prof Josh

I was relaxing at the Boudreau. I had just finished mowing the field behind the house for my *petanque* court and sat down with a cool Stella Artois. Lemieux found me in my favorite *chaise de jardin,* a wooden lawn chair Pierre built several years ago. Cushions by Rosemarie.

"I have something for you, Prof Josh, something precious and important."

"Don't tell me, let me guess. You have decided to build a new soccer stadium for De La Salle? Or you came early for dinner?"

Without a word he handed me Boney's journal. I was speechless. I looked at the book and back at Roger. He smiled. I held it like it was the Blessed Sacrament.

"I have not read it, my friend. But maybe the Harkis did. Or maybe they made a copy. This seems to be the original, *n'est-ce pas?*"

I opened it reverently and flipped through to get an idea of the length and the dates. It covers the seven months before Boney's death. My hands trembled a little more than usual.

"Thank you, Rog. Now seriously, want dinner? I'm baking a ham."

"Thank you Prof, but I have to go. You need private time I think to read Boney's words. *Bon courage!*"

His Landrover dug its way out of Boudreau's gravel drive. I turned to the first page.

12 August Toulon

Joel and Francois picked me up 6:45. We drove to a farm where a Madame Fourvier was waiting in a panic for us to remove several German grenades from her overgrown hedge. They were still in the original belt holder, as if they were just dropped while someone was on the run, or inadvertently left there when the troops moved out. If the groundskeeper had struck them while clipping he may have been blown up. We never know. We took them in the truck. She hardly said 'merci.'

11:23 Vence

We have lunch in our usual restaurant. Before we finish four guys come in and sit at our big table. They made us a proposition. They said those Godfather words, 'you cannot refuse.' But we did refuse. A great brawl began. I was bloodied a bit but we had the better of them and drove off. Without dessert.

In the afternoon we checked the regional deminage site, found it all in order, placed the grenades inside the old fort. Ran up to Gorges du Loup to remove a shell from under a large tractor. The farmer did not see it buried just below the surface until he was directly over it. He had been on his tractor since early morning, yelling for his wife who finally noticed he did not come in for noon meal. She went to look for him and learned some new pre-WWI words not sanctioned by the Academie. Anyway, we were able to get him off the tractor and for two hours dug around and under the machine and the shell. Francois and I lifted it out. George backed the Rover as close as possible. Just as we had it in the proper rack the same four guys drove up with a truck full of junk. There were old tires, car parts of all types, from boots to hoods to roofs to doors. Again they made their proposition: "Take this load of junk to Lac Bleu." Again we said 'non" and once more, like ill-mannered school boys we boxed, and kicked, our three against their four, actually a fat four. When they were all on the ground, breathing heavily and moaning about various hurts, we helped each other toward the truck. A hiss came from the truck and we demineurs hit the ground. An explosion blew the Landrover's doors out. Francois' leg was torn off at the knee. He screamed. Poor Francois! We applied all the first aid we knew. Our emergency equipment is the best and Joel had raised a 'copter pilot with his radio.

5 September Digne-les-Bains
    Joel and I were furloughed for a week. Army inspectors have interviewed us at length. We have been reprimanded for fighting! Four Algerians have been arrested on a charge of possession of illegal firearms and attempted

murder. They are singing to the army investigators. We identified them as our Vence brawlers. Many deminage soldiers and their families have been spending time at the home of Francois. They will be taken care of financially but his kids now have a hero papa instead of a live one. I am very sad. Rosemarie knows Francois is/was on my team. But I will not tell her how close I came to being killed. She worries enough as it is. The details of the dangers, written by Joel and me, are in our files. She will never see that official personnel file. I would rather let her think I am a *godiche* or a stupid *balourd*, (I think Josh would say klutz). Rosemarie thinks God protects klutzes and clumsy oafs.

Rosemarie

After three hectic days in and around Boudreau and the Avrille field of devastation, L.V. and I had to get back to our teaching. I left a few days supply of cooked food in Boudreau for Josh and the many folks he is feeding these days. I have an advanced seminar on The Parlement Européen, an evening class which has brought together many Angevins from different walks of life. It seems the university dean forgot the class number was to be set at thirty-five and now we are forty-two in a cramped room designed for thirty.

Shortly after arriving in my apartment last night a member of the class arrived unannounced at my door. He was evidently one of those allowed in after the class should have been closed because I did not recognize him right away.

"I am sorry to disturb you madame. I have a gift for you from your husband. Please accept this."

He handed me an envelope in which were stuffed about seventy pages of hastily written notes I recognized as my Boney's handwriting. I was somewhat taken aback, sat down and invited him to do the same.

"I thank you for these, monsieur, but I must confess I am confused. Did you join the Parlement Européen seminar tonight? Your name must be on my tentative class list. Would you mind telling who you are?

"My name is Ahmed Ben Bella, madame professeur. I am honored to be your student and I will study and try to contribute to the class."

"Fine. But how do you know where I live and how did you come to have my husband's journal?"

"Madame professeur, I am a French citizen of Algerian descent. My family came to France during the internal French-Algerian struggles. Now, earning my doctorate is very important to me.'

I tried to relax while observing him. He was wearing a white shirt and dark necktie, blue suit, black unshined shoes. He smiles easily, is very intense in conversation, seems manly and strongly built. But back to my question.

"Ahmed, where did you get these pages?"

"I was able to copy them madame, from a friend of mine. We are Harkis, madame, and we help each other whenever we can. My friend had the journal. He will turn it over to the brother of your husband. I am sure he does not mind my having a copy made for the wife of the brave deminer. That is about all there is to that madame, *c'est ne pas grand chose, madame, pas complique.* It is nothing, madame; it has been no trouble. I am happy to be of service. I will just go now."

I spent the rest of that night reading Boney's marvelous journal. It is written with feeling and perception. He was writing for himself, for me, and for the Department. During the reading I cried and laughed at various subtle turns of phrase. He was suspicious of any civilian who expressed an interest in Lac Bleu. Boney was intelligent and as it turned out so totally devoted to his dangerous work. All that is shown in the journal. Oh dear God, I still miss him terribly.

The next day I asked Ahmed to meet me in the library after class. There, in a remote corner of the reading room, I asked him to tell me what he knew of my husband. It turned out he knows a great deal.

"Normally, madame, I am a quiet guy who never talks about himself. But these are very unusual circumstances. I am here in this class specifically to help you."

"How do you intend to help me and why?"

"Madame, eight years ago when your husband was killed I was with him. He died in my arms."

I was shocked.

"Once again Ahmed, I have to ask you: Who are you?"

"My name is really Ahmed Ben Bella, madame. My parents named me after the great first president of Algeria. He was decorated for bravery after World War II for heroism in the French army. My father fought alongside him and together they helped organize the Algerian National Liberation Front. They both made sure I was educated at the Sorbonne and monies they invested are still paying for my education. When I finish my studies here I will return to Algiers in some political capacity."

"And in the meantime you will be studying here and 'helping' me?"

"Yes, that is my plan. I want you to know all there is to know about your husband's early life and the significance of his death."

I paused and looked at him. I thought he will probably make a successful politician some day.

I said, "significance?"

"Yes madame. He did not have time to write all he had in mind. You see, I was a deminer. We worked well together. You most likely have my name on the final reports you received from the government after his death. It was George Lablanc. Unofficially I have been investigating details surrounding his life and death off and on for these many years. Because I am a French citizen and an Algerian I have experienced racial intolerance many people from my country have come to expect in France. Immigration from Algeria has been rather heavy and many French are biased against us. After all, madame, the French lost well over 9,000 soldiers during those horrible years, 1954-59, while we were fighting for our independence. The native French have reason to distrust people like me."

"Well, I must say Ahmed, you certainly have surprised me with these revelations. I never did meet the man who carried my Boney out of the explosion area and into the nearest town. You then accompanied him to the hospital where he was declared dead on arrival. Then you, this George Lablanc, disappeared. The *Département du Déminage* have said they have no such name on their records."

"That is correct madame. I went underground for them. I have had several identities since that day. I have been employed in various ways by Interpol here and abroad. In your class I am Leonid Mabuti."

"I must go now to my office appointments. Monsieur Mabuti I will think seriously about all you have told me. I may have to take Boney's brother, Professor Josh Baker, into my and your confidence."

"That is fine madame. I know of this man. He is *vaillant,* madame, *un vrai brave.* I trust him. He is like his brother."

"Au revoir, monsieur Mabuti."

"Au revoir, madame. And please, do not fail to boil your drinking water. Some stomach problems have become apparent in town, madame. Some of those sprayed by the lake water have skin rashes also. Be careful."

Prof

Rosemarie was quite shaken by the visit of Ahmed Ben Bella AKA Leonid Mabuti AKA George Lablanc. She had not slept a wink, she said, since reading the journal. Neither had I but I did not mention it. Now was the time for us to share our thoughts about the death of Boney. It was an emotional trip for us when it happened eight years ago. Now much of that experience was upon us again. With some trepidation we began going over the details of that horrible day.

She spread out some family papers on the table. I picked up the original report of Boney's accident. That day a request for a demining team had come from a prestigious hotel near the Annecy lake. A boater had sighted the flat end of an *obus*. When Boney and Lablanc arrived the former entered the lake in hip boots and shouted back to his partner that it looked like a shrapnel shell from a howitzer. Lablanc's testimony then says he yelled back, "Okay, I'll bring out the shovels." Boney leaned over to get a better look and that's when it blew.

"I remember," Rosemarie said, "wondering about how the body was moved from the site of the explosion to the hospital in Annecy. According to the Dossier of 15 May 2001, the accident took place in a shallow part of *Lac d'Annecy*. A deminer named George Lablanc, of whom there is no further record, carried Boney from the three-foot deep shallows to the shore and on out to the nearest road at the western end of the lake. Here a couple had stopped to view the *Cret de Chatillon* perched on the summit of Semnoz Mountain. They were interrupted in their love making by a man carrying a smaller man out from the trees onto the road. This Lablanc shouted at them and they responded quickly, albeit somewhat disheveled and embarrassed. At the hospital in Annecy Lablanc filled out all the proper forms and a staff person notified the Département de Déminage. Two deminers were there in about a half-hour. Lablanc was nowhere on the premises. He had seen Boney into surgery and was gone. The remainder of the Dossier contains the signed statements of the couple, Rick and Linda Quinn of Dublin. They had been on their way to a restaurant in the lakeside village of Talloires. The report mentions the significance of the manner of Lablanc's carrying Boney. Instead of putting the wounded man over his shoulder, as most men would have done, Lablanc was carrying him in both arms, hugging him to his chest. The report recorder, a Major Roman Philippe, comments there at the bottom, that the two responding deminers were not well acquainted with Lablanc. They considered him a quiet, efficient team member."

"Considering we are dealing with the déminage department we are fortunate to have this much info," I said. "You know how they detest anyone asking questions about demining work."

"I wonder if they keep any records beyond this meager report about Boney. Of course they have all our family history, no doubt, and his service record, etc. But as to demining I think you are right, Josh. We only have what the department considers a detailed Dossier on a minor aspect of the department's overall mission. Amen."

"But I'm wondering Rosemarie. Now that Lablanc, in the person of your student Leonid Mabuti, seems to have reappeared, could we not trust him enough to begin regular talks with him about his demining service experience? What do you think?"

"He told me about bad water and skin rashes, Josh, facts the media have not mentioned since the explosion. He somehow knows a lot more than the controlled media. And is willing to talk to us. I'd say yes, let's trust him, when and if Smith and Beauchaine can vett him to our satisfaction."

It was a few weeks later that I received the background check on Ahmed Ben Bella. Smith and Beau were able to discover only what Interpol and the Sûreté wanted them to find. With that caveat understood, we read with interest the Ben Bella, Ahmed DOSSIER.

Born: 1950 in Maghnia, Algeria in 1959.
Residence: Since completing his bac (honors, languages), has lived in numerous cities in the Middle

East and Europe, particularly Algiers, Paris, Rome. Baghdad.

Family: Only child. Unmarried. No offspring. Harki. Cherished by, and brought up by his father. Always working for Algerian independence, his father and grandfather were right hand men to The Paladin himself, Ben Bella, the first President.

Financial stability: Always seems to have plenty of money for his trips, causes, gifts. Spends little on himself. No outstanding debts.

Personal: A man of mystery with obvious but unheralded connections to the Deminage Department, MI 5 and Interpol. It is assumed that the DGSE, *Direction Generale de la Securite Exterieure* has used him, but of this there is no record. A master of *le masque,* a pro at disguises of all kinds, including eye color, penmanship, voice, laugh, dialect, language, physical appearance. Often wears gloves. Finger prints are difficult to come by.

There is some evidence, but no proof, that he was involved, through one or two international agencies, in:

- selling French arms and ammunition to Iraq;
- negotiating the cancellation of debts owed France by many of the poorest nations;
- deliberated with foreign conglomerates for the rich oil fields of the Sahara;
- had dealings with three *genista* gentlemen concerning the smuggled gems amid the munitions in Lac Bleu: Professor Antonio

Barardelli, Abbot Deman Baume, and Commander Laurent Boulanger, all deceased.

Note: All these *genistas* wanted the lake to be emptied of ordnance. Several serving Prefets want the lake to remain filled. Their cry remains: *Il ny'a aucun danger.* There is no danger. Graft charges are pending on several of these politicians concerning unrelated issues.

Reading this report on Ahmed helped us to realize that a mysterious international man of many talents has become interested in our Avrille. Where will these interests lead? It's consoling to learn about the accident and last hours of Boney. I am grateful for that. It is because of his devotion to my brother that I will endeavor to remain in contact with Ahmed, as difficult as that would seem to be. I need to fill Pierre in on these developments.

Pierre's busy with one of his outside activities. Today he is repairing some altar statues in his church, St. Eustache. He will be here the day afer tomorrow. In the meantime I called upon the Mayor of Avrille, Monsieur Jean-Baptiste Fabre. He received me in the recently renovated office 'complex' which has received much media attention since the Day of the Big Blow. So far the print media have called the incident by many names but *Aucun Risque d'Explosion,* A.R.E., seems to be the most popular in the cynical press. Fabre informed me that next week will mark the start of a new Avrille movement, called, in English, Our Enduring Milestones. He means to convey to the public that this abominable experience the city has had will forever be remembered in its history books. It is to be understood as "enduring," as in *durable*. Because each year a city celebration will recall the horror and the survival of Avrille. It's a disaster in a long string of remarkable historical "milestones" in Avrille-Angers-Anjou.

"Well," he said, "so much for slogans."

"Mr. Mayor, as a citizen of Avrille, how can I assist your Enduring Milestones project?"

"Professor, let me share something with you, on a very personal note."

With that he moved a beautiful Claude Monet painting, *Les peupliers, automne,* and opened the wall safe behind it. He handed me this message, written in cursive free-flowing penmanship.

Pleaserefrainfromanyefforttodrainthelakewelikeitfullme rcilfitgoesloweryourhousewillblowup

While I held the page he wiped his sweaty face and hands with a large handkerchief. The poor mayor had outgrown his three-button suitcoat some years ago. Maybe that was why his fat face was bulging and brightr red. He was extremely affected by this politely presented threat.

"If I had enough money," the mayor began, "I would reconstitute the Lac committee to further investigate suggestions; for example, a strong wall around the lake and inside the lake itself to protect us in the event of another explosion. I would like to offer financial help to those many families who lost all their doors and windows in the blast. If we are going to live here we should have *anti-bruit* screening shields, and earthworks, like American earthen dikes and levees. And what about all our sick and injured?"

He put his head down and wiped his face again, opening his tightly buttoned coat in an effort to release strain on the buttons. An overweight mouth-breathing mayor is not a pleasant sight.

"And now," he continued, "I am threatened with extinction if I lower the lake, as if I have any power to do that now that Chirac's government has taken over direct control of a part of my city."

"Who do you suppose, Mayor Fabre, wants the lake lowered or emptied?"

"I suppose," he answeed, "those anti-pollution people, CACTUS, and the genistas, and now perhaps most of Avrille and Angers. They want the area cleared of all war debris."

349

"And who's against it, Mr. Mayor?"

"The self-serving politicians who have forever promised us they would take our demands under consideration. Announced excuse: lack of funding. And of course those who, it seems, have caches of valuable materials down there they wish to preserve for future use."

"Well put, Mr. Mayor. 'Preserve for future use.' After all, diamonds are forever. Even in buying and selling arms."

He smiled and wiped. Just then the mayor's assistant came in with a fax. Again, he read it, handed it to me, and wiped his whole head and both hands. The fax read:

Lucien Pitie has announced his retirement from the ecology ministry.

Pitie was the *Ministre de l'Ecologie et de Developpement Durable* for *Maine-et-Loire.* There's that word 'durable' again. Ol' Lucien wasn't too. Durable, I mean. Or enduring. Poor guy. Maybe he received a threatening note like Fabre's. French ecologists are not 'long lasting' these days.

I thanked the mayor, knowing he was having a very bad day. From the public phone I called Lemieux and summarized the conversation I just had with the mayor. Roger said he would put one of his cruisers in Fabre's neighborhood. I returned to Boudreau and was preparing a large pot of beef stew for the next several meals when a motorcycle slid into the driveway gravel. A man I did not recognize dismounted and approached Boudreau's *porte de grenade.* I instinctively felt for the American Army Colt .45 Automatic in the small of my back as I slowly opened the door a few inches.

"How do you do Professor Emeritus Josh Baker? I was told I would find you here. I am Ahmed Ben Bella. Could I have a word with you, please?"

"Who told you where to find me?"

"My seminar professor, Madame Rosemarie Baker, your sister-in-law, sir."

"Of course, monsieur Ben Bella. I was expecting you one of these days. Please come in. Welcome to Boudreau."

I motioned him to a seat in front of the fireplace. The *pot-au-feu* needed my attention for a moment as I turned off the stove and covered the bread. I could observe him from the kitchen, a well-built fellow, dressed in the *de rigeur* black leather outfit common to bikers around the world. Black hair, brown eyes, sunburned face and arms, heavy leather boots. Sounds like a native speaker of French from the Lyon region.

351

"So what brings you to charming Avrille, monsieur?"

"Professor, please call me Ahmed. I am here to talk to you about your brother. Madame Baker, to whom I presented her husband's journal, encouraged me to meet you.

"Ah yes, she mentioned that. My copy came from an Algerian Harki just yesterday. I am sure we are both very grateful to finally see what he has written. It has been very moving, to hear his voice, as it were, on his favorite topics."

We talked for three hours, with time out for a bowl of beef stew and fresh country bread. He drinks only coffee when at the helm of his huge bike. He had just been riding around *rue de la Terniere,* the road that runs closest to Lac Bleu. The city's garbage brigade, never very large, has been working around the clock for several days and the road, he says, is still a mess. Along the drainage canal on Terniere's edge he spotted several articles of clothing. He dismounted for a short walk and found a man's shirt sleeve in some bushes. It will take weeks more, we guessed, for Avrille to look clean again, once one of France's award-winning little cities. He was relaxed; Boudreau has that effect, even on strangers.

He said as he was picking about the roadside weeds, contrary to traffic control mandates, he was accosted by the Prefet's car, fender-flags flying. Two *carriers,* quarrymen, got out of the car and drew what looked like Italian Berettas. He told them he was unarmed, looking for the town's garbage collection center. "They called me stupid because I was unable to smell the garbage a short distance from the famous Lac Bleu. The garbage dump, had, of course, been blown all over the city when the lake blew up."

Ahmed smiled and shook his head. He had learned a great deal by interacting with the quarrymen. He saw the cordoned-off Terniere still has piles of debris. The Prefet's men, formerly unemployed quarry workers, are patrolling the area. No vehicular traffic allowed; no gawkers or junk collectors either. The Prefet's political clout has risen in direct proportion to the lake's disastrous upheaval. The area now seems like a small war lord's domain, complete with armed thugs as patrolmen, operating in official Prefecture cars with *sous-prefets* in charge. These are the guys who want the lake to remain loaded with ordnance and whatever else needs to be hidden from the public eye.

We decided to take my Avant and tour the Terniere. Ahmed took his briefcase from his motorcycle. I moved the bike close to Boudreau's eastern side. He gave me shortcut directions to the Angers airport.

"The airport?" I said.

"If we want to see the damage and get some idea of what can be done about it we might as well see it all from above."

"But isn't the government doing that?"

"The Assembly is discussing the amount of funding necessary and allowable. It will be at least a year of compromise-*merde* and speech-making before the Avrillais see any actual government help. After that decision is made graft and corruption follow closely. In the meantime the political cover-up is working just fine. Anyway, you and I, Professor, have no power to do much. But at least we can see for ourselves. No?"

"I agree. By the way, Ahmed, do you fly?"

"Oh, oui, I mean, sure Professor, I fly, now and then."

He smiled, glanced at me, winked, and opened his briefcase on his lap. He took out some papers, leather gloves, a cap with a visor.

"I guess you noticed my briefcase is carrying," he said. A Walther with a Carswell silencer. I seldom have guns on my person. I prefer to use my hands. But my briefcase always carries. It is always on the bike."

354

I didn't mention my little Army Colt in my belt. Flying over this area is a great idea, I thought, and I began to anticipate the joy of flying. I began to realize how much I miss my American Cessna Skyhawk in the little Midsouth AVIA Alliance airport near Memphis.

As we drove into the Angers small-plane airport Ahmed pointed to the office door.

"Just park there. I'll sign in and try to get us a new Horizon copter."

After ten minutes he came back with his briefcase in one hand and papers in the other.

"Ours is that Horizon just over there. We can park here and lock up."

"The army rents its copters?" I asked, amazed at so easily securing the use of military property.

He noticed my surprise. "I know a guy. Let's rev her up."

We were cleared, and whipping up our personal wind storm, we slowly lifted off.

"This is a fine little copter, Professor. The Horizon System gets its name from *Helicoptere d'Obervation Radar et d'Investigation sur Zone.* The army uses this for surveillance, just as we are doing."

France uses copters developed for use in Warsaw Pact and NATO plans?"

"Oh oui. As you probably know Professor, the French army has been undergoing some restructuring, as they call it. Their military theoreticians have moved from a purely defensive stance to one more dedicated to, if you'll pardon the word, *A C T I O N.* They want an army of about 140,000 regular troops, with about 16,000 officers. These can be divided into ten brigades. Right now there is one Franco-German brigade whose operational language is *Anglais,* my friend. How about that for progress? France is ok with a NATO-led high intensity operation anywhere it's needed in Europe. The French are justifiably proud of this new army."

As we gracefully glided over Angers I couldn't help but notice that French cities have a plethora of churches, schools, and museums. One more of them and the people will have no place to walk or drive. I picked out the Musee Pince, the Cathedrale Saint-Maurice, and Catholic University of the West. The Maine lake and river had boaters gladly maneuvering in a gusty wind. Ahmed gestured toward Avrille, five kilometers away.

"Let's take a look at disaster city," he said. "'Disast her hell, man; damn near killed her.' Sorry, Prof, I learn such expressions from G.I.s. They enjoy teaching American English."

And then as we swerved over toward Avrille, he continued. "Driver stops just short of running down two lady pedestrians. 'Almost hit them in the ass. No says his friend, you rect 'um.'"

Coming over the now world-famous little Lac Bleu we became silent, bug-eyed, tense. The area around the lake was totally ruined, including the Technical Center, the Sports Complex and the beautiful Rond-Point where four grand avenues come to a circular conclusion. It looked like a very large charge of Semtex blew up, destroying everything for thousands of yards in all directions. Ahmed leveled off and hovered over the lake. With the sun in the right direction we could see metallic reflections from a few feet below the surface. Oxidized copper and brass shell casings. Unexploded munitions? Exploded and fallen back down into the lake? Anyway, we now know that inside the high wall the army has built there are tons of mysterious junk still piled high right to the water level.

As Ahmed turned gently east over the Poney-Club we took some small arms fire from below. *Incroyable.* Unbelievable. It was as if we had suddenly entered a war zone. Bullets pinged under our feet, against our sides. Two windows were blown out. As he turned the copter we took several more hits, this time through the floor and walls. Helicopters. They are wonderful flying machines, but unarmed, as we were, they are easy targets. He lifted us quickly and began a wide circle, yelling out that "we are going back to Angers."

But over Avrille's Ecole St. Exupery one of our blades broke off. We began to spiral helplessly. Ahmed screamed in Arabic and slumped over in his seat. He shook himself a little when I pulled him back upright.

"I'm hit in the arm and shoulder, my friend. I think in the leg too."

He slumped over again, bleeding profusely. I unstrapped and tried to grab control. We were going down. In the school yard. I strapped in and prepared for a pulverizing death. The little Horizon crashed directly into the school's outdoor swimming pool. There was a terrific, shocking splatter. Copter parts ripped and tore off, flying all over the cabin. Several heavy objects hit me in the head. I sat in the disintegrated trash pile, formerly a healthy Horizon. Chlorine-laden water came up to my chest. I became faint, heard shouting around the pool. I reached over to check Ahmed. He wasn't there. I heard some kids yelling. The last thing I remember was the great scrabble word: *flotsam.* I think I was chuckling as I passed out…flotsam.

Lemieux

I arrived at the school's outdoor pool about ten minutes afer we heard and saw it swirling around above the town. I positioned several officers around the school premises, convinced the Principal to send the students home, and ran out to the copter. Two school profs were lifting a helpless body up out of the water and laying it gently next to the diving board. An ambulance drove up and three attendants soon had things under control. One of them handed me the wallet of the victim. I was horrified to read: Josh Baker, Professor Emeritus, Memphis, TN, USA. I bent over the stretcher as it was being carried into the ambulance. It was Prof Josh, alright, breathing, but that's about all.

I called the hospital emergency and gave them a quick summary of what to expect. Ordered two of my motorcycles to lead the ambulance and remain with Prof. Got Rosemarie on the University phone, and raised L.V. about to go into her regular lecture. I promised to call again with up-dates. Two detectives from my office and two experts from the Angers airport were on their way. I decided to wait for them to arrive.

We were immediately struck by the fact that the pilot's seat was soaked in blood. The medical examiner's office had dispatched a photographer. She was clicking away and noticed numerous bullet holes in all parts of the wreckage. Strands of hair, blood samples, finger prints, and so on were being collected. An expensive leather briefcase was found between the seats—empty. All the usual vital detective work was underway when I left for the hospital. I kept thinking I do not remember Josh ever saying he knew how to fly a copter. Especially not a French army Horizon. So where was the pilot? And what were they doing? Just cruising about on a joy-ride? Josh up-grading from a USA Cessna jockey to a French copter pilot? *Mon Dieu,* I sure had a lot of questions for him.

I know many of the doctors and nurses at our fine Avrille hospital. I went right to the main *triage* desk. The nurse saw me coming in and shouted a room number. I found Josh was surrounded by a medical team trying to rouse him. Vital signs unsteady, unable to speak or recognize anyone or any thing. Maybe a skull fracture? Concussion? Maybe amnesia? Temporary? That's something I have heard, on CNN, American quarterbacks experience. 'His return to the game is questionable' is the way the announcer warns the fans. 'The team coach is asking him what day is it, what team are we playing?' One announcer told us it was a 'shocking of the brain.' When I hear that, several times a season I think 'they should be playing soccer football.' I was brought back from my musings by the chief doctor.

"Roger, your friend has a concussion. We cannot predict how badly he is hurt at this time. Maybe tomorrow we'll be able to run additional tests. Right now you can tell his friends to pray for his recovery because that is what I will do. *Je suis désolé, malheusement, nous ne pouvons pas faire grand chose.* I'm truly sorry, Rog, there is little we can do."

"Thanks doc, I know you will be doing your best. You have my number. Call any time, day or night. I must go now to see his sister-in-law. *A bientot.* I'll see you."

Bon soir, mon ami. "

We shook hands.

I talked to myself all the way to the car. 'Who in the world was piloting the Horizon?' And, "Where is he? How did he get away so quickly without anyone seeing him?' Rosemarie was pacing her university apartment when I rang the doorbell.

"Roger, come in. Talk to me. What happened?"

We kissed cheeks.

"The med team thinks Josh has a concussion, Rosemarie. He's in a coma. It could be serious or he could be in the game again in a few days, all A-OK."

"So we really don't know anything! Right?"

"Well we don't know what he was doing in a copter when it crashed into the school pool."

I went over the details for her, as much as I could with any certainty. While having *quiche a la Rosemarie* my office called with additional info. There was another person piloting the plane; Josh was a passenger. Some kids saw a guy walk up to the shallow end of the pool, up the steps, and out the school gate. A few students heard him say over his shoulder: "Call SAMU 15. My friend seems to be hurt." Then he just walked down the street. Naturally, the kids were more excited about the man still in the wreckage but maybe one of them called the emergency number. None of the kids could supply a description of the man who walked out of the pool. They did say his long hair was soaked and he had a visor pulled down over his eyes. His jacket was observed to be of several different colors depending on which student you were asking. All agreed on one thing; he had a great pair of good army boots, the same kind many school boys love to wear. The key question is, why did he just walk away from the scene of the accident, leaving his injured passenger in the pool? Two men were checking airports for rental Horizons. Nothing. Then they went to the military Flight and Training School. Sure enough, there was one Horizon missing, taken out just that morning for a 'tuning up' exercise. The signature of the 'exerciser' was blurred, the identification number meaningless. Detectives were putting the crime into the KIDNAP column, with a footnote indicating an outright THEFT of government property.

Meanwhile, back at the hospital...

L.V.

I raced right over after my class. It had begun to drizzle. I guessed Rog was over giving Rosemarie an up-date. From what I gathered from nurse Eileen Taylor, nothing much is done while a person with a concussion is resting. The doctors here emphasize the definition of 'shaking violently resulting in brain injury.' Coma is the same in French and English. I should call Beau and Smith and see what the agency has to say about what the news now has called a bungled job. "Skyjacking Kills One." "School Children Endangered." "Well-Known Professor Involved." Several of the best newsmen and journalists of West France are on the case. "Missing Pilot Alleged Terrorist" led one afternoon paper. "Horizon A Failure." Two hours later that story was found to have been placed by the competitors for a French army helicopter-building government contract.

Beauchaine and Smith met me in La Roche Boulangerie, just around the corner from the hospital. It's a cute little place, frequented by pretty Filipino nurses. We three Josh fans told each other as much as we knew about the story and the injury. I couldn't help noticing Beau's great looking Calvin Klein trousers

363

while we were silent for a time, munching *croissants.*
While slurping hot *café-au-lait* we quite naturally
began to raise rhetorical questions concerning the
missing pilot. Beau left for the airport to get a copy of
the form the pilot is reported to have completed.
Maybe there are other signatures of that blurry style on
other flight-plan papers, credentials, etc. Hopefully
there will be a finger print or two. Smith called a
fellow agent to help Lemieux's men search the
neighborhood around the Ecole St-Exupery for
witnesses who may have heard shooting or seen
shooters. He excused himself and hailed a taxi to go
back to the crash site to look at the wreckage's bullet
holes. He really wanted to identify what kind of guns
were used. It began to rain hard.

"See you later, L.V. This is too bizarre."

"Yeah, I know. Like I'll be here near Prof. Good
luck. And remember Agent Smith, the palindrome of
the day: 'Nurses run.'"

Over the next three days Rosemarie and I took turns
with morning and afternoon sessions with Josh. Our
car went back to the U., and I used Josh's Avant. Each
day we sat next to the bed and quietly read the
newspaper to him. We played some of his favorite
arias and Debussy's Prelude to the Afternoon of a Faun.
Nurses and doctors talked to us about 'coma' and
'comatose.' Lemieux called every day. So did Leonid
Mabuti, Rosemarie's evening class student, who missed

a few classes since he crashed his motorcycle into a deer. An Algerian acquaintance of Josh's, a guy named Marami, called too, in his heavily accented French. Both these men were like very interested. I like thanked them for their concern, whoever they are. We also kept a joint journal so he can read it when he feels better. The constant downpour this past week has not done much to raise our spirits. It is really dark outside again today.

Beauchaine

During the week following the crash Smith and I were given the pleasant task of cooperating with the Avrille-Angers Commissariat, using Lemieux's new offices as our headquarters. Rosemarie insisted on setting us up at Boudreau where we can conveniently meet with Pierre, L.V. and of course, Chief Roger. Her evening program students came by and we discussed the hazards of motorcycle driving in rural Maine-et-Loire. It is evident they have great respect for Rosemarie and brought her several pounds of prepared mutton, a traditional Algerian gift for someone feeding many people. At least that is what Mabuti told them to do. Rosemarie had said she prefers mature sheep to young lambs for big dinners. Mabuti expresses sincere interest in Josh's condition but has not been around. He missed today's wonderful *blanquette de veau* dinner. Rosemarie placed the meat in the center of a large platter, surrounding the veal with veggies and rice. Pierre opened a couple of great white wines for this characteristic French meal. At Boudreau, of course, there is always fruit, cheese, chocolate mousse and coffee.

We grouped around the *entrée* fireplace and L.V. recited a palindrome in honor of Robert. This Operation Entrée custom is now considered our *l'habitude*, and has the force of habit, one way we respect our fallen Gagne comrades. As she tossed a white pill into her mouth: "Lonely Tylenol." A brief applause from the group brought on her signature hair toss and bow. "Like thank y'all. The reports to the group then began.

Smith is into tracing bullets and guns and had determined the guns used to shoot the copter down were very powerful Berretta hunting rifles, quite unlike the usual government issue. Hospitals and doctors' offices had been checked for info on a bearded guy in army boots. No leads there at all. The entire story of the missing Horizon and its crash at the school was supressed by the Army officials under the issue of 'secret national defense research,' making it impossible for the press to expose it. All the kids who saw the crash were disappointed when nothing was ever mentioned in their hometown papers. When they returned to school on Monday there was not a speck of copter debris to be found anywhere. The swimming team had regular practice in a normal St. Exupery school day. The airport attendant who apparently signed out the Horizon to Josh's pilot was found at *La*

Bravade holiday procession in St-Tropez. The local police reported he had been spending great sums of money. Smith had him brought back to Angers where he has said nothing about anything, so far. Pierre left for Angers where a friend in the flying school was to give him some investigative tips. He is very shaken by Josh's continuing condition.

That afternoon it was L.V.'s turn to visit Josh. She went to the Boudreau garage to see if Josh's Avant had gas enough to reach the hospital and back. As she passed the side of the house she was surprised to see a shiny Harley-Davidson parked there. She made a mental note to check with us later about that and roared out to the hospital. After all the dish-washing and kitchen-cleaning Rosemarie and I were about to lock up when Pierre returned, excited about the contents of his briefcase.

"Bonjour mademoiselles, ca va?

"Hi, Pierre," I said, "Sorry you missed a great dinner."

"I have eaten, thank you my dear Beau."

"So what's the big rush? And the official briefcase?" asked Rosemarie.

"I told you I was going to visit a friend, a co-worker. Well, not exactly a co-worker, that is, I serve

B. J. LUCIAN

him at my place of work and he helps by ordering
doubles. Today he has been very helpful. I called
Lemieux, he's on his way to hear this tip."

"What's a tip in your world Pierre?"

"My dear, a tip is something someone leaves on the
bar, a euro or two. But this tip I'm speaking of is an
'alert,' a 'cue,' or a 'tip-off.' In NYPD, a 'heads-up.'"

"Wow, our Parisian friend is an American
dictionary," I said,

"You are going to love it, both of you. And
Lemieux too," who just walked into Boudreau's Salle
de Grenade at that moment.

After a few minutes of *bavardage,* idle gossip and
chatter in French, Pierre reaches into the briefcase and
takes a seat.

"How does 15-16 February 2003 have a significant
Lac Bleu connection?' he began. "Anyone wish to
venture a good guess?"

We three were silent, staring at the ceiling, the
floor, out the window.

"Okay. I will tell you. On this day, it was a
Tuesday, the great Antwerp Diamond Center robbery
took place. Now, do you recall?"

"Right," said Lemieux. "I believe a Dutch woman and three Italian guys were arrested just a few days after the theft. Right?"

"Correct, monsieur Lemieux. It was the largest haul of gems ever stolen from Antwerp, which is, after all, the gem trading capital of the world. Since the 16th century, *n'est-ce pas?* The thieves actually completely emptied one-hundred and twenty-three different vaults. Must have taken them the better part of the night. And heavy to carry too."

"All those gems in one place?" asked Rosemarie.

"Yes, that's true," responded Lemieux. "For generations dozens of gem trading companies have used that one facility. After all, it is, or was, recognized as a most secure place. The numerous companies are all established in the basement of a well-known heavily guarded Antwerp building. Diamond cutters and dealers store their stuff in the ADC."

"Yes, and besides live guards around the clock there were many alarms and cameras. Special passes were needed to enter. The motto of the Antwerp Diamond Center was something like 'Security is our strong point.'"

"Didn't the High Diamond Council give some publicity to the charge that it was an inside job?" asked Roger.

"Yeah, most everyone agrees now it was an inside job. But the four suspects have said nothing," Pierre said, smiling.

"Why are you smiling? asked Rosemarie.

"Because now I get to the 'tip'"

"What's the tip, Pierre? Come on, you have our interest," I urged.

"Okay, this is the big alert to us from my colleague and friend," Pierre replied, now openly laughing. "My friend believes the 2003 Antwerp heist is now hidden in Lac Bleu!"

We were stunned for a few seconds. Then all three of us seemed to shout simultaneously, "But that was blown up."

"Well, we know diamonds rained down on the crowd that day. That was one container, one small part of the total Antwerp loot. The explosion was meant to give the suggestion everything was destroyed or lost. No use looking for diamonds there. All gone. But, my friends, the main cache is still in place, as are most of the explosives. The big Sunday rally explosion gave the impression there is nothing left. But nowadays it is safely intact, surrounded and guarded in Lac Bleu by the army. And the insiders can get any gems out any time they choose. Under government protection."

"This is a masterfull cover-up, a scheme of monstrous proportions, if this is true," I said.

"Oh, it's true, Beau. The amount stolen is estimated to be in the millions of euros. So they spread a few hundred thousand around the grass in that spectacular Sunday show. The small amount the thieves planned to lose in their explosion that day exemplifies the adage, 'You have to spend money to make money.' *N'est-ce pas?*"

"I suppose it would be useless to question your tipper for additional details. Has he any tangible proof?"

"I was waiting for that, *mon commissaire*. I have here an estimate of what each company lost, losses which their insurers are hoping can be recovered. The insurers know full well the Lac explosion did not destroy the entire lot. The insurance companies, it is said, have employed private investigators to work along with their own company people. The hiring of special detectives for a covert mission of this magnitude tells me loud and clear the jewels are still in our blessed little lake."

"Are you saying, Pierre, that the army is in on the cover-up?" asked Rosemarie.

"I suppose a few of the key officers are, my dear. They had walls and electric fences built. They most likely have an inventory to present to the committee working for the National Assembly. That will further dampen any doubts about Lac Bleu being a danger to Avrille. The fake inventory will undoubtedly show only a few grenades, for example, within the new protected strong-wall system. *Aucun riske* has come true. There is no danger anymore to anyone. The lake has become a diamond vault guarded by the army. *Finis!*"

.

"Okay, finis for the moment," said Lemieux. "But what you said about investigators interests me, Pierre. If the insurers are convinced their insured gems are being guarded in the lake and they hire spies to uncover information about that, that means our town will have strangers skulking about, looking under every rock. After all Boulanger Camp is heavily guarded by sincere young soldiers who won't know they are working for a multi-million-euro gang of thieves. What will a so-called private investigator do around here if what you say is so well covered up? And by the way, L.V. taught me the word skulking."

"You are right," I said, enjoying Roger's serious study of English. "A skulker goes about stealthily spying in a secretive manner. All Roger has to do is like pick up all skulkers for questioning, thus exposing their skulkiness."

"I will give you these papers, Roger. You have a safe in your office, *n'est-ce pas?*"

"If this is true, Pierre, you will be the hero of The Gem Lake Story, soon to be a best-seller and a movie. Yes, I will place them in our new safe in the *commissariat.* I'm sure we will all be very grateful for this 'heads-up.'"

"I'm sure Smith too will be thrilled with Pierre's breakthrough. But I'm also sure the Sûreté will want to eventually talk to your colleague, Pierre," I said, giving him a grateful hug.

"I will never be able to do that, you know, Beau. I had to give him my word. So my saying anything further about my source is not an issue here. That is closed. *Finis.*"

Pierre was congratulated by Roger and Rosemarie. We agreed to meet back at Boudreau the next afternoon.

L.V.

When I took my place beside Josh I held his hand and whispered his name. I said the Hail Mary slowly, and close to his ear. There was no movement or signal of any kind from him. After one decade of the Rosary I walked around the room for a minute and a doctor, on entering, noticed my tears. I pretended to be looking out the window. We both said "hi."

"I believe I'm seen you here before. You are the professor's student?"

"Yes, sir, former student. I graduated three years ago. He taught me psychology."

"The professor is fortunate to have a devoted, grateful student. You must be very good friends."

In the meantime he was adjusting things here and there above Josh's head. We both stared at the heart blips. He has an English accent; perhaps London educated.

"What do you think, Doc? Will he be okay soon?"

"Well, as you know Miss Campbell, we never really do know for certain in cases like this?"

"Like this?" I said sadly.

"Yes, you see concussion of the brain, that is, injury to the brain from a blow to the head, is not completely understood by medical science. We know increased brainstem pressure causes some suspension of respiration and the reduced pulse rate that follows a concussion. Other symptoms include the pallor you see on the professor here."

"When he comes out of it, as he will, what then?"

"Aftereffects such as dizziness, headaches and nervousness may last for a time. Maybe amnesia and some loss of memory may result. Recovery from a concussion is usually complete, especially when prompt assistance was available."

"Was 'prompt assistance' available to the prof?"

"That's what I understand, miss, and that is all to the good for the professor. The brain cannot be very long without oxygen."

We then went on to discuss coma in general, that state of unconsciousness in which a person does not respond to external stimuli. Respirators are used when patients lose the power to breath normally. Comas have been known to last for long periods of time.

"I read about Karen Quinlan and the right to 'die with dignity.' Fortunately Karen did live. Because of that case wasn't there some kind of legal precedent set?"

"Right, you have done your homework. When there is no electrical activity in the brain cortex the life support respirator may legally be removed."

At this he gestured toward Josh. We both looked up at the TV-like screen above Josh's head. There seemed to me to be plenty of electrical activity. Josh is a long way from being brain dead. Then he said.

"It is common for most people and hospitals to consider that the irreversible loss of brain activity is the sign that death has occurred."

"Emphasis on 'irreversible,' right?"

"Right, miss. Does the professor have a Living Will? Would you know that?"

"Yes, he has. I have a copy of it right here in my bag. We had a copy made of the original in Boudreau."

"Boudreau?"

"Yes, like that's the name of his residence. Boudreau."

"May I see the paper please?"

I handed him the paper, noting his name tag, 'G.E. Jones, Internal Medicine.'.

"I say, he does have it all organized. This Living Will written in Tennessee and signed by him, states, and I quote:

If at any time I should have a terminal condition and my attending physician has determined that there can be no recovery from such condition and my death is imminent, where the application of life-prolonging procedures would serve only to artificially prolong the dying process, I direct that such procedures be withheld or withdrawn, and that I be permitted to die naturally with only the administration of medications or the performance of any medical procedure deemed necessary to provide me with comfortable care or to alleviate pain.

Well, that's the lot miss. Your professor covered all the necessary aspects of death and dying. The staff seem to know him, or at least they know about him. A very special fellow they say."

"He's one great man, doctor. We all love him."

He took my hand, gave me the Will, and stepped back. "I must be continuing on my rounds miss. I wish you and him," nodding at Josh, "all the very best, you know." He walked out very deliberately, with a slight favoring of the right leg.

I went back to whisper to Josh, like, 'Let's go prof, it's time we hauled ass out of here, we need you, what's a little bump anyway, you're okay, *andiamo, allons y.'* Then I said another Hail Mary.

I thought I saw an eye lid flicker but the brainy tv didn't register anything new or different. A nurse came in.

"How long have you been here miss. I would have brought you a coffee if I had known. Do you wish something now?"

"No I'm alright thank you Miss Oglevie. I had a fine talk with Dr. Jones. He helped me a lot."

"Dr. Jones?"

"Yeah, the good looking limpy-gimpy guy. Internal Medicine. Like he sounds English."

"We have no Jones on staff."

"You sure?"

"Positive. My roster at the central desk has no Dr. Jones. Maybe he was a family friend on his lunch hour. That sometimes happens. I see he entered nothing on the professor's chart."

"Yeah, thanks."

She checked a few things around the bed and left. I sat back down, took Josh's hand, and cried.

**Who pities a snake charmer when he is bitten,
or anyone who goes near a wild beast?**
SIRACH 12:13

PART VII

L.V.

The next day I drove in again, in the morning. Rosemarie was due to arrive after her afternoon seminar. There was the usual hospital hustle and bustle, sort of a quiet efficiency coupled with quick soft-footed maneuvers. Nurses learn to walk a certain way as if on thick-padded carpets, like the old style nuns. One minute they are there and the next minute they appear two doors down. It was like that when nurse Taylor came in to check the drip and smooth the bed and read the chart and offer the coffee and take the temperature and display the smile and whisk out the door, all in one smooth coordinated move.

I took up my position next to the bed and began to read the sports page to Prof Josh. The first page had a good article on European Soccer At Its Best In The Blues. I jumped when I heard a voice over my shoulder.

"Good morning Miss Campbell."

"Yikes, Doc, like you always scare people that way? Anyway, yeah, good morning sir."

"How's the patient today?"

"Maybe you should tell me."

"Okay, let's see."

"He read the chart at a glance. Then he lifted Josh's eye lids and flashed a light in his eyes. He took pulse and heart beat and blood pressure. He put both hands very gently on each side of Josh's head and leaned over him, almost touching forehead to forehead. He was very intense, concentrated.

"Professor," he said very softly, "Miss Campbell is here to bring you up to date on the Blues. Would you like that, prof?"

It seemed as if he was observing Josh's brain waves through his skull. He forgot to write anything on the chart.

"Anyway," he continued whispering to prof, "you have rested enough now and it's okay if you want to wake up and discuss the Blues. Whatever you think. Whenever you're ready, professor."

Doc Jones straightened up, walked around the room for a couple of turns, then looked at me.

"Keep reading quietly into his ear. He likes it and will soon respond. I think this morning he will be hungry. I will pass by the Nurses' Station and order him a big breakfast which you can encourage him to eat. You should eat too. Goodbye now Miss Campbell."

I thanked him as he walked out the door towards the nurses. Like great bedside manners, I thought. I went back to reading the paper, in the controlled whisper he had used.

The hospital chaplain came in. We talked about prof. The priest read a few prayers for the sick. He blessed prof, made the sign of the cross on prof's forehead, and smiled at me.

"All the best to you too miss," he said in French.

"Merci mon pere."

He was gone too. Back to reading.

"I'm pretty hungry, L.V."

I dropped the paper, leaped up, knocking over the chair, and grabbed the buzzer. I gave it several long buzzes.

"Prof, my God, Prof you are going to be okay. Oh God."

I was leaning over him, hugging him around the neck, when the nurse came running in shouting, *"Arret, arret, tu fais mal!* Stop, you're hurting him."

"He's okay, Prof's okay," I yelled.

He had a silly grin, shrugged, made a sound like 'phew.'

Two other nurses came rushing in, took all the vital signs Doc Jones had done, wrote them down, told Josh to rest easy, not to move. An attendant came in with some broth and crackers, and a soft-boiled egg on toast. While the nurses all talked at the same time one began to feed him a little soup. I ran into the hallway with my Nextel and left a message for Rosemarie. Then I asked Roger to please call the others. Rog said:

"I knew he would come back to us if you were there to receive him, L.V."

Of course I cried again like only for a minute with him on the phone. When I returned to the room Josh was joking with the nurses, slurping soup and asking for some real food. His doctor was there reading the chart the nurses had just written. Then he asked Josh some silly questions to test his memory. After a few minutes of that Josh said:

"I remember we crashed into that school's swimming pool. And now I'm here eating. That's it. Nothing between the crash and this minute. But I feel fine, thank you. Curious, but fine."

The hospital doc explained what had happened since the crash, told him about concussions and comas, how he should go easy for a few days, how fortunate he was. After a few questions from Josh the doc told him he would probably recover totally. Everyone in the room was smiling. It was a wonderful Josh moment.

Nurse Taylor asked what he meant by 'curious but fine.'

"I mean how is Ahmed, the pilot? Why were we fired upon? By whom?"

When Pierre arrived, a few minutes before Beau and Smith, the doc said Josh could sit up in bed. There was a lot of French hugging and hand-shaking. Josh attributed his being awake to my ministrations. I told them I just happened to be there when he awakened naturally, having slept for a few days. Beau said it was my constant urging that brought him out of the coma. They congratulated me. I was embarrassed, wishing Roger was there. Josh, always the prof, suggested we bring the Sûreté up to date. Pierre did not have to be coaxed to explain again about the Antwerp heist. He emphasized that the gems are *probablement* in the lake.

"That could explain the shooting. You may have been hovering over the spot where millions of gems are resting," explained Smith. "Anyway, we have questioned dozens of folks who live in the area and could not find a living soul who heard or saw anything.

Of couse the army base is completely deaf, dumb and blind."

"So where in the pilot?" asked Josh. Everyone looked at Smith. "We have no idea."

"Well, let's see here," offered Beau. "This Ahmed Ben Bella, a covert agent for numerous entities, a loyal Harki Algerian, has many names as we know. He is Leonid Mabuti, intrepid graduate student of Rosemarie. He was George LaBlanc as a *démineur*. We have seen those three pictures in Lemieux's office. No resemblance at all to each other. When you set them side by side you see three totally dissimilar faces. And three reported accents and mannerisms. And according to our agents he was badly injured in the copter crash. But no Angers doctor or hospital has seen him. And the guy who signed out the Horizon machine knows nothing."

"I think I have a fourth persona. During my bedside stints a Dr. G.E. Jones, Internal Medicine, came in twice," I said.

I went on to tell them as much about this guy as I could put into words. I mentioned the slight limp, the English accent, his wonderful bedside manners, his knowledge of the case. We called the Nurses' Station and again no record of a Dr. G.E. Jones. Smith searched the hospital phone book and the Angers area M.D. internet list on the Nurses' Station computer.

This confirmed that there is no such medical doctor. When Rosemarie arrived she said Mabuti missed one class last week but tonight he was in the seminar and presented an outstanding paper to the class.

"And that mortorcycle you saw at the side of Boudreau, L.V. It is not there now," added Rosemarie.

Nurse Taylor came in to tell us visiting hours are over. We all left amidst more hand-shaking and hugging. Josh crawled back into his newly made bed. Taylor assured us the doctor would sign his release if he promises not to exert himself at all for several days. After the group entered the corridor to discuss what restaurant we were now going to, I slipped back into the room, signaled the nurse "two seconds." She waited patiently as I whispered to Josh, "I didn't get a chance to finish the story. The Blues won."

As I left the room I heard him explaining to the nurse how significant that international soccer-football news is to him. They both laughed. In the meantime the group decided we would meet at *Restaurant La Ferme,* at *Place* Freppel, described as hectic-frenetic and outdoors-rustic. Beau and Smith swore by the Ferme *coq-au-vin.* Rosemarie had heard their white Anjou wine is remarkable. We were in a most joyful mood. I told Lemieux we'd be waiting for him there. He said he'd try to join us. I sort of like knew he would do that. Despite the torrential rain.

In the parking lot Beau decided to come with me in Josh's Avant. As we pulled out she said, "What, no appropriate palindrome?"

"Oh yeah, like thanks for reminding me Beau. I'm having the Bird Rib."

Prof Josh

I spent the next few days in the Colbert. It was a nice change to experience Paris again. My Colbert suite has always been another home to me. Pierre has become a most meticulous hotel manager-director. The place is spotless and the help is superb. As in all of France, the rooms are smaller than some Stateside hotel rooms. But the service is always extraordinary.

Many of our old friends came to visit my Suite 84-A. I tried to keep my promise to the doctors and curtailed my social activities, took naps, and walked slowly. One day a very old lady who told Pierre she was an old school chum of one of my aunts was admitted to the suite. She was a sprightly old doll, smelled of too much Cashmere Bouquet floral fragrance, and liked my vodka. After twenty minutes of airing our mutual geneology and sipping Absolute, she began to laugh and smile. My 'old Aunt' was Ahmed Ben Bella.

I called Pierre in to meet the disappearing copter pilot. Ahmed removed his wig and he and Pierre began to exchange war stories about Algerian independence. I was happy to see them enjoying each other's company but I had to break into the dialogue for a simple question.

"Where in the hell did you go when we landed in the pool, my friend?"

"That's why I came to talk to you, professor. I am glad your long-time *ami, monsieur le director LeGrand* is here. You, sir, should know what the professor has been through. I am not sure he will remember the details so I will attempt to acquaint you with how your long-time friend behaves when under pressure. But first I apologize for dressing this way. I am being followed by an Algerian or two. We will have to continue my being an Aunt for a few more days. I have let it be known on the street that you, professor, are very near death and that as your Aunt I am here to make family funeral arrangements with Pierre. It would be well, *monsieur le director,* to alert your Avrille-Angers friends to what we will now talk about. *D'accord?"*

"Yes, okay, Ahmed, explain away. We have questions for you, as you probably expect."

"Yes, professor, and thank you for your gracious patience. Your little Lac Bleu is still the center of events, as you shall see."

Ahmed then took on an un-Aunt-like attitude. We sipped café au lait, an occasional drop of kir, and ice water, (for me).

"The professor is a, uh, I think you say, cool customer. He kept his head while I demonstrated the ability of the Horizon to perform some tricky maneuvers over Angers and Avrille. We were about ready to return to the Angers private airport when we suddenly took lots of rifle fire. Prof did not panic. The shooting was a complete surprise to me; I had thought the hot-heads guarding the lake were under the control of the military. Apparently the military has lost control under pressure from higher government authority or from a very powerful and influential entity of some kind. Anyway, they blasted away at us, an unhappy sitting duck. Our little copter was decorated with many holes. Luckily we both remained conscious even after being hit. We plopped rather heavily into the school pool. Prof here kept me from falling out of my seat after being hit several times. I cringed and crumpled and bled dreadfully but stayed awake long enough to see that prof too was bleeding. I knew, as usual, that my services for good would be abruptly ended if the authorities brought me in. I made sure prof was not mortally wounded, slipped out of the pool, told some boys to call SAMU, and quickly managed to contact my covert Interpol medical station."

"I would not have appreciated being abandoned there like that, Ahmed, if I had known I was left in the wreckage. But I know you have the bigger picture in mind, understanding more than all of us the intrigue and danger of the entire Lac Bleu situation."

"Were you submitted to the *procés-verbal?*" Pierre asked me.

"Yes, but questioned very leniently. After all, the local *gendarmerie* knows me quite well by now." I glanced at Ahmed.

"They know me too, but they don't know they know me," Ahmed added, smiling.

"So what's next?" asked Pierre. "You two guys are on the mend, thanks be to God. But there are millions of euros in diamonds in the lake, buried with the old ordnance. The lake is now totally flooded, the main streets of the base and the town are under several feet of water. The gem-consortium, or whatever the thieves have established, is committed to killing anyone who comes near the lake's diamond cache, no questions asked."

Ahmed smiled and looked from me to Pierre and back to me.

"You know, professor, your old buddy here really has a spy's incisive mind. Pierre, the thieves who successfully emptied the diamond center of its treasures are sophisticated professionals who know how to organize multi-national financial operations. The actual diamond robbery in Antwerp is part of a gigantic conspiracy to sell the lot to the highest bidder. Right now, on the illegal but so-called 'open market,' there are national groups in several nations bidding and haggling over prices, payoffs, transportation, delivery, products available, etcetera. In the meantime the goods for sale are being guarded most assiduously, as we have experienced."

"Is it possible," I asked, "that our circling over the lake was a threat to the security of the hidden cache. They became so nervous they just opened fire? Now they can claim that the copter posed a danger to the school so they acted to protect the childen from danger. The pilot escaped and his colleague is officially out of his mind. So case closed. The diamond protectors come off as an alert security force for which the school headmaster is now very grateful. How does that sound?"

"Like the morning papers, *mon ami*. I think you are interpreting the day's editorials, *n'est-ce pas?*"

"Right Pierre. I did have time to scan the Avrille news reports."

"But the luck of our conspirators may be running out," said Ahmed. "This flooding is calling attention to the lake, attention the conspiracy definitely does not want."

He paused, sipped coffee and looked at Pierre.

"Would you be willing to come with me to get a close look at the base debris? Prof must still rest for some time yet. I know of your exploits and prof vouches for your skills. How about it, monsieur?"

"I would be willing to continue to help Josh in his search for answers to the basic Lac Bleu controversy if I knew more about the entire situation. You must admit Josh that when we began we did not consider meeting up with bad-mannered international jewel thieves, kidnapping, death and destruction."

"You're right of course, Pierre," I said. "It has become somewhat more dangerous, many times more complicated. I'm not at all sure what the jewel heist has to do with the world situation, except that there are millions of dollars or euros at stake. There are too many aspects of demining and Lac Bleu that I still don't understand. But I am excited, by darns, to find out. You and me Pierre, *la stupeur et la stupide.*"

"Wonderful," shouted Ahmed. "You two have the brains and brawn of trained CIA agents. The bravery, willingness, togetherness—all there. Let's talk more about the Lac situation."

Ahmed did talk. He was sincerely interested in sharing his views. He spoke quietly for about thirty

393

minutes with barely a pause. I felt he was taking us completely into his confidence. Before he finished he had made a believer out of me.

"When the world first heard of Lac Bleu of Avrille, near Angers, it was considered a local problem. It consisted of citizens getting together for a Sunday afternoon protest of polite proportions. Then politicians came into view and experts appeared on both sides. Bullhorns, soap-box harangues, lawn chairs and divers showed up. An energetic group with the acronym CACTUS organized the populace. The Maine-et-Loire Minister of Ecology killed himself. Anti-pollution groups, such as the quiet but influential *genistas,* worked to clean up demining stock piles. Did the sunken munitions propose a great risk to the community? Was the government really responsible for many years of neglect and indiffernce? Were there really tons of unexploded munitions stored too close to private homes? The debates in the press emphasized two expressions. The people said things like *un vrais scandale qu'on laisse des armes dormir.* Government spokesmen replied *aucun danger tant qui'il y a de l'eau.* The lake is a scandal, but there is no danger.

"The National Assembly refused at first to consider gathering demining data. Then an Assembly woman was kidnapped and threatened so she would drop further efforts at official government demining data-gathering. A diver found a gem. People were shot and jailed, the munitions blew up, little Avrille was on

CNN. And so was Antwerp. These days they are on together, a typical tiny French town and the diamond center of the world share newscasts.

"From Cambodia to Albania there are brave citizens risking their lives to clear their countries of land mines. Will France, Europe's battle ground, ever be free of unexploded left-overs from its wars? Some countries are beginning to cooperate with men and technology, engineers are teaching mine detection. Some monies are forthcoming. But it will be years before the earth will be free. And now comes a new phase of an ongoing disaster—hiding stolen diamonds in the demining storage sites. What a genious mind-exercise that is!"

Ahmed excused himself to visit the WC. Pierre walked to the window and looked out over Place de Notre Dame des Victoires. I slowly moved toward the fridge to begin testing my new supply of Chablis. I put fresh glasses and two cheeses on the coffee table. It was a very quiet and thoughtful five minutes, a rare experience when Pierre and I are in the same room.

Ahmed returned. "Any questions, gentlemen?"

"Assuming the Antwerp gems are actually in Lac Bleu," I asked, "what does the consortium intend to do with them? Will they just keep them closely guarded until news reporters and law men finally forget about them? Or do they need to be moved soon? What's a reasonable time schedule?"

"Typical question from a French student of American culture," laughed Ahmed. "A time schedule!"

"Sorry, I'm just wondering if we are in a hurry to act. Call in the marines today or infiltrate by marrying into their families over the years?"

"I had an opinion before this flood began, professor. Now I'm not sure. It is of the utmost importance for the consortium to discover what the changing conditions will mean for the loot. No doubt they will have to send divers down now, under cover of military secrecy, and ascertain the stability of their treasure. They may need to remove them to a safer place, another demining site, for example, since they seem to have infiltrated the *Département du Déminage.* Rival thieves will certainly be wary of raiding another site after seeing what happened at Lac Bleu's explosion. Maybe a demining site is the safest hiding place one can find nowadays.

"Do we have any idea how the stuff is bought or sold?" asked Pierre.

"Interpol and other governments' agencies seem to feel we are talking about diamonds for arms. Gems will be exchanged for munitions, perhaps, or the diamonds will be laundered into US dollars for purchase of a whole directory of current military hardware."

"Who buys and sells such stuff legally these days?" I said. "Who are the big arms makers?"

"Information of that type is on everyone's internet, easily accessible. In 2000 international arms sales hit the 40 billion dollar mark. Stats on hand? Sure, in the Congressional Research Service. Also, the Library of Congress. It figures, you know. The U.S. is the world's biggest arms dealer."

"So it's possible that these gems will end up paying for arms made in the U S of A?" said Pierre.

"Correct sir. U.S. sales accounts for about one-half of all weapons sales. Two other big dealers are, of course, France and Russia. Russia's biggest customers? India and China, also Iran, Iraq, South Korea. What are they buying? Whatever they want. Aircraft, tanks, SAM missiles."

"Does the U.S. sell much to Israel?

Definitely. And helicopters to Singapore. Germany, Britain and Italy also sell to countries developing their military hardware. And remember, any small nation with money or diamonds can sponsor small warlord munition supplies, in Africa, Asia, the Balkans. Don't forget Pakistan has had to keep up with its neighbors too. And the rivalry never ends. The richest companies in the world are the munition makers. But sometimes we have to say we know nothing about arms sales. Government security and secrecy, you know."

"And Lac Bleu and the deminers are involved, one way or another?"

"Right, my friend." Then he put his glass down, wrote a phone number on a paper napkin. "In case you really get lonesome," he said, handing me the cocktail napkin. "I hope to visit you again in a few days, maybe next week. Thank you for your hospitality, professor. Continue to improve, in mind and body," he said smiling. "Personally, informally, I think the Lac explosion was completely accidental. Amen."

He flipped on his wig, adjusted some of his garments, took a deep breathe and became an old lady, struggling to shuffle out the door and down the hall. We watched him from the window. On the curb he tripped slightly, caught himself, used the cane. Amazing sight, worthy of a *Palme d'Or* or even an Oscar.

Each day I walked a little further and slightly faster. My headaches had ceased and thus I became bold enough to resume my lifetime habit of walking a couple of miles each day. One afternoon I drove to the *Musée d'Orsay,* found a good parking place, and went straightaway to the escalator. I had decided to spend some time in the beautifully lit middle level where one of my very favorite Rodin's is gloriously displayed. The world knows the d'Orsay contains the most astonishing collection of impressionist art on its upper level. For many years now when strolling the museums of Paris I plan my walk ahead of time so that I am not distracted from my pre-selected art work for that day. I have strolled the impressionists several days for many miles lately. This day Rodin beckoned. So after a *plat du jour, sans dessert,* in the excellent d'Orsay restaurant, I proceeded past Gauguin's Breton belle and Toulouse-Lautrec's Jane Avril, to the end of the Lille Terrace where Rodin's incomparable cast Gate of Hell occupies the hall's anchor spot.

Here is a place to reflect and meditate. The wooden bench helps. In this magnificent Gate casting Rodin included two famous works he had already completed to rave reviews, The Thinker and The Kiss. I was resting comfortably, going over in my mind some of the Lac Bleu connections Ahmed had talked about. The Gate end of the hall was free of chattering school groups. The rest period, though, was ended when two large swarthy dudes found my bench and sat, one on each side of me. The bench was at once crowded with our three pairs of wide hips. I was instantly on the alert. Pickpockets? Tired Rodin fans? Art critics?

None of the above.

"Professor, you will come with us. Now sir."

The garlic-laden breath got my attention before I felt a prodding into the left and right rib cages. They arose; their crushing closeness was enough to carry me right along with my feet off the ground. The guy on my right held tightly to my elbow. The one on the left had his hand on his gun. In this formation we made our way back past Jane Avril, toward the escalator. Between Jane and Breton belle I stomped very hard on the shin-foot region of the guy on my right. For an instant he staggered. I grabbed his gun, shoved him down, spun around with my left fingers in the other guy's eyes. The first guy was struggling to stand when a kick in his face sent him sprawling. Knowing these guys could easily take me in a fair fight, I dashed for a hiding place among the many recessed niches. As I fled past Henri Rousseau's *La guerre,* I stumbled over a body. It was a museum guard, his body curled up or stuffed behind a marble pedestal. I ran on, looking for a similar temporary hiding place. I could hear running feet behind me, loud in the empty hall. Then the firing began. They really wanted to get me, one way or another, *immediatement.* I was running down the Seine Terrace, back toward the Gate when I saw the recessed area devoted to Homer Winslow. I decided to duck in there, and hide behind a statue of St. Michael slaying a dragon. The guy whose eyes were poked had dropped out of the race and stayed back near Jane Avril, cursing in Algerian accented French. The one I kicked twice was firing as he ran at me, holding his gun in both hands extended arms-length out in front. Shooting on the dead-run, so to speak, is difficult. He shot the arm off Michael. The flying arm smacked me in the head. I fell to my knees, dizzy and confused. As the shooter came rushing up I grabbed St. Michael's copper arm, wound up and winged it side-arm. It hit him in the forehead. He staggered and fell face down at the statue's feet. I stood up and looked for the other swarthy. He was just leaping off the down escalator and making for the entrance with museum guards trailing, side arms drawn. I wiped off the gun I had been holding and dropped it near the copper arm. Then I walked back over to the Rodin Gate of Hell and resumed my seat. In a minute three guards came dashing up, guns out. They asked me if I had heard any shooting. I waited until they asked me twice more, shouting now. I nodded 'no' and returned to my *Musée Pocket Guide*. One guard stayed with me as the others ran towards St. Michael's statue, yelling into their phones. The guard who sat with me, panting noisily, explained that there had been some disturbance but the danger is over now. Again I nodded pleasantly, went up close to the Rodin, and examined it carefully with my pocket magnifying glass in one hand, official guide in the other. After a few minutes the guard sort of waddled and toddled off. Nice man, very polite. He turned, weaving, and said, *"Bon jour, monsieur."*

I was seated once again when another guard told me I would have to exit the museum. As he was directing me to a little-used exit from middle level to first floor a public announcement informed us the museum is closing early today. There were many gendarmes now in the lobby, ambulance people on the escalators, museum visitors getting their money back from a nervous museum administrator.

It occurred to me that guard service companies must hire a high percentage of overweight people compared to other occupations. Of course, this is especially true in the States. How often have you seen guards, in stores, public athletic events, banks, and casinos, in the States as well as in Europe, who could not run ten yards. Guard services are humane companies that give huge eaters the opportunity to earn money while dressed in unique tight-fitting uniforms. "Guard Pride" is their motto. Inaction is their creed. They observe people in between naps. They have time to read the paper each day. They guard.

The next day Operation Entrée met in a conference telephone call on the speaker-phone. Lemieux, Beau and Smith, with Pierre and me at our end. I reviewed the d'Orsay day.

"This is Smith, prof. We have determined the two guys who came after you are the Harki Algerians who first surfaced at the CACTUS picnic-explosion. They are being held on charges of 'disturbing the peace in a public place.' They are Marami's men, the guy who said he was CIA trained. Beau remembers their names."

"Alque and Bernudo, prof. They seem to have gone over to the services of the highest bidder, in this case, the gem movers and shakers of Lac Bleu fame. They'll be talking in jail but the simple charges of 'disturbance' will protect them from the anger of their bosses. No one has come to claim them; no visitors so far. Anyway, they are out of circulation for a while."

"Lemieux *professeur, comment ca va? Très bien j'espere!*"

"Thanks to y'all for being available together," I said, truly grateful to hear their enthusiastic voices again. "I'm doing okay and, according to my doctor, will be completely recovered soon."

"According to your Paris *gendarmarie p.v.*, your pitching arm remains in good condition," from Lemieux.

"*Oh oui,* he's fine," Pierre. "What can you tell us about the flood?"

"It is another Lac Bleu calamitous event," from Lemieux, who managed the 'calamitous' quite well, considering he probably just heard it from L.V. Then he added. "According to L.V. the Lac demining site is a physical and moral washout. This is a pun, no?"

"Yes, thanks Rog" I said, over the giggles from the listeners. "What's the condition of Camp Boulanger today? The Paris papers have little coverage these days."

"According to my informants and my officers who cruise about the area constantly, flooding has now reached many Avrille homes. Evacuations have begun. Army men and boats are helping. The high waters are not receding yet. There is much property destruction. The Camp is rather open now because of the arrival of many small pontoon boats, many of which have been assigned to Avrille citizens. More rain is forecast."

"Officially," Beauchaine, "the *Départment du Déminage* is reporting floating debris from the lake. Some grenades, shell casings, and wooden crates are surfacing, increasing danger to the lives of Avrillais. Deminers are working overtime, gathering as much of the junk as possible and assembling piles in a new site beyond the flooded area. From there Department trucks are taking it away to other undisclosed sites. Life is very exciting these days in ol' Avrille. Beauchaine out."

"I remember," Pierre said, "when government officials said there is no danger to the citizens as long as the munitions remain covered with water. Okay, now they are definitely covered with water. There is still danger?"

"Yes." This from Smith. "There is danger because no one knows how many of the total unexploded shells actually blew up recently. There could still be enough down there to explode again, causing an even larger catastrophe. We need more info on what the lake looks like now, today. We need an inventory. The deminers are occupied removing ordnance, creating another collection site. But in the meantime, while deminers are doing their jobs as usual, the lake is undergoing what environmentalists call Pollution Stress. That is, the lake waters have been disturbed first by the explosion, now by rushing flood waters. The contents of the lake, if there are any ordnance 'contents' still down there, are most likely in unpredictable topsy-turvy condition, being tossed around in mud, in impenetrable darkness, bouncing off rocky edges, against each other. Diving is impossible. Much of their technical equipment has been damaged. What a mess."

"What if the jewels are in a container that could float?" I suggested. "Wouldn't that be worrying the thieves? What if they are in a container that will never float to the surface but that could be bounced about in the turbulance? Don't you think there are representatives of the Antwerp dudes watching that lake surface twenty-four hours?"

Lemieux coughed, begged pardon, and broke in.

"I will keep you informed about the Lac Bleu events. You know how to reach me. But I think we should give some thought to the Harki *types, les méchants, no?* Why are they continuing to harass prof Josh?"

"Right, we need to address that," Beau and Smith together. "The Algerians are in the arms race, as are dozens of nations. The intelligence organizations of each of these nations feel that prof Josh has a lot to say about what happens to the jewels."

"Remember, the reason they took him and others to the Maginot Line last month was to find out where the jewels were. They were convinced he knew. After the explosion they still suspect him because underground intelligence still thinks Boney knew all about gems and Lac Bleu. The same is true of Mitchel Joseph. His technology would have assisted the anti-pollution Avrillais. Now, of course, all the arms merchants know about the gems on the open market, the deals being made to arm each other, helicopters or surface to air missiles, buyers and sellers—they know about us, all of us in Operation Entrée."

"So we are putting Josh under twenty-four hour guard from now on. That means prof, one Sûreté is with you At All Times. Pierre, that means the Colbert Suite now houses two men, prof and an agent. Prof, I'm repeating, At All Times."

"Okay." I said, reluctantly. "I hope the guards like Paris museums."

Pierre

On the advice of all his friends Josh decided to spend a week or so at the Ma in Aix-en-Provence. His two guards, known to us as Tim and Ter, were very understanding, intelligent, and vigilant. We never talked to them together since one of them was always sleeping. This did curtail much of our after-kir loud story telling but in general we were a pleasant group. Rita promised to visit us in a few days.

The villagers became used to the jovial gentlemen from "the professor's mas," who strolled about, shopping for antiques, sitting for coffee, foraging through the weekly outdoor market. A few of the more alert elderly ladies began to suggest dinner menus, explaining that they just happened to have the exact item needed to complete a most marvelous meal. We slowly picked up on local phrases, but mostly we all spoke French. Tim and Ter knew a few words and understood most of what they heard. We jogged, played card games, watched American and Italian movies, listened to classical music and read history on rainy days. Ter was the *petanque* champion.

In fact it was during a particularly close bowling session that Rita arrived at Ma. She had rented a CV 2 also and brought many cheeses, along with mail for us Colbert residents. From several shopping bags she unloaded the elements of her special rice salad. While she and Tim put together her luncheon masterpiece Josh served two white wines and several cheese and cracker combinations for the 'hired help,' as the Sûreté men referred to themselves.

Rita's Salade Extraordinaire was a tossed mélange of rice, tuna, hard-boiled eggs, black olives, cubed bits of Swiss cheese, *cornichons,* American gherkin pickles, capers, tomatoes, anchovies, green peppers, and French mustard vinaigrette. Ter had her identify each ingredient but she said the secret was in the mixing and in her 'added stuff' which she could not devulge and Tim did not see. Amidst compliments from all, Rita blushed, accepted victory, and went for a walk along the shaded forest path. I went with her to be sure she would not contaminate the sacred killer-dragon arena. Josh and Ter were on luncheon clean-up. I promised to perform miracles with the Ratatouille Dinner I had planned.

However, when Rita and I returned Ma was empty. The three guys were nowhere to be found around the house.

"Probably walking off the wonderful lunch," I said, hopefully. Our rentals were all still in the driveway.

"I'll unpack and take a short siesta," Rita said.

"Okay, I'll read here. There is a new John Le Carré I want to start. *A bientot.*"

I guess I dozed for a while. When I awoke the house was still quite empty. Rita was knitting on the patio.

Josh

I guess it happened only about five minutes after Rita and Pierre had left for their walk. Thank God. It seemed to be perfect providential timing. Marami, it turns out, only wanted the Sûreté guys and me. They probably would have felt it necessary to execute Rita and Pierre and anyone else we had invited to lunch that day.

I recognized Marami the moment he came crashing in from the patio. "CIA-trained" he had said. That had struck me because I had no idea what it meant. Trained for what? I thought. And why you? I wanted to ask. Well, now I didn't have to ask. He told me.

"Me and my men are here to hold you for ransom. I am a trained hostage negotiator. I have done this work in many places around the world. In Vietnam, Cambodia, New York, Zaire, Philippines. First time in France. Lovely country professor. Thanks for this opportunity."

Holding some new kind of a gun that looked like a rapid-fire two-handed pistol-rifle machine, Marami, and three others had us surrounded in seconds. They had found all our doors, front, back, and patio, open to the fresh air and apparently to them too.

Tim and Ter were flaming angry and refused to get up and place their hands on their heads, as ordered. Tim had been napping. His gun was on the table next to him. Ter's gun was in his belt. Both guns were placed in Marami's back pack, and both agents were slugged hard in the stomach. They fell forward and retched and coughed and were miserable.

Marami kept his position over me where I sat while his three bums took care of the kicking. Then he said, "Well, we meet again professor."

"What a hell of a great opening line Marami. Are you broadway trained as well?"

"Good opening line from you professor. Do you know why I am going to hold you for a while?"

"You want all my money?"

"You are trying to demonstrate that you are calm, cool, collected, eh? Keep it up, sir, you will need it."

"Okay, let's go," yelled Marami. "Bring the cars around. Dump those two in the trunks, one in each car. Come on prof, we'll wait out on the road."

And just like that we were moving down A8, from Aix to Nice, no food stops, little conversation. I prayed that Tim and Ter would survive in their car trunks. I hoped for a positive outcome of this Nice venture. Obviously I had time to think. And worry. After three hours of safe driving and winding road along the Provencale River we arrived at our hotel. Imagine, taking over several rooms in one of the most expensive hotels in Europe, the Negresco. Nothing like a modern kidnapping hideout in a *Belle Epoque* hotel of true *grandeur*. One could presume Marami is planning on a short stay.

Ter and Tim were rousted out of their confinement in the parking lot. Their keepers gave them a WC break, telling them to "wash up and look good." Marami went to the desk and had a chat with the manager and the concierge. We six waited off in a corner of the lobby. I could see the three at the desk nodding and smiling and shaking hands. Finally Marami joined us with baggage handlers who took all Marami's luggage and gave us our keys. I was staying in a gorgeous suite—with two of Marami's thugs. I was assigned the pull-out coach, near the bathroom. Each of my guards had king size beds. A half hour later food service carts came clattering. A dining table was set up in Marami's giant connecting suite. Steak and lobster was on his menu. The rest of us had hamburgers. And fries. French fries.

He told the three guards to decide their watch times. I was never to be without one of them. Then he sat me down while Tim and Ter watched the tele with the guards.

"I want you to understand exactly what you are doing here. You will tell your Commissaire Lemieux what has happened. He is to make all the arrangements for your safe return. The Sûreté is to remain far in the background. This is what you tell Lemieux now: we will release you when the Antwerp gems are delivered to us in their entirety. We will tell him where. That's all you have to say. Your life depends upon how fast the *grand genistas* can react. Here's the phone. Call. You know the number, no?"

"He will have a few questions for you Marami."

"Not now. Just give him the message. Only the message."

I dialed, Lemieux's Sergeant answered. Lemieux came on.

"Hello, Roger. This is Josh. I have a brief message for you. No, don't interrupt, please. We will be released when all the Antwerp gems are delivered to Marami period end of message."

"Oh, I almost forgot," said Marami. Please remind Lemieux that one Nice person will be die mysteriously each day until we receive our gems. Tell him that now."

I repeated it. Then Lemieux said "Let me talk to the bastard." Marami grabbed the phone and slammed it down.

"Very good, professor. Now you may rest; remember you are recovering. *Bon soir.*"

After dinner the guards cleaned up the suite. The next morning Ter, Tim and I were allowed out onto the terrace overlooking the *promenade des Anglais,* and the continuing *Quai des Etats Unis.* From here we could see all along the coast. Sunbathers were beginning to descend from the promenade to the water's edge and the smooth-stone beach below. Along the coast the radiant tiled dome of the *Cathédrale Ste-Réparate* reflected the rising sun over the bay. Nice was having a beautiful morning.

Ter whispered, "I don't think this is one of those kidnapping cases where the kidnapped become enamored of their kidnappers, do you guys?"

"You know," said Tim, "our captors lack charm. Is that fair to say?"

"Okay, shut up and come on in gentlemen." This from Marami.

"Today's another day," he whispered menacingly, "so that means if we don't have good news by tonight we have to kill someone. I have been looking at the telephone directory of this place for an idea. Now I know. Our victim tonight should be a diamond dealer. Clever, no?"

"Brilliant Marami. Now can we eat?" asked Ter.

"Sure. Call for the morning hamburgers, Arasi."

Arasi did so and twenty minutes later we had burgers. Arasi really liked them and could eat several. He became the Burger King of the group. Most of that day we read, watched the tele, read sports pages. So far, our disappearance has not been reported by any media.

Around 1800 hours Marami had me call Lemieux again. I was to repeat the same message. This time I was able to have the classical coastal radio station on during the call. I turned up Verdi's *Nabucco* overture, which must have gone out loud and clear over the phone.

Around midnight Arisi and one of the other guys left the hotel. They were back in their rooms at 0200. We were awakened by Marami delivering the morning paper. I was able to turn on the radio near my pull-out. With one wrist handcuffed to the floor lamp I managed to spread out the front page of the local gazette.

Stanislaus Villafranche, noted Nice diamond merchant, was found beaten to death on the steps of the Chagall Museum on the far north side of town. Monsieur Villafranche had been a philanthropist in favor of underwriting fishing vessels for impoverished Asians living along the coast. He had been a good man, according to all reports. Now he was dead because of what Lac Bleu did or did not contain. That day, our second with Marami, killer burger czar, not a word was heard among the guards. I stayed with my lamp, slept, read, listened to Mozart.

At 1800 I was told to ask Lemieux if he had any news. He said "We are working on it." Then he added, "Tell the SOB the local Algerians in Angers-Avrille were sorry to hear their good friend Stan Villafranche was killed. They are angry, tell him, very angry."

Again Marami slammed down the phone.

"Okay, professor. Would you like to choose the one to die tonight? How about just choosing a name at random. Someone, let's say, who lives in Avignon. I will call a pal of mine and he will perform the service while we rest easy here in the glamorous Negresco. Go ahead, select any common name likely to live in Avignon."

"Thanks," I said. "I'll pass."

, professor. I will choose. The person to die
      ill be the Jules Labonte family of Avignon.
Surp.. .d? That guy broke up the Maginot Line plan
we had gone to great trouble to set up. He crashed in.
He beat up my men and caused them to be deported. I
don't like him. It's pay-back-Labonte time, professor.
Lemieux will pay attention after this."

He went into his room with the phone. When he
returned he was smiling. *Bon nuit à tous.*

The next morning during our hamburger breakfast,
me dining elegantly one-handed, spread out on my pull-
out, a Horizon copter hovered outside our balcony. A
couple of ski-masked guys with rifles were looking
directly into our windows. They waved. Tim, Ter and
I waved back, totally confused. The Horizon stayed
around for a few minutes, then pulled up and
disappeared from our sight, apparently over and around
the back of the Negresco. Marami and our guards
bustled about in a turmoil of activity. They broke out
weapons I never knew they had in all that luggage.
They raced around arranging furniture in a *feng shui*
defense mode. My pull-out couch became part of the
improvised fortress. I continued to finish my burger
because I could not get up unless I hauled the huge
floor lamp around with me.

"Okay, professor. What the hell is that? Who are
those guys? Did you give Lemieux some message
while I was asleep?"

"Swift thinking Marami. During the night I have been sending Morse code and semaphore messages for help out over the harbor to all the ships at sea. How I did that without a bulb or a flag is a mystery even to me."

The three guards huddled with Marami. African-Arabic accents swirled around the room. The sounds were gruff and sharp, controlled but vehement, with lots of gestures. It seemed like they were having a discussion in which each guard spoke up decisively, while the three victims watched, fascinated at their apparent democratic exercise of free speech.

Marami finally broke the huddle, determined, but ready to call an audible if need be. Each guard loaded their collection of artillery, side arms and shiney new sniper rifles. Then we heard the copter again. It appeared from above this time, hovering right outside our suites. Marami's men froze. The copter guys waved again. We waved back. The guards looked at Marami, at us waving, at the smiling, waving copter passengers. Flustered.

Marami yelled. "Okay professor. Who the hell are these clowns?"

"Maybe they are here to deliver the Antwerp loot, genious," suggested Tim.

"Maybe they want something to eat," said Ter.

"Maybe they are going skiing," I said, smiling at Marami. I had no idea what all this meant. I was as perplexed as Marami was.

"Seriously, Marami, how about calling the concierge, your friend, for a bull horn or some such gadget they use here in Nice in these situations. I will go out on the balcony and ask them what's going on. Undoubtedly your hotel director is concerned too."

From where I was standing I could not see over the balcony, but I guessed by now a crowd of curious onlookers must be gathered under our window.

He nodded to Arisi who immediately dashed out the door, slamming it. Just then we heard "Attention suite 715. Don't shoot. We can see you have plenty of fire power in there. We come in peace."

Marami yelled at me. "Okay, ask them what is going on."

"They won't be able to hear me until errand boy Arisi returns with a bull horn. Then we'll talk. Relax Marami, aren't you used to this kind of pressure?"

Arisi ran in, horn in hand. Marami pointed to me. I took the horn in my left hand and the damn lamp in my cuffed right. Ter held the blowing balcony curtains and

I stepped out. I was really scared and uncertain myself but could not resist asking, "Hey Marami, you want me to ask them for a light bulb?"

The copter crew had been watching all this and talking and laughing back and forth. Now I could see two people up front and two sitting behind them, all staring at our balcony. Searching for an opening line, I tried, "You guys come here often?"

"We have something to say to Marami, professor. Tell him to get his ass out here so we can see him while we talk."

The bull horns were working perfectly. Not only could Marami hear them but I supposed so could all the other patrons on this side of the hotel and the gathering crowd of vacationers watching and listening on the *promenade* below.

"I can hear from here, tell them professor."

I told them and shrugged, with the Gallic 'phew.'

"Okay Marami. Here's the deal. You let Ter, Tim, and the prof go now, immediately. When we see them free down on the beach we will accept your surrender. To show our good will we will toss a small bag of Antwerp diamonds onto your balcony. The gems will be considered your property and will provide you some support when you get out of jail several years from now. But today you will go to jail to await trial."

"What the hell, professor. This is not okay. If they do not leave now we will kill all three of you."

I relayed this to the copter pilot.

"We suggest Marami, you look outside here. Just come to the balcony and look down. There are fifteen police cars down there, accompanied by a small army of Interpol and national police. Look into your suite's corridor. Police, armed and waiting. We lay siege. You will starve. Take a time out, consider our plan. I will toss you a small diamond bag right now. Here you are."

With that one of the masked guys flipped a bag of something heavy through the open French doors. The bag had "Antwerp" printed on the outside. Marami opened it, gently poured the contents on the coffee table in the center of their fortress. He produced a diamond dealer's eye glass and studied a few pieces. Again the huddle. Everyone talked. The huddle broke. Arisi and the other guards came out onto the balcony, shoving the three of us in front of them. Marami took the bull horn.

"Now you see what you have done. We will kill these three men right here in front of you and toss the bodies over into the crowd you have gathered. To prevent that, go away, dismiss the law men you have needlessly gathered. Announce to the media and Interpol that we have reached an agreement. We will walk out to our cars, taking the professor with us."

"We can't do that Marami. You are finished as a free man."

"Okay professor," he said addressing me. "We have no choice."

He made to turn me around. I resisted and brought the lamp down hard on his head. He slumped a little but did not go down. Two shots came from the copter and he fell dead. Tim and Ter were wrestling the three guards. The copter guys shot two guards. The remaining kidnapper was Arisi. He opened fire on the copter with his Czech Cesca. I saw one shooter fall back on the floor of the Horizon. Arisi got a few more shots off before he fell under a rain of bullets from the copter.

The three of us were okay, just a little bruised, and it turned out Lemieux has a great talent for organizing spontaneous details when in a most complicated situation. The Interpol people and the local police chiefs truly appreciated his ability and were moved to ask in French, "By the way, where is Avrille?" L.V. was overjoyed at seeing Prof Josh alive and rather well. But Lemieux's takeover of what the press called the *Junk Jewelry Junket* was a wonderful surprise to her. When she saw him dictating orders over several phones

421

to numerous offices she was moved to hit him with the palindrome of the day: Roger, Drab Bard indeed! Pierre and Rita Mary Tomasino closed up the Ma and headed up to Boudreau where Rosemarie was preparing for a fine homecoming party. Marami and his pals were turned over to the Interpol for identification and eventual burial in their beloved Algeria.

Smith and Beauchaine

Madame Catherine Didier profited politically from the *"J.J.J."* Her committee was prominent in current discussions among all Assembly parties relative to environmental activities, and was honored to have a member of the *Département du Déminage* permanently assigned to her sub-committee. The long-standing covert condition of that department became ever so slightly open to public scrutiny and justifiably to public respect. Papers began running articles informing their readers about the extraordinary service the Department regularly renders. Television journalists and talk show hosts discovered new ground when Verdun farmers were paid to tell their countrymen how the *demineurs* removed unexploded shells. Widows told of husbands being blown to bits while plowing. People came forward with forty-year-old grenades they never knew could still be lethal. In the weeks following the Nice incident the Department became known for its well-deserved bravery. And the tabloids made lots of money out of very wide publicity.

Madame Didier revealed government plans to mount several statues in various French cities where demining work had been especially compelling. Annecy would be honored to set aside a hectar for a life-size replica of Jean-Luc Napoleon Baker. A ten foot high cactus plant was to be erected between Angers and Avrille. *Le Courrier de l'ouest* reported on the controversial CACTUS in its op ed pages.

It is about time this paper acknowledges the good done to this community by the Collectif Angevin pour le tracé urbain sud, the noisy organization which called itself CACTUS. The word cactus in French carries some of the 'stickiness' of the word in English. Characterized as the spiny-leafless plant *Cactaceae* which often produces beautiful flowers, Cactus called our attention to the scandalous environmental catastrophe known as Lac Bleu. With that in mind and out of respect for the many deaths resulting from the recent explosion, this paper encourages its readers to contribute to the construction of a giant cactus replica on a site still to be decided.

After everyone had time to rest and recover from the shocks provided by recent events we all met at Boudreau. It had been a week since we had seen each other and all of us were prepared with comments about the national and international press coverage. Everyone brought wine and/or cheese for Rosemarie to disperse as her menu dictated. Her daughter, Delynne, was briefly free of Sorbonne studies and was on hand to assist her mom in Boudeau's up-keep. Delynne has her mother's smiling eyes and copper-colored hair, while she favors her father in physical stature, athletic ability, pert nose. When Rosemarie and Delynne stand near each other Pierre and Rita have trouble telling them apart. Delynne is presently writing a short speech she will give next fall at the unveiling of her father's statue. Rosemarie is writing the script to appear at the base of the small monument to Boney's bravery.

When we all gathered for vodka-tonic cocktails a la Emeritus, the conversation covered many topics but finally settled down to a few Lac Bleu clarifications. Tim and Ter, the guards assigned to be with Prof, Rosemarie and Delynne, Pierre and Rita, L.V., Chief Lemieux, the LaBontes of Avignon, and us, Beauchaine and Smith, made thirteen for dinner that sunny Sunday afternoon.

"Overindulgence is greatly underated," began L.V.

"I think you're right," agreed Rita. "This seems like a good time to have a long and leisurely traditional meal. How may I help?"

"You can put out the wine glasses, if you wish, Rita," said Rosemarie. "Delynne guarantees they have been washed and shined and are ready for heavy service. We have two sets, red and white."

That set the pace for the hours to come. During that time Lemieux asked a few good questions.

"In the official testimony we read that the Labontes were selected to be killed. Do you all know why they survived that threat?" Lemieux asked. He was smiling, at ease in his new Armani slacks and sports shirt.

We all looked at Jules and his wife.

"Because we weren't home. We were on the TGV to Aix-en-Provence. We knew nothing about Nice," Jules replied.

"You missed an exciting week-end, Jules. Unusual for you, right?" asked Prof. Jules gave Prof a hug and mumbled something about another rescue being one too many.

"Now that the rains have stopped, what do you think will happen to Lac Bleu?" said Lemieux.

"Well, Rog," Pierre ventured, "news at the Colbert confessional says we are still confused about the part demining has played in this country since two world wars."

"What do you mean, confused?" asked L.V.

"Well," Pierre continued, "Rumors from Avrille Army officers and the official Département rumors on just what to do with Lac Bleu. The army wants to keep it as Camp Boulanger. The Department tends to listen to politicians these days. And that source says the sooner we abandon that particular *déminage* site the sooner the town can begin selling real estate again. Politicians want to sell real estate. So maybe the *déminage* lake site has to go."

"Wonderful," shouted Tim, from the bar, "isn't that what y'all have been wanting for years?"

"Yes," smiled Lemieux, we just wanted it sooner with less loss of life."

"So maybe you are getting what you Avrille citizens and CACTUS fought for?" asked L.V.

"I think we are close, L.V. But a few more things have to be made clear. And my Colbert-Paris rumors are usually correct. Maybe this came from Didier herself. I heard the lake will be drained and the munitions will be removed to the Calais area. How about that?"

"Let's hope you are right, my friend," said Prof. "We need to clean up poor ol' beat-up Avrille and give it a chance to move on, grow, integrate infrastructure, and so forth, without tons of explosives lying around."

At this point Beauchaine and I could restrain ourselves no longer. We nodded, took deep breaths and told them that next week the lake is to begin draining until totally dry. The national government has decided in session late last night to fill it in and construct a modern family park with thrill rides for the kids, tree-lined paths for strolling elders "like this group," with a prominent band stand in the center, surrounded by picnic tables.

"How do you know this?" Rosemarie shouted from the kitchen.

"It will be in tomorrow's news. The Sûreté was there to assure the Assembly members that the criminal element and the contemptible shadow of the Antwerp heist are no longer of any concern. The gem heist is a non-issue in Avrille. So is the lake. A dry lake is a done deal."

"That would be great, but what about the gems?" from L.V.

"Well, that's part of my Colbert-Paris rumor," answered Pierre. "If the explosion sent all the gems all over Loire-et-Maine, then the Lac's value to the diamond industry has diminished, right? If there are gems, the Antwerp heist placed there, let's say, after the explosion, then they will be found as the lake is drained. Army engineers have worked out a feasible plan along with some American dam construction technology for perfect water control. The Antwerp gems are in large cases, not in small bags. If they are still there they will now be found. The Army's Special Forces will be on hand with the demining department. Gems will not get through."

"If gems are found who owns them?" asked Prof.

"They will be confiscated by the national police and the Sûreté and sorted out with the help of the European Court," explained Lemieux. "That would take forever, of course. Owners will come from all over the world. It will be a legal-political circus, like the stolen Jewish art work after Hitler."

"And if no gems at all are found when the lake dries will that prove the Antwerp loot is somewhere else?" continued L.V. "I'm interested because I have a bag of junk jewelry collected after the explosion. I have had them appraised. Glass, but attractive, like so much other stuff that went flying that day."

"Actually, that's a good point," said Lemieux. "If the genuine diamonds are in containers they may have been sunk to the bottom of the quarry, maybe covered with tons of stone. In a few weeks they will be covered with tons of rocks and dirt, with grass, swings and a huge musical carousel. Antwerp will be failed history. Ditto for the Army Camp."

"Attention tous le monde. Voila, le diner." This from mother and daughter in the kitchen.

We spread ourselves around the grand table in the dining room. First, the ladies presented us with a choice of fish soups, a *bourride,* a garlic fish stew, or *bouillabaisse,* an original Marseille soup. Rosemarie's local fish included monkfish, snapper, mullet, scorpion fish and conger eel. Those who chose traditional *bouillabaisse* were served the broth first. The fish followed, separately. Meanwhile Pierre was serving wines, Josh hung with his vodka-tonic.

After while the *doubière* appeared amidst cheers and applause. This is a scalding-hot pot-bellied casserole filled with beef stew. The red wines were opened. This was followed by Delynne's special *Salade Nicoise* and her *Tarte au Citron.* Stuck in the center of each piece of this delicious French pie was a fresh sprig of *genet.* We clapped and cheered. Again Rosemarie had forgotten nothing. We lifted our broom sprigs, dipped them in wine and splashed and sprinkled each other in the manner of a padre using holy water at High Mass. Cheeses, coffees and after-dinner drinks were served on the patio. All of us helped carrying plates and dishes under Josh's direction.

When we were all settled again, informally lounging and sipping, about to doze, perhaps, Rosemarie came out with a sealed envelope for Josh.

My fine graduate student, left this for you. He said you should read it aloud to us if he is not here with us by this time today."

To my trusted friend Professor Josh Baker. If I do not appear by the time Professor Rosemarie Baker gives this to you I will be dead.

By now, my dear professor, I hope you have recovered completely from the results of our pool landing. I have told Middle-Eastern wedding producers time and time again to cease and desist from the ancient custom of firing rifles into the air during wedding parties. One day an Iraqi war could be accidentally begun in this stupid manner.

I must also apologize for the ill treatment afforded you in the Negresco. Time was running out for me, the patience of my masters in Algiers was at an end. We always thought, professor, that you knew where the diamonds were hidden. We had to try one last time. Whether you do or do not know is a moot point now, isn't it? In any case, sir, you have won. I salute you.

Your many friends among the local authorities should also be congratulated. Lemieux is a fine man with a sharp policeman's mind. Pierre, your life-long friend, was of no help to us either. These last few days I made sure my Assembly contacts were able to get Didier's measure passed. She is innocent of any chicanery. Her nephews definitely are not.

During this past year the Bedards played both sides, the pro-government stance in favor of non-interference in the Lac Bleu pollution problem, and the pro-consortium interest in illegal diamonds. As for the first stance, I could not care less. As to the latter I literally became the consortium when the stupid Bedards managed to eliminate themselves. I became a kind of illegal diamond corporation-sole. And that's when I came into your lives.

Lastly, the jewelry most people picked up at the explosion is worthless, albeit attractive, tawdry trash. Save it for the next Mardi Gras. However, the bag of gems hidden in Elvee's apartment book shelf is worth millions. Use it with my blessing on your good fortune. If you are reading this be assured my fortune is over.

There were six signatures in various distinctive hands, penmanship to match each personality of his several identities. He signed only last names.

Lablanc

MABUTI   Ben Bella

Marami   Genèt   Jones

A long discussion ensued about each 'character.' Rosemarie spoke about Mabuti's desire to better himself, hoping for a good grade towards his doctoral studies. Pierre is convinced Genèt is his name for the old lady 'Aunt' he used so effectively. Ben Bella was the masterful creature of the CIA, an Interpol source, a trusted French National Police officer, working in conjunction with law enforcement agencies everywhere.

"Dr. G.E. Jones was a great help to Josh in the hospital," said L.V.

"Yes, that's right. He literally ordered me back to reality."

"Marami was, like all the others though, eventually just a jewel thief. Do you think he would have shot you professor, there in the Negresco?" asked Lemieux.

"The Ahmed Ben Bella I thought I knew would not have done so. No. But, under pressure, I think Marami or one of his thugs would have. Yes."

"This whole Ben Bella story gives new meaning to the *mot juste: couvert.* Covert." Lemieux went on. "He was certainly a master of his trade. We met only a few of his personalties. Imagine, over many years, he could have had dozens of careers. Perhaps his very best one was that of *démineur.*"

"*Sous le couvert,* always playing a part, fake or real, facade or genuine, how could he go on day after day?" asked Rosemarie, who had become very pensive.

432

"How could he ever be sincere? How do we know that this final letter means what it says? We really don't, do we?"

"We know he's dead," said Lemieux. Finally the U.S. State Department has shared with us their collection of his finger prints, DNA, and a disguise gallery directory. He is wanted for questioning in several countries on suspicion of just about everything."

"And in the last year everything about the Avrille-Lac Bleu scene has changed greatly. Last summer," reminisced Prof Josh, "remember, we were all concerned about the government abandoning us to our Lac Bleu pollution problems. Ministers wanted nothing to do with the lake because there was no danger as long as the ordnance was under water. Ordnance and tons of unexploded munitions were important. Murders were committed because of them. Then jewelry brought to light another international interest—stolen gems, hot items on the black market. More people were killed. Now, this summer, we may see the end of Lac Bleu and the beginning of a new peaceful Avrille."

"Aren't we all thinking I should check out my apartment right about now?" asked L.V.

Beau said she would go with her. Driving carefully they should be back in an hour. In the meantime I will contact the Sûreté gem expert. He's in Angers and can follow them back here to Boudreau in time for the post-siesta Petanque Tourney. I'm sure the Tourney can wait for a decision on whether we all join the Junk Jewelry Junket or really celebrate the arrival of actual gems.

Prof Josh

Small talk turned around other recent events less stressful. My historic Avant, a truly great French car, was returned in excellent condition thanks to Lemieux's influence in certain Maine-et-Loire body shops. I sat in it after the huge dinner and walked around it several times, touching it reverently here and there. Ter commented on the marvelous picture of Catherine Didier on the front pages of our papers. She was wearing a flamboyant hat entering the Assembly, smiling and waving and holding on to the hat in the wind. She looks marvelous. Her sister's twin sons were not mentioned.

Smith, stretched out on a Pétanque Court bench, speculated on how the ordnance would be transported. The Army Special Forces, Deminage Department, would, of course, be in command of the official escort from the Lac to the new site being readied at Calais. Land Rovers and other, larger trucks, would be employed, together with hundreds of regular army units spread out along the route. As the Lac dries additional heavy earth-moving equipment and cranes will be on the scene, working cautiously, delicately. Pierre, between practice pétanque tosses, suggested that these

Avrille events will have some political consequences as well. "For example," he said, "you can't expect the voters to re-elect those bumblers who for years disregarded the advice of experts concerning the dangers inherent at demining sites. I'll bet the political careers of many Maine-et-Loire office-holders will end at the next election. Bets, anyone?"

About that time I noticed several people glancing at the big clock in La Salle de Grenade. Others were checking wrist watches when casually changing pétanque practice sides. It was about time L.V. and Beau should be getting back.

After another half-hour the Sûreté diamond expert arrived with his black equipment case. He said he found L.V.'s apartment unlocked and empty so he came directly to Boudreau. He and Smith went into a quiet corner, both talking rapidly. Then we all sat and continued to wait. But not for long. There was too much adrenaline in the group.

"What do we do?" asked Rosemarie. "There's no answer at L.V.'s."

Smith was on Beau's cell phone. No answer. The gem guy was nervous and wanted to get back to his office. Lemieux said we all stay right here for another few minutes.

"My men have been to L.V.'s apartment," he said, between several quick calls. "As the doc here said, door open, no one around. The area is now under surveillance. Wait here."

The phone rang and I clicked on the speaker phone.

"Hi prof, this is L.V."

"Where in the world are you girl, we have been worried."

"I'm okay. I'm like stranded in Chalonnes, about 18-20 miles out of Angers."

"I know where that is. What do you mean stranded?"

"Beau just left me here. She took the jewels. She's gone."

"Hey, slow down dear. What do you mean she's gone?"

"Prof I'm sorry and like very angry. That witch just took me at gun point in her car. When we were near Chalonnes she tried to force me out of the car. I'm like, 'I'm not leaving.' She pushed me out and is long gone. That's it. Can someone come get me please?"

"Smith just bounded out the door with Lemieux. They'll be there in a few minutes. Stay where you are."

"Okay Prof, thanks. I'm like, I can't believe this, Prof. And Prof, I am mad as hell!"

"Understood. Keep calm. Watch for the police car. We'll see you soon."

In a few minutes Lemieux told us his men were now searching Beau's apartment. "Everything is there, clothes, food, books, television, and so forth."

He called a few minutes later with a very distraught L.V. in the car. Roadblocks were set up, airports and train stations covered within a half hour. Her Sûreté office supplied Beau's dossier pictures and documents. Her boss was stunned. Interpol has been notified. They were furious. "There are many angry people around here right now," Pierre repeated every couple of minutes. Every time he said that I responded, *Mais oui, mais oui.* Personally, I felt numb. I thought Smith was having a heart attack.

Rosemarie prepared a cool glass of orange juice and two aspirins which L.V. took when she arrived. The gem expert left, Smith and Lemieux took to the international phone books, Rosemarie and Rita took L.V. to a guest room where she tried to relax. Soon an Interpol agent appeared, then two gendarmes from the National Police. All interviewed L.V. at length. The feeling in Boudreau that night was one of complete 'stupefaction,' and 'outrage,' two terms used that evening on the tele. Gratefully, the Avrille police kept reporters at bay. Lemieux hired Rosemarie to be the spokesperson for the reporters. She worked successfully out of an office in the new Avrille *Commissariat* complex and looked wonderful on the tube. The French Deborah Norville and Anne Sawyer in one beautiful sister-in-law.

After days of hypertension and activity Boudreau became calm again. Pierre had to get back to the Colbert. Smith was suspended for ten days and then posted to Auderville to help supervise French ferries in the English Channel. Rita returned to her Paris research job, L.V. to her University classes. At our last Boudreau lunch that summer she got off the palindrome of the year.

"What do you guys think of what Beau did? Did she Borrow Or Rob?"

Months later nothing had been seen or heard of the Antwerp gems. Sûreté agent Celine Lorraine Beauchaine had dropped out of our lives and/or off the planet. Forever.

Pierre

Rita and I are trying to join the 1.5 million speakers of Occitan. To do this, especially at my retard level, we had to study intensively, a totally new experience for us. We were doing this because we had decided that if we are to spend summers and other weeks in Aix-en-Provence we would like to speak the so-called 'local' language. Rita is bright and a quick learner. My years learning all the continent's bad slang at the Colbert confessional worked against me when it came to "languaging it," as our professor put it.

I have been visiting Prof Josh at Boudreau this fall. He is busy preparing a new second semester course for his psychology department in Memphis. It is tentatively called in the directory Impulse Control Disorders. He thinks it will sell well in his graduate department, and will include a section on Impulse Control in the Stealing Situation. "Contrary to common belief," he says in his notes "people with stealing disorders do not necessarily have other underlying personality or emotional disorders." He wants to make a strong point of this in the course.

The *Département du Déminage* has been doing a remarkable job, day and night, in removing the *materiel* from the rocky bowels of the lake. Last summer's big explosion left tons of debris, often indistinguishable from the still dangerous unexploded kind. Now that the quarry is totally dry spectators have been watching great tons of junk being picked up by huge machines and gently set down onto special army trucks. Much of the work of sorting is, of course, still done by hand, one mustard gas shell by one eighty-year-old 75 mm shell, one by one. Reminders to the workers say things like, "Easy does it boys." One sign reads *Doucement monsieur. Avec douceur.* Gently.

Yesterday, early in the morning, a group of *démineurs* spent an hour wrestling a Minewerfer into place for transportation to Calais. The Minewerfer is that horrible 250 mm German shell. Fortunately there are few of those down there. Crates of 'potato mashers,' grenades made famous by the Boudreau incident, are still being hauled out. So far, thanks be to God, no injuries among the unbelievably brave guys down there in the quarry. Occasionally, when a particularly difficult maneuver has been accomplished, the inevitable crowd of sidewalk engineers cheers and claps. *Démineurs* wave to the crowd in gratitude, happy for the encouragement and support. They are on television news shows and interview forums each night. For the first time in the history of demining in France the public gets to see and appreciate the outstanding work of this hitherto little known group of heroes. Demining is going on these days in many parts of the world as technical knowledge spreads from very busy French engineering schools. And as you would expect, plainclothesmen from the DST mingle among the onlookers: *Direction de la Surveillance du Territoire.* Avrille's Lac Bleu will always have the attention of the French equivalent of the FBI. Some fans of Avrille have quoted a Canadian motto on an informal sign on the fence surrounding the deminers' working area. It epitomizes the pride and the hopes of Avrille, Maine-et-Loire.

Un monde de beauté naturelle à quelques minutes d'ici!

You're just minutes away from a world of natural beauty!

And from what I hear at the Colbert confessional, Interpol and an exiled Sûreté agent named Smith have never stopped looking for the Lac Bleu gems.

And my best buddy, Prof Josh, often sits out in front of Boudreau looking out towards the former Lac Bleu, with a prolonged and perplexing smile on his face. It's as if he knows something we don't.

The crown of old men is wide experience;
their glory, the fear of the Lord.
SIRACH 25:6

EPILOGUE

Laura Veronica Campbell and Roger Lemieux were married ten years ago. They live in Angers, near the university. She is on the language faculty and Roger runs their Dive Shop. Their three girls are two, four, and six years of age. They are tri-lingual, (English, French, and Occitan), and show promise of becoming good swimmers and divers.

Rita Mary Tomasino and Pierre Le Grand live in Place des Victoires, Paris. They are regulars at St-Eustache, where their two sons are altar boys. He continues to manage the Colbert. Rita is a head departmental researcher in the Bibliotheque Nationale.

Rosemarie Evangeline Baker and her daughter Delynne now own and operate four bakeries in and around Avrille. Rosemarie has written two best-selling cook books.

Agent Matthew Smith has retired to St-Paul-de-Vence where he grows vegetables and investigates anything having to do with diamonds. His partner, Celine Lorraine Beauchaine, has never been found.

Jean Didier and Jeanne-Clotilde Bedard are both still in jail.

Professor Emeritus Josh Baker spends four months a year at Boudreau. He continues to put threads in each doorway and window and checks them occasionally. He has written the definitive volume on the *Département du Déminage*. Operation Entree meets there every August for several days. In the winters Prof Josh studies the *zither* in Fargo. C'est la vie!

NOTE

The quotes from the Book of Sirach are attributed to the author Ben Sira. He was a professor. The contents of Sirach give us the impression of a teacher lecturing in an actual classroom preparing his Jewish students for life in a Hellenistic world. Scholars generally date Sirach in the period between 195 and 180 BCE, Before the Common Era.

Slightly more than two-thirds of Sirach has survived in Hebrew manuscript. Other fragmentary and mutilated scrolls have been discovered.

(The Book of Sirach, page 603-867. The New Interpreter's Bible, Vol. V, Abingdon Press, Nashville, 1997)

ABOUT THE AUTHOR

B. J. Lucian, FSC, has been a member of the international Order of the Brothers of the Christian Schools, (De La Salle Brothers), for fifty years. He has been a psychology teacher/counselor in the U.S. and the Philippines. Nowadays he reads and writes history and teaches zoology for the Memphis Zoological Society. He is Professor Emeritus at Christian Brothers University, Memphis, Tennessee.

ABOUT THE AUTHOR